AS LONG AS I'M THE ONLY ONE

BY:
CHENELL PARKER

Published by Chenell Parker

OTHER TITLES BY CHENELL PARKER
(IN ORDER)

HER SO CALLED HUSBAND PARTS 1-3
YOU'RE MY LITTLE SECRET PARTS 1-3
YOU SHOULD LET ME LOVE YOU
CHEATING THE FUTURE FOR THE PAST PARTS 1-3
YOU'RE NOT WORHT MY TEARS
WHAT YOU WON'T DO FOR LOVE
CREEPIN': A NEW ORLEANS LOVE STORY PARTS 1-3
COMPLICATED PARTS 1-3
NEVER KNEW LOVE LIKE THIS PARTS 1 & 2
HATE THAT I NEED YOU
I HEARD IT ALL BEFORE
I DON'T WANT YOU BACK

Chapter 1

Marlee blew out a breath of frustration as she listened to her boyfriend of three years, Tyson, trying to argue his point. After the intense, animalistic sex that they'd just had in and out of the shower, he just had to go and ruin the mood.

"You act like I go out of town every weekend. It's been two months since I've had to do this," Marlee huffed.

"It don't matter how long it's been. I'm just not feeling the shit no more," Tyson replied with a scowl, as he slipped on his boxers.

"It's just work Tyson. You act like I'm going party or something," Marlee reasoned.

"Oh, so it's work now? Whatever happened to it just being a hobby? You already have a job," Tyson reminded her.

Marlee and her best friend, Sierra, had always expressed interest in becoming physical therapy assistants since they were in elementary school. They'd both obtained their associates degrees from their local community college, but they were having a hard time finding a job. Sierra had no problem going back to the retail store that she'd worked in previously, but Marlee took a different route. Although she'd never worn much makeup herself, she was a natural when it came to beautifying others. Marlee learned the basics from YouTube, but she took a three-month cosmetology course to gain more knowledge and experience. It started out with her practicing on her close friends and family, but she quickly made a name for herself.

Even though Marlee had found a full-time job as a physical therapy assistant at a local clinic, she still made lots of money on the weekends when she was off. A few times, a bride-to-be would solicit her services, but the weddings weren't always local. Marlee got paid good money to travel, and her traveling expenses were always included. Tyson hated when she took jobs out of town and he was very vocal about it. What started out as a hobby was paying Marlee almost as much as her day job, but he didn't care. He had taken care of her for the past three years and that wasn't going to change.

"I know baby, but it's good money," Marlee replied as she shook away her thoughts of the past.

"You ain't hurting for no money like that though, Marlee. I got whatever you need, and you already know that," Tyson said.

"I know you do Tyson, but it's too late for me to back out of it now. I've already committed, and the wedding is next weekend."

"I would never want you to go back on your word, but I don't want this year to be like the last. You were gone almost every month, and I hated that shit. I don't care about you giving up a few hours on the weekends, if you're local. It's a wrap on that out of town shit after this though," Tyson demanded.

With Marlee's flip mouth and feisty attitude, Tyson expected a snappy comeback. He probably would have gotten one if her phone hadn't started ringing soon after he'd finished talking.

"That's Kim," Marlee said when she looked at the name that flashed across her screen.

Tyson had two kids, ages five and seven, and his son's mother, Kimberly, and Marlee got along great. His ex-wife and mother of his daughter, Taj, was another story. Tyson's daughter, Tyanna, was a sweetheart, but her mother was a bitch. Taj wanted to call all the shots whenever her daughter was with them, and Marlee wasn't having it. She took very good care of Tyanna when she and Tyson had her and that should have been good enough for Taj.

"The fuck is she always calling you for? My phone is sitting right here," Tyson snapped angrily.

"You should be happy that your girlfriend and the mother of your child get along. Or would you prefer our relationship to be like the one that I have with Taj?" Marlee asked him.

"Fuck Taj! And Kim is wasting her time calling because Ty can't come over here this weekend," Tyson frowned.

"Why not?" Marlee questioned.

"What kind of stupid question is that? I'm trying to spend some time with you, since you're gonna be gone next weekend. Ain't nobody coming over here," Tyson replied.

Tyson was a great boyfriend, but the same couldn't be said for him as a father. Taj seemed to always have a problem with Marlee, but she should have been grateful instead. If it weren't for Marlee, her daughter probably would have never seen her father. Tyson was always there financially, but he didn't care about spending time with his kids. If he saw them for one hour every week, he would be cool. His mother, Tracy, got her grandkids often, but he just didn't give a damn. He would rather smile up in Marlee's face all day, rather than spend time with his only two kids. Most women probably would have been okay with that, but Marlee wasn't one of them. It was sad that his son had a closer bond with his mother's husband than he did with Tyson, but that was his own fault.

"Hey Kim," Marlee answered the phone as she shook her head at his comment.

"Hey girl. Did I catch you at a bad time?" Kim asked her.

"No, I'm good. What's up?" Marlee asked as she walked into her closet to find something to wear for the day.

"Nothing, but Ty is trying to come over there next weekend. He wanted to come this weekend, until I told him that we were going to the zoo," Kim chuckled.

"Lil spoiled ass," Marlee laughed. "But, I'm gonna be in Atlanta next weekend. I'm doing a wedding."

"Oh, well, that's a wrap on that. I don't trust Tyson with my baby all by himself," Kim noted.

"That's a damn shame," Marlee replied as she walked out of the closet with her clothes in hand.

"You know my baby don't like his fat ass. He probably wouldn't even stay if you weren't there anyway," Kim said.

"Probably not, but I've been wanting to get him and Tyanna and go to the water park or something," Marlee said, as Tyson snapped his head around to face her.

"When?" Tyson questioned loudly.

"Tell his pathetic ass to shut up. He probably don't even want them to come over there," Kim snapped.

"You already know," Marlee agreed without saying too much in his presence.

"Oh, and me and my sister need to make an appointment for next month. It's her anniversary and she's having a party. I'll text you the date and you can invoice me for the deposit," Kim said.

"Okay, I got you. And tell my baby that I'll see him when I get back," Marlee replied before they disconnected.

"When did you tell her that he can come over?" Tyson questioned.

"I didn't, but I'll probably get him the weekend after my trip," Marlee replied.

"Damn man. We can't never have no time to ourselves. Why don't she just bring him to my mama like Taj does with Tyanna?" Tyson asked.

"That's not Tracy's son; he's yours. You really need to do better as a father," Marlee fussed as she dropped her robe, revealing her naked body.

"Give me a baby and I will," Tyson replied.

He licked his lips lustfully as he watched her putting on her black thong and bra. Marlee was sexy as hell with her short frame and protruding ass. Her breasts weren't all that big, but they were enough for him to grab a hand full and be satisfied. She had a medium brown complexion with big doe shaped eyes. Marlee had a style like no one else that he'd ever met, and that shit was a big turn on. She didn't conform to images and she didn't care about the latest trends. In the days where most women were rocking fake hair down to their asses, she opted to keep her naturally curly hair cut into a mohawk. It was always dyed a different color at the top and, this month, she was rocking a honey blonde color. The sides were cut low and she always had a different design cut into it. This time, she only had a few straight lines put in, but it was still the shit. She didn't see the resemblance, but Tyson always compared her to the singer Keri Hilson. She was even prettier to him, but she hated the comparison.

"I love you baby, with my whole heart," Tyson said as he wrapped his arms around Marlee's waist.

"I love you too boo." Marlee smiled, loving when he always said that he loved her that way.

To most people, Tyson would be considered ugly, and Marlee didn't disagree. He didn't have the best facial features, but certain things made him attractive to her. What he lacked in looks, he made up for in style and swag. He was a big boy, but he dressed better than the average male model.

"What do you feel like doing today?" Tyson asked once they were both dressed.

"I told you that I want to go get my shoes. You know the other color came out today," Marlee said, referring to the pink, yellow, and silver Giuseppe high tops that she wanted.

"We can do that tomorrow. Ain't nobody rushing to spend nine hundred dollars on no shoes," Tyson replied.

"But, I was supposed to be going shopping with Desi tomorrow," Marlee whined, referring to her cousin Desiree.

"Let's go before I get pissed off," Tyson said as he grabbed her hand and led her out of their condo.

Aside from her sister, Mat, and best friend, Sierra, Marlee had three cousins that she hung out with religiously. Her mother had three sisters and she and her cousins were close. Marlee was close with her entire family and they were always doing something together. Her mother, stepfather, and aunts ran a very successful home health care business, so most of them worked together as well. Tyson didn't have a problem with their close bond, but he didn't like it when her people interfered in their time together. He loved to have Marlee all to himself and he tried his best to always make it happen.

After going to see a movie and getting some things that she needed for her trip, Marlee and Tyson headed over to his mother's house. Tracy lived across the street from Marlee's sister, so she never had a problem going over there.

"You already know I'm not going in your mama's house now. I'm going by Mat. Just call me when you're ready to go," Marlee said when they pulled up and saw Taj's car parked in front of Tracy's door.

"Man, you're bringing your ass right in this house with me. You can go see Mat before we go home. The fuck I look like going in here without you on my arm?" Tyson replied. His ex-wife would have been happy to see that, but he wasn't giving her the satisfaction.

"Alright, but don't get mad if I fuck your baby mama up. I might swing on your ass too, for insisting that I come up in here," Marlee said, making him laugh.

That was nothing new to Tyson though. Marlee was a live wire and she didn't mind swinging on him or nobody else. He'd been ducking shoes, perfume bottles, and everything in between during their three years together. It didn't matter what it was. If Marlee was pissed enough, she would throw it at him, no questions asked.

"What's up y'all?" Tyson asked when he and Marlee walked into his mother's house.

"Hey y'all," Trinity, his sister, spoke up.

At twenty-six years old, Trinity was the same age as Marlee and four years younger than Tyson. She was still tight with his ex-wife Taj, but she loved Marlee as well.

"Marlee!" Tyanna yelled as she ran up and hugged her father's girlfriend.

"Hey baby." Marlee smiled as she leaned down and kissed the seven-year-old beauty.

She ignored the frown on Taj's face because that was nothing new. Taj hated her for whatever reason, but Marlee never understood why. She and Kim had hit it off from day one, but Taj was always a bitch.

"Speak to your daddy, lil girl. Standing there acting like you don't see him," Taj fussed at her daughter.

"Hey daddy," Tyanna said as she released Marlee and gave him a hug.

"Why your mama always gotta make you speak to me? You know how to speak when you call to beg," Tyson said as he kissed her cheek and walked away.

Taj's eyes stayed on him the entire time as she licked her lips lustfully. Truthfully, Tyson wasn't the best-looking nigga that she'd ever met, and he was nowhere near being the finest. But, she still loved her ex-husband unconditionally and that much was certain. She and Tyson had been on and off since they were fifteen years old and that was fifteen years ago. They made the mistake of getting married when they were twenty and that turned out to be a disaster. They were both too immature for that kind of responsibility and everyone told them so. They cheated on each other so much that Tyson demanded a blood test when she got pregnant with their daughter.

When Tyanna was a year old, Tyson went to jail for a year. While in there, he decided that staying married to

Taj was no longer what he wanted to do. He sent her some divorce papers, and she stupidly signed them. She regretted that decision then and she was still regretting it now. It was cool for a while though because he still gave her all the benefits of being his wife. Tyson used to be in a relationship with his son's mother, Kim, but he never left Taj alone. He took care of them both, and Taj was fine with that. Unfortunately, Kim just couldn't deal. She left Tyson alone and moved on, but he didn't run back to Taj like she thought he would. He played around with a few women for a while until he met and settled down with Marlee. At first, Taj didn't care that there was a new woman in his life. She knew that Tyson would never be done with her, but she was sadly mistaken.

A few months after getting a condo with Marlee, his ass started acting brand new. It started out with him telling her not to call at a certain time because he wanted to be respectful. That was never a problem before and Taj wasn't feeling it. He used to pop up at her house all the time, but it didn't take long for that to stop too. If he did come over, he always made sure to have Marlee with him. The money that he used to give her slacked up until it stopped altogether. It was then that Taj knew that he was really in love with the bitch. He had never done anything like that before with any of his other women.

All hope wasn't lost though. She still got a taste every now and then whenever Marlee had to go out of town. He was a faithful and devoted man other than that. He tried acting like she was a nobody in his girlfriend's presence, but she knew the real him. Trinity had mentioned something about Marlee going out of town again soon, so Taj was sure that she would be hearing from him. That was, if he didn't already have somebody else in mind. Tyson's views on cheating were stupid as hell. In his mind, sex wasn't considered cheating, as long as feelings weren't involved. If he didn't love or care about you, then he wasn't cheating. Taj knew that it was all bullshit because he would die if Marlee did the same.

"I'll be right back baby. Let me go see my sister and Sierra right quick," Marlee said as she headed for the door.

"Don't be all day Marlee. I'm ready to get something to eat and go home," Tyson replied.

"Just text me when you're ready," she said.

"I'm ready right now. As soon as I go back here and speak to my mama, we can go. I told you that I'm trying to lay up all weekend," Tyson said, making Taj roll her eyes and frown.

"I won't be long. Tell your mama that I said hello," Marlee said, right before she walked out of the house and crossed the street to her sister's house.

She knocked for a few seconds before Mat opened the door and let her in.

"What's up lil sis?" Mat asked as she walked back over to the sofa where she was lounging.

Marlee returned the greeting before sitting down next to her. Mat looked like a cute boy at first glance in her loose-fitting basketball shorts, tank, and perfectly lined dreads, but she was all woman. She had always been a tomboy ever since Marlee could remember, so her being a lesbian didn't come as a surprise to anyone but their father, Matthew. What did come as a surprise was when Marlee learned that her best friend and sister decided to get into a relationship. Sierra had confessed her love for girls to Marlee when they were only fifteen years old. She wasn't attracted to boys like most girls her age, but that was never an issue for Marlee. She loved her regardless, and she didn't care about that. It was weird for Marlee seeing her sister and best friend together at first but, after them being together for five years, it was as natural as breathing now. They were good for each other and she loved their relationship.

"Where's Sierra?" Marlee asked.

Before her sister could answer, Sierra walked into the room wearing only her boy cuts and a sports bra. She handed Mat a plate of food and took a seat right next to her.

"You want something to eat friend?" Sierra asked.

"No, bitch, but why don't you ever have on clothes?" Marlee asked.

"Like you got room to talk," Sierra laughed.

"At least I get dressed when company comes over. Your ass be half naked in front of anybody," Marlee replied.

"Girl, bye. Besides you and your family, nobody else really comes over here. You know they don't fuck with us like that," Sierra said.

"Don't even start that dumb shit Sierra. I'm not even in the mood," Mat fussed with a frown.

"I'm just saying. It's not a lie." Sierra shrugged sadly

Marlee felt bad for her girl because she didn't deserve to be ostracized like that. Sierra was the sweetest person that anyone would ever have the pleasure of meeting, but her overly religious family didn't care about that. They had basically disowned her when she got with Mat, and she hadn't seen or talked to them in years. Her mother pastored a church not far from their house and Sierra wasn't even welcomed there. It was sad that a place where a person was told to come as they were, closed the door in the face of one. Holidays and birthdays were always a sad time for her, so Marlee and her family made sure to always do something special during those times.

"When do you leave for Atlanta?" Mat asked.

"Next weekend. I wish my bestie was coming with me though," Marlee replied.

"You already know that shit ain't happening. If you were staying in a hotel it would be cool, but not with his ass," Mat said, referring to their father.

Just like Sierra's family, their father, Matthew, didn't approve of his oldest daughter's relationship either. Mat, short for Matilyn, had never tried to hide who she was from anyone. Their mother, Tiffany, loved her daughter regardless and she loved Sierra as well. Matthew lived in Atlanta with his girlfriend, but he and Mat didn't talk or speak to each other at all. Marlee kept in contact with him, and she and Desi were staying with him when they went there the following weekend.

"It's cool sis. You know I understand. Desi is coming with me. It'll just be the two of us, since Yanni and Kallie have to work," Marlee said, referring to her cousins.

"I know Tyson ole fat, insecure ass is having a fit," Sierra spoke up.

"You already know he is. And stop calling my man fat. He's just big boned," Marlee laughed.

"All his bones are big too. Nigga acts like y'all are joined at the hip or something." Mat frowned.

She hated how Tyson acted over her little sister. Marlee was a smart girl, and Mat pictured her with a college educated working man instead of the dope boy that she had fallen in love with. Tyson got on everybody's nerves with the way he followed Marlee around like a stray dog. He didn't care if it was all girls in attendance. He didn't mind being the only male in the crew, as long as he could be up under Marlee. He was good to her sister, so Mat tolerated him, even on the days when she wanted to knock his clingy ass out.

"That be that snapper that makes him act like that," Marlee laughed as she did a little dance in her seat.

"Don't even remind me that you're having sex. I don't need to hear that shit." Mat frowned.

"I'm twenty-six years old Matilyn. Stop with the dramatics," Marlee replied.

Mat was only four years older than her, but she swore that she was Marlee's mother. When they were growing up, she was so overprotective that boys used to be scared to approach her little sister.

"You want some more to eat baby?" Sierra asked as she got up and grabbed Mat's now empty plate.

"Nah baby, I'm good," Mat replied, right as someone knocked on the door.

"Let me go. That's probably Tyson," Marlee replied.

"Ole pussy whipped ass nigga," Mat hissed.

"You just got here. Tell his disgusting ass to calm down," Sierra fussed.

"We were across the street by his mama's house. I just came to see y'all for minute, but we're about to go home. I'll call you later Sierra," Marlee promised before she opened the door and walked out.

Just like she'd assumed, Tyson was standing on the porch waiting for her. A few dudes from the block were out there playing basketball on a makeshift goal, but their eyes landed on Marlee as soon as they saw her. Marlee knew most of them as friends of Mat's, so she smiled and waved as they headed to Tyson car. He instinctively wrapped his arm around her waist as he opened the car door and ushered inside.

Taj stood on the porch and shook her head in disgust. Taj just shook her head at his nerve. Tyson was good to Marlee, but he wasn't a saint. He got mad when another man looked at her but, most times, he did more than just look. He was acting brand new now but, as soon as Marlee was out of town the following weekend, Taj would probably end up at her house and in her bed once again, just like before.

Chapter 2

"I told your greedy ass not to eat that food from them Chinese people. That shit looked like it was old. You got me about to throw up too." Marlee frowned as she clamped her hand over her mouth in disgust.

"Stop being so extra Marlee. You work in the medical field. This shouldn't be nothing new to you," Desiree replied, as she held their cousin Yanni's hair in her hand while she threw up in the toilet.

"I'm a physical therapy assistant, not a nurse. That shit is turning my stomach," Marlee replied as she turned up her nose.

Marlee, Tyson, and her two cousins were walking through the mall, when Yanni suddenly rushed off to the bathroom. Marlee and Desi ran behind her because they didn't know what was wrong with her. When Yanni ran into the stall and started throwing up, Marlee felt like she was about to start doing it too. Forever the nurturer of the trio, Desi rushed into the stall to assist her. Yanni was greedy as hell and she was always trying something new. Marlee hated the food in the mall, but her cousin just had to get it anyway.

"Bitch, I feel like I'm dying," Yanni said when she stood up and walked over to the sink.

"You look like it too," Marlee replied.

"Are you okay boo?" Desi asked as she handed her some wet paper towels.

"Yeah, I'm good, thanks to you. This bitch ain't good for nothing," Yanni said while pointing at Marlee.

"I'm sorry cousin, but you know I got a weak stomach," Marlee replied as she helped Yanni fix her disheveled hair.

"I should have stayed my ass at home. That's what I get for following behind you to get those ugly ass shoes," Yanni argued.

"Bitch, I didn't ask you to come. I wanted Desi to come with me and you invited yourself," Marlee snapped.

"Alright y'all. Let's not do this right now," Desi said, stopping her two favorite cousins from bumping heads like they usually did.

Usually, their other cousin, Kallie, would be there to help keep the two of them apart, but she had other plans.

"You always got something to say about me tagging along, but Tyson be all up your ass and you be fine with that," Yanni retorted.

"Tyson is my man and the one who's paying for those ugly ass shoes, as you called them. You sound like you're mad. Get you a nigga who can do more than just buy you something to eat. Maybe then you can stop riding the bus," Marlee quipped.

"That dope money only last for so long honey," Yanni replied.

"And that's exactly why I work four days a week for ten hours a day to make sure that I have my own," Marlee retorted.

"Can we have one day without the two of you going at it?" Desi begged.

"I'm fine. Iyana seems to be the one with the problem, just like always. They need to come up with a cure for jealously. It's obviously a disease," Marlee spat.

"You ain't got shit for me to be jealous of." Yanni frowned.

"Okay. Keep telling yourself that until you start to believe it," Marlee smirked, right as her phone rang.

Tyson was waiting for them outside the bathroom, so he was probably trying to see what was going on. Marlee stepped away to take his call, as Desi turned to Yanni and started fussing.

"Why do you always have to start with her?" Desi asked.

"How did I start with her? I just said that I should have stayed my ass at home and I should have," Yanni replied.

"Yeah, but did you have to call her shoes ugly? It's like you love provoking her for whatever reason. We're too grown for all that arguing all the time. She goes out of her way to be nice to you, but you act like you hate your own cousin," Desi noted.

"I don't hate her but, unlike the rest of y'all, I'm not kissing Marlee's ass. She got you and Tyson doing that enough," Yanni snapped.

"If I didn't know any better, I would think that Marlee was right. You do sound like you're jealous," Desi replied.

"Of what? Marlee don't have shit that I want. I might not have a huge walk-in closet full of designer labels and fancy perfume, but I'm happy with my life just the way it is. Who puts mirrors on all four walls of their closet? That bitch is obsessed with her damn self if you ask me," Yanni noted, as Desi looked at her sideways.

Truthfully, she was a little envious of her cousin, but she would never admit it. Marlee was a beautiful girl and she had a style that couldn't be compared to anyone else. She was bold and wasn't afraid to try anything once. While Yanni barely graduated from high school, Marlee had gone to college for two years and got her associates degree. She would have gone back for two more years but, when she started to make a name for herself in the makeup industry, she quickly abandoned the idea. She had money coming in from two different incomes, not that she had to use any of it. Tyson had her spoiled rotten and she never had to buy anything for herself. He wasn't all that cute in Yanni's opinion, looking like Kodak Black with a fade. Then, he was fat on top of that. He could dress his ass off though and he had enough money to make a woman overlook his appearance. Their entire family felt that Marlee could have done better, but he treated her well, so they all liked him. Yanni didn't have the best luck in relationships, but she was hoping for her luck to change soon.

"Let's just go," Desi said as she opened the bathroom door and walked away.

Marlee was still standing there on the phone, but Tyson wasn't with her.

"Okay baby. I'm going to Saks to see about my shoes. Just meet me over there when you're done," Marlee said before she hung up the phone.

"Where's Tyson?" Desi asked.

"He went to look for a belt, but he'll meet us in Saks," Marlee replied.

"Okay, let's go," Desi said.

"Do you feel better Yanni? You want some ginger ale or something to settle your stomach?" Marlee asked her cousin.

Marlee hated arguing with her cousin, but Yanni was always coming for her. She never had an issue with any of the other cousins, but Marlee stayed on her radar. Even still, Marlee was always the bigger person. She would always try to make amends with Yanni, even though she was never the one who started it.

"No, I'm good," Yanni replied as she and Desi followed her to the overly priced store.

Everything in Saks was high, so Yanni never even bothered to look at anything. Desi always picked up shoes to see the price, but she never even bothered to buy any of them. Marlee's closet was full of overpriced clothes and shoes that she barely wore. Even her perfume cost two hundred dollars and up. Yanni sat down, while Marlee went up to the counter with a shoe and asked the clerk for her size. Desi sat down next to her after a while and watched as Marlee tried the shoes on.

"Yes bitch, these are gonna be cute with my ripped jeans and halter top," Marlee said as she admired the shoes in the mirror.

"They look so cute on your feet cousin," Desi complimented.

"Thanks cousin." Marlee smiled.

"Girl, I know you ain't about to spend almost nine hundred dollars on that shit. They look too plain to even spend half as much," Yanni said as she scrunched up her face.

"I'm not spending a dime; Tyson is," Marlee laughed.

"He got you too spoiled to complain about anything," Desi replied.

"They're not even all that cute to be so high. They look like space ship shoes." Yanni frowned.

"That's your opinion, but I love them. Let me call my man and tell him that I'm ready," Marlee said as she grabbed her phone.

"Just one pair today Marlee? You know we got two colors in instead of one," the clerk who knew Marlee by name said when he walked up.

"What other color? Let me see," Marlee begged.

"That's a damn shame when the store clerk knows you by name," Desi laughed.

"You know I love this store," Marlee replied, right as the clerk came out and handed her another box.

She gasped when she opened it and saw the hot pink, blue, and gold beauties that were inside. Marlee wanted to cry because now she was torn. She had just gotten two pairs of expensive shoes the week before and she didn't know if Tyson was going to do it again.

"Oh shit! How do I look? Is my hair straight?" Yanni asked as she pulled some gloss from her purse and coated her lips.

"You look fine. What the hell is wrong with you?" Desi questioned as she looked around.

When her eyes landed on the two men who had just walked into the store, her question was answered. Yanni was always looking for a come up and she could spot a nigga with money from a mile away. Things never worked out in her favor, but that never stopped her from trying.

"Girl, that's RJ," Yanni said, like her cousins were supposed to know who he was.

"Who?" Marlee asked.

"RJ Banks. I work for him. Well, I work for his father, but he's part owner or something like that. All I know is that he signs the paychecks honey," Yanni answered.

"Oh." Marlee shrugged uncaringly.

"They own the parking garage company that I work for," Yanni noted.

Yanni worked as a cashier for Banks Parking Garage, and RJ and his father owned the place. They owned about four of them, but Yanni worked at the main location in the central business district where their offices were located. The location where she worked made about one hundred grand per month or more, especially on the days when there was a festival in the city. RJ was rolling in the dough and Yanni wanted to help him spend it.

"He's handsome. They both are," Desi complimented.

"I think the one with the dreads is his cousin or something. He's always at the job for one thing or another. That nigga RJ is paid out the ass and he's not married," Yanni replied.

"As if that would have mattered if he was," Desi snickered, right as the two men came closer.

"Hey RJ," Yanni cooed when the two men walked pass them.

"What's up?" a man who looked almost identical to Jayceon Taylor, or The Game as he was known to most, spoke back.

He didn't have the facial tattoos and he didn't look as mean as the other man that he was with, but he could pass for the rapper's cuter but younger brother. He looked to be over six feet tall and he was sexy as hell. Desi wasn't even interested in getting with anybody, but even she had to do a double take. The other man that he was with was handsome too but in a more rugged kind of way. The man known as RJ sported a low cut, while his accomplice had shoulder-length dreads that were dyed red at the tip. Both men looked at Marlee briefly, but she was too busy admiring her shoes to notice. Yanni kept her eyes on her target the entire time until they were out of sight. She fell back into her seat dramatically as soon as they were out of view.

"Bitch! That nigga is too fine for words," Yanni said as she fanned her face.

"What nigga?" Marlee questioned, like she was hearing it for the first time.

"One of the niggas that was just looking at you," Desi replied.

"He was not looking at her," Yanni snapped angrily.

"I don't care if he was," Marlee said.

"You better not care. Don't get nobody fucked up in here," Tyson warned when he walked up on them and kissed Marlee's neck.

"Come see baby. They have two new colors and I can't decide which ones I want. Which ones do you like best?" Marlee asked as she modeled one shoe on each foot.

"I like them both," Tyson replied as he wrapped his arms around her waist.

"I know Tyson, but which ones do you like best? I need to make a decision," Marlee whined.

"No, you don't. Get both pairs," Tyson said like it was nothing.

"Are you sure Tyson? You just spent close to two grand on shoes last week," Marlee reminded him.

"I know baby, but you're worth it. I don't have a limit when it comes to you," he replied as he kissed her lips.

"Aww, that's so sweet," Desi smiled, as Yanni rolled her eyes up to the ceiling.

"I can't wait to hit those Atlanta clubs next weekend," Marlee said as she took the shoes off and put them back in their boxes

"Me too cousin," Desi agreed.

"Don't be trying to look too good for them ATL niggas. Just remember that you got a man at home," Tyson replied.

"You don't have to remind me of that every time I leave. Ain't nobody getting this but you boo," Marlee said as she backed it up on him.

"Damn baby. Let me go pay for this shit, so we can go home," Tyson said as he licked his lips in anticipation.

"It's about time," Yanni said as she stood up and walked away.

"The fuck made you invite her jealous ass? Bitch can't stand to see you happy," Tyson fussed.

"I didn't invite her nowhere. That's all on Desi," Marlee replied.

"You know it's all love with us cuz, but leave her hating ass at home next time. She gon' keep playing with my girl and get herself fucked up," Tyson said while looking at Desi.

"Y'all know how Yanni is. She don't mean no harm," Desi defended.

"Fuck her. That bitch got it in for my baby and I'm telling you what I know," Tyson fumed.

"What do you know that I don't? Did that bitch say something about me to you?" Marlee asked.

"Hell no, baby! You think I would let anybody talk about you in my presence? She don't have to say shit. Her actions show it. She wants to be you," Tyson said, right before he walked off to the cash register.

"That bitch better thank God for you. I would have been laid her hating ass out if you wouldn't always stop me," Marlee said to Desi.

"I'll have a talk with her," Desi promised.

"I'm tired of always being the bigger person. She acts like I did something to her. If so, I would much rather her tell me and let's get past the shit," Marlee fumed.

"I really don't think it has anything to do with you, Marlee. Yanni is not happy with her own life right now. She's always complaining about not making enough money at her job and she's tired of living with auntie Yvette," Desi said, speaking of Yanni's mother.

"But what does any of that have to do with me, Desi?" Marlee questioned.

"Nothing, but I think she just takes her frustrations out on other people." Desi shrugged.

"Don't say other people because it seems to be just me. You can make all the excuses in the world, but I see shit for what it really is. She doesn't seem to have an issue with you and Kallie. Our relationship has been rocky for the past two or three years and I'm tired of trying to figure out why," Marlee noted.

"We all need to just sit down and have a talk. Our family is too close for this to even be happening," Desi replied.

"The way I feel right now, we can take it to the streets and box it out. The bitch knows she can't handle me, so I don't know why she's always coming for me," Marlee said.

"You ready to go baby?" Tyson asked when he walked up holding Marlee's bags.

"Yeah, I'm ready," Marlee replied, as he grabbed her hand and walked away.

Desi walked with them, as Yanni trailed behind talking on her phone. Her attitude seemed to have disappeared, letting Marlee know that it had to be a man on the phone. That was the only time that she smiled and seemed to be happy. Marlee was happy that she had to work and couldn't accompany them on their trip to Atlanta. She didn't come when they went to Florida two months before and Marlee was fine with that too. She never really helped anyway. Desi and Kallie always helped Marlee set up, while Yanni sat around and looked.

"Call me later so we can go over our checklist for next weekend. Since it's just the two of us, we have to make sure that we don't forget anything," Desi said to Marlee when they got to their cars in the parking garage.

"Okay cousin, I will," Marlee promised before she and Tyson walked away.

"I'm tired as hell." Yanni yawned once they got into Desi's car. She turned up the music and danced in her seat as Desi drove away.

"We need to talk," Desi said as she lowered the volume and prepared to have a long overdue talk with one of her favorite cousins.

Chapter 3

"Hey daddy!" Marlee yelled when her father opened the door for her and Desi.

She and Desi had caught an early Friday morning flight to Atlanta, but they rented a car at the airport. Marlee had already shipped all her work items to her father's house, so she didn't have that to worry about. Marlee was happy that the wedding was on a Friday because she only worked Monday through Thursday. She and Desi planned to hit up some clubs that night and sleep all day Saturday, before flying back home that Sunday afternoon.

"Hey baby, with your pretty self," Matthew said as he pulled his youngest daughter in for a hug.

It had been six months since he'd seen Marlee, although they talked on the phone daily. Matthew hadn't been to New Orleans in two years, but Marlee came to visit him a few times. He still had family in New Orleans, but work didn't let him visit as often as he wanted to.

"Hey Matthew," Desi said as she hugged her former uncle.

"Hey, my girl. What happened to all that pretty hair that you used to have?" Matthew asked as he ran his hands over Desi's low, neatly lined fade.

"It's been gone for over a year now. I got tired of dealing with it, so I chopped it off. This is low maintenance. A trip to the barber and I'm done," Desi replied.

"It looks good on you too," Matthew said as he ushered them inside.

"Thanks." Desi smiled, as they followed him into the living room and took a seat.

"Is your girlfriend home? I want to meet her," Marlee said as she looked around.

Her father lived in the same apartment when she last visited, but he had a different woman at the time. Matthew had lived in Atlanta for about fifteen years, and Marlee lost count of how many women he ran through. Matthew and her mother, Tiffany, were married before Mat and Marlee came along. Matthew was a brick layer and he had an abundance of work at one time.

Things changed when Marlee was seven and Mat was eleven. Matthew got laid off from his job and money was running low. At the urging of his brother, they went to Atlanta to look for work and lucked up on a good job. It was only supposed to be temporary and Matthew flew home every weekend to spend time with his family. Whenever school was out, Tiffany would pack up their daughters and spend a few days in Atlanta with him. It didn't take long for Matthew to get promoted on his job and he was making more money than ever.

He decided that he wanted to make Atlanta his home and he begged Tiffany to pack up the girls and move there with him. School had just started, so Tiffany decided that it wasn't a good time. Matthew wasn't able to come home as often with his new position, but Tiffany didn't mind making the weekend trip. The distance was putting a strain on their relationship, but she tried her best to make it work. She felt Matthew slipping away so, when his birthday rolled around, Tiffany left her kids with her sister and decided to surprise her man with a visit. Unfortunately, she was the one who was surprised when she got there and another woman answered the door.

Tiffany was heartbroken, and Matthew didn't make it any better. He basically told her that it was her fault that he'd cheated. If she would have moved like he told her to, he wouldn't have felt the need to seek companionship elsewhere. There was nothing else that he needed to say. Tiffany went back to New Orleans and filed for divorce the very next week. It took her two years before she started dating again, but she was happy that she did. Her second husband, Alvin, was a Godsend and he loved her and her daughters more than anything. They had been married for ten years and she was looking forward to many more. She and Alvin got government funding to start a home healthcare agency and things had been going great for them since then. Tiffany made sure that her family were employed, and Alvin did the same for his.

"No, she's at work, but you'll see her later. What time do you have to be at the hotel for the wedding?" Matthew asked.

"Not until two. The wedding is not until seven and I need a nap." Marlee yawned.

She had six faces to do, including the bride, but that wouldn't take her long at all. It was only a little after eight and she had been up since five. She and Tyson had been getting it in all week, but that was nothing new. He was acting like she was leaving for a week, instead of just the weekend. He was complaining too much and getting on her last nerve. Marlee never took off from work, so she promised him that she would take two days off just for him. He was too excited, and Marlee was happy that she could make his day.

"How's Tiffany?" Matthew asked his daughter, referring to his ex-wife.

"She's good. Just working as usual," Marlee replied.

"What about your sister?" Matthew inquired, like it killed him to call his daughter's name.

"Mat is fine too," Marlee replied.

"Matilyn. Her name is Matilyn, not Mat," Matthew corrected. "That was my late mother's name and that's what I'm calling her."

"Okay daddy. Well, Matilyn is fine," Marlee replied.

"You know I love your sister, Marlee. I just don't approve of her lifestyle. That's not how I was raised and I'm not apologizing for that," Matthew spoke up.

"Let's not do this right now daddy. Let's just agree to disagree. I don't want to argue," Marlee replied.

She didn't care how her father felt; her feelings would always remain the same. In her opinion, his love came with limitations. Her love was unconditional. She didn't care who Mat decided to spend her life with. She loved her regardless.

"Okay baby. Go get you some rest and we'll talk later. I'm sure you and Desi are hitting up some clubs tonight," Matthew laughed.

"You already know we are. I hope your girlfriend don't have a problem with us coming in late," Marlee replied.

"Nah, she's cool, but I'll give you a key anyway," Matthew said as he made sure that they were comfortable in his spare bedroom.

Desi was out as soon as her head hit the pillow, but Marlee talked to Tyson for a few minutes. As soon as she hung up with him, she climbed into bed with her cousin and drifted off to sleep.

***

"Cousin, you are a miracle worker," Desi said as she and Marlee got dressed to go out for the night.

They had just come back from the hotel where Marlee did the makeup for the wedding and they were ready for a night of fun.

"What do you mean?" Marlee asked.

"That was not the prettiest bride, but you made her look like a queen," Desi laughed.

"Girl, I didn't want to say nothing but damn," Marlee laughed with her.

"But, she got a husband, so hey. He obviously loves her just the way she is." Desi shrugged.

"Yep and she just found out that she's pregnant," Marlee replied.

As soon as the words spilled out of her mouth, she wished that she could take them back.

"Oh, well that's good," Desi replied as she looked away sadly.

"I'm sorry Desi. I wasn't trying to be insensitive or nothing," Marlee apologized.

"It's okay Marlee. People get pregnant every day. I can't get in my feelings every time I hear about it. It won't ever happen for me, but I'm happy for other women who get to experience it," Desi replied.

Although it wasn't intentional, Marlee felt like shit. After being raped by her mother's live-in boyfriend at only eight years old, Desi had been left unable to have children. Desi was an only child and her mother, Dionne, had her spoiled rotten. She had dated Corey for two years before she let him move in with her and her then five-year-old daughter. Desi was crazy about Corey at first, but then things seemed to change. She didn't like to be around him when her mother wasn't there, but Dionne didn't pay attention to the signs.

One night after being called in to work unexpectedly, she put Desi to sleep and left her in Corey's care. Usually, Desi would stay at Marlee's house when her mother worked, but it was a spur of the moment kind of thing. Dionne made it all the way to her job when she realized that she forgot her access card to get into the office. She had to turn all the way back around and it was a good thing that she did. She crept into the house, hoping not to wake anyone up, but sleep was the furthest thing from Corey's mind. When Dionne heard her baby crying, she got her gun from her safe and crept down the hall to Desi's bedroom. Her heart broke and her rage took over when she walked down on her man lying on top of her daughter.

Corey's eyes were closed, like he was enjoying the pain that he was inflicting on her baby. Desi begged him to stop, but he was moaning and groaning like he was fucking a grown ass woman. Dionne didn't even think twice as she pulled him off her daughter and emptied the clip to her gun in his naked body. She didn't even think to call the police to tell them what she'd done. She grabbed Desi and rushed her straight to the emergency room with the gun still in her hands. It wasn't until the police were called to the hospital that she told them about Corey's dead body that was in her house.

Everyone thought sure that Dionne was going to get off for killing him, but she was charged with manslaughter instead. She ended up doing six years in jail, while Desi stayed with Marlee and her family. Desi was traumatized for months and she refused to talk to anyone. She couldn't go to school, so Tiffany had to hire a teacher to home school her. Everyone was okay with her not talking to them, but Marlee wasn't. She and Desi shared a room, so Marlee would climb into bed every night and talk to her. Even when Desi used to wet the bed, Marlee never made her feel bad about it. She simply helped her take a shower and changed her sheets.

After a while, Desi opened up, but Marlee was the only person who she would talk to. That was fine with the family because Marlee became the mouth piece for them both. Once her mother, Dionne, was released from prison,

Desi was flourishing like a normal teenager and doing well. Dionne was so overprotective of her one and only daughter, and she still had a hard time letting Desi be an adult. Thankfully, counseling and lot of love from her family helped Desi through her tough time. She'd also been volunteering at a local grief counselling center, hoping to help people who were just as lost as she once was. It took a while, but Desi didn't mind telling her story to anyone who wanted to hear it.

"I'm ready to drink til I drop," Desi said as she did a little shake in the mirror.

"You look too cute," Marlee complimented.

"Thanks cousin and so do you," Desi replied.

"Them niggas gon' be on you tonight," Marlee said as she hit her cousin on the butt.

"They can keep the drinks coming, but I'll pass on everything else," Desi replied.

"Every man is not like Jerry, Desi. You'll never know what's out there because you're too afraid to try," Marlee said.

"Can we not talk about this right now Marlee? I'm ready to enjoy myself without feeling depressed," Desi replied.

Jerry was Desi's ex-boyfriend and Tyson's good friend. She honestly thought that he would be her husband someday. That was, until he was hit with child support papers for a baby that she didn't even know he'd made. Desi was crushed, especially since she knew that a child was something that she could never give him. That happened over a year ago, and Jerry was still begging for her forgiveness. He swore that it would never happen again, but Desi didn't want to hear it. As much as she loved him, she just couldn't see herself taking him back. And as much as she loved children, she couldn't see herself welcoming a baby that he'd made by cheating on her.

"Sorry cousin. I won't bring it up again," Marlee promised, shaking Desi away from her depressing thoughts.

"Are you ready Marlee?" Desi asked her.

"Yep," Marlee said, right as Tyson was calling her on Facetime.

He had been blowing her up since they got there earlier, and he couldn't wait for Sunday to come. Tyson usually slept all day and hustled all night until Marlee came back home. He hated to sleep alone.

"Don't forget the key. I don't want to wake anybody up when we get back," Desi whispered, while her cousin talked on the phone.

Marlee held the key up for her to see, as she continued her conversation. She still hadn't met her father's girlfriend because they were asleep when she got in from work. When Marlee and Desi left for the hotel, Cara was taking a nap by then. When they got back, she was out with her friends, so Marlee wasn't looking forward to meeting her until the following day.

After telling her father that they were leaving, Marlee turned on her GPS and headed to their first destination. She hung up with Tyson as soon as they pulled up to the club. She and Desi checked their appearances before they got out of the car and joined the crowd of people who were partying inside.

Three more clubs and many hours later, Marlee and Desi were drained. They drank and danced the night away and they were ready for the bed. It was after six the next morning when they got back to the house and the sky was about to turn a different color. Marlee tried to be as quiet as she could when she inserted the key, hoping not to wake anyone up. Her father told her that his girlfriend was off that day and she didn't want to disturb her.

"Oh shit, Desi. The key ain't working," Marlee mumbled to her cousin.

"The hell you mean it ain't working?" Desi asked.

"Just what I said. I'm turning it, but the door still ain't opening," Marlee replied.

"Let me try it," Desi said as she snatched the key from her hand.

She did the exact same thing that Marlee had done and got the same results.

"I told you. The shit ain't working," Marlee noted.

"That's because they locked the deadbolt. Call your daddy and tell him to let us in," Desi suggested.

"I don't want to wake his girlfriend up. It's after six in the morning," Marlee noted.

She knew that the woman was home because her car was parked right next to Matthew's truck.

"What the hell are we gonna do then, Marlee? I'm not sleeping in no damn car. I gotta pee," Desi complained as she shifted her weight from one foot to the other.

"Calm down girl. Let me call him. I hope his ass answers," Marlee said.

"He better," Desi said as she started doing a dance to keep her urine at bay.

"Hello," Marlee whispered when someone answered the phone. "Daddy, it's me. Come let me in. The key ain't working."

"What?" Desi asked when she saw the look on Marlee's face.

"His ass hung up on me," Marlee replied.

"Girl, Matthew better stop playing. I'll piss in his front yard and kill all these damn flowers," Desi threatened, making her cousin laugh.

She was just about to call back when she heard the locks to the door being undone. Desi breathed a sigh of relief when the door was swung open for them. Marlee was ready to thank her father for his help, when she looked up into the face of his angry girlfriend, Cara.

"I'm so sorry Cara. I didn't mean to wake you," Marlee apologized as she and Desi walked into the house.

She expected the other woman to say something, but she turned and walked away instead. They never even got to really look at her because it was dark, and she was gone before they really had a chance to. When she slammed the bedroom door, Marlee and Desi looked at each other in shock. They knew that she was probably upset, but they didn't expect her to react the way that she did. Marlee hated that her first interaction with the other woman wasn't a pleasant one. Hopefully, Cara would be more accepting of her apology later after she'd rested up a bit.

"The fuck is wrong with that bitch?" Desi asked as she and her cousin headed to the room that they were sleeping in.

"What do you think is wrong with her? We come busting up in here at six in the morning and broke the lady's rest. And your drunk ass needs to calm down," Marlee giggled, as her cousin raced to the bathroom.

Desi was always the calm one of their crew, but she had no problem getting ignorant when and if she had to.

"I understand her frustration, but that's not our fault. Your daddy gave us the key, so we wouldn't disturb her. It was probably her ass who put the deadbolt on," Desi fussed.

"I don't even know girl. I'm about to take a shower and prepare to sleep my day away." Marlee yawned as she grabbed some clothes from her duffle bag.

Once she showered, Desi did the same while Marlee talked on the phone with Tyson. He had been out all night as well and he planned to sleep his day away until she returned home the following day.

"Can we please go to sleep without music for once?" Desi yawned as she snuggled under the covers.

Marlee nodded her head as she rolled her eyes up to the ceiling. Everybody knew how much Marlee loved music. She didn't do anything without it, and that included sleep. She had been doing it so long that Tyson could no longer sleep without music either. Desi didn't have to worry though because she wasn't going to do that in her father's house, especially after having already disturbed Cara's sleep. She had her earplugs prepared to listen to her music on her phone.

"I'm going to bed Tyson. I'll call you when I get up, but that won't be any time soon," Marlee said, right before they got off the phone.

She turned on her R & B playlist and put her plugs in her ear, right before getting comfortable in the king-sized bed with her cousin. She and Desi had planned to sleep their day away, but things didn't quite happen the way that they planned.

Chapter 4

Besides the smell of something cooking, the loud arguing coming from inside the apartment woke Marlee up much sooner than she anticipated. It was a little after two that evening, but it felt like she'd only slept for a few minutes. Her head was pounding, but she managed to lift it slightly to see if Desi was up or not.

"Desi!" Marlee called out when she saw the spot that her cousin was in was vacant.

"I'm right here," Desi said as she zipped up her duffle bag.

Marlee was shocked to see that her cousin was dressed and packed, like they were leaving that same day instead of the next.

"The hell are you doing up already? I'm still tired as hell." Marlee yawned.

"You can fly back home tomorrow if you want to, but I'm driving back today. I've already made arrangements with the rental car company," Desi noted, making her cousin jump up despite her pounding head.

"What's wrong Desi?" Is everything okay?" Marlee asked in concern.

"I'm good, but your daddy's girlfriend is about to get knocked the fuck out," Desi fumed.

"I'm confused or maybe I'm just tired," Marlee said, looking at her in confusion.

"That bitch has been going off for a while now. Her and your daddy's arguing is what woke me up. She's in her feelings about what time we came in this morning. Your daddy was asking her why she locked the deadbolt and it was on from there."

"Girl, fuck her! Nobody was trying to wake her up. That's why my daddy gave me a key. She got the wrong bitch if she thinks she gon' talk to me crazy. Give me a minute to get dressed and we can get the fuck up out of here," Marlee ranted.

She forgot all about her pounding head as she went to the bathroom to freshen up. Once she was dressed, she packed her duffle bag and made sure that all her work supplies were in their proper places. Since they were driving, she didn't need to have her father ship everything back to her. She could pack it in the rental car and be done with it.

"I'm hungry as hell, but I ain't eating nothing from her ass." Desi frowned.

"We can stop and grab something before we head out. We can take turns driving, so we can get some more rest," Marlee suggested, right as someone knocked on the door.

Her father didn't wait to be granted entry before he slowly made his way inside the room. Marlee and Desi were making the bed, but he didn't miss their packed bags that sat in the middle of the floor.

"What's up baby girl? You're leaving?" Matthew asked.

"Yeah, I think it's best before we have a problem," Marlee replied.

"Don't trip off that dumb shit that Cara is saying. She just be in her feelings sometimes," Matthew said in a whisper. He was looking behind him to make sure that Cara didn't hear him.

"No, it's fine daddy. I would never want to disrespect anyone in their own house, so it's best that I leave. You already know that I'm not good with holding my tongue. We're gonna just drive back today and I can rest when I get home."

By then, they all heard Cara on the phone talking loudly about Marlee and Desi. She was saying that she didn't know how they did things in New Orleans, but they were going to respect her as the woman of the house. Right then, Marlee knew that she and Desi had made the right choice when they decided to leave. Things were going to turn out bad if they didn't.

"This is my house and you don't have to leave if you don't want to," Matthew said lowly.

"The fact that you're whispering lets me know that that's not true," Marlee said as she grabbed her bag.

"It's not even like that Marlee. I'm in a bad position right now," Matthew replied while he grabbed her work supplies to carry them out.

"It's cool daddy." Marlee shrugged like it was no big deal.

She loved her father, but she had to keep it real. He hadn't been in her and Mat's life like he should have since they were younger. Their stepfather had three other kids, but he was more of a father to them than Matthew ever was. Matthew was always full of excuses and Marlee was used to it by now. She had to call him most of the time or they probably wouldn't have talked as often as they did.

"Thanks for letting us stay here Matthew." Desi smiled as she followed her cousin out the bedroom.

Marlee wanted to laugh when she got into the living room and saw the tall, skinny woman who was standing there talking on the phone. Marlee was a little over five feet and she was considered short to most. Matthew was much taller than his daughter and he was considered average height for a man. The fact that Cara towered over them both was hilarious to Marlee. Her natural hair was pulled back into a fluffy ponytail, and her drawn on eyebrows resembled the Nike symbol. Marlee was sorry that she was leaving because Cara could use a makeover and she would do it for free. She didn't get a good look at her the night before, but she was a hot mess.

"Seriously daddy?" Marlee questioned as she and Desi looked at his girlfriend and laughed.

Matthew had been with several women in the past, but none of them looked like Cara. She was nothing like the women that he usually went for, and Marlee was shocked.

"Make sure you get the house key back Matthew. And make this the last time you give it to somebody who doesn't live here," Cara snapped as she looked at Marlee and Desi in anger.

Cara was looking forward to meeting Marlee when she first learned that she was coming to visit. Her eagerness quickly turned into anger when Marlee had the nerve to disrespect their house the way she did. Cara was ready to snap on her man when his phone rang at six in the morning.

When she answered and Marlee begged to be let in, she was livid. There were certain things that she didn't play, and she didn't care if her man's daughter had a problem with it.

"You come get it. All that hot shit you were talking on the phone. Come say that shit to my face. I bet I lay your pencil thin ass out," Marlee threatened.

"Marlee chill," her father begged as he ushered her outside.

"You better listen to your daddy, lil girl!" Cara yelled, as Marlee and Desi walked out the front door.

"Come outside and pop off, so you can catch these hands hoe. You talking all that shit and he gon' have a new bitch living up in here next month," Marlee said, knowing exactly how her father was.

"Calm down baby girl. Don't even worry about what she's saying," Matthew begged as he walked his daughter to the car.

"Fuck that bitch! You don't ever have to worry about me coming to your house again as long as she's here," Marlee swore.

"She won't be here much longer, but I need her right now. I lost my job a few months ago and I'm just starting a new one. I need to get my money up before I can do anything. She's paying all the bills for me right now," Matthew admitted.

That explained why he was entertaining her tall, ugly ass in the first place. Marlee just shook her head in disgust, but she wasn't surprised. She was so happy that her mother no longer had to deal with him and his bullshit. It didn't matter that he was her father. He was not the man that she would have wanted her mother to spend the rest of her life with.

"I'll call you when I make it home daddy," Marlee promised once everything was loaded in the car.

She gave her father a hug before she and Desi left to head back to New Orleans. They were both tired, but they stayed up the entire time that it took to get back home. They took turns driving, but they kept each other company so the ride wouldn't be too boring. Besides stopping for gas and food, they drove straight through and made it to Louisiana right as the sun set. It was still early, but they were both in desperate need of more sleep. Marlee was driving, but she could see that Desi was fighting her sleep in the passenger's seat. Marlee had tried calling Tyson twice before, but he never answered. He was probably getting the rest that she and her cousin were lacking. He had her messed up if he thought he was going to keep her up though. She already knew that sex was going to be the first thing that he wanted, but it wasn't happening.

"You wanna stay by me until tomorrow? I can follow you to turn in the rental and bring you back home?" Marlee offered.

"Girl, that's fine with me. I don't feel like driving no more anyway." Desi yawned.

"And I'll make sure to turn the music off, so you can sleep," Marlee giggled.

"I'll probably be too tired to hear it," Desi said, waving her off.

They made one more food stop before getting on the bridge to get to Marlee's house. Desi was thankful for her cousin's second bedroom and bath because all she wanted was a shower and a bed. Tyson and Marlee's cars were in their assigned spots, so she parked the rental behind them before they got out of the car. Desi grabbed her bags from the back seat, but Marlee planned to send Tyson out to get hers whenever he got up. As soon as they entered the house, Desi laughed when she heard the slow jams pouring from their speaker in the bedroom.

"I'm going turn it off," Marlee promised as she sat her food on the kitchen counter.

"Girl, I'm good either way. I can't tell nobody what to do in their own house," Desi said as she sat at the dining room table and started to eat her food.

Marlee walked down the hall to their bedroom to bring Tyson his food, before she went back to the dining room to eat with her cousin. Tired or not, she knew that he was about to wake up and devour the wings that she'd just purchased for him. Tyson was a big boy and he didn't turn down food.

"Baby, wake up, I got you some food," Marlee said when she swung the door open and flicked on the light.

Tyson was in bed, but he was doing way more than just sleeping. Marlee was in shock. The drink that she'd been holding fell from her hand and stained their tan colored carpet a bright shade of red. The music was still on and, had she not turned on the light, her man would have probably continued to fuck another woman in their bed. He didn't hear when she came into the house and he never heard when she entered their bedroom.

"Shit!" Tyson yelled as he jumped up from his compromising position and reached for his boxers.

He was fucked and there was no lie that he could tell to make the situation better. Hearing about it would have been one thing, but to have Marlee standing there witnessing it with her own eyes was an altogether different story. She wasn't due home until the following day, and Tyson wondered why her plans had changed. Marlee was in a daze as she looked right past him and into the eyes of the woman who he was entertaining. He knew that look in her eyes all too well. She was in attack mode and no one was spared once she got like that. Tyson made a move to grab her arm and that was the worst thing that he could have ever done.

"Get the fuck off me!" Marlee screamed as she started to swing on him.

Tyson was dead ass wrong, so he stood there and took the blows that she was delivering to his face and chest.

"I fucked up baby," he admitted as tears of regret rolled down his chubby cheeks.

"Fuck you, nigga! I hate you! I regret the day I ever met your sad ass," Marlee cried.

"I made a stupid mistake Marlee. I don't even know what to say or do to fix this," Tyson admitted.

"There ain't no fixing it. It's bad enough that you got another bitch in my bed, but my cousin though nigga!" Marlee cried and screamed.

Desi heard all the commotion over the music and ran down the hall to see what was going on. When she got to the room and saw Marlee swinging on Tyson, she had a look of confusion written across her face. That was, until she saw their cousin, Yanni, nervously hurrying to put on her clothes. Desi wanted to say that she was shocked, but nothing that Iyana did surprised her anymore. She'd slept with one of her best friend's husband a few months after she served as the maid of honor in their wedding. As wrong as Yanni was, when the girl came to her house with a car load of other chicks, Desi, Marlee, and Kallie were the ones who went out there and fought with her.

"Bitch, I know you didn't," Desi fumed as she looked at her cousin in disgust.

"Man, come help me with this girl Desi," Tyson begged through his busted lip.

Marlee had picked up the speaker that the music was playing from and smashed it across his head, silencing the melody. Blood was rolling into his eyes, making it almost impossible for him to see.

"Fuck your fat ass. You better be lucky that I'm not helping her," Desi fumed.

Marlee didn't need any help because she was fucking Tyson up all by herself. Yanni looked scared out of her mind, but Desi didn't feel sorry for her. For days, she had replayed their conversation in the mall over in her head. Something that Yanni said stood out to her, but Desi didn't know if she was making too much out of the situation or not. Marlee and Tyson had lived in their condo for a minute, and Desi couldn't recall one time that she'd ever seen the inside of her cousin's closet. The fact that Yanni knew the space as well as she did raised a red flag, but she brushed it off. She wasn't even as close to Marlee as Desi was, so that was odd.

"No bitch, don't try to run!" Marlee yelled, snapping Desi out of her thoughts of the past.

Yanni was trying to ease her way out of the room, but Marlee pulled her back by her shirt. Desi felt no remorse for her, as Marlee pummeled her face and slung her around the room. Tyson wiped his bloody face with his shirt as he begged and pleaded for Marlee to calm down. He was apologizing and trying to explain himself, but she wasn't trying to hear it.

"Desi, get her. Help me," Yanni begged through her tears. She was trying to hold Marlee's hand, but that was a waste. Marlee was enraged and she didn't plan on stopping until she was good and ready.

"Nah boo, take that ass whipping. It ain't like you don't deserve it," Desi replied.

"All that shit you was talking and you were fucking him all along!" Marlee yelled as she repeatedly pounded on her cousin.

"Marlee please, stop," Yanni begged, sounding pathetic.

"No bitch, don't beg now," Marlee raged.

"Please, I'm pregnant," Yanni cried as she balled up into a fetal position.

It was as if someone had poured cold water onto a smoldering fire once Yanni revealed her news. Marlee let her go and backed away from her. Hurt wasn't a strong enough word for how she was feeling. Being betrayed by one person you loved was bad enough, but she got it times two.

"Bitch, pregnant by who?" Tyson asked angrily.

"Oh, my God," Desi said as she covered her mouth with her hands.

Her heart broke for Marlee. She could see that her cousin was crushed, and she didn't have the right words to comfort her. Desi had gone through something similar with her ex, but Marlee's situation was different. Desi didn't know the other woman who her ex cheated with, but Tyson cheated with their cousin. Now, she knew why Yanni always threw Marlee so much shade.

"That bitch is lying baby. I swear to God she's lying. If she is pregnant, it's not mine," Tyson said, like that was supposed to make a difference.

"Let's go. I'll come back to get my stuff later," Marlee said to Desi as she turned to walk away.

"Baby, I'm sorry. I know that I was wrong for going there with your cousin, but it ain't like I got feelings for her or nothing. It was just sex and she came at me," Tyson swore.

"Is that supposed to make me feel better Tyson? You better learn to love that bitch because you're her problem now. I'm done with both of y'all trifling asses. I'm just thankful that I wasn't dumb enough to have a baby by your pathetic ass," Marlee spat angrily.

Yanni looked like a fool, as she pulled herself up from the floor while covering her bloodied mouth. She didn't have a pot to piss in, but she was always fucking somebody else's man.

"I don't want her!" Tyson yelled as he cast an angry glare in Yanni's direction.

"Too bad because you got her. And if he is your baby's daddy, you should be prepared to do everything by yourself. This nigga probably would have never even seen his kids if it wasn't for me. But, that's what you get for always trying to walk in another woman's shoes. Shit always looks better when you're peeping through the window, instead of living in the house," Marlee spat as she and Desi left them in the room and walked out of the house.

Clad in nothing but boxers, Tyson ran behind them, begging Marlee to hear him out. He looked like a damn fool on his knees with tears streaming down his face as he held on to her legs. Desi couldn't believe the performance that he was putting on, considering what he had done. He was screaming to the top of his lungs for Marlee not to leave him and making a fool of himself in the process. His pleas fell on deaf ears, as both women got into the rental car and sped out of the driveway. They had barely turned the corner before Marlee broke down and cried. Desi felt so bad for her cousin because she didn't deserve that kind of betrayal.

"Get the fuck out of my house!" Tyson barked as he grabbed Yanni's arm and forcefully pulled her out of his room.

Her stupid ass had the nerve to be sitting on his bed holding a towel to her face like it was all good. He shouldn't have been mad with her since he was just as guilty, but he wasn't thinking rationally. In his mind, Yanni was the enemy. Granted, he'd met her months before he ever laid eyes on Marlee, and they had sex after their second encounter. When he met and started dating Marlee a little while later, he was shocked to know that she and Yanni were first cousins. He made sure that Yanni kept her mouth shut and Marlee was none the wiser. He and Yanni played the game and they never had any problems. It wasn't until about two months ago when Marlee went out of town for a job did they even go there again. Yanni showed up at their condo on some friendly shit and they ended up in bed together soon after.

She swore that she wasn't, but she was so jealous of Marlee. Tyson remembered coming out of the shower and finding her in Marlee's closet spraying on her perfume and looking at her wardrobe. He went off on her for invading Marlee's privacy and he hadn't dealt with her since then. When Marlee left to go out of town again, it was basically a repeat of the time before. Yanni showed up to their house and he'd been fucking her in every hole on her body since then. Having Marlee come home and catch them in the act was something that he never thought would happen. The fact that Yanni was now claiming to be pregnant was another problem that he wasn't trying to deal with. He knew that they used protection, but he wasn't sure that they used it every time. If she was pregnant by him, she had to be at least two months, or she had the wrong man.

"What are you getting mad with me for? I didn't know that she was gonna come home, just like you didn't," Yanni said, bringing him back to their present situation.

"I don't know why your nasty ass even showed up over here in the first place," Tyson growled.

"You sure didn't turn me away," Yanni replied.

"I should have with that garbage ass pussy," Tyson snapped.

"Why keep coming back for it then?" Yanni questioned.

"Get your hoe ass out of here before I slap the piss out of you," Tyson threatened as he opened the door for her.

"Look, you can feel how you want to feel about me, but we still have a situation to address. I'm pregnant and you're the only person who I've been with in the last three months."

"You think I believe that shit. Bitch I know your background better than anybody," Tyson noted.

"Like yours is any better. Like I just said, we're having a baby, no matter how you feel about it," Yanni said as she stood outside by the front door.

"Yeah, well, you can go ahead and kill that and kill yourself while you're at it," Tyson fumed as he slammed the door in her face.

Yanni felt like a fool as she walked away from the house and called a cab. She was a nervous wreck about everything because she knew that she was in over her head. Having Marlee upset with her was nothing compared to what was in store when the rest of the family found out. Her mother was going to be pissed and she was not ready to deal with the backlash. She came from a very close-knit family and she just made herself the black sheep of it.

Chapter 5

As much as Marlee prayed for a different outcome, things didn't go quite like she had hoped. Yanni was almost nine weeks pregnant and she swore that Tyson was the father. It was no coincidence that it was around the same time as Marlee's last out of town job. Marlee was done with him either way, but that was even more confirmation that she had done the right thing.

An entire week had passed, and Mat had successfully moved all of Marlee's things out of his house. She had some of the dudes that she played basketball with help her and they did it while Tyson wasn't home. He had been blowing Marlee's phone up and blocking his number did nothing to stop him. He was calling just about everybody in her family to get to her, but they had no words for him. Yanni's mother, Yvette, was so heartbroken, and she kept telling Marlee how sorry she was about everything. She was pissed with her daughter for bringing that kind of drama to their otherwise peaceful family existence. The entire family was upset with her, and Kallie was really the only person that she talked to. Kallie was like a dog who carried a bone, so Marlee was careful about what she said around her. She tried to play the neutral roll, but she talked too much in Marlee's opinion.

"Did you eat your soup and sandwich cousin?" Desi asked when she walked into Marlee's bedroom and laid down in the bed with her and Sierra.

Marlee hadn't gone back to work or left out of her room since everything happened. She was severely depressed, and she did little to try to hide it. She was thankful for all the vacation time that she never used because she really needed it right now. Her supervisor was a close friend of her mother and step-father and she assured her that it was okay. She knew all about what happened, and she didn't try to rush her back to work. Sierra picked up the slack and she came over to chill with her girl every evening when she got off. Desi was a receptionist at their family's health care agency and Marlee's house was the first place she went to after work as well.

"Not yet, but I will," Marlee said, knowing that it was a lie.

"You really need to eat something Marlee. You can't be taking medicine on an empty stomach. I know you're hurt, but Tyson ain't worth all that," Desi replied.

As if she wasn't in enough emotional pain, Marlee had to endure physical pain as well. Her cycle had made an appearance and the cramps were kicking her ass something serious. Her eyes burned from crying so much and her back felt like it was broken, right along with her heart.

"Fuck Tyson! Fat, ugly, knock-kneed bastard!" Marlee fumed as she twisted her face up in anger.

"Newsflash friend. He was fat, ugly, and knock-kneed when you were with him. You just loved him too much to see it," Sierra said, making her friend laugh.

It felt good to see her friend smile and that was Sierra's goal. Mat was ready to murder somebody over her little sister and she had to always talk some sense into her. Heartbreak was a part of life, but having it done by her own cousin was the hardest part of it all. Their family was always doing something together, so it was impossible for the two women to stay away from each other. Their mothers were not only sisters, but they were best friends too.

"Girl, you should see him when he's crying. It's even worse." Desi frowned.

"I don't know what I ever saw in that fat fucker," Marlee said.

"Three years later and I'm still trying to figure that out," Desi replied.

Tyson was nowhere near Marlee's type, but she overlooked his appearance because his personality drew her in. He was a gentleman and he spoiled her with whatever hear heart desired. He respected her and that's what she loved about him the most.

"Fuck theses niggas. I'm about to be on my hoe shit from now on," Marlee ranted.

"Girl, bye. That ain't even you and you know it," Sierra said, waving her off.

"Yeah, well, it's about to be me from now on. It seems like these hoes are winning out here and I'm about to join them. Three strikes and these niggas are out," Marlee said, referring to how many failed relationships she's had.

Her first boyfriend and sex partner, Westley, was good to her, but he was a certified mama's boy. His mother wasn't the overbearing type, but he didn't know how to balance being there for her and being in a relationship. Marlee didn't mind him cancelling dates to do things for her, but she had a breaking point. The last straw for her was when he answered the phone in the middle of sex to see what his mother wanted. It was nothing major and she told him so, but he got up, leaving Marlee in his bed ass naked to go see why her toilet was leaking. Marlee was gone when he got back and that was the end of that relationship.

Her second boyfriend, Anthony, seemed like a Godsend and he treated Marlee like a queen. He wined and dined her, even a year after they were together. She loved that he still did the same things that he did in the beginning of their relationship. He didn't switch up on her once he had her, like so many other men did. She really thought he was the one until he went to his brother's bachelor party and decided to fuck a stripper. He would have gotten away with it too, if his brother's girlfriend wouldn't have ratted him out. Marlee was done with him too and she never looked back. Four month later, she met Tyson and that relationship ended even worse than the two before. She was over it all and she didn't want to be monogamous anymore.

"Have you talked to your father yet?" Sierra asked, breaking Marlee away from her thoughts.

"Nope. The phone rings once and goes straight to voicemail right after," Marlee replied.

"I know you don't think so cousin, but he got you blocked. It was probably his bitch, but I'm sure he knows what's up," Desi noted.

"He probably don't know nothing. It ain't like he ever called me anyway. I was always the one to call him," Marlee noted.

"That's my point cousin. You call him every other day and you've never let an entire week pass without doing so. He should be trying to see what's up, especially since you never called to say that you made it home. Matthew is full of shit. That bitch probably told him to do it and he probably listened. He already said that he was in a bad position since he hadn't worked for a while," Desi pointed out.

"That's true Marlee. He should have at least called to make sure you made it home safely," Sierra agreed.

"Call from your phone and see what happens Desi," Marlee requested.

She called out her father's number and watched as her cousin dialed it from her phone. As soon as the phone started ringing, Desi placed the call on speaker to let everyone in the room here what was happening. After the third ring, Marlee was shocked when her father answered the phone. Desi quickly said wrong number before she hung up on him.

"I told you, bitch. He is wrong for that bullshit," Desi fumed.

Matthew was foul as fuck and she lost all respect for him after that. He was too old to be playing those kinds of games, as if her cousin wasn't going through enough.

"It's all good. If he let that nappy headed toothpick dictate to him who he can and can't talk to, that's on him. I can't miss what I barely had." Marlee shrugged.

"You know how Mat is when it comes to you. She was ready to book a flight and lay somebody out when I told her about what happened. Shit, I feel like she's just as depressed as you are, the way she's been moping around the house lately," Sierra laughed.

"I know. My sissy loves me." Marlee smiled.

It had been years since Marlee saw her sister shed tears, but Mat cried right along with her when she found out what Tyson and Yanni had done. Marlee was her baby and she hated to see what she was going through. Just like most of the family, Mat also worked at their family's company. She and Kallie did transport, making sure that their clients got to and from their appointments. Sometimes, they had to bring them to grocery stores and other places, so her hours varied depending on the day. Marlee knew that as soon as she was done, she would be walking through her bedroom door soon after, just like the others.

"We need a girl's day out. It doesn't have to be at a club or nothing. Maybe we can go to the nail salon or have drinks and just chill," Desi suggested.

"That sounds like a good idea after the week we've all had," Sierra agreed.

"I guess," Marlee mumbled, right as her bedroom door flew open.

"Did you eat something?" Mat asked as she walked in and greeted Sierra with a kiss.

"Hello to you too Matilyn," Marlee sarcastically replied while rolling her eyes.

"Stop calling me that old lady ass name. You only do that shit to piss me off," Mat fussed.

"That's your late grandmother's name and that's what I'm calling you," Marlee joked, repeating what their father often said.

Mat hated her name and she cut it short when she was only eight years old. Their father swore that it was because she wanted to be a boy, but that wasn't quite true. She always said that it sounded old fashioned, and Marlee had to agree. The name didn't even fit her, but Mat was perfect.

"Don't tell me shit about that nigga or that name." Mat frowned.

"You know he blocked me, sis. Well, him or his bitch did," Marlee announced.

"How do you know that?" Mat questioned.

"I got Desi to call and he answered the phone. When I call, it rings once and goes straight to voicemail. It's all good though," Marlee said, even though she was hurt.

"Fuck him and his bitch. On God, I better not ever run into her ass. You know how much me and Sierra be in Atlanta," Mat replied.

Sierra and Mat had mutual friends who they visited in Atlanta, but Mat never even bothered to tell her father when she was there. He didn't accept her, and she wasn't trying to force him to.

"You don't even know how she looks," Marlee noted.

"Just picture a Q-tip with a nappy afro," Desi said, making them laugh.

"You still didn't answer my question Marlee. Did you eat?" Mat asked again.

"Not yet, but I will," Marlee replied.

"Baby, go warm up the food that I got for her earlier. Her ass is about to eat, even if I have to shove it down her throat," Mat said while looking at Sierra.

She didn't have to tell her twice because she hopped up from the bed and went to the kitchen. About five minutes later, she came back with a food tray with Marlee's soup, sandwich, and a bottle of water. Marlee didn't know what kind of soup it was, but it smelled good as hell. Besides a few crackers every now and then, she hadn't really been eating much lately. Her stomach let her know just how neglected it was when it started growling loudly. Mat didn't have to force anything on her because Marlee was starving. She took all of ten minutes to finish her meal and was asking for seconds. Her stepfather cooked, so he fixed her a plate of spaghetti to enjoy right after. Mat was satisfied that her sister was feeling better and she had something that would make her smile even more.

"What's this?" Marlee asked when her sister handed her a white envelope.

"Open it and see," Mat smirked.

"Seriously Mat?" Marlee smiled bright as she sat up in bed.

"Hell yeah!" Desi yelled as she snatched the envelope from Marlee's hand and saw what was inside.

"Thanks sister. You always know how to make me feel better," Marlee said as she wrapped her arms around Mat's neck.

"That's what big sisters are for." Mat smiled while hugging her back.

Marlee felt better that day than she did all week. She was still hurt, but it was time for her to get back to her old self. She was sure that Tyson wasn't sitting around moping over her and she was tired of feeling weak. Mat always did know how to lift her spirits since they were kids and it appeared that nothing had changed.

***

"Hey cousin," Desi said, answering the phone for Kallie.

"Hey boo. I was looking for you when I came into the office, but you were already gone," Kallie replied.

"I left early. Me and Marlee went to the mall," Desi replied.

"Thank God. I'm so happy that she got out of the house," Kallie said.

"Yeah, she's feeling better, so I'm happy for that," Desi noted.

"I just wish her and Yanni can get past all this mess and move on," Kallie sighed.

"There's nothing to get past. Yanni is a sad ass bitch and nobody fucks with her like that but you," Desi ranted.

"I'm on my way over there now to check on her. Auntie Yvette has been on her ass and she's really going through it. You know Tyson is trying to make her have an abortion," Kallie said, talking all over herself like always.

"That's good for her dumb ass. That nigga didn't want her. She was just some free pussy. I don't feel sorry for her at all."

"I know that you and Marlee have a special bond, but that's still our cousin. She was wrong for what she did, and I already told her that. This is not the time for us to choose sides though, Desi. You and I should remain neutral," Kallie reasoned.

"Fuck being neutral. That bitch was dirty and that's all there is to it. You already know where my loyalty is, so I don't have to waste my time telling you," Desi snapped.

"I just hate that this is happening to our family," Kallie said sadly.

"Again, that's all Iyana's fault. Don't call me expecting sympathy because she gets none," Desi replied.

"Well, I just pulled up to auntie Yvette's house. I'll stop by your apartment before I go in for the night," Kallie said before they hung up.

Kallie and Desi lived across the street from each other in the same apartment complex. They always hung at each other's houses with Marlee and Yanni, but things were going to be different now. Kallie hated that she had to hang with her favorite cousins separately, but that's how things were going to be from now on.

When she walked up on the porch, she heard her auntie yelling before she even got to the door. Before she had a chance to knock, Yvette swung the door open and was walking out.

"Hey baby," she said, as Kallie gave her a hug.

"Is everything okay auntie?" Kallie questioned.

"All this shit with Yanni and Marlee got me so stressed out. My sisters and I don't have this kind of drama in our lives."

"I know auntie, but it'll get better. We're family and nothing will change that," Kallie replied.

"How fucking stupid could Iyana be though, Kallie? That boy should have been off limits, no questions asked. I know what it was though. She saw all the shit that Tyson was doing for Marlee and thought he was gonna do the same thing for her. He fooled her ass though. That nigga don't want nothing to do with her or her unborn child. That's what she gets for being jealous of her own cousin," Yvette fussed as she walked down the steps and up to her car.

Kallie watched as she pulled off before she walked into the house. Iyana's two older brothers were sitting in the front room watching tv, so she spoke to them and headed upstairs to her cousin's bedroom.

"Yanni!" Kallie called out while knocking on the door.

"Come in!" Yanni yelled out, right before Kallie walked into her room.

As soon as Kallie saw her, she knew that Yanni had been crying. Her eyes were red, and she looked as if she'd had a rough day. Her hair was pulled into a ponytail and she was still in her pajamas.

"Are you okay cousin?" Kallie asked.

"I just can't wait to get out of her house. Her and my brothers act like they're so perfect. People do stupid shit sometimes. I'm not proud of it, but it happened," Yanni sniffled.

"This is hard on everybody Yanni. You and Marlee were so close and nobody expected this to happen," Kallie replied.

"Marlee and I haven't been close for three years now. If it weren't for Desi always dragging me along, she and I wouldn't even be in each other's company," Yanni admitted.

The day her cousin came to their family picnic with Tyson on her arm was the day that she decided to stop fucking with her. Marlee didn't know that her cousin and her new man had history, but Yanni was salty about it. She had seen Tyson several times at the club and he always went home with a different chick. Yanni was thrilled when she happened to be the one who he chose to take home one night. He wasn't much to look at, but he had money and status. Yanni used some of her best tricks on him that night and had him screaming like a bitch. Tyson cuddled with her that night and even took her to breakfast the next morning.

Yanni thought for sure that they were about to be together, but he dropped her off home and acted like he didn't know her after that. She was pissed to see that he was doing for her cousin all the things that she wanted him to do for her. She hated going to their house, but Desi always insisted that she come along whenever she went. He had her fucked up if he thought she was getting an abortion though. Her baby was about to be her meal ticket and Tyson was going to pay.

"She's so hurt by what happened though," Kallie said, interrupting her thoughts.

"Boo fucking hoo. That bitch is lucky that I didn't press charges on her for hitting me while I'm pregnant," Yanni fumed.

"What's going on with Tyson? Is he still saying that the baby is not his?" Kallie asked.

"I don't give a damn what he's saying. He's the only person that I've been with in the past few months. I got pregnant when Marlee went out of town a couple of months ago."

"God, Yanni. What made you even go there with him?" Kallie questioned.

"I don't need any more judgement Kallie. I'm getting that enough from everybody else. Besides, I had him before Marlee even knew that he existed," Yanni informed her.

Kallie listened, as Yanni ran the entire story down to her about how and when she met Tyson. She was shocked to know that she had known him first, but that still didn't justify her actions. Kallie was sure that if Marlee knew their history, she would have broken it off with Tyson and never looked back. Instead of saying something, Yanni chose to be conniving and sleep with him behind her cousin's back.

"This is crazy," Kallie said while shaking her head.

"Yeah, but shit happens." Yanni shrugged uncaringly.

"Let me ask you a question Yanni, and don't get offended," Kallie said.

"What?" Yanni quizzed as she looked at her.

"Are you really sure that the baby you're carrying is for Tyson? Like one hundred percent sure?" Kallie asked.

"No, I'm two hundred percent sure that it's his," Yanni replied matter of factly.

"Okay, well, he needs to take responsibility. You don't have to wait until the baby is born to do a paternity test. Do your research and see about getting a DNA test done before the baby comes," Kallie said.

"Can I really do that?" Yanni asked as she sat up and looked at her cousin.

"Yes, you can and you should. He was just as wrong as you were, and he shouldn't get a pass. Make his ass start paying before the baby even gets here," Kallie replied.

Yanni's interest was piqued and her cousin had her undivided attention. Kallie pulled up some info on her phone, and Yanni read over the details. It appeared that having a paternity test before the baby was born wasn't uncommon. Several women did it and the risk for miscarriage wasn't as great as it was before. All she had to do now was get Tyson to agree to having the test done and, hopefully, pay for it too. Since he was so adamant about her baby not being his, he shouldn't have had a problem. She wasn't far enough in her pregnancy to have it done now, but she couldn't wait to shut him up when and if the time ever came.

Chapter 6

RJ's leg bounced nervously as he talked on the phone with his best friend, Kassidy. His girlfriend of four years, Aspen, was in the bathroom and he was impatiently waiting for her to come out. Ten minutes had passed, and she had been quiet as a mouse.

"What's going on RJ?" Kassidy asked him.

"I don't even know. She's still in the bathroom," RJ replied.

"It doesn't take that damn long. Ask her what's up," Kassidy said.

"Nah man. Some shit ain't even worth the rush," he noted.

"You know how impatient I am. She needs to hurry the hell up," Kassidy argued.

"Calm your nervous ass down girl. You seem to be more worried than I am. I don't know why my mama even told you anything," RJ said, right as the bathroom door slowly opened.

"Because I'm your best friend nigga. You obviously weren't going to tell me," Kassidy replied.

"Who are you talking to?" Aspen asked when she walked.

"This is Kassidy. What happened?" he questioned while looking at her.

"I don't want her in our business RJ. She already knows too much as it is," Aspen argued as she rolled her eyes.

"She makes me sick. It ain't like I won't find out anyway. Call me later," Kassidy said before hanging up the phone.

Kassidy and RJ had been best friends since high school and nothing changed once they graduated. Although they went to different colleges, they stayed in touch and hung out whenever time permitted. Both friends were certified accountants and that had always been RJ's plan. While he worked with his father running their parking garages, Kassidy landed a decent paying job with the IRS. For some reason, she and Aspen hated each other, and it had been that way since they first met. Aspen had the crazy idea that Kassidy wanted him as more than a friend, no matter how many times he tried to convince her otherwise. Kassidy, on the other hand, felt that Aspen was trying to come in between their friendship and she didn't like it. Both women often clashed, and he was tired of playing referee.

"What happened?" RJ asked as he sat on the bed next to Aspen.

"It's negative," she said, referring to the pregnancy test that she'd just taken.

When Aspen missed her cycle the month before, she just knew that her dream was about to become a reality. Giving RJ his first child and having his last name was all that she wanted. He claimed to not be ready but, once he laid eyes on his first born, she was sure that all doubts would be removed. He was only saying that he wasn't ready because he was too busy partying to do anything else. He didn't want any more responsibility.

"Cool," RJ said calmly, as if it were no big deal.

"You could at least pretend to be upset Ryker," Aspen said, calling him by his real name.

"The fuck you want me to do Aspen? You know I'm not ready for kids but, if it happens, I'm gonna handle my business. I know what the possible outcome is when we have unprotected sex. It doesn't matter if you're on birth control or not. Shit happens," RJ replied.

"We're both gonna be thirty years old in two years RJ. What the hell are we waiting on to start a family?" Aspen questioned.

"I'm waiting until I'm ready," RJ replied as he stood up and walked over to the mirror.

Aspen was pissed when he picked up his brush and started brushing his waves. RJ was the most nonchalant man that she'd ever met. Nothing seemed to bother him, and he kept it bottled up if it did. Here she was ready to get married and start a family, and he was having trouble picking out a house to purchase. RJ had his own house when they met, but he sold it when a hospital offered to buy him and his neighbors out to put a rehabilitation center on their block. He alternated between her house, his mother's, and his father's, instead of buying another one right away. He didn't care that he wasn't stable, and he didn't seem to be in a hurry to get another place to stay.

Working as a paralegal, Aspen had hopes of being accepted into law school soon. Being an attorney was her lifelong dream and she wasn't stopping until it was accomplished. Career wise, things were great. She only wished that she could say the same about her relationship.

"I can't do this anymore RJ. It's been over four years and we're still in the same position that we were in when we met. You're afraid of commitment and I just don't get it," Aspen sighed dramatically.

"How am I afraid of commitment if I committed to you?" RJ questioned.

"Being my boyfriend is not the same as being my husband. You won't even live under the same roof as me. Not to mention, I have to share you with Kassidy and Murk all the time," Aspen said, referring to his best friend and cousin.

"You don't have to share me with nobody, but you knew that I wasn't a homebody when we first met. I had a life before we got together, and nothing has changed. And living under the same roof won't change nothing about our situation. I'm not letting you rush me to do nothing that I'm not ready for. I'll get married and start a family when the time is right."

"I'm done RJ. It's obvious that I'm wasting my time with you and I'm getting too old for it. I just have to accept that we want two different things out of life," Aspen said sadly.

"Cool. Come lock your door, I'm out," RJ said, not bothering to reply to what she had just said.

It wasn't like it was the first time and he was sure that it wasn't the last. Every time something didn't go her way, ending the relationship was how Aspen dealt with it. RJ used to entertain her dramatics in the beginning, but he got over it quick. He wasn't the arguing type and she already knew that. If an argument is what she wanted, she had the wrong man.

"Stupid ass bastard," Aspen fumed once he was gone and she locked up her house.

She loved RJ to death, but she was tired of going through the motions. She had a good man who was willing to give her the world and everything in it. She felt like a fool to have left him for a man who barely wanted to share space with her. When her phone rang a few minutes later, Aspen blew out a breath of frustration before she answered for her ex, Aaron. He was calling from a different number, but she knew that it was him.

"What's up beautiful?" Aaron asked when she answered the phone.

"Nothing Aaron. Didn't I tell you not to call unless I called you first? What if RJ had been here?" Aspen questioned.

"I'm sorry baby, but I didn't call from my cell phone," Aaron replied.

"It doesn't matter Aaron. Just don't do it again," Aspen snapped.

"Okay, I won't," he conceded.

At thirty years old, Aaron used to be everything that Aspen wanted. They'd met her freshman year of high school and had become fast friends soon after. Just like her, Aaron had lost both of his parents at a young age. Unlike her, he became a ward of the state since he didn't have any relatives to take him in. Aspen was blessed to have two older sisters and an aunt who raised her from a year old up until she was old enough to care for herself. She didn't remember her parents since they both died when she was so young. Just from looking at the pictures that her family showed her, she was a carbon copy of her mother, who favored the actress Regina Hall to her. Sadly, her father was a mystery, since she had heard conflicting stories about who he really was. Her mother lost her life behind that mystery when her husband killed her and the man she'd cheated on him with, before killing himself. Aspen didn't know who was responsible for the other half of her DNA and, unfortunately, she would never find out.

Aaron didn't know anything about his genetics. He was left in the hospital as a newborn and had been bounced around from home to home since then. When he was sixteen, he was placed in a home with an abusive foster parent that he ran away from. Aspen's family loved him, so it was nothing for them to give him a stable place to stay. Aaron ended up dropping out of school, but they made sure that he got his GED. When he turned eighteen, he decided that he wanted to join the military and make a career out of it. Aspen didn't want him to go, but she didn't want to stand in the way of his dreams. She stayed in contact with him and she visited him in New York where he had been stationed as often as she could.

Their relationship was almost perfect, and Aaron was talking marriage. That was until Aspen met RJ a little over four years ago and decided that she wanted something different. Aaron was devastated. Aspen was all that he knew, and he couldn't see himself being with anyone else. His friends called him a fool, but they just didn't understand. Aspen and her family were all that he had, and he would be lost without them. Every holiday, birthday, and important event in his life was celebrated with them. Her family thought that she was selfish for continuing to string him along while she waited for RJ to come to his senses. Aaron was like her puppet, so she knew that he wasn't going anywhere. He was her comfort zone and she always ran back to him when things with RJ got rough. And, as always, Aaron welcomed her with open arms. He tried to move on several times, but it never seemed to work out.

"I'm sorry Aaron. I didn't mean to snap on you. RJ and I just broke up and I'm not in the best mood," Aspen said after a while.

"Why do you keep doing that with him? He's obviously not ready to settle down. We could have been married with kids by now if you weren't wasting your time with him."

"Please don't do that right now Aaron. I already have a lot on my mind," Aspen sighed.

"Can I see you, Aspen? You don't have to come here. We can go out to dinner somewhere if you want to," he suggested.

"I don't know Aaron," she replied.

"Please baby, I really miss you. The only time I get to see you is when that clown makes you mad," Aaron noted.

"I need a massage," Aspen said, making him smile on the other end of the line.

"You got it baby. Anything you want," he replied eagerly.

He didn't care about what people said. His heart only beat for one woman and that was Aspen. He didn't care about RJ either. He would be out of the picture soon and that much he was sure of. He was pushing Aspen away with his actions, and Aaron was right there to welcome her back whenever she was ready. It was deeper than what the average person saw between the two of them. Aspen and her family were all that he had. He wasn't going to give that up for nobody, especially RJ.

"Give me about an hour to freshen up and I'll be over there," Aspen said before she disconnected the call.

Aaron's massages were heaven sent and she really needed one now. What she didn't need was the nagging that usually came along with it. She wasn't in the mood to hear him begging her to leave RJ and take him back. Yeah, she broke up with RJ not too long ago, but that was nothing new. After a few days apart, she would go crazy without him and go running back. She hated that he never made the first move, but it was cool. Since she ended things, it was only right that she put them back together.

***

"She should be happy that she's not pregnant. I wish I would have a baby by a nigga who doesn't even want one with me," Kassidy said as she and RJ sat in the restaurant and enjoyed their meals.

He took too long to call her back, so she blew his phone up until he finally answered. RJ was always vague with his answers and he never elaborated on his relationship with Aspen. Besides telling her that she wasn't pregnant, he didn't really say much of anything else. He didn't even tell her that there was a possibility, but his mother, Ivy, kept her well informed. They always shopped and went to the nail salon together, and Ivy was usually full of conversation.

"I don't want to talk about that right now," RJ said, dismissing her comment.

"I'm surprised her crazy ass didn't break up with you again," Kassidy remarked, not letting up.

"Man," RJ said as he fell out laughing.

"She did break up with you, huh?" Kassidy asked as she laughed with him.

"Let it go Kassidy. You know I don't do all that gossiping shit."

"Stop lying. You and Murk gossip all the time. You tell him everything, so don't even go there," she said, calling him out.

"We don't gossip, we just talk about shit. He's a man, so it's different. The fuck I look like telling you all my business anyway, knowing that you don't like the person who we're discussing. Everything that comes out of your mouth will be negative, just like always," RJ noted

"I'm not negative; I'm just honest." Kassidy shrugged.

"Ain't shit honest about you always being up in my business. I know what your problem is though," RJ said as he looked at her with a smirk.

"I'm just dying to hear this. What do you think my problem is RJ? It's obvious that you know something that I don't."

"You need some dick. It's been a minute since you've had some and that's why you're always worrying about somebody else. Them lames down there at the IRS ain't hitting it right. You need to get you a nigga from the hood to break your back in right," RJ replied.

Kassidy laughed, but there was only one man who could do that for her. Unfortunately, he didn't see her the same way. RJ had put her in the best friend zone since high school and that was probably where she would always remain. It killed her over the years having to watch him with different women, but she had to play if off and act like she was unbothered. Besides being the most handsome man that she'd ever laid eyes on, RJ was smart as well. He was a genius with numbers, which was why his bank account was overflowing with riches. RJ wasn't boastful like most men his age. Besides the Bentley truck that he drove sometimes, no one would ever know that he even had it like that. He didn't drive the truck every day because he still had his Navigator. His father was a self-made millionaire and his lastborn child and only son was following in his footsteps.

"I'll pass on the hood nigga. I had one already," Kassidy said after a while.

"One? That ain't shit. You should have given my dog a chance when he wanted you. It don't get no more hood than Murk," RJ said as he finished the last of his food.

"Murk!" Kassidy yelled. "You mean your crazy killer cousin with the five kids and four baby mamas? The same one who puts his house arrest anklet on his dog whenever he wants to sneak out of the house after hours?"

Kassidy played it off in his presence, but she was scared to death of Murk. His name spoke for itself and his reputation was known all over New Orleans. His mother and two brothers were just as bad, but RJ acted as if it was normal. Murk had a reckless mouth and he didn't care what came out of it. His mother, Iris, and Ivy were sisters, but they were nothing alike.

"You make the man sound worse than he is," RJ laughed.

"It doesn't get any worse than Murk. The nigga went back and robbed the dice game because he lost of all his money. Who rides around with a ski mask in their car?" Kassidy questioned.

"I can admit that he moves a lot different than the average nigga. My dog got a good heart though," RJ defended.

"Yeah, a black one," Kassidy mumbled.

She was happy to be spending time with RJ without Murk or Aspen being a distraction. She wished it could be like that all the time, but that was just wishful thinking. RJ wanted the house and kids, but he wasn't sure that Aspen was the one who he wanted it with. He always claimed to be waiting for the right woman to come along, but she had been right in front of him for years. Kassidy was just waiting patiently for him to realize it.

Chapter 7

"What's up pops?" RJ said when he walked into his father's office.

He was seated behind his massive black lacquer desk with the phone glued to his ear. As usual, his smile was bright enough to replace the sun when his son walked into the room.

"Sweetheart, I have to go. Our son just walked into the office. I'll see you in a little while for lunch," he said, letting RJ know that it was his mother on the other end of the line.

It was crazy to him how his parents were together, even though his father had a wife at home. Ryker Sr., or Banks as he was known to most, was a complicated character. His father and his wife, Lauren, have three daughters together with his sister, Raven, being in the middle of them, born to a different mother. It was weird to explain to anyone and RJ hated to even try. His sisters, Faith and Hope, were Lauren and his father's oldest two girls. Raven's mom, Camille, gave birth to her when Hope was only three months old. A year later, Lauren welcomed her last daughter, Joy, and Ivy had RJ six months later. They were all right behind each other, with RJ being the youngest and only boy. He didn't agree with his parents basically having an affair, but there was nothing that he could do about it. Ivy loved his father more than anything and the feelings were obviously mutual. RJ had never known his mother to have another man and his father would probably lose it if she even tried.

Being a six-foot five giant with dark brown skin and even darker eyes, Banks gave new definition to the phrase ladies' man. Born in Africa to a Nigerian father and American mother, he came to live in the states when he was only ten years old. While things were different in America, Banks' father had embedded in his son some of the cultures of his homeland. His father wasn't big on monogamy and neither was Banks. He wasn't as bad as his father who had fathered multiple children in and out of the states. Banks' infidelity came as a result of wanting a son, or heir, as he often called it. The birth of a male child was considered a source of pride and honor in Nigerian culture, and Banks' father stressed the importance of that to him.

Banks was an impatient man. When Lauren gave him his first daughter, he loved her unconditionally, but he needed his son. When he started up the affair with Camille, he and Lauren were already trying for baby number two. He didn't expect both women to be pregnant at the same time, but he was ecstatic to think that one of them might be carrying his son. Sadly, that wasn't the case. Lauren was hurt about him fathering an outside child, but she wasn't giving up. As soon as her body healed from the birth of her second daughter, she was ready to try again. By then, Banks had started dealing with Ivy and Lauren was hit with more bad news. She was pregnant with another girl to add to the three that her husband already had. Banks never made her feel bad about it and he treated their daughters like royalty.

Lauren beat up on herself more than anything because she couldn't give her husband what his heart desired. She almost bled to death when she gave birth to her last child and had to have a hysterectomy. Apparently, she wasn't giving her body enough time to heal in between pregnancies and that was the result. She wasn't surprised when she had her daughter and learned that Ivy was four months pregnant with her husband's child. What crushed her sprits was when she found out that the other woman was giving him his first and only son. Without even knowing it, Ivy had secured an irreplaceable place in her husband's heart that even she couldn't compete with.

"So, I had to hear from your mother that there was a possibility that I could have been a grandfather," Banks said as he stretched his long legs out and crossed them at the ankles.

"Man, that lady tells all my business," RJ chuckled as he took a seat on the black leather chair that was right next to him.

"You might have Murk and Kassidy, but let's not forget who your real best friend is," his father reminded him.

"I know pops, but it wasn't that serious for me to say anything. I didn't even tell my mama; Aspen did. I wasn't saying anything until I knew for sure."

"That's understandable, but I still like to be informed about everything that has to do with you. I don't want to hear it from Ivy," his father noted in his deep voice.

To the average person, Banks looked intimidating. He towered over most people that he stood next to, but he was the nicest person that anyone could ever meet. He was a gentle giant with a heart of gold. Money didn't change him because he was born with two silver spoons in his mouth. His father was a millionaire and so was his mother. He was their oldest son and the only child for his mother, just like RJ was for Ivy. He had to share some of his father's riches with his siblings, but he still walked away with the most, just like his father planned it. He inherited every dime of his mother's money and he was set for life. RJ never had to work a day in his life, but he still chose to do so. He hated to be babied, but his father couldn't help it. After four tries, he finally got his son, and nothing was too good for him. He doted on him, but that was to be expected.

"You got that pops," RJ replied after a while.

"Your mother and I are going to lunch. You wanna join us?" his father asked.

"Nah, I'm good," RJ declined.

It was crazy to him how his father had a wife but was dating his mother like it was no big deal. He didn't have multiple women like he did back in the day, but his wife knew all about Ivy. Banks prided himself on honesty and he instilled that in RJ as well. Lauren knew that he spent lots of time with his son's mother and most of his weekends usually belonged solely to her.

That was what she was afraid of. Ivy had secured a place in his life with the birth of RJ and she hated her for it. Lauren also hated RJ, but she tried to hide her feelings. Her husband took very good care of her, but there was nothing special about it. Not when he did the same things for his woman on the side. Banks tried to keep both women happy and, in his mind, he was succeeding. The thought of his wife being miserable never crossed his mind. Lauren and her daughters didn't have much of a relationship with his outside kids and that would never change. It didn't matter that they were all siblings who came from the same father. Lauren wasn't their mother and that made all the difference in the world.

Lauren was an eighteen-year-old flight attendant when she and Banks met. He wanted her when he first laid eyes on her and he made it possible. After months of flying back and forth to her home town of Denver, Banks started sending for the honey brown hued, freckled faced beauty to come to him. That lasted for months until they discovered that she was pregnant. Banks demanded that she quit her job and move to New Orleans with him. Lauren's family was against it from the start and threatened to disown her if she did what he requested. Unfortunately for them, Lauren made the move anyway. Her family made good on their promise for years and they hadn't talked to her. It wasn't until her father took ill and died about ten years ago did they reach out and reconnect with her. Once they saw how well she was doing for herself, the past was quickly forgotten. They visited New Orleans quite often and they always had their hands out when they did.

"What are you doing in the office on a Friday anyway?" Banks asked his son.

"I'm meeting up with Murk. We're about to hit up Saks to see what's new. I might step out for a little while this weekend and I wanted to get something to wear."

"You and Aspen made plans?" his father questioned.

"Nah, she's on that dumb shit again. I need some time away from her ass, so this breakup came right on time. I got enough on my plate as it is," RJ said, making his father look over at him.

"Like what? Your problems are my problems and I wasn't aware that we had any," Banks said sternly.

"It's nothing really, but I'm ready to be in my own house again," RJ replied.

He didn't mind at first but going from house to house was starting to get on his nerves. He needed stability again.

"Isn't Raven helping you with that?" Banks asked, referring to his daughter who was a real estate agent.

"Yeah, but her schedule has been kind of tight. You know her clientele has doubled since she helped that basketball player find his house. I just gotta wait until she has time."

"That's bullshit! She should always have time for you. If she can't make it happen, then I'll hire somebody else who can," Banks snapped angrily.

RJ shook his head, regretting even saying what he'd just said. He knew how his father was and he didn't need him calling Raven and going off on her. RJ was a grown twenty-eight-year-old man, but his father still acted as if he were a child. RJ would be the first to admit that he was spoiled rotten, but the shit wasn't cute anymore. It wasn't the same as when he was in high school and he showed up with the finest of everything to make his peers envious. He didn't need his father speaking up for him or fighting his battles. He could do that all by himself.

"Come on pops. Let it go. Raven is doing her job and she's doing it well," RJ said as he slumped down in his chair.

Raven was his favorite sister and the only one that he was close with. His sisters by Lauren didn't fuck with him too much, but that was cool with him. Their mother hated him and, apparently, they did too. They were great actresses because they were full of love whenever his father was around. His sister, Joy, worked as the receptionist at their office, but she barely said two words to him most days.

"See, this is what I don't like. Your facial expression, your posture. What's bothering you, son? If it's Aspen, then be done with her ass and move on. I like her and all, but not if she's not making you happy."

"Aspen is the least of my worries," RJ said, waving him off.

He regretted the statement as soon as it left his lips. That was about to be another issue that his father blew out of proportion. RJ was good, but his father was never convinced. It's like he wanted him to walk around with a smile on his face twenty-four seven, and the shit just wasn't normal.

"That's my point RJ. You shouldn't have any worries. I work hard to make sure of that. Tell me what the problem is so I can fix it," Banks demanded as he stood to his feet."

"There is no problem to fix," RJ chuckled. "But, if there was, I'm a grown ass man. I can handle myself pops."

"I know you can RJ, but you're my only son. I want the best of everything that life has to offer for you."

"I know you do and I'm good. Rest your nerves and stop stressing over nothing," RJ replied, hoping to ease his mind.

"Maybe you need a vacation or something. Get Murk and take a trip somewhere. Put it on the company card," Banks suggested.

"Chill out pops. If I need a vacation, I can pay for it myself. Do I need to drop my boxers and show you how big my dick is?" RJ asked, making his father laugh loudly.

"You don't have to do that. You're my son, so I know you're working with a monster," Banks laughed, right as Joy buzzed his phone.

"Ivy is here to see you, daddy," Joy snapped over the intercom.

"Okay baby, I'm coming," Banks said, either oblivious or ignoring the attitude that his daughter displayed.

RJ walked out with his father to greet his mother, who was standing there smiling. Joy was livid as she watched her father kiss his other woman before RJ did the same. Banks grabbed Ivy's hand and the three of them walked out of the building together and she called her mother as soon as they did. It wasn't like Lauren was going to do anything. She was a kept woman, so she let her husband have a woman on the side, no matter how much it hurt her. Banks never lied about his relationship with Ivy. And sadly, he never had to.

***

"Bitch got me fucked up fam. I hate these scandalous ass hoes out here," Murk fussed as he and RJ walked through the semi-crowded mall.

"How she got you fucked up if she's asking you for money for your child, nigga?" RJ asked.

"You're missing my whole point bruh. The bitch asked for four hundred dollars to help pay for my daughter a party. She came back two days later with hair sewed in down to her ass. Then, she gon' tell me that she decided to do some cake and ice cream at the house because she didn't feel like being bothered with all that other shit. I still ended up coming out of pocket with more money because my mama gave my daughter a party at our house. Then, her hoe ass had the nerve to show up like it was all good."

"And what did you do?" RJ questioned with a smirk.

"The fuck you mean? I cut that shit out of her head and sent her home with the fucking braids. Bitch trying to get cute for the club on my dime. She got the wrong nigga. Any money that I give her is for my daughter. That's what's wrong with these hoes now. Bitches want to make sure they look good and don't give a fuck about the kids. I'll kill that bird before I let her neglect mine," Murk ranted.

"Man, that's exactly why I'm happy that I don't have none. I ain't trying to be arguing with nobody like that every day. Shit is annoying as fuck," RJ replied.

"Keep fucking with Aspen and you won't be saying that shit for long. She look like a trapper," Murk noted.

"I already know. Her stupid ass went a whole week without taking her pills. She didn't think I paid attention, but she was too dumb to cover her tracks. I fucked around and went in her unprotected a few times, but I'm smooth on her now. She's switching to the three-month shot, but I still don't trust her sneaky ass. I don't even want to use her condoms no more. I'm bringing my own shit from now on," RJ replied.

"I hate condoms. It don't make no sense to get pussy if you can't feel the real thing." Murk frowned.

"And that's exactly why you out here cutting weave out of people's heads and shit. Five fucking kids later and you still ain't learned your lesson."

"I love my kids, but their mamas can choke on a dick and die, especially Christie," Murk fumed.

"Yet, she's the only one that you got two kids with and you're still fucking her," RJ reminded him.

"I know man. The bitch got dope between her legs or something. The shit is addictive, but I hate that hoe," Murk fussed.

"You can have that shit. I'm a single nigga and I'm bout' to act like one all weekend. I'm turning the fuck up," RJ announced.

"Man, I need to get away for a few days. These hoes got me stressing and I'm tired of going to same clubs every weekend. If it ain't Jay's or the Second Line Bar, ain't really nothing else to do. I don't fuck with them other clubs too much. I need to stay around niggas who I know," Murk reasoned.

"My pops was trying to get me to book us a trip on the company card. That nigga swears I'm still a lil ass boy," RJ laughed.

"What did you tell him nigga?" Murk asked as he stopped walking to look at him.

"I told him that I was good. If I want to go somewhere, I can pay for the shit myself," RJ replied.

"Aww man, you on that bullshit cuz. Nigga know you're grown but damn."

"The fuck you getting mad for nigga? You got a big ass house arrest bracelet on your ankle, so you can't go far anyway," RJ remined him.

"Fuck this bracelet. I can strap this shit on Killa and be on the next flight out," Murk said, referring to his Rottweiler.

"Keep doing that shit if you want to. Stupid ass gon' be going right back to jail," RJ warned.

"I don't give a damn about that dumb shit. We could have been hitting up some clubs in Vegas this weekend," Murk noted.

"We still can. I don't need my pops to make shit happen. I got my own money," RJ reminded him.

"The fuck are we waiting on then? Let's do this shit," Murk replied excitedly.

"I'm on it nigga," RJ said as he pulled up the Delta Airline app on his phone.

"See, we're like Prince Akeem and Semmi. We're about to be on our Coming to America shit," Murk said, as RJ made their arrangements.

Since they were trying to leave out the same day, he was sure that the tickets were going to be expensive, but RJ didn't care. He was just happy to be getting away for a while, and Murk felt the same way.

Chapter 8

"Man, these hoes deep up in this bitch!" Murk yelled over the loud music.

He and RJ had arrived in Vegas around eight that night and they had just walked into their first club. They packed up everything that they'd purchased from the mall and decided to buy whatever they didn't have. They were lucky to find a nonstop flight and even luckier that the Bellagio had a room to accommodate them at the last minute.

"Hell yeah," RJ agreed, as they made their way to the bar.

The club was in the lobby of their hotel and it was jumping. The music wasn't what they would have chosen, but the atmosphere was live. After getting their drinks, Murk and RJ maneuvered through the thick crowd and found a wall to lean on so that they could people watch.

"Damn man. I should have gotten my own damn room. I'm hitting one of these hoes in here tonight, even if I have to do it in the bathroom," Murk swore.

"You better be happy that we were able to get a room at all. I'll hit up the casino if you need the room for a while. Just make sure you stay on your own bed nigga," RJ warned.

"The fuck I need a bed for? They got a sofa and a chair up in there," Murk noted as he spotted a chick dancing in the crowd.

She wasn't a local and that much he was sure of. The way she twerked her ass to the beat let him know that she was a Nola girl for sure. The DJ had switched to a bounce track that he was sure the Vegas people knew nothing about. The song had uptown DJ written all over it. Murk saw two other chicks standing by the DJ booth, so he was sure that it was them who made the music request. Soon after, they joined the other girl on the dance floor, and the crowd parted like the red sea while they did their thing. Murk had seen them somewhere before and he never forgot a face. He was just trying to remember when and where.

"What nigga? Something got your attention. You been stuck staring in the same direction for a minute," RJ observed.

"Man, I know them hoes from somewhere," Murk said as he pointed to the three women who dominated the dance floor.

"Stop always calling female hoes, bruh. I got sisters, nigga," RJ fussed.

"Besides Raven, fuck them hoes too. And their mama," Murk replied.

RJ's sisters and step mother hated Murk just as much as they hated him. Since RJ stayed at the house sometimes, Murk often came there to visit. His sisters had their own house, but they hung under their mother like they had no life outside of her. They were weird as hell too. Their father wanted to purchase them all a house, but their slow asses decided to get one big house and live together. It was like one brain was shared among three women. They didn't do anything without each other except for work. Raven was nothing like them, though. She had a daughter and husband, but his other sisters had no kids or man.

"Damn! They ain't playing with it," RJ said as he watched the three women do their thing. One of them had a drink in her hand that she finished off before signaling to the waitress to bring her another.

"Ole girl with the red hair can get the dick any way she wants it," Murk said as he kept his eyes glued on his prize for the night.

When the waitress passed by, RJ stopped her and asked her what the woman on the dance floor was drinking. When she told him, he gave her some money and told her to let the woman know that it was on him. Ole girl was on the short side, even with heels on, but she was pretty with lots of sex appeal. She was rocking the hell out of her mohawk, and he was feeling her style. The skirt that she had on had a ripped look to it and the belly shirt that she wore matched. She had a design cut in the side of her head that gave her an edgy, bad girl look. He was intrigued, and he couldn't take his eyes off her.

"Shorty with the mohawk is fine as fuck," RJ noted.

"They're all fine. Even the lil bald head one. My hair is longer than hers, but she can get it too," Murk said as he racked his brain trying to see where he knew them from.

"I want her lil bad ass," RJ exclaimed as he continued to stare.

"That's it!" Murk yelled out.

"What's it?" RJ asked him.

"I knew I saw them hoes somewhere before. They were in Saks with that other thot bitch that works for you and your pops. The one that be trying to throw the pussy at you all the time. They're probably all hoes, but that's even better. No commitment. Just stick and move," Murk replied.

"I ain't trying to wife her or nothing. One night and we can pretend like it never happened. We're in Vegas nigga," RJ reminded him, just as he watched the waitress give her the Long Island that she ordered.

When the waitress pointed to him, the woman looked over and smiled. He raised his drink in the air and winked, while she lifted her glass and did the same.

"Bitch! That's that RJ nigga that Yanni hoe ass was falling out over," Desi said as she watched Marlee flirting with the man.

"His fine ass can get it," Marlee replied.

"Bitch please. Just because he got you a drink," Sierra said as she made her way off the dance floor.

She was tired as hell and sweating up a storm. They had been there since the day before, thanks to Mat, who'd surprised them with the tickets. She was there with them, but she was upstairs in the room relaxing. Mat was a homebody, so Sierra wasn't surprised when she took her firestick and chilled when they went clubbing. Sierra wasn't complaining because she loved the change in her. Mat used to run the streets from sun up to sun down a year or two ago, so she welcomed it. She paid for them all to go to Vegas in hopes of cheering Marlee up, and it seemed to be working.

"That's what hoes do, huh? Buy me a drink, get the pussy," Marlee said, as Desi fell out laughing.

"Well, that's my cue to go back up to the room. It's almost two and I'm surprised Mat hasn't called me yet." Sierra yawned.

She couldn't talk about her girlfriend because she was a homebody too. Her goal was to make sure that Marlee had a good time and that was accomplished.

"You better not tell Mat anything Sierra," Marlee warned.

"Bitch, do I ever? Don't try to play me like I'm a snitch Marlee. You were my best friend before Mat became my girlfriend," Sierra noted.

"Okay bitch, I'm sorry," Marlee apologized. Sierra was right. She had always kept Marlee's secrets before and after she got with Mat.

"And you need to make that your last drink Marlee. Your ass is tipsy enough," Sierra said, right as Desi got excited about something.

"Bitch, they're coming over here! I hope the lil funny looking Lil Wayne look alike don't try to talk to me. I am not interested," Desi said as she turned her back.

"Now you're wrong for that. He's handsome in a thugged out kind of way," Sierra laughed

"Yeah, he is, but I'm still not interested," Desi replied, right as the men approached them.

Although he was wasting his time, she was happy to see that the man with the dreads walked up to Sierra, while the other man headed straight for Marlee. Desi didn't know what Sierra told him, but she walked away and left him standing there soon after.

"What's up beautiful?" RJ flirted when he walked up to Marlee.

"Hey handsome." Marlee smiled as she flirted right back.

"I'm RJ. What's your name?" he asked as he grabbed her hand.

"Marlee," she replied as she watched him bring her hand up to his lips and kiss it.

"I like that. It's different," RJ replied as he smiled at her.

From there, their conversation flowed effortlessly. Marlee looked even better up close and personal, and she was thinking the same thing about him. She was happy to see that Desi wasn't being too difficult and was conversing with his cousin, who they now knew as Murk. Desi wanted to stop Marlee from ordering another drink, but she was already sipping before she had a chance to. She was getting a little too cozy with that RJ character, but Desi didn't want to ruin her cousin's fun. She was happy to see her smiling and all, but that hoe talk wasn't flying with her. Desi was already uncomfortable with what she was seeing. Marlee was on the bar stool, while RJ stood in between her opened legs. He was whispering in her ear while she giggled. He was feeling her up a little too much for Desi, but her cousin was encouraging it.

"Where are you staying?" RJ asked Marlee as he planted wet kisses on her neck.

"I'm staying here," Marlee replied as she titled her head to give him better access.

"Uh, maybe we need to get going to our room. Are you ready Marlee?" Desi asked.

She didn't like the direction of their conversation and she was trying to stop her cousin from making a stupid mistake. She got it, Marlee was hurt, but fucking a random nigga was going to do nothing to ease that pain.

"She's good man. I hope you ain't one of them hating types," Murk said with a frown.

"Fuck whatever you think. That's my cousin and we don't know you niggas!" Desi barked.

"Bitches have been slapped for saying less, but you get a pass since this is our first interaction," Murk noted.

"Am I supposed to be scared nigga?" Desi questioned.

"Chill out cousin. I'm good," Marlee giggled, as RJ's hand made it up her skirt.

"Really Marlee?" Desi asked angrily. She was tipsy and behaving like a totally different person.

"Do you need some dick? I usually don't fuck broads if they don't have no hair to pull, but I'll make an exception for your uptight ass," Murk snapped.

"Nigga, you couldn't even fuck me with a dildo," Desi snapped.

"Oh, alright. That's what you like. Now I see why you're rocking that nice ass fade." Murk nodded like he understood.

"Fuck off loser," Desi said as she flipped him off.

Murk only laughed because he had never had a woman talk to him like that. Desi had a slick ass mouth, but so did he. She would never outdo him when it came to talking shit, but he didn't mind if she tried.

"Calm down Desi," Marlee ordered.

"Don't tell her bald head ass nothing. I slide hoes too," Murk warned.

"Well, slide yourself hoe. Broke ass probably depended on your cousin just to get here," Desi fumed.

"Chill out Murk," RJ said, chuckling at them going back and forth.

"Are you ready Marlee?" Desi asked as she stood to her feet.

"Come chill in my room with me," RJ requested.

"Hell no, nigga! We don't know you!" Desi yelled.

"Who the fuck is we? He didn't ask your small head ass," Murk replied as he stood up too.

Desi gasped when she looked over and saw RJ and Marlee engaged in a heated lip lock. Marlee wrapped her legs around his waist, as he carried her out of the club and through the casino. Desi had her purse, so she ran out behind them, with Murk hot on her heels. People were staring at them, as RJ walked with Marlee wrapped around his tall, muscular body. They never came up for air as they rode the elevator up to the rooms and stopped on a floor that was two floors beneath where Desi and Marlee's room was.

"This is not our floor Marlee. Let's go. You are not going to some random man's room. We don't know anything about these niggas," Desi said as she blocked them from getting off the elevator.

"Chill out Desi. I'm just walking him to the room and I'll be right back," Marlee replied.

"Okay, well, I'm staying right here. That shouldn't take you long," Desi said as she moved to allow them to pass.

She stood right there in the hall with her arms folded, waiting to see just where RJ was going. She'd heard of too many horror stories to let him play games with her cousin. He was going to have to kill them both because she was not budging. They had cameras in the hall, so at least their killers would be identified.

"Go to the room Desi. I'll be up in a minute," Marlee promised.

"Fuck no!" Desi yelled defiantly as she made a move to go get her.

"Bring your bald-headed ass back in here and stop trying to block," Murk said as he yanked her petite body back into the elevators and closed the door.

"Ahh! Help me! Somebody help!" Desi screamed like she was crazy.

"The fuck is wrong with you, girl. Shut the hell up before somebody think I'm kidnapping your crazy ass," Murk said as he covered her mouth.

"You are, and your boy kidnapped my cousin," Desi mumbled with his hand still covering her mouth.

"Your cousin ain't complaining. Hell, she looks like she wants it more than my nigga do. What floor y'all room on?" Murk questioned as he continued to cover her mouth.

"Get your nasty ass hands off of me," Desi snapped as she bit his hand.

"Bitch!" Murk yelled as he rubbed his hand on his jeans.

"Your mammy is a bitch and you ain't bringing your disrespectful ass in my room."

"Girl, you got me fucked up. Your girl is in our room and I'm coming to yours. Nigga ain't trying to fuck with your confused ass. I'm tipsy and I'm ready to get some sleep," Murk noted.

"Your dirty ass can get on the floor because you ain't getting in none of our beds," Desi said as she pushed the button for their floor.

Murk ignored her because he wasn't in the mood to go back and forth with her. She was obviously dick deprived and he didn't mind helping her out. When they got off the elevator, Desi rushed down the hall to their room like she was trying to leave him. Murk's legs were longer, so he had no problem keeping up.

"Baby girl, I've been running from the police since I was ten years old. I can sprint better than the average track star. Fuck you thought," Murk said as he stood behind her in front of her room.

"Just shut up and don't touch shit when you get in here. My card is on file nigga," Desi snapped.

The room was stocked with liquor and snacks, but none of it was free. Desi had given the front desk her card to take off the three-hundred-dollar deposit that was required. Whatever they used came out of her money and she didn't know his ass well enough to pay for his shit.

"You need to ask around about me when you get back to New Orleans. Your flip ass mouth is gon' be the cause of me splitting your wig. Shit ain't gon' be hard since you ain't got no hair," Murk noted as he fell out on the bed.

"Get your dirty ass up out of my bed. Nasty ass didn't even take a bath. Get in the other bed," Desi ordered.

"Man, fuck!" Murk yelled out angrily as he jumped up from the bed and got into her face. "Bitch, I'm warning you. Shut the fuck up and leave me the fuck alone."

"Or what, you bad breath bastard? Get your hand out of my face with them dirty ass fingernails," Desi replied as she slapped his hand away.

She maneuvered around the room to get her night clothes ready to take her shower. Murk got into the other bed, and she headed into the bathroom. About twenty minutes later, Desi was dressed down in her pajamas, ready to get some sleep. When she got back into the room, her face twisted in a mask of anger when she saw Murk sitting there with a bottle of Grey Goose turned up to his mouth. She knew that he got it from the room because he didn't have anything when they left the bar. Desi attempted to call Marlee a few times, but she never got an answer. She was pissed, and she couldn't wait to see her ass.

"No the fuck your broke ass didn't. Did I not tell you not to touch anything? I'm responsible for that liquor that your drinking. You're about to pay for that shit nigga," Desi fumed.

"I swear, I wish I had my gun on me," Murk sighed as he fell back on the bed.

"Me too nigga. That way you could kill yourself. You're paying for that liquor," Desi demanded.

"Here man, fuck!" Murk yelled as he jumped up.

He pulled a knot of money from his pocket and peeled off three hundred-dollar bills. He knew that was how much the deposit was and he made sure to cover the entire amount. He wasn't in the mood to go back and forth and he just wanted her to shut up.

"Now you can help yourself to whatever," Desi said as she stuffed the money in her purse. She straightened up the room before sending Marlee a text. When she got down on her knees to say her prayers, Murk spoke up and interrupted her.

"Say one for me too," he requested as he continued to drink.

Once she was done, Desi got into bed and prepared to go to sleep. She had her box cutter under the covers with her, just in the case her uninvited guest tried anything. She was prepared to get a few good hours of sleep in, but Murk had other plans. He talked to her for hours about shit that she had no interest in. Admittedly, he turned out to be cool, but Desi was tired as hell. When Murk finally stopped talking, Desi looked over to find him sleeping peacefully. As much as she enjoyed their conversation, she was happy for the little things.

Chapter 9

"Damn it," Marlee hissed as she tripped over something in the middle of the floor.

The room was dark since the curtains were closed, and she was having trouble finding her clothes. Her intentions weren't to stay in RJ's room so long, but it was almost one that evening when she got up. The heat from his body being wrapped around hers had her sweating bricks. Thankfully, he was in a deep sleep, making it easy for Marlee to slip out of bed. RJ was her very first one-night stand and that nigga did not disappoint. He worked her body over something serious and she was still feeling it now. She would have loved to blame it on the alcohol, but she wasn't drunk. Tipsy, maybe, but she knew exactly what she was doing. She got it out of her system and it was over. A broken heart made people do some stupid things, and Marlee was living proof of that. She was sure that Desi was mad with her and she knew that she had a lot of apologizing to do.

"Fuck it. I'll get my shoes later," Marlee whispered to herself as she tried to make her way to the door without disturbing RJ.

She was dressed, but she couldn't find her underwear and bra. She had her phone and Desi had her purse, so she was good for now.

"Where are you going?" RJ asked, scaring the hell out of her.

She didn't even hear him get out of bed and it was too dark to see him. When he opened the curtains a little, Marlee covered her eyes to shield them from the sunlight.

"I'm going to my room. I need to take a shower," Marlee replied.

"I have a shower in my room too, you know," he laughed.

"Yeah, but I don't have any clothes here," she replied as she picked up her underclothes since the sunlight allowed her to see better.

She and RJ took a shower together a few hours ago before going to bed, but she needed another one. She still didn't feel fresh since she had to put her dirty clothes right back on.

"I got you covered on that too," he replied as he opened his duffle bag.

He handed her a brand-new pair of basketball shorts and a t-shirt. When he opened his pack of socks, he gave her a pair of those too.

"Thanks, but I need my own clothes. I don't plan to stay in this hotel all day," Marlee replied as she walked towards the door.

"Why not?" RJ asked as he pulled her back.

The way he looked at her was always so intense, but Marlee never looked away. She wasn't shy, so there was no need to pretend. He took the items that she was holding from her and threw everything on the floor. They had gone at it at least four times since they got to the room, but Marlee didn't mind one more round. RJ undressed her and pushed her back on the bed. Marlee scooted back until she was near the headboard and watched as he got undressed. He climbed into the bed slowly, kissing his way up her body as he did. They had quickly become familiar with each other's bodies, so he knew just what to do. RJ spread her legs wide and eased his head between her thighs to taste her. Marlee's scent was intoxicating and he inhaled her with every flick of his tongue.

"Umm," Marlee moaned as she pulled him in deeper while he feasted on her goodies. She rotated her hips and thrusted her body upward to meet every stroke of his tongue. After a few minutes of ecstasy, she pushed him away and flipped him over. She switched her body to the upside-down position before dropping her love box right in his face. This time, when he pleased her, she was able to please him too.

"Fuck," RJ moaned as he repeatedly slapped her ass.

Marlee was working him over, and he was doing the same to her. The sounds of their moans filled the room as they tried to outdo each other orally. Marlee would never admit it out loud, but RJ was clearly winning with the way he snaked his long tongue in and out of her honey pot. That nigga was a fool with it and Marlee knew that she was going to miss that once they went their separate ways. Marlee had stopped sucking him because he was giving her the business. He had her screaming as she held on to his legs for support. When he stopped, she thought she had a minute to catch her breath, but he never gave her time to recover. He pulled her up and placed her on her back while he rolled on a condom.

"Ooh shit!" Marlee screamed when he entered her.

RJ had both of her legs on his shoulders as he stroked her body with expertise. Marlee held on to his forearms for leverage as he beat her shit out the frame. Once he got tired of that position, RJ flipped her over to get on top without even pulling out. He sat up on his elbows and watched as Marlee bounced up and down on him with no hands. She was sexy as hell, and RJ didn't want their time together to end. Marlee was leaving the next day, but he and Murk were staying until Monday. RJ planned to make every minute count and he was doing a damn good job so far.

"Damn," RJ moaned as he threw his head back in pleasure.

He bit his bottom lip as his face twisted up in a sexy frown. Marlee loved his sex faces and she kept her eyes on him the entire time. She knew that he was enjoying it, so she picked up the pace and had him really going crazy. When RJ grabbed her around her neck, she met him halfway and engaged in a sloppy kiss. He was moaning, letting her know that he was nearing the end, and she felt the exact same way. A wave of euphoria rushed over her, right as RJ released into the condom. Marlee wasn't too far behind as her body shook, and she collapsed on his chest.

"You're draining the life out of me," Marlee panted as she tried to catch her breath.

"This is only the beginning. Come hop in the shower with me right quick. Round two will be even better," RJ promised.

"We're way past round two," Marlee replied.

"When it's this good, who's counting?" RJ asked as he picked her up.

"I can walk RJ," Marlee giggled as she wrapped her arms and legs around him.

He made her feel like a child, but she loved every minute of it. He towered over her and she felt light as a feather in his arms.

"I know you can, but I like holding you," he replied as he put her down in the shower and started the water.

About an hour later, Marlee was dressed in his shorts and t-shirt as they took the elevator up two floors to her room. RJ was tall as hell, so his shirt looked like a dress on her short frame. She had to roll the shorts up three times to make them fit and the socks swallowed her tiny feet. When she knocked on the door, Desi opened it and just stared at her. She was already dressed for the day and Marlee was ready to do the same.

"It's about time nigga. I need a shower. Got my nuts all sweaty and shit," Murk fussed when he saw RJ standing there with her.

"What are y'all getting into today?" RJ asked while looking at Marlee.

"I don't know. I need to get dressed and put something in my stomach," she replied.

"Cool. I guess we can link up later," he said as he gave her a kiss on her lips.

As soon as he and Murk left, Desi closed the door and turned to her cousin.

"I already know Desi. I made a stupid mistake and it won't happen again," Marlee said before her cousin could start fussing.

"That wasn't just stupid Marlee; it was dangerous. We don't know them like that. Not only did you stay the night with a complete stranger, but you forced me to do the same. Murk is cool and all, but I don't know anything about him other than the little that he told me in conversation."

"I know cousin and I'm sorry. I got being a hoe out of my system and I'm good," Marlee replied as she looked for something to wear.

"I can't believe you. Taking the walk of shame wearing a stranger's clothes," Desi said, making her laugh.

"I know but, bitch, it was well worth it. That nigga is the truth!" Marlee yelled.

"And I want all the details over lunch. I'm starving," Desi said.

"Me too. I just got out of the shower, so I won't take long to get dressed," Marlee promised.

"Mat called me asking for you. She called your phone but didn't get an answer," Desi informed her.

"Shit. What did you tell her?" Marlee asked.

"That you were getting dicked down by a nigga that you met in the club last night," Desi replied.

"Bitch!" Marlee yelled, making her cousin laugh.

"I told her that you were hungover and still sleeping. Her and Sierra were going out for breakfast and wanted us to join them," Desi replied.

"Oh okay," Marlee said.

She grabbed her khaki joggers with her belly shirt and laid it on the bed. After knocking a few wrinkles out of it, she got dressed and put some mousse in her mohawk to make the curls more defined. She decided to do a little light makeup on her and Desi, and they were ready to go. Sierra and Mat had gone back to sleep, so it was just the two of them.

***

"Lil bald head bitch finessed me out of three bills. She better be lucky that I didn't double back and rob her ass," Murk laughed as he and RJ walked the strip.

He was telling his cousin about Desi and what happened when they were in the room alone. Once RJ and Marlee parted ways, he and Murk got dressed and hit the Vegas streets. After getting something to eat, they did a little shopping and went back to their room. Once they took a nap, they went back out, looking for something else to get into. They were getting hungry again, so they were currently trying to find somewhere to eat.

"The fuck you mean nigga. I ain't never met a broad good enough to do no shit like that. Even your baby mamas have to lie and say it's for the kids," RJ noted.

"Man, you know I hate all that fussing and nagging. She was getting on my fucking nerves, so I handed the shit to her."

"Fussing for what though?" RJ asked.

"She was going off about me drinking the liquor in her room. Bitch got a vicious ass mouth too," Murk noted.

"She must have given you some head," RJ assumed, thinking that his cousins statement had an underlying message.

Murk was always saying that a chick had a vicious mouth and that usually meant that she was good at oral.

"Fuck no! She made it clear that nothing was shaking between us, so I didn't even try. She cool as fuck, though. She ain't feeling a nigga like that, but I'm cool with it. We can do the friend thing. At least I don't have to worry about her secretly being in love with me and shit," Murk replied.

"What you trying to say nigga?" RJ asked.

"Dog, you can't be that dumb. Kassidy be damn near drooling at the mouth when she's around you. Bitch ain't want to give me the pussy, but I bet she serve it to you on fine China."

"Kassidy and I are friends and that's all we'll ever be. I'm not even attracted to her like that," RJ said, waving him off.

"Yeah, but she's damn sure attracted to you. Maybe I need a female friend with no strings attached. I need somebody who ain't scared to tell me about myself. Shit keeps a nigga like me grounded," Murk replied.

"Man, listen, her cousin is the fucking real deal," RJ stopped and said dramatically.

"She must be something serious for you to let her stay that long. The last bitch you had when you and Aspen broke up didn't even last for two hours," Murk laughed.

He and RJ had gone to New York a few months before, but they got separate rooms that time. They both met somebody and took them back to their rooms, but RJ wasn't with the bullshit. Once he got what he wanted, he wanted ole girl gone and ended up fucking up Murk's plans. The chick that he was with was her friend, so she had to leave and go home with her girl.

"She's sexy as hell with that mohawk and she ain't shy," RJ said as they passed by a hookah bar.

"Let's vape something nigga," Murk said as he walked over to the door and pulled it open.

The inside of the bar was dimly lit and cloudy as hell. They had a huge bar with lots of top shelf liquor and a small restaurant styled area in the back.

"Wings and Hennessey on deck. This is my kind of spot," RJ said as he looked around and nodded his head.

"Yep and shit just got better, look," Murk said as he pointed to Desi and Marlee who were seated in the rear of the building with hookah pipes in their hands.

They had a bottle of liquor sitting between them, but the bottle was still kind of full. Two dudes were standing there trying to talk to them, but Desi didn't look interested as usual. Marlee wasn't smiling, but she seemed to be the more cordial of the two.

"Bitch, you in here trying to cheat on me!" Murk snapped when he walked up on them.

He was looking right at Desi, making the man that was closest to her step back. Desi narrowed her eyes at him, as RJ and Marlee laughed. RJ bumped into the other man as he took a seat next to Marlee and wrapped his arm around her.

"You trying to replace a nigga already. It ain't even been twenty-four hours yet," RJ said with a sexy smirk.

"Not at all." Marlee blushed as she took a sip of her drink.

The two men who were standing there quietly walked away, right before Desi went off on Murk.

"Call me another bitch and watch I stab your skinny ass," Desi threatened as she pulled out her box cutter and flipped it open.

"Stop trying to be a thot out here in these Vegas streets. Bald head ass know you don't like men," Murk said as he grabbed her cup and sipped her liquor.

"Give me my shit. I don't know where your nasty ass mouth been!" Desi yelled as she snatched her cup back.

"Is ole girl with the red hair your cousin too?" Murk asked Marlee.

"No, she's my sister-in-law," Marlee replied.

"How many brothers do you have?" RJ wanted to know.

"I don't have any brothers. It's just me and my sister," Marlee answered.

"I thought you just said that red head was your sister-in-law," he said.

"She is," Marlee replied, looking at him like he was slow.

"Oh okay, I got you." He nodded in understanding.

"So, that's why she ain't give a nigga no play. I knew something had to be up," Murk said.

"Boy bye. Stop acting like every female that don't want you is a lesbian. Maybe a bitch just ain't buying the bullshit that you're selling," Desi snapped.

"That's not the only reason, but ninety-nine percent of the time it is." He shrugged like it was true.

RJ and Marlee were back at it, just like they were the night before. She claimed that she got all the hoe out of her system, but Desi wasn't convinced. RJ had pulled her on his lap while they shared her hookah pipe and liquor. They were kissing like they'd been lovers for years, knowing that they'd only met the night before.

"It ain't gon' be a repeat of last night Marlee. This talkative bastard is not sleeping in our room again," Desi fumed.

"Let me fuck you straight. You can put the dildo up and get the real thing. You ain't gon' even be into girls no more when I get through with you. I'm telling you, one night with me will change your life," Murk said as he winked at Desi.

"It probably will when you infect me with your germs. Get the fuck on Murk," Desi said as she mushed his head.

RJ and Marlee were in their own world and didn't pay their arguing any mind. They stayed in the hookah bar for hours, laughing and enjoying each other's company. Murk was actually fun to be around when he wasn't being disrespectful. Desi had to put him in his place a few times until he finally got it. He threw the word bitch and hoe around too much, and she wasn't feeling it. He kept them laughing with his stories, and RJ confirmed that everything that he said was true. He had too many babies and baby mamas for Desi to keep up with and she was happy that they were only friends.

"Y'all want to go grab something to eat before we go back to the room?" RJ asked, as they walked along the strip.

"Most of this shit out here is nasty as fuck. I keep wasting money because I keep throwing my food away," Marlee complained.

"Let's go to Chili's. They can't possibly get that wrong," Desi suggested.

Marlee wasn't a big fan of their food, but she could tolerate the appetizers. They shared more laughs over food and drinks before they all walked back to their hotel. Desi was happy that Marlee wasn't tipsy and seemed to be in her right mind. When the elevator stopped on RJ and Murk's floor, she was happy when they both stepped off. She was ready to climb into bed and talk shit with her favorite cousin until it was time for them to leave. RJ just stood there and stared at Marlee until the elevator doors started to close. He seemed to be battling with himself, but the fight didn't last too long. Before the door closed all the way, he reached inside and pulled Marlee out. He picked her up and she wrapped her arms and legs around his body as he walked away to his room.

"Looks like it's me and you again tonight bestie." Murk smiled when he got back onto the elevator and pressed her floor.

"Ughh! Life is such a bitch," Desi groaned in frustration as she got off the elevators and stomped all the way to her room.

"Your bald head ass is a bitch," Murk snapped.

"Nigga, what?" Desi yelled as she turned to face him.

"Nothing, just open the door," Murk replied as he followed behind her and prepared to piss her off until it was time for her to catch her flight.

Chapter 10

"How was your trip? You know, the one that I wasn't invited on," Kassidy said as she talked to RJ on the phone.

She found out through Ivy that RJ and Murk had taken an impromptu trip to Vegas, and she was salty about it. They were supposed to return that Monday but came back on Tuesday instead.

"I needed that shit. I feel more relaxed than I've felt in a while," RJ replied, ignoring her comment about not being invited.

He knew how it went down when he and Murk were together, and he would never invite Kassidy to come along. She was cool to chill with at times, but she wasn't a nigga. He wanted to have fun and he didn't need her in his ear all the time because she didn't agree with the decisions that he made. She would have had a lot to stay about his interactions with Marlee while in Vegas and that's what he didn't need. He had never cheated on Aspen but, when they were broken up, he was free to do his thing. He was always careful and that was all that mattered.

"Yeah, well, I guess I can forgive you for not telling me. But, you owe me dinner and I want it tonight," Kassidy said, pulling him away from his thoughts.

"I got you, but it can't be tonight. I'm on my way by my pops right now. Nigga acting like he ain't seen me in years," RJ chuckled.

"Didn't you come back yesterday morning though?" Kassidy asked.

"Yeah, but I stayed at my mama's house. I damn near slept the day away since I barely got any rest in Vegas," RJ noted.

"I'm afraid to ask why," Kassidy chuckled.

"I wouldn't tell you if you did," RJ countered.

"Some best friend you are," Kassidy whined.

"Man, fuck," RJ hissed when he pulled up to his father's house and saw Aspen's car parked out front.

Lauren and Aspen's aunt were close, and Aspen was close with his sisters. Aspen's aunt, Patrice, visited Lauren a lot, but Aspen was never with her. That was, until Lauren decided to throw a small dinner party for her birthday that Patrice invited Aspen to. That was the same day she met RJ and they started dating soon after. RJ had a few girlfriends before her, but he was really feeling Aspen. They had chemistry in and out of the bedroom and she loved sports just as much as he did. The first two years of their relationship was almost perfect.

When they entered year number three, things took a turn in a new direction. Aspen started talking about marriage and babies, and that was a conversation that RJ wasn't ready to have. He wasn't sure if he wanted what she wanted, and he wasn't going to let her rush him into doing anything. They were both still in their twenties, but Aspen swore that they were old. They had lots of time to plan for their future, but she didn't see it that way. If it weren't for his father wanting to see him so bad, RJ would have turned around and went back to his mother's house. He wasn't in the mood to have another 'where is this relationship going' conversation with her right now.

"What's wrong?" Kassidy questioned.

"Nothing, I just pulled up to the house. I'll hit you up later," RJ said before he hung up the phone.

He sighed as he got out of the car and headed to the front door. Lauren hated when he used his key, so he pulled it out and let himself inside, hoping to piss her off. Lauren's face was the first one he saw, followed by Aspen and his sisters. They were all sitting around the living room talking, but all conversation came to a halt when he walked in.

"Good evening," RJ spoke as he made his way down the hall to the family room.

He felt their eyes on him, but he really didn't give a damn. He was sure that Aspen put them in their business like always, but she was the one looking like a fool. She always broke up with him then came running back to apologize a few days later. The last year of their relationship had been an emotional roller coaster that RJ had become accustomed to. He loved Aspen, so he always forgave her and moved on until it happened again. The shit was getting old though and he was getting tired of it. When he walked into the room, his father was stretched out on the sofa with the phone pressed to his ear. As soon as he saw RJ, he sat up and smiled.

"Yeah baby, he just walked through the door. Enjoy your movie and I need to hear from you the minute you get back home," Banks said to who he knew was his mother on the other end of the line.

RJ listened as his father professed his love to his mother while his wife was in another room. As much as he loved his father, RJ didn't want that kind of life for himself. He wanted his only kids to come from the woman he married, and he didn't want any other women on the side. He didn't want that for his mother either, but she was content with being the side chick. She had played her position for more than twenty-eight years and she didn't have any plans of stopping. Banks took care of her the same way he did his wife, and she had no complaints. He couldn't spend all of his free time with her, but he made sure that she always had something to do. He was always paying for Ivy and one of her sisters or friends to take a trip somewhere. If he didn't do that, he paid for spa days, shopping trips, and anything else that her heart desired. Ivy had given him his only son, and nothing was too good for her in his eyes.

"Who is she going to the movies with?" RJ asked when his father got off the phone. His mother was getting dressed to go somewhere when he left, but she never said where she was going.

"One of the ladies that she goes to the hair salon with," Banks answered.

"What if she meets somebody who wants to take her out on a date? How would that make you feel?" RJ asked his father out of curiosity.

"Stop wishing death on people RJ. Any man that's crazy enough to even ask her out doesn't value his life. How was your trip?" his father asked, changing the subject.

"It was good. I needed that," RJ replied as he picked up the remote and turned the tv.

"Did Murk behave himself?" Banks asked.

"Does he ever?" RJ countered.

"I talked to Raven. She has a few houses that she wants to show you," Banks announced.

"Yeah, she told me how you called going off on her. I told you that I was good, but you never listen. Now, you got Raven mad at me because she thinks I sent you at her on some dumb shit," RJ fussed.

"Mad at you?" Banks repeated.

"Is that all you heard just now? I really need you to stop doing that pops. I'm a grown ass man and I don't need you to handle my business for me. You get mad when I don't tell you stuff, but that's why."

"Okay son, I get it. I'll take a back seat and let you run the show from now on," Banks promised.

RJ knew that he was lying, but he let it fly. He lost count of how many times they had that same conversation and he was sure that this time wasn't the last. He knew that his father loved him, and he appreciated that he was always there. So many other black men couldn't say the same, so he was fortunate.

"How long has she been here?" RJ asked, referring to Aspen.

"Not long. She claims that she came to see Lauren and your sisters, but I know the truth. Are you staying here tonight? I can get Lauren to fix you something to eat," Banks offered.

"I might stay, but I'm good on the food," RJ replied.

He didn't want Lauren going out of her way to do anything for him. She did whatever her husband told her to, so RJ was sure that it would have gotten done. Lauren was a damn good actress in his father's presence. She pretended that RJ was just as important as her daughters and she had him fooled for a long time. It if weren't for Aspen telling him how they really felt about him and Raven, he would still be believing that lie. His sisters confided in Aspen a lot and pillow talk was a muthafucka. He never told his father because Lauren would have probably had a one-way ticket back to Denver if he did. He just handled her and his sisters accordingly. He spoke and kept it pushing.

Two hours and lots of conversation later, RJ stood to his feet and prepared to leave. He told his father that he might spend the night, but he changed his mind. He had a room at both his parents' houses, but he decided to utilize the one by his mother.

"Can we talk RJ?" Aspen asked, as soon as he opened the door and stepped into the hall.

Banks was behind him, preparing to walk him out, so he kept walking to give them some privacy. RJ led her into the family room and closed the door behind them. He sat down on the leather sectional and she took a seat next to him.

"What's up Aspen?" RJ asked, even though he already knew.

It was like a never-ending cycle of break up to make up. It was draining, and he was tired of doing it.

"I just wanted to apologize for-" Aspen started before he cut her off and interrupted.

"Let me stop you right quick Aspen, and make no mistake about the shit that I'm about to say. I want a wife and kids someday, no doubt about it, but I can't tell you when that day will be. I love you, but if me taking too long to give you what you want is a problem, then I'm obviously not the man for you. All this breaking up every other month and getting right back together is for the birds. I'm not your ex. You can't walk in and out of my life when it's convenient for you. So, the next time you feel like you want to break up, make that shit permanent. The next time is the last time. Ain't no more coming back and that's on God," RJ swore.

Aspen's heart beat in her chest like a drum. The look on RJ's face was like none that she'd ever seen before, so she knew that he was serious. With Aaron, even if she mentioned them breaking up, he bowed down and gave her whatever she wanted. She had to realize that they were two different men and what worked for one didn't necessarily work for the other. After spending two days with her ex, Aspen was missing RJ something serious. Aaron's constant whining about them getting back together was driving her crazy. She left and went to find RJ to make things right again. When she found out that he was in Vegas, she was ready to lose her mind.

"I know baby and I'm sorry. I overreact sometimes, and I have to do better. It's just that all of my friends and family are getting married and having kids and I feel so left out. It's like I'm always a bridesmaid and never a bride"

"That has nothing to do with us though, Aspen. Shit happens when it happens. You can't base what we do off what other people are doing. They obviously were ready to do what they did, but I'm not. And if you're tired of being a bridesmaid, say no when they ask you. That's a simple solution."

"I understand baby and you're right. I'm sorry for making you feel like I'm rushing you. I just want us to go back to the way we were four years ago," Aspen said as she wrapped her arms around him.

"Yeah, me too," RJ said as he pulled her onto his lap.

"I love you so much baby. I promise to do better," Aspen swore as she planted a kiss on his lips.

"I love you too," RJ replied with a smile.

***

It was back to business as usual once Marlee returned from Vegas. She behaved like a hoe all weekend, but it was time for her to get her life back in order. Three weeks had passed since then, and she was happy that she had gone back to work. She didn't have as much idle time and she didn't think about Tyson as much because she stayed so busy. He seemed to be on some stalker shit, and Mat was ready to kill him. He was popping up at Marlee's job and just about everywhere else she went. Even when she went to Walmart with Desi, he was begging her to hear him out and take him back. Marlee was so embarrassed that she left her basket with everything in it and went home. Sierra had started picking her up for work just so he wouldn't see her car in the parking lot.

Yanni was three months into her pregnancy and that should have been what he focused on. Kallie told Desi that they had done a non-invasive prenatal paternity test to see if Tyson was really the father. The results hadn't come back yet, but Marlee already knew what they would be. She couldn't see Yanni going through so much if Tyson wasn't the father. She hated the strain that her and Yanni's rift put on their family, but that wasn't her fault. They had all gone to their uncle's fiftieth birthday party the week before and the tension was thick. Yanni sat at a table all by herself and Kallie was the only one who she even bothered to talk to.

"What's for lunch and don't say you don't care. You always say that and then complain when I buy something that you don't like," Sierra said when she sat next to Marlee at the desk.

They had both just finished with a patient and Marlee was doing her paperwork. She was happy for the interruption because she was feeling herself getting depressed again.

"That's because you always want to try something new," Marlee replied, never lifting her head up.

"What about Burger King?" Sierra suggested.

"That's cool with me. You already know what I want," Marlee replied.

"I can't go bitch. My next appointment is in twenty minutes," Sierra replied.

Marlee always set her appointments up early since they opened at six, but Sierra hated working at that hour. She usually clocked in and went back to sleep in the break room for a few hours before she got her day started. Then, she got mad when she had to stay late to finish all of her appointments, but that was her own fault. They had to take a total of six or more patients each day, and Marlee sometimes had to help her best friend out. There were only five of them in the office and their supervisor was never really around.

"Your lazy ass need to stop waiting all late to do shit. And don't tell me what you want either. You better eat whatever I bring you," Marlee fussed.

"That's why I love my bestie. You fuss all day, but you always come through," Sierra said as she kissed her cheek.

"Don't try to butter me up." Marlee blushed.

After getting her wallet from her purse, she grabbed Sierra's keys and headed for the door. When she walked outside to the car, Marlee stopped when she saw Tyson standing there leaning against his. He didn't see her car in the parking lot, but he knew that she was there. Marlee never missed days from work, so he tried his luck and waited around to see if he could catch her. He knew her routine for breakfast and lunch and he was happy to see that nothing had changed.

"Can we talk Marlee, please?" Tyson begged, just like always.

"We don't have shit to talk about Tyson. I'm trying not to get a restraining order taken out on you, but don't push me," Marlee warned.

"Come on Marlee. You know I would never do nothing to hurt you," he swore.

"Too late," she replied as she walked away to the car.

"Can I just explain? Even if you don't take me back, I owe you that much."

"What is there to explain Tyson? You fucked my cousin and got her pregnant nigga. Not just some random bitch on the streets, but my first cousin. I would have left you either way, but at least the shit wouldn't hurt as bad. Imagine how the fuck I feel having to be around that bitch at family functions and shit. Even if you did feel the need to cheat, my family should have been off limits. I regret the day I introduced y'all," Marlee said as tears rolled down her cheeks.

"You didn't introduce us. I met her months before I met you," Tyson confessed as he lowered his head in shame.

"What?" Marlee questioned as she looked at him for an explanation.

She stood there and listened as Tyson replayed the entire story of when him and Yanni met and the first time they had sex. Yanni was always the promiscuous one of their crew, so him fucking her was nothing new. She got around and she never tried to hide that fact. It pissed Marlee off that none of them cared to enlighten her of their dealings before things got too deep between her and Tyson. Yanni was one of her favorite cousins. If she would have said something, there was no way in hell that she would have still been with his ass. Any man that her cousins or friends dealt with in the past were off limits to her.

"She used to flirt with a nigga behind your back and shit, but I always put the bitch in her place. When you went out of town a few months back, she came over there acting like she didn't know that you were gone," Tyson said.

"And you fucked her," Marlee said as more of a statement than a question.

"I'm sorry," Tyson said as he looked away.

"Yeah, you really are, but why confess now? It's over between us and the damage is already done."

"I just wanted you to know the truth about when me and Yanni first met. I was foul as fuck for what I did, but don't sleep on her either. That bitch is a hater and you're who she hates on the most," Tyson noted.

"Yeah, well, she doesn't have to hate no more. She won. She wanted you and you're all hers now." Marlee shrugged as she attempted to walk away.

"I don't want her though, Marlee. I made a mistake, but I just need you to forgive me," Tyson begged as he grabbed her arm.

"Okay Tyson, you're forgiven. As a matter of fact, I forgive you and Yanni," Marlee replied.

"Are you trying to be funny or something Marlee?" Tyson asked while looking at her skeptically.

"No, I'm dead ass serious. I forgive you both. You and Iyana are not even worth my sanity. The sooner I move on from this situation, the sooner I can heal."

"I love you, baby. I love you with my whole heart and I always will. I'll do whatever you want me to do to get us back to where we were before," Tyson said as he tried to pull her into a hug.

"I don't think so Tyson," Marlee said while pushing him away.

"But, you just said that you forgive me," Tyson said, looking as if he was confused.

"And I do, but that don't mean that I fuck with you. Forgiving you doesn't mean taking you back. You got my cousin walking around carrying a seed that you planted in her. This is a done deal. I'll never take you back," Marlee said, breaking his heart all over again.

Tyson's eyes watered, but Marlee walked away before he could shed any tears. His emotions didn't move her, and she didn't care how he felt. He obviously didn't care about how she would feel when he fucked her cousin in their bed.

Once she got into Sierra's car, she dialed Desi's number and pulled out of the parking lot.

"Hey cousin," Desi said when she answered the phone.

Marlee heard all the noise in the background, so she knew that her cousin wasn't at work. "Where the hell are you?" Marlee asked.

"I'm on my lunch break. I'm getting me something to eat. Why? What's up?" Desi asked.

"Girl, ask me why Tyson's big, fat nasty ass just showed up at my job," Marlee said.

"What happened? Did he try to do something to you? I'll make Murk whip his fat ass!" Desi yelled.

"Who?" Murk asked in the background.

"Bitch, I didn't know that you were with his crazy ass. I'll tell you about it later, but he didn't try to do nothing to me," Marlee replied.

"Didn't I tell you about putting your nasty ass lips on my drink? Order your own shit," Desi said fussing at Murk.

"Shut your bald head ass up," he replied.

"I can't believe y'all stayed in contact with each other. Your ass is just as crazy as he is," Marlee laughed.

Desi and Murk exchanged numbers before they left to go back home. They didn't like each other romantically, but they had been hanging out just about every day since then. Desi would never date someone like Murk, but she liked him as a friend. He kept her entertained and there was always something new with him. She never had a platonic male friendship before and it felt good. Marlee couldn't believe it when her cousin told her about all his babies and baby mamas. She also learned that RJ didn't have any kids, but he did have a girlfriend. According to Murk, they had broken up right before they went to Vegas, but they were back together now. Marlee didn't feel no kind of way about the information that she was given. RJ laid pipe like a professional plumber, but that was the extent of their relationship. They didn't exchange numbers and that was cool with her. Murk told Desi that he asked about her, but Marlee wasn't trying to go there again.

"He just needs some home training and he'll be alright," Desi replied.

"Well, enjoy your lunch cousin. And call me when you get off," Marlee said.

"I might pass over there after work," Desi replied.

"Okay, I'll talk to you later," Marlee said as she hung up the phone and pulled into the parking lot of the fast food restaurant.

She tried not to let it, but she felt the depression trying to creep up on her again. She had been fine for the past few days, but seeing Tyson had her feeling down again. She no longer had an appetite, so she ordered food for Sierra only and headed back to the job.

Chapter 11

Desi talked, but Marlee wasn't listening. She was in another world and she never wanted to come back to the one that she was forced to live in. Marlee thought back on her entire twenty-six years on earth and tried to remember what she had done so wrong for her to have so much misfortune. Her first two relationships didn't work out and she had to live with that. She also had to live with the fact that her first cousin was walking around carrying a baby for her now ex-boyfriend. The test was confirmed, and Tyson was indeed the father, just like her cousin had been saying. That was a hard pill to swallow, but that too was something that she could live with. Eight weeks was how long she and Tyson had been broken up and her days and nights were getting better or, so she thought. Now, just when she was starting to see a sliver of light at the end of the dark tunnel, life had a way of kicking her while she was still down.

"Marlee!" Desi yelled while waving her hand in front of her face.

"God Desi. What am I gonna do?" Marlee cried as she looked down at the two pink lines on the home pregnancy test.

"I thought you said y'all used protection. And I thought you were on birth control," Desi said as she paced her bedroom floor.

Marlee had missed her cycle, and Desi's house was the first place that she thought to go. She didn't have any symptoms of being pregnant, so she was caught off guard when it happened.

"I am on birth control. Well, I was up until everything happened with Tyson and Yanni. I was stressing and taking pills was nowhere on my mind," Marlee cried.

"Are you sure it's not Tyson's?" Desi asked.

"No, Desi. I had a period after Tyson and I broke up," Marlee reminded her.

"That doesn't mean anything, does it?" Desi questioned.

She didn't know how true it was, but she'd heard that some women have a cycle while they were expecting. Maybe that was the case with Marlee.

"This can't be happening to me. Please God. I didn't mean it. I don't really wanna be a hoe," Marlee cried as she got on her knees and prayed.

"Why didn't you use condoms Marlee? You didn't know him well enough to have unprotected sex with him. Hell, you didn't know him at all," Desi fussed as she pulled her up from the floor.

"We did use protection Desiree! You think I'm that reckless!" Marlee yelled as she paced the floor with her.

"Every time?" Desi asked her through narrowed eyes.

"Yes, except in the shower," Marlee confessed.

"The shower! You took a bath with him too!" Desi yelled.

"God, Desi! I don't need to hear that shit right now!" Marlee snapped angrily.

"Okay cousin, let's both just calm down and think," Desi reasoned.

"I can't even think straight right now Desi. All that stupid talk about me wanting to be a hoe was a joke, but this shit is real."

"I know Marlee, but it's gonna be okay. The first thing you need to do is tell him," Desi said.

"How can I tell him anything? I don't even have his number. Hell, I don't even know the nigga's real name. This is just so fucked up," Marlee said as she dropped down to the floor in a fit of tears.

She was so embarrassed and ashamed of herself. Never in her entire life had she behaved the way she did in Vegas and now she was paying for it. There was no way for her to justify her actions and she wasn't going to try. She could no longer call Yanni a hoe because she was no better than her cousin.

"It's okay Marlee. I can get all of his information from Murk," Desi offered.

"Desi, no, please don't tell him anything. Promise me that you won't," Marlee begged.

"I won't say anything, I promise," Desi swore.

"I don't even know if he wants kids or not. Not to mention, he has a girlfriend. I just feel so stupid," Marlee sobbed.

"He still deserves to know Marlee. It's not fair for you to deny him of something so important. Are you trying to be a single mother?" Desi questioned.

"I'm not trying to be a mother at all. I know how you feel about this Desi and I'm sorry, but I can't have this baby," Marlee said as she looked at her.

She saw the pain flash across Desi's face, but she wasn't trying to hurt her. She was in a bad position and she was trying to figure a way out of it.

"If that's what you want to do, then I can't stop you," Desi said lowly.

"Please don't do this to me, Desi. I really need you right now," Marlee begged.

"You can't possibly be that insensitive Marlee." Desi frowned.

"What do you mean?" Marlee questioned.

"Are you seriously asking me to go with you to have an abortion?" Desi asked.

"No, Desi. I would never do that. Even though you might not agree, I'm just asking you to understand why I have to do it."

"First off, you don't have to do shit. You're doing it because you're selfish and you want to. And, no, I don't agree and I'll never understand. You can see yourself out. I'm about to shower and go to bed," Desi said, dismissing her.

"Desi, please," Marlee begged.

"Good night Marlee. Do me a favor and lock up when you leave," Desi said before walking into the bathroom and slamming the door behind her.

Marlee felt like shit, but she was sure that Desi felt even worse. She loved her cousin like a sister and she would never do anything to intentionally hurt her. She was torn and now she had no one else to talk to. She and Desi argued all the time but, by the next day, they would be back like nothing had ever happened.

***

It was now day three and Desi still wasn't talking to Marlee. She answered the phone for her, but she always told her that she would call her back. Of course, she never did, but that never stopped Marlee from calling again. She was going crazy without her favorite cousin and she was ready to make her talk to her. Kallie tried calling to make small talk, but Marlee was always vague with her answers. Kallie was sweet, but she talked too damn much. She didn't mean any harm, but Marlee would never tell her any of her personal business. She played both sides and Marlee couldn't get with that.

"Desi, I know you see me calling you. Please call me back. I'm sorry, okay. I love you and I miss you," Marlee said as she left her cousin yet another message.

It was Friday and she was off from work the entire day. She usually spent it with Desi, but she wasn't feeling her right now. Marlee spent the entire morning calling abortion clinics, but she was torn about what to do. She had just come back from seeing a doctor and found out that she was six weeks pregnant. Two weeks after breaking up with her boyfriend, she went out and got pregnant by a stranger. If that wasn't a hoe move, she didn't know what was. She had been battling with herself about what she should do, but she hadn't made a definite decision yet. She was tired of trying to figure it out and she was just ready to go home.

As soon as she pulled up to their house, Marlee's face lit up like a Christmas tree. Desi's car was parked out front and Marlee couldn't be happier. When the front door opened and Desi walked out, Marlee jumped out of the car and ran straight to her.

"My cousin!" Marlee squealed as she wrapped her arms tightly around Desi's neck.

"Bitch, stop being so dramatic all the time," Desi laughed.

"I'm not being dramatic. I missed you. I hate when you're mad at me," Marlee pouted.

"Yeah and I hate when you make me mad," Desi countered.

"I'm sorry cousin, but it wasn't intentional," Marlee replied.

"So, what happened? Did you do it? On second thought, I don't want to know," Desi said, waving her off.

"No, I didn't do anything yet," Marlee replied. She made sure to say yet, letting Desi know that it was still a possibility.

"Oh," was all Desi could think to say.

"I did go see an OBGYN today though," Marlee said.

"And?" Desi quizzed, encouraging her to say more.

"I'm six weeks in, so it's definitely not for Tyson. We broke up eight weeks ago," Marlee pointed out.

"Wow. Do you plan to tell RJ? I can get his number from Murk. I'm about to meet up with him right now," Desi said.

"No, Desi, and you promised not to say anything," Marlee reminded her.

"I know I did and I won't," Desi swore.

"You know I love you, right Desi? You're like my sister and I would never do anything to hurt you," Marlee said as she grabbed her cousin's hand.

"I love you too cousin and I don't want you to be mad with me," Desi replied.

"You didn't do anything for me to be mad at you. I was the one who messed up," Marlee admitted.

"I have to go Marlee. I'll call you later or maybe I'll come back and spend the night," Desi said as she walked off towards her car.

"Yeah, come spend the night so we can watch movies and pig out like we use to." Marlee smiled.

"Sounds like a plan. I'll be back in a few hours," Desi promised before she got into the car and drove away.

Marlee was all smiles until she walked into the house and everybody stared at her like she was on display. Her grandmother, mother, stepfather, Mat, and Sierra were all there and they didn't look too pleased.

"Did you do it?" her mother asked as she stood up and walked over to her.

Tiffany was known to swing first and ask questions later, so Marlee backed up a little.

"Did I do what?" Marlee asked.

"Don't play dumb with me, Marlee. Did you have an abortion?" Tiffany asked.

Now she understood why Desi said she didn't want her to be mad. That lil bitch sold her out and rushed out of there soon after.

"Answer the question Marlee. Did you have an abortion or not?" Mat spoke up.

"No," Marlee replied as she looked away.

"How far along are you?" Tiffany asked.

"Six weeks," Marlee replied.

"Does Tyson know?" her mother asked, as everyone else sat around waiting for her to answer.

Apparently, Desi just told them that she was pregnant and that was it. She couldn't have gone into detail if they were asking about Tyson.

"Tyson is not the father," Marlee said as a few tears fell from her eyes.

"I know he hurt you, baby, but don't deny him a chance to be in his child's life. Low down bastard got two of my grandbabies pregnant. I'm still trying to see what y'all saw in his ugly misfit ass," her grandmother fussed.

"Tyson is not the father grandma. We broke up eight weeks ago and I'm only six weeks pregnant," Marlee announced.

"Do you even know who the father is?" her mother asked, making her feel like more of a hoe than she already was.

"Yes," Marlee answered as she broke down and cried.

As usual, Mat was the first one to offer her comfort. She jumped up from the sofa and moved their mother out of the way. She wrapped her arms around her baby sister and let her soak the front of her shirt with her tears. Marlee was so ashamed, but she took a seat and told them the entire truth. Sierra was shocked to know that the mystery man from Vegas was the same one who had fathered her best friend's child. She saw him and Marlee flirting back and forth, but she didn't think it had gone that far. She and Mat did their own thing for the duration of their trip, and Marlee and Desi did theirs.

"Does he know about the baby?" Alvin, her stepfather, asked.

"No and I don't want him to," Marlee replied.

"I know you're grown and all Marlee, but I don't think abortion is the right thing to do. This baby didn't ask to be created, but it happened. It's a gift from God, no matter how it was conceived. You know we're all here for you, baby. Just think before you do something that you'll regret," her mother pleaded.

"You know I got you, sis. Whatever you need, I got you. I'm not trying to be all nice and sweet like mama. I don't care if you're grown or not. You ain't having no damn abortion," Mat fussed, making her laugh.

"Don't do it friend. I've heard too many horror stories about abortions and I don't want that to be you," Sierra spoke up.

"Just have the baby Marlee, please," Alvin begged her.

"Okay," Marlee said, making her mother and sister visibly relax.

"Thank God," her grandmother sighed.

"My first grandbaby!" Tiffany yelled excitedly as she pulled Marlee in for a hug.

"Your first and only unless it's coming from baby sis," Mat corrected.

Marlee was nervous, but she trusted that her family had her back. They always did, and she was sure that nothing would change. After seeing her grandmother off, Marlee talked to Mat and Sierra for a while. Once they left, she went to her room and quickly dialed a number on her phone.

"I'm sorry Marlee. Don't be mad with me," Desi said when she answered the phone.

"I should kick your ass for what you did. I know you didn't agree with me having an abortion, but you didn't have to rat me out. Had me in there explaining my one-night stand in front of grandma. I see a promise means nothing to you," Marlee argued.

"I promised not to tell Murk and I didn't. I never promised not to tell anyone else though," Desi pointed out.

"Bye Desi. I ain't fucking with you no more," Marlee fussed.

"Wait cousin. I'm in the store getting us some snacks. I'm coming over to spend the night with you and my God baby," Desi replied.

"Your snitching ass ain't being my baby's God mother," Marlee replied.

"I got you a bucket of chocolate almond ice cream," Desi said.

"Okay, let's negotiate," Marlee said, making her laugh.

Once she hung up with Desi, she took a long, hot shower and curled up in her bed to wait for her cousin.

Marlee didn't know what obstacles she was about to face being a single mother but, with her family, she was happy that she didn't have to face it alone.

Chapter 12

"Girl bye. I don't even believe that shit. That bitch is only claiming to be pregnant because I am. Ole bothered ass hoe. She claims she don't want Tyson, but now she's pregnant with his baby. Yeah, okay," Yanni laughed as she talked on the phone with Kallie.

"I don't know girl. My mama said that's what grandma told her. She said she thought I already knew and that's why she didn't say anything before now," Kallie replied.

"If she is pregnant, it ain't for Tyson. Bitch probably don't know who her baby's daddy is, but I'm the hoe," Yanni said.

"Tyson is a real low life. He's just making babies all over New Orleans like that shit is cute. I'm sorry that you're having his baby and I pray that Marlee's baby is not for him too. That's probably the only one he'll be bothered with anyway," Kallie said, making Yanni green with envy.

"You sound crazy. That nigga don't even be bothered with the baby that he made with his wife. The fuck makes you think he gon' be bothered with a baby just because Marlee's the mama," Yanni snapped.

"Why are you so happy to be having a baby by him if you know that?" Kallie asked.

"My baby is a blessing, no matter who the father is. I'm not happy about being pregnant by Tyson. I'm just happy to be having a baby, period," Yanni said, knowing that she was lying.

Tyson might not have spent much time with his kids, but he was always there financially. When she used to hang with Marlee a lot, Yanni saw that for herself. One Christmas, he and Marlee got them a ton of clothes and he gave both of his baby mamas a thousand dollars each to get them some toys. He gave them money for his kids weekly and Yanni was about to be rolling in the dough, right along with them.

"I guess. Did he ever answer the phone for you? I mean, since he knows for sure that you're carrying his baby, that's the least he could do. While he's running around here chasing Marlee and she don't even want his ass," Kallie said.

"You need to stop believing everything that you hear," Yanni said, getting frustrated with her cousin.

"Nobody told me nothing. He was the one who called me begging me to call her on three-way for him. Talking about how much he loves her, but he obviously didn't love her enough."

"Did you call her?" Yanni questioned.

"Hell no! Marlee is done with him and that's exactly what I told him. I think he ended up going to her job to see her though."

"When?" Yanni wanted to know.

"Girl, I don't know. My mama be telling me stuff after she talks to auntie Tiffany. I heard that Marlee was talking about getting a restraining order on him," Kallie answered.

"His fat ass is pathetic." Yanni frowned.

"Did he go with you to your doctor's appointment like you asked him to?" Kallie questioned.

"Nope and I don't give a fuck," Yanni snapped.

"Does his mama and sister know that you're pregnant?" Kallie asked.

"Yeah, but they're not too happy about it. Only because I'm Marlee's cousin. It's nothing against me. He gave his mama my number and she called me. She said that she's going to be here for her grandbaby, but she didn't agree with what me and Tyson did. She told me to keep her updated on my progress and my baby shower and stuff."

"She seems to be more concerned than her son," Kallie pointed out.

"I'll call you later Kallie. I'm about to call his fat ass right now," Yanni said.

"Call him for what?" Kallie asked.

"Because I can," Yanni replied before hanging up.

She was pissed about Tyson chasing after Marlee like he was. She shouldn't have been surprised because he always did. Her being pregnant by him changed the way she felt about it though. Not to mention his failure to show up at her doctor's appointment earlier that day. She texted the information to him more than once and he never bothered replying or showing up. Yanni had some words for him, but he probably wouldn't even answer the phone to hear them.

***

"This bitch." Tyson frowned when he saw that Yanni was calling him yet again.

"Who is that?" his sister, Trinity, asked when she saw the frown that appeared on Tyson's face.

Since Marlee left, Tyson's place had been a mess. She was the one who kept everything in order and Tyson was lost without her. Trinity took it upon herself to help her brother out. She called him to pick her up, since she didn't have to go to work that day. After cleaning the house and washing clothes, Tyson was bringing her back home. Taj tried to snake her way back in by offering to do it, but Tyson wasn't having it. He wasn't even in the mood to entertain another female and he wasn't sure when he would be. It was crazy because he was free to do whatever he wanted, but he didn't have a desire to do anything. Taj wanted dick and that was all that he gave her before sending her on her way. Another relationship was out of the question. He hadn't really seen his kids too much either, since Marlee was the one who always got them to come over. Whenever he did see them, Marlee was the first person who they asked about. They missed her, but not more than he did.

"That was that stupid bitch Yanni. She got me fucked up thinking I'm going to a doctor's appointment with her ass. I didn't even do that shit with my other two kids. That bitch ain't special," Tyson replied after a long pause.

"She seems to think otherwise since she's pregnant. I don't like the bitch and I probably never will. You know how big I am on family. That was fucked up what she did to Marlee. You were dead ass wrong too, but Marlee is her blood. I'm gonna love the baby, but that bitch better stay away," Trinity said, right as they pulled up to their mother's house.

They spotted Trinity's boyfriend, Craig, outside playing basketball, but he started walking over to Tyson's car when he spotted it.

"That bitch was jealous of my baby. I don't know what the fuck I was thinking when I hit that," Tyson said, shaking his head.

"You not only hit it, but you hit it raw," Trinity reminded him.

"Dumbest shit I've ever done," Tyson admitted with a sigh as they got out of the car.

"What's up baby?" Craig greeted when he walked over and planted a kiss on Trinity's lips.

"Hey boo." Trinity smiled.

"What's popping Tyson? Nigga, you don't know how to shoot blanks, huh? You gon' have a whole basketball team full of kids if you keep this shit up," Craig teased.

"Man, don't even remind me. Of all the bitches I could have knocked up," Tyson said, shaking his head.

"Shit, I thought you would have been happy," Craig replied.

"Happy for what? I can't stand Yanni with her hoe ass." Tyson frowned.

"I'm talking about Marlee," Craig spoke up.

"Marlee?" Tyson questioned with a puzzled look on his face.

"Damn nigga. You didn't know that Marlee was having your baby?" Craig asked.

"Who told you that?" Tyson asked.

"You know her sister be out here shooting hoops with these niggas. She must have said something because that's been the talk. I'm surprised you ain't hear it yet. Niggas saying you knocked two cousins up at the same damn time," Craig laughed.

"I didn't hear nothing. Marlee is trying to play games and I don't have time for that shit. She can hate me all she wants, but she got me fucked up if she thinks she can keep me away from my baby," Tyson fumed.

"Mama is about to die for sure. She was already pissed about Yanni and this will only make things worse," Trinity noted.

"Don't even say nothing to her. I'm not in the mood for her mouth right now. I'm about to go to Marlee's job and see what kind of bullshit she's on," Tyson said as he checked his watch for the time.

He had about forty-five minutes before Marlee was scheduled to get off and he was praying that traffic was light. He understood her being upset with him, but she was taking shit too far now. After leaving his mother's house, Tyson broke the speed limit trying to get to his destination.

When he arrived, he was happy when he saw Marlee's silver Charger parked in the lot. He parked his black one right next to it and got out. It was only six months ago that he'd purchased the matching cars and surprised her when she got home from work one day. He loved doing things to make her smile and he hated that he'd ever made her cry. After checking his watch again, Tyson saw that it was a little after four. He saw two of her co-workers walking out, followed by Marlee and another lady. When she saw Tyson standing there, Marlee paused for a few seconds before she started walking to her car again. She waved goodbye to a few people before turning to face him.

"What do you want Tyson?" Marlee asked with an attitude.

Of all the days that Sierra decided to call off, it had to be that one. Marlee ended up driving herself to work and she was sorry that she did. She wasn't feeling well, and Tyson was the last person that she wanted to see. Marlee never threw up, but the nauseous feeling was the worst. She would have rather thrown up every day than to constantly feel like she wanted to. Her doctor told her that the prenatal vitamins would help, but they hadn't helped yet.

"What kind of games are you playing Marlee?" he questioned.

"What the hell are you talking about Tyson? I'm about two seconds away from getting a restraining order on your ass," Marlee snapped.

"You can kill all that noise my love. There's no piece of paper that you can get that will keep me away from my baby," Tyson replied.

"What baby?" Marlee asked.

"So, you really gon' stand here and play dumb with me, Marlee? You didn't think I was gon' find out that you were pregnant with my baby. How long did you think you could hide that shit?" Tyson questioned.

"I'm not trying to hide shit. Yes, I am pregnant but not by you," Marlee replied as she tried to walk around him to go to her car.

"Look, I know I hurt you and shit and I'm sorry, but ain't no way in hell are you keeping me from my baby," Tyson fumed.

"This. Is. Not. Your. Baby," Marlee spoke slowly, clapping her hands after each word to make him comprehend.

"So, what, you cheated on me, Marlee? Is that what you're saying?" Tyson had the audacity to ask.

"The fucking nerve of you to even ask me some shit like that. I might be a lot of things, but a cheater is not one of them. I was faithful to your fat ass, even though you didn't deserve it. Get the fuck out of my way before I pull out my mace and spray the fleas off your dog ass," Marlee threatened.

"When's your next doctor's appointment? I want to be there," Tyson said, ignoring everything that she'd just said.

"Are you fat and slow? This is not your baby. Go to the doctor with that bum bitch Yanni. She's the one who's having your baby, not me!" Marlee yelled.

"Okay, so prove it," Tyson challenged.

"Tyson, listen and listen well. I know the timeline is mad close to the last time that we had sex, but I promise you that this is not your baby. My cycle came down after we broke up and I had sex the week after that," Marlee confessed.

"That's bullshit Marlee. That ain't even your style," Tyson noted.

"As much as I hate your ugly ass, I wouldn't lie about something so important. You think I would want to be a single mother. I would be happy to let you take care of your responsibility," Marlee said.

"I'm sorry that I hurt you, Marlee. I regret that shit every day, but I can't take back what happened. But, please don't do this to me. Don't keep me out of my baby's life," Tyson begged.

"God help me," Marlee sighed as she looked up to the heavens.

"I miss you so much baby. My kids miss you too. It's fucked up how you just abandoned them like you did," Tyson said.

"My relationship with your kids came about because of my relationship with you. As much as I love them, I can't be in their lives because I'm no longer in yours. Now, for the last time, get away from my car before I call the police," Marlee threatened.

"It's all good Marlee, but you already know this shit ain't over. Hate me all you want to but keep my innocent baby out of it. That shit ain't right. You never struck me as the type to use a child as a pawn."

"And you didn't strike me as the type to have a low IQ. Obviously, you do since you can't seem to comprehend what I keep saying. You have a good day Tyson," Marlee said once he moved and let her pass.

"You do the same and I'll see you tomorrow and every day after that until we get some shit clear!" Tyson yelled with a smirk as she got into the car.

"Fat, retarded bastard," Marlee fumed as she sped away from her job.

She couldn't wait to call Desi to tell her about her uninvited guest. Tyson was a whole ass mess to be coming at her like he was. He was trying to assume responsibility for a baby that wasn't his, when he didn't even want to claim the one that he had really fathered. Although Marlee was going to be a single mother, she welcomed that any day over having a baby with Tyson. She didn't know what Yanni thought, but she was going to see real soon. It was Marlee who made sure that his kids were straight because Tyson just didn't give a damn. Of course, she did it with his money, but he was always complaining about how much she spent. He had no problem buying her thousand dollars shoes, but he complained when she made him give his kids the same amount for Christmas. Yeah, being a single mother beat that any day. At least she knew that her child would have nothing but the best, and Marlee wouldn't have it any other way.

Chapter 13

"Are you feeling better Marlee?" Sharon, her co-worker, asked her.

Marlee had entered her third month of pregnancy the day before and the nausea just wouldn't subside. Her doctor switched her prenatal vitamins at her appointment and she was hoping that it worked. Thankfully, she threw up a few minutes before, so she was feeling fine now.

"Girl yes. I just needed to get it out, but I'm straight now." Marlee smiled.

"Okay, good. Sierra went to get breakfast, but she said she'll be right back," Sharon replied, right as the front door chimed, alerting them of a visitor.

Marlee was waiting on a patient and she was sure that's who it was. When Sharon asked the woman if she needed help, her assumptions were correct. Marlee already had the room set up, so she welcomed her customer back. After telling her what they were going to be doing, Marlee had her sign a few consent forms and got right to work.

"What happened to your hand?" Marlee asked the woman as she started doing the massaging techniques that she had been trained to do.

"I broke my wrist in a car accident a few months ago and had to get surgery, but it's still been paining me at times. It's not as bad as it was in the beginning, but the pain is still there. My doctor said that I should do physical therapy so here I am." The woman smiled.

"Okay, just let me know if I'm hurting you," Marlee said as she and the woman made small talk.

She admired Marlee's hair and makeup, and Marlee started promoting her business from there. She gave her a few cards for herself and to pass along to her friends. When the door chimed again, Sharon got up to assist whoever it was.

"That's probably my boyfriend. He had to run across the street to the bank," the woman replied.

"That's cool. He can come back here if he wants to," Marlee offered.

"Give me a minute to go get him," the woman said as she got up and went to the front.

When she came back a few minutes later, Marlee regretted saying that her man could come to the back. When she locked eyes with RJ, Marlee's heart skipped a beat. She knew that it was a possibility that she'd see him again but not like that. Desi and Murk were like besties now, so seeing him again wasn't impossible. The fact that his girlfriend was her patient just made everything seem so uncomfortable.

"Baby, this is Marlee. Isn't that a pretty name?" Aspen smiled.

"What's up?" RJ said while nodding his head in her direction.

"Hi." Marlee smiled shyly, as if she didn't have his dick down her throat only twelve weeks ago.

The tension in the room was thick, as Aspen dominated the entire conversation. Marlee was all into it before, but she barely said two words now. She prayed that the timer hurried up and went off, signaling the end of their session. As soon as they left, Marlee was going to give Aspen to Sharon and take one of her patients. She didn't want to run the risk of being in RJ's company if she didn't have to. The hour-long session seemed longer than usual and Marlee kept checking the timer to see how long before she was done.

"This feels great. I should have been come to see you," Aspen said as she closed her eyes and enjoyed Marlee's skillful hands.

Marlee felt RJ's eyes on her the entire time, but she pretended to be engrossed in her work. When Sharon walked in a few minutes later, she was happy for the temporary distraction.

"Hot chocolate with caramel and two ham and cheese croissants, courtesy of Sierra," Sharon said as she sat the food down in front of Marlee.

"Two croissants? That's too much for me to eat," Marlee replied, even though she was going to eat it all.

"It wasn't me, boo. I'm just the delivery person. Sierra said that she had to make sure her niece or nephew eats something. I just hope you can keep it down with that terrible morning sickness," Sharon said, making Marlee want to choke her.

"Aww, you're pregnant?" Aspen asked with a smile.

"Yeah," Marlee said, as RJ's eyes got wide and his eyebrows rose in surprise.

His gaze traveled down to her stomach, but there was really nothing there to see. Marlee didn't look pregnant unless she was completely naked, so it was hard for anyone to tell.

"How far along are you?" Aspen quizzed.

"Twelve weeks," Marlee said, as RJ looked down deep in thought.

He was counting down the time since he had been with Marlee in Vegas. When he looked up at her again, his eyes held a million questions that he needed answers to. When the timer buzzed, Marlee wanted to jump for joy. Aspen didn't seem like she was in a rush, but Marlee was ready for her bounce.

"Congrats on the baby. What do you want the sex to be?" Aspen asked her.

"As long as it's healthy, it doesn't matter," Marlee replied as she stood to her feet, hoping that they got the hint.

"That's a good attitude to have, but I want a boy if I ever get pregnant. Boys are a big thing in my boyfriend's family, so that's what I want to give him," Aspen said, as Marlee walked them up to the front.

She made Aspen another appointment with Sharon before seeing them off. Marlee released the breath that she'd been holding, right before she grabbed her food and rushed off to the break room. She had to tell Sierra what happened because it was unbelievable if she had to say so herself. She knew that Desi was going to be shocked and she couldn't wait until she got off to tell her too.

***

"You think he suspects that the baby is his?" Sierra asked as she drove her and Marlee back to work after their lunch break the next day.

"I really don't know, but I could tell that he was thinking about it," Marlee replied.

"Girl, this is so weird. And Tyson's fat ass needs to go sit down somewhere. I'm happy that the baby is not his. I don't want my niece or nephew looking like his ugly ass." Sierra frowned.

"His other kids are cute, so I wouldn't have worried about that. It would have been just my luck to have a baby come out looking just like his ass though," Marlee laughed.

"But, you said RJ doesn't have kids though, right?" Sierra asked.

"I don't think so, but I don't know for sure. Murk told Desi that he doesn't. I know his girlfriend doesn't have any, but she wants some," Marlee noted.

"Do you think he assumes the baby is his? You said he looked like he was thinking about it," Sierra pointed out.

"I don't know Sierra. Murk and Desi hang out and talk all the time. If he wanted to know anything about contacting me, he could have asked Desi. Maybe he just doesn't give a damn and that's fine with me," Marlee said.

"Or maybe he wanted to talk to you himself," Sierra said when they pulled up to the building and saw RJ leaning up on a Bentley truck.

"Bitch, don't leave me out here with him by myself," Marlee panicked.

"Shut the hell up Marlee. I wasn't with your ass when you fucked him the entire weekend in Vegas, was I?" Sierra asked.

"Okay bitch, but you better be peeping out the window or some shit," Marlee said as they got out of the car.

"Don't be scared now. You weren't scared when you gave up the goods. Just see what he has to say," Sierra suggested.

They walked up to the building, but they had to pass by RJ's truck to get there. He stood up straight when he saw Marlee and stuffed his hands in the pockets of his cargo shorts. Sierra didn't understand where all the shyness was coming from. According to Marlee, they fucked like rabbits in Vegas, but they were acting like scared teenagers now. Marlee stopped, but Sierra waved at him before walking into the building.

"Hey. The lady inside said that you were at lunch, but you would be back soon. I decided to wait around. I hope you don't mind," RJ spoke up.

"No, it's fine. So, what's up?" Marlee asked.

"That's what I'd like to know. Twelve weeks ago, we were together in Vegas and now you're twelve weeks pregnant. I'm not trying to offend you or nothing, but I just want to know if there's a chance that it could be mine," RJ replied.

For someone who wasn't trying to offend her, RJ was doing a great job. Marlee understood his position though. They didn't know each other, and he didn't know her history. She fucked him the first day they met, so she couldn't get mad about him questioning her.

"Look, I understand your position. We don't know each other outside of the bedroom, so I'm sure you have lots of questions. And yes, there is no doubt in my mind that the baby is yours. I don't expect you to take my word, so I have no problem doing a blood test," Marlee said.

"Can that be done before the baby is born?" RJ asked.

"Yeah, I know somebody who had it done. I just have to find out how to go about doing it," Marlee replied.

She knew that Yanni had the test done to prove that Tyson was her baby's father. She didn't have a problem doing the same for RJ.

"I'll pay for it, so don't even worry about that. Can I get your number to keep in contact with you?" he asked awkwardly.

"Yeah," Marlee replied as she called it out to him.

It was crazy how uncomfortable they seemed around each other with clothes on. When they were naked for the entire weekend, they weren't as shy.

"Lock me in," RJ said when he called her phone so that she could have his number too.

Marlee promised to look into having the test done and call him when it was time. RJ had a lot on his mind, so he went straight to work to have a talk with his father. He had tossed and turned all night and he couldn't get Marlee's pregnancy off of his mind. RJ knew that they used protection, but he would be lying if he said they used it every time. He pulled out when they were in the shower, but he didn't even remember if he did that every time either. Aspen was going to die if he ended up getting another woman pregnant, especially since she had been begging for a child of her own. He wasn't ready for kids, but he had to man up and handle his business if Marlee's baby was his.

When he pulled up to the building, RJ saw the same woman who Marlee was in the mall with a few months ago. He never paid attention before, but her round belly was on full display in her uniform now. She always broke her neck to speak to him, but he never paid her much attention. She was a bird and her actions always showed that. She was too thirsty, and she never tried to be discreet about it.

"Hey RJ," she cooed as she twirled her hair around her finger.

"What's up?" RJ spoke back as he looked at the name on her name tag.

He never knew her name, but he knew her face from seeing her around the office all the time. It was rumored that she'd gotten around with a few of the men who worked there, but he didn't know how true it was. When RJ walked up to his father's office door, he stopped when he heard his sister, Joy, mention his name.

"I only asked for two days off daddy. You never make RJ fill out a form when he wants to take off. He just doesn't show up and nothing is ever said. That's not fair," Joy whined.

"RJ doesn't do the same job that you do Joy. I never said that you couldn't have the days off. I just asked you to fill out a time off request form. This is a business and I'm running it as such. I can't have personal feelings getting involved and I won't," Banks replied sternly.

"It's always personal with RJ. You don't even try to hide the favoritism," Joy complained.

"I don't show favoritism Joy. I love all of you the same, despite what you and your sisters say. I don't understand why y'all all seem to be so envious of your only brother."

RJ was tired of the back and forth, so he tapped on the door and cut their conversation short. He had something important to talk about and Joy was only whining like always. Out of all his sisters, she was the most spoiled. She didn't mind having a tantrum if things didn't go her way.

"Sorry, am I interrupting something?" RJ asked as if he didn't just hear part of their conversation.

"No, come on in son." Banks smiled.

"Daddy!" Joy pouted. "I wasn't done talking."

"You can have the days off Joy. Just let your assistant know when so she can be prepared to handle your work and hers," Banks replied to his youngest daughter.

RJ always wondered what the hell his sister needed an assistant for, when she never really did anything her damn self. The only thing she did was boss the other girl around and complain all day.

"Thank you, daddy." Joy smiled as she kissed his cheek.

When she turned and faced her brother, her smile faded, but that was nothing new. RJ didn't even bother speaking and neither did she. Banks always noticed the tension that existed amongst his kids, but he never really spoke on it. There was lot of jealously there and he'd seen that from the beginning. RJ was his only son and his daughters always called him out for showing favoritism. Although he always denied it, Banks knew that it was true. RJ was a younger version of him, so he couldn't help it.

"I didn't think you were coming in today," Banks said when RJ flopped down in the leather chair that was next to his desk.

"I had to take care of something first," RJ sighed as he ran his hand down his face.

"What's wrong son?" Banks asked in concern. RJ looked stressed and he needed to know why.

"I got some shit going on right now," RJ confessed.

"Like what? Talk to me, RJ," his father demanded as he sat up and looked at him.

"So, when I went to Vegas, I hooked up with a chick that I met in the bar. She chilled with me in my room the entire weekend, but I never heard from her again once we left. Murk kept in contact with her cousin, but that was about it. Yesterday, I went with Aspen to physical therapy for her wrist and the chick that I hooked up with in Vegas works there," RJ rambled.

"Oh okay. So, what, she told Aspen about y'all messing around in Vegas?" Banks asked with a smirk.

"No, it's nothing like that," RJ replied.

"You and Aspen weren't together at the time anyway. She broke up with you, so she shouldn't have anything to say," Banks noted.

"No, that's not the problem," RJ said.

"What's wrong RJ?" his father asked.

"She's pregnant," RJ announced.

"By you?" his father yelled as he stood up from his seat.

"She says it is," RJ replied.

"I hope you didn't fall for that bullshit RJ. This girl slept with you during a weekend in Vegas and now she's claiming that you're the father of her child. I see dollar signs written all over this mess," Banks fumed as he paced the floor.

"She offered to have a DNA test done," RJ said.

"She offered, or you asked?" his father inquired.

"No, she mentioned it first. She's gonna set it up for us to have it done."

"How far along is she?" Banks asked.

"Twelve weeks. The same amount of time it's been since I was in Vegas," RJ replied.

"I can't believe that you were so careless RJ. How could you have unprotected sex with a woman that you'd just met? In Vegas of all places. You need to be doing more than just having a DNA test done," his father argued.

"It was stupid of me, I already know," RJ replied.

"When is this test being done? I want to be there," Banks announced.

"No pops, I don't need you to be there. I can handle it. I'll let you know everything once I talk to her."

"What's her name?" his father asked.

"Marlee," RJ replied.

"Marlee what?" his father asked, hoping that he could get some background information on the woman who would possibly be the mother to his only son's first child.

"Damn man. I don't even know," RJ admitted.

"Un-fucking-believable. How in the hell am I supposed to explain this to your mother, RJ? This is crazy," Banks said while shaking his head, right as RJ's phone rang.

"This is her. Don't say nothing pops," RJ said, right before he answered the phone.

He listened, as Marlee gave him all the information to the DNA testing center that he should go to. She and

Sierra started looking online as soon as RJ left, and she had the perfect place in mind. Their results yielded one hundred percent accuracy and their turnaround time was the fastest. RJ grabbed a pen and paper from his father's desk and wrote down everything that she told him. He and Marlee didn't have to be tested at the same time, but he wanted it done as soon as possible.

"What did she say?" Banks questioned as soon as his son got off the phone.

"She gave me the info to go get tested. I can do it at any time, but she's going today when she gets off since they close at seven."

"When do you plan to go?" his father asked.

"I don't know," RJ replied as he leaned his head back and sighed.

"What don't you know about RJ? Why can't you go now?" his father asked.

"Yeah, maybe I will," he replied.

"What's the address? I'll drive," Banks offered.

"Pops, no, I got this. I'll let you know what's up when I get back."

"I don't want to hear that shit RJ. I got questions to ask and I want answers directly from them. I need to know how accurate this test is. You have too much money to just let some random woman claim to be having your baby."

"But, what if it is my baby?" RJ asked, just to see what his father would say.

"Then, he or she will be one of the riches babies ever born in New Orleans," Banks replied as they headed out the door to his car.

"I hope I get this damn house that I want," RJ sighed.

"You will, don't worry. You got the one thing that it takes and that's money. If you have a baby on the way, you damn sure need it," his father said, as they got into the car and pulled away.

Chapter 14

"I want to meet her. When can she come over to see me?" Ivy asked as she looked at the paperwork that her son had just handed her.

She was ecstatic, and she couldn't wait until her first grandchild arrived. Four days after having the test done, RJ got the results that he and his father had been waiting for. It was official, and he was going to be a father. Although his mother was happy, RJ had mixed emotions. He didn't know Marlee that well, and he prayed that they could co-parent and be civilized with each other. Murk had the baby mamas from hell and he didn't want to go through that. Other than that, the idea of fatherhood both excited and frightened him. He didn't know the first thing about kids, but he wanted to be a good father. He really had to get his shit together and get him another house now.

"I don't know ma, but I'll ask her. Honestly, I need to get to know her better myself. I'm about to have a baby with somebody and I don't know anything about her," RJ replied.

"That's the first thing you need to do RJ. You have to spend time with her to get to know her. Hopefully, Aspen will understand your position," Ivy said.

Aspen. That was another thing that had RJ bothered. He heard what his mother said, but there was no understanding where Aspen was concerned. Giving RJ a baby was as important to her as breathing. RJ knew that they were headed for a breakup, but he meant what he said. If she broke up with him again, there was no coming back.

And as much as he loved her, he couldn't put her before his child. His father wasn't having that, even if he tried.

"If she doesn't understand, then she's not the woman for you," his father spoke up.

"Don't tell him that baby. Aspen is a sweetheart, and this is going to hurt her," Ivy said.

"I know it will, but his child comes first, no exceptions," his father said, looking at him to make sure he understood.

"I know that pops," RJ replied.

"Honesty RJ. If you don't do anything else, always be honest. No matter how it makes you or the other person feel, you should always tell the truth. Either they accept you or they don't," Banks lectured.

"I just want to meet her. Maybe she can come keep me company sometimes, so I don't be in this big ole house bored all the time," Ivy suggested.

"Bored?" Banks asked as he turned to face her.

Ivy was a natural beauty with her amber colored skin and Asian eyes. She had a slender nose with full pouty lips that Banks could kiss all day. He never dreamed that him going into her family diner one day would lead to him falling in love with someone other than his wife. He'd been going to the same diner for months, but he had never run into the seventeen-year-old beauty before. He found out that she was only filling in for her sick cousin for a few days, but he was happy that she did. He wined and dined Ivy for months until she gave him her virginity on her eighteenth birthday six months later.

Nine months later, RJ was born, and she was set for life. Whatever her heart desired was hers and he made sure of it. He never hid his feelings from his wife and he never tried. Ivy had given him something that no other woman had. That alone made him love her unconditionally. Truthfully, he loved her even before then. It pained him to see her broken hearted and crying when she learned that he was married. There was no way that he was letting her leave him, so he was patient and waited until she finally decided to stop hating him.

"Yes, bored, and no I don't want to take a trip anywhere. I'm tired of vacationing with my friends and sisters," Ivy said after a while. She was thankful for Aspen and RJ's best friend, Kassidy, who often stopped by to visit her.

"Where do you want to go sweetheart? I'll take you anywhere and you know that," Banks said while looking at her.

He hated when Ivy said stuff like that because he felt like he wasn't doing his job as her man. She was forty-six years old and her son's father was the only man that she'd ever been with. Banks didn't want her to have idle time on her hands because he didn't want her mind to wander. That was why he made sure that she stayed busy during the week when he couldn't be there with her. It seemed as if that wasn't enough, but he didn't mind doing more. If he had to take off from work to accompany her on a vacation, he would gladly do so, no questions asked.

"Ask her when she's free to come over RJ. I want to meet her," Ivy said, referring to Marlee.

She ignored what Banks was saying, but she knew that he wasn't going to let up. Making her happy was all that he cared about, but it got lonely not having him there with her all the time. Ivy was young and naïve when she got with him, so she didn't know what she was doing. It never dawned on her that she had signed up to be a married man's kept bitch, possibly for the rest of her life, especially since she didn't even know that he was married until after her son was born.

"Are we going to talk Ivy? Tell me why you're not happy," Banks said, never taking his eyes off her.

RJ already knew what time of day it was, so he stood up to leave. Just as he did with him, his father treated his mother like she was a baby. He wanted her happy at all times and he tried his best to fix whatever problems stood in the way of that.

Once he left his mother's house, RJ sent Marlee a text, asking her if she needed anything. She told him that she was good, so he called to see where Aspen was. There was no need to avoid the inevitable and he was ready to get it over with. When she said that she was at home, RJ told her that he was on his way. She sounded so happy when he said that but, sadly, he knew that her mood wouldn't last very long.

***

"I guess everything is all good with y'all now since I haven't seen you in a few weeks," Aaron said as he talked on the phone with Aspen.

"Don't start Aaron. I told you that we got back together a few days after we broke up," Aspen replied as she sprayed her body down with perfume.

As soon as RJ said that he was on his way, Aspen took a quick shower and slipped into her silk night shirt. She didn't bother putting anything on under it because she was sure that she wouldn't have it on for long. When the phone rang again, she thought it was RJ saying that he was outside. She was pissed when she answered for Aaron, who had called from another number. No matter how many times Aspen told him not to, he still called her before she called him. He started using an app so that his number wouldn't show up, but she didn't even want him to do that.

"Where does that leave me, Aspen? You swear that I'm what you want, but I'm not too sure anymore. I'm trying to let you get this shit out of your system, but my patience is wearing thin."

"Aaron, you were my first everything. Anything that I experienced in life, I did it with you. I just felt like I was living in a bubble and I hadn't experienced anything that life had to offer. You should be happy that I'm doing this now, versus when we get married and have kids."

"I understand baby, but for how long? We could have been living our best life right now, but you're still playing these games. I wish you would just be honest with me, Aspen. If this is not what you want anymore, just let me go be happy with someone else."

Aaron had to be the dumbest man on planet earth. No other man in their right mind would have bought the bullshit that Aspen was selling. Truthfully, she had love for him because of the history they shared, but she wasn't in love with him. She couldn't let him go just yet, though. Not until she and RJ walked down the aisle and made things official. Aaron was her comfort zone and she didn't want to lose that.

"I don't think I've ever loved another man as much as I love you and I probably never will," Aspen said, telling him what he wanted to hear.

"I love you too, baby. When am I gonna see you again?" he asked, right as there was a knock on Aspen's door.

"Hopefully soon, baby, but I gotta go. My auntie is calling, and you already know how she is," Aspen said as she hung up and powered her phone off.

With a big smile on her face, Aspen glided over to the door to let her man in.

"What's up?" he said when he walked in and gave her a peck on the lips.

"Hey baby," Aspen said as she closed and locked the door behind him.

She felt weak in the knees as she caught a whiff of his expensive smelling cologne. She didn't know what fragrance it was because RJ had so many. When he sat on the sofa, Aspen straddled him and started planting kisses on his neck. He palmed her ass and threw his head back, enjoying her juicy lips on his flesh.

"We gotta talk Aspen," RJ said, trying hard not to moan.

"Dirty talk?" Aspen asked as she tried to lift his shirt over his head.

"No, it's serious. Raise up before you make me change my mind," RJ said while tapping her thigh.

"We can talk later. I need to feel you right now," Aspen cooed sexily in his ear.

"You will baby, but we really need to talk," RJ said, making her look at him.

The serious look on his face made her nervous. She prayed that he wasn't telling her that something was wrong with him health wise. The thought of losing him had her feeling physically sick and he hadn't even said anything yet.

"What's wrong RJ? You're scaring me," Aspen worried.

"Damn man," RJ sighed as he ran his hand down his face.

He didn't even know where to start, but he had to be honest with her. His father taught him the importance of honesty at a young age and he tried his best to always be truthful. RJ would rather not answer a question before he lied to someone.

"What is it RJ? Are you cheating on me or something?" Aspen asked, dreading his answer.

"No, but today I found out that I have a baby on the way," RJ said, making Aspen gasp in shock.

It felt like all the air had left her lungs and tears immediately stung her eyes. She wanted to believe that he was joking, but the serious look on his face let her know that it was real. RJ was really having a baby with another woman.

"You just said that you didn't cheat on me. I can't believe that you would hurt me like this," Aspen said as she broke down and cried.

Yeah, she was doing her thing with Aaron, but that was mostly when they were broken up. That was exactly why she kept him around. RJ was too undecisive and she couldn't let her for sure thing go for someone who couldn't make up his mind.

"I didn't cheat on you. We were broken up and I was in Vegas," RJ replied.

"Wait, so you took a woman with you when you went to Vegas?" Aspen questioned.

"No, we hooked up while we were both there," he admitted.

"That was months ago RJ. How far along is she?"

"She's three months," he replied.

"How long have you known her?"

"I met her in Vegas," RJ said, feeling embarrassed.

He never bothered telling Aspen that she'd already met the woman when she went to her physical therapy appointment. He knew that Aspen would be going back to the clinic where Marlee worked and he didn't want there to be any drama.

"Oh God! You got your one-night stand pregnant!" Aspen yelled in anger.

"Basically," RJ replied truthfully.

"Are you even sure that the baby is yours? You had a fling and now she's trying to pin a baby on you. Trick probably saw dollar signs and decided to trap you. I don't believe her," Aspen argued.

"She had an amniocentesis test done," he noted.

"A what?" Aspen questioned in confusion.

"I read up on it and it's a test that's done on pregnant women to determine if their baby is healthy and stuff. It can also be used to test paternity," he answered.

"Are you sure that the test is even accurate?" Aspen asked, grasping at as many straws as she could.

"It's very effective and their accuracy rate is almost perfect," RJ pointed out.

He'd done his homework, so he knew all there was to know about the testing. No matter how Aspen tried to spin it, he was going to be a father in six more months. He didn't want to hurt her feelings, but he wasn't apologizing for that.

"Almost doesn't count RJ. We need a second opinion," Aspen said as she got up and paced the floor.

"What for Aspen? The results are going to be the same," RJ said, getting frustrated with the entire conversation.

"I don't care. I think you need a second opinion," Aspen replied.

"That's not going to happen. The procedure already carries a slight risk of miscarriage when it's done so early. I'm not taking a chance by having her do it again."

"Are you even listening to yourself RJ? You act like you want her to have your baby," Aspen said as she stopped pacing to look at him.

"She's already having it Aspen. Like it or not, in six more months, I'm going to be somebody's father," RJ pointed out.

"All this time you've been telling me that you weren't ready for kids, only for you to knock up the first bitch you meet in Vegas. You make sure to strap up when you fuck me, but you go in a stranger raw."

"Don't act like we've never slipped up and didn't use condoms. You just had a pregnancy scare a few month ago," RJ reminded her.

"Yes, but I've also been your girlfriend for over four years," Aspen pointed out.

Her first thought was to end their relationship, just like she always did when she was upset. The only thing that stopped her was what RJ told her after their last breakup. She knew that he was tired of the back and forth dance that they'd been doing over the past year. Breaking up with him again meant breaking up forever and she couldn't have that.

"I don't know what else to say Aspen. I didn't do anything wrong and I didn't cheat. This pregnancy wasn't planned but, like I always tell you, shit happens. No matter what happens, I'm going to be the best father that I can be. The baby is innocent, no matter how guilty you think I am," RJ said, breaking her away from her thoughts.

"Where does this leave us, RJ? I don't want this to come in between our relationship. I've heard stories about how bitter baby mamas can be and I don't want to go through that."

"I don't either Aspen, but I don't think she's like that," RJ assumed.

"How can you say that RJ? Do you even know her well enough to know how she is?" Aspen questioned.

"No, but I plan to get to know her," RJ answered truthfully.

"What the hell is that supposed to mean?" Aspen yelled.

"Lower your voice Aspen and it means just what I said. I'm about to have a baby with a woman that I barely know anything about. As fucked up as it sounds, that's what it is. I just found out her last name when we had the test done and that's unacceptable to me. I don't know where my baby will be living at or nothing else. This shit is stressing me out already," RJ said while massaging his temples.

"Do your parents know?" Aspen asked as she sat down next to him and spoke calmly.

"Yeah. I had a talk with them before I came over here. I wanted to wait for the test results to come back before I said anything. They want to meet her," he noted.

"Wow. It sounds like y'all are about to be one big happy family," Aspen said sarcastically.

"It's not even like that Aspen, but my baby is my family. I'll never turn my back on my child and I hope that's not what you expect."

"No, I would never want you to do that. We're gonna be married someday and I plan to love your child like it's my very own. I just don't want this to come in between us, RJ," Aspen said sadly.

"It won't if you don't let it," RJ replied as he kissed her hand.

"The baby's mother, does she know about me?" Aspen asked.

"Yes, she knows that I'm in a relationship. I'm not a liar Aspen. I don't have anything to hide," RJ said as he pulled her onto his lap and kissed her.

He wanted to tell her that they'd already met, but he didn't want things to get weird. Aspen still had a few weeks of physical therapy left and he didn't need her and Marlee clashing before then.

"Just promise me that things won't change between us, RJ," Aspen said as she looked deep into his eyes.

His response was to pull her close and kiss her, but she wasn't satisfied. RJ couldn't lie and tell her that because he really didn't know what was going to happen. Aspen knew her man all too well. She knew that RJ would never answer a question that he wasn't sure about. He was right about one thing; he wasn't a liar. He told the truth, even if it meant hurting someone's feelings and he got that attitude from his father. Aspen prayed that that was the only thing that he got from his father. She couldn't take it if her man adapted to his father's womanizing ways.

Banks was something else altogether. Lauren was a damn fool to know that her husband was spending his time and some of his nights with his side chick. She was a kept woman, so she never did make a fuss about it. It was crazy because he didn't mess with a bunch of women. It was only Ivy and his wife, and he didn't try to hide it. Lauren confessed to her how his actions hurt her, but what could she do? Everything that she had was given to her by her husband. Without him, she had nothing.

Aspen was happy that she had her own money and degree. That way, she didn't have to depend on a man to take care of her. The women in her family were independent and they stressed the importance of that to her. She made good money and, when she became a lawyer, she would be making even more.

Chapter 15

"What did he say?" Sierra asked when Marlee got off the phone with RJ.

"His mother wants me to come to dinner at her house this weekend," Marlee replied.

"My girl is all in the family. Get it bitch!" Sierra yelled excitedly.

"Girl, bye. It ain't even like that with us. We're getting to know each other for the sake of this baby and that's it," Marlee said, waving her off.

Over the past month, she and RJ had formed a friendly bond and they talked multiple times a day. The awkwardness that existed between them in the beginning was gone and they were comfortable around each other. Marlee had met his parents and his mother was cool. She couldn't say anything about his father other than he looked scary. He was a big, tall, dark skinned man who looked like he would kill someone with his bare hands. When he spoke, although his voice was deep, he wasn't as frightening. He asked Marlee a bunch of questions that she had no problem answering. RJ looked so much like him and she could tell that he loved the ground his son walked on. Ivy was more talkative, and she never wanted Marlee to leave. Marlee had gone to Ivy's house twice after that, at her request, without RJ or Banks being present. Ivy had a beautiful home, courtesy of RJ's father, who she affectionately referred to as her man. She confided in Marlee all about her crazy situation, but she couldn't judge.

"Another delivery for you, Marlee!" Sharon yelled when she walked to the back carrying a huge edible arrangement.

"This nigga," Marlee sighed, already knowing who it was from.

"I ain't never seen no shit like this before in my life. It's usually the man saying that he's not the baby's father when the woman swears that he is. I've never seen a nigga claiming a baby and the woman telling him that he's not the baby's daddy," Sierra laughed.

Marlee was in her fourth month of pregnancy and Tyson had become a pain in her ass. He showed up at her job whenever he felt like it or he had shit delivered every other day. It was crazy how he didn't really be bothered with Yanni and she was the one who was carrying his daughter. She was always putting on a show for Facebook and that nigga had yet to accompany her to a doctor's appointment. He kept telling Marlee that he wanted to do a DNA test and he thought she was lying when she told him that she did it already.

"He's so fucking stupid. What did I ever see in his crooked leg ass?" Marlee frowned.

"I don't know honey, but you made up for it with your baby daddy," Sierra laughed.

"Bitch, stop acting like you're into men before I tell my sister," Marlee joked.

"I don't have to be into men for me to give a compliment. The nigga is fine and even a lesbian like me can see that," Sierra said, making Marlee laugh.

"Pass me the scissors. I might not want his fat ass no more, but I'm about to tear into this edible arrangement," Marlee said right as the door chimed, alerting them of a visitor.

RJ's girlfriend, who she now knew as Aspen, walked in smiling and waving at everyone. That was like her third or fourth time coming there, but Marlee no longer assisted her. RJ still hadn't told her that Marlee was the woman who carried his child and she didn't feel that it was her place to do it. He claimed that he was going to tell her when she got released from the clinic the following month because he didn't want to bring any drama to her job.

"Hey girl. That stomach is popping out," Aspen said when she looked over at Marlee, as Sharon led her to the back.

"Yeah, it is." Marlee smiled awkwardly as she touched her protruding belly.

She didn't do anything wrong, but she felt like she was being fake. She hated feeling like she was smiling in Aspen's face, knowing that she was having a baby with her man. The shit just seemed shady and she didn't do shade. RJ didn't even accompany her to her bi-weekly visits anymore and that made the situation seem worse. She was happy when Sharon led Aspen to the back.

"When do we find out the sex?" Sierra asked, interrupting her thoughts.

"I don't know. I didn't even ask. Maybe he'll do it when I go back for my five-month checkup," Marlee replied

"You know Mat wants a boy, but I want a girl. Did you think of any names yet?" Sierra asked.

"No, but I hope it's not a boy. I hate his name. What the fuck is a Ryker?" Marlee asked with a frown.

"I think it's cute and different," Sierra laughed.

"I just keep thinking of Ryker's Island," Marlee replied.

"Maybe he doesn't want the baby named after him if it's a boy," Sierra said.

"Girl, bye. That's the first thing he said when we discussed it. He's a junior and he wants to keep it going. I'm hoping for a girl, just so I won't have to do it."

As if on cue, her phone rang and the name 'baby daddy' popped up on her screen. Marlee stepped into an empty room before she picked up.

"What's up baby mama?" RJ asked as soon as she answered the phone.

"Nothing, just waiting for my next client to get here," Marlee replied.

"Come outside," RJ demanded.

"For what?" Marlee asked.

"I must be out here if I'm telling you to come outside," he replied.

"You do know that your girlfriend is here, right?" Marlee asked.

"Yeah, I know. I see her car parked out here," he replied.

"Okay, I'm coming," Marlee said before she hung up.

She told Sierra where she was going before she made her way outside. She spotted RJ's copper colored

Bentley truck the moment she walked out. That truck got anyone's attention, even if they weren't trying to look. There was a woman on the passenger side looking her up and down with a frown on her face. Marlee smiled and waved, but she didn't return the gesture.

"Hot chocolate with caramel and two ham and cheese croissants." RJ smiled as he walked up to her and handed her the food.

"Aww, you remembered." Marlee smiled.

"Yep," he replied as he rubbed her growing baby bump.

"Who is that you're riding with?" Marlee questioned.

"Oh, that's my girl, Kassidy, that I was telling you about," he answered.

"Oh okay, so that's why she's booting me up. She got a lil crush on my baby daddy. Just fuck her and get it over with. That's obviously what she wants." Marlee smirked.

"It ain't even like that my baby. That's been my best friend for years," RJ pointed out.

"You might be her best friend, but she wants to be more than yours," Marlee noted.

"Let me find out my baby mama is jealous," he chuckled.

"Never that. I'm just calling it how I see it," Marlee replied with a shrug.

"I hear you, Marlee. I'll see you in a few hours for lunch," RJ said as he kissed her forehead and walked back to his car.

"Yes indeed. We're giving forehead kisses and shit," Kassidy said when he got back into the truck.

"Mind your business lil girl." RJ smiled as he pulled off and drove away.

"What are you smiling for? Don't tell that me you're crushing on your baby mama," Kassidy said.

"Look at her. Why wouldn't I?" RJ asked, like she should already know.

"Maybe because you have a girlfriend already," Kassidy pointed out.

"Is that the only reason Kassidy? You make me think you're feeling a nigga as more than just a friend," RJ said while cutting his eyes in her direction.

He wasn't blind, and he knew that Kassidy was attracted to him. He didn't see her like that though, not that she wasn't attractive. Kassidy was beautiful with her smooth milk chocolate skin and big brown eyes. She could have probably had any man she wanted, but she was still single. She swore that she hadn't found the right one yet, but RJ wasn't so sure that was the real reason.

"I'm just trying to be the voice of reason here. Aspen and I don't always get along, but I still wouldn't want you to do her dirty," Kassidy replied, not bothering to reply to his other comment.

"What about if I was doing her dirty with you?" RJ asked, trying hard not to laugh.

"Whatever RJ," Kassidy said, waving him off.

She would gladly be to him what Ivy was to his father, but that was only wishful thinking. She saw by the look on his face that he was only playing, but she was dead ass serious.

"Let me stop fucking with you before you get in your feelings. But, real talk, Marlee is the shit. I can't even front like I'm not attracted to her. I can't lie to nobody else and I'm damn sure not about to lie to myself."

"I mean, she's cute, I guess." Kassidy shrugged, trying to hide her anger.

RJ was starting to piss her off. Marlee was a one-night stand who lucked up and got pregnant for a nigga with money. She was a hoe, in Kassidy's opinion, but he was talking like she was more than that.

"Cute?" RJ yelled. "We ain't talking about no kittens Kassidy. She's fucking beautiful."

"She just doesn't seem like your type," Kassidy replied.

"Since you think you know me so well, what's my type?" RJ questioned.

"Well, she's much shorter than any girl that you've ever dated."

"I love that shit though. I had fun picking her up when we were in Vegas. What else?" RJ questioned, wanting her to continue.

"I've never seen you date a girl with short hair before and especially not that wild color," Kassidy said.

"As long as she got enough for me to pull when I hit it," RJ replied.

"Eww." Kassidy frowned.

"What else?" RJ pressed, wanting her to go on.

"Forget it RJ. I can see that you feel like playing," Kassidy replied.

"I'm not playing, but I'm trying to get you to see something. I don't have a type and I never did. Aspen likes to get that long ass hair sewed in her head, but that never mattered to me. She can shave the shit off and it wouldn't bother me one bit. And honestly, Marlee's hair was the first thing that stood out to me when I first saw her. I loved the fact that she sets her own trends and doesn't try to be like everybody else," RJ admitted.

"It sounds like Aspen has some competition on her hands," Kassidy chuckled, trying to make light of the situation.

RJ could tell that everything he'd just said went right over her head, so he didn't even bother continuing. His comments were really aimed at Kassidy, since she always did what she saw others do. Even in college, she was swayed by what others did and ended up changing her major. She had originally planned to attend school for business management, but she quickly switched over to accounting so that she could follow in his footsteps, even though they went to different schools. RJ was always a wiz at math, but Kassidy struggled for a while. He stayed up tutoring her many nights and he often wondered why she changed her major to something that she wasn't too familiar with. His sister, Raven, made it clear to him that Kassidy only did it to be closer to him, and RJ believed her. He tried his best to treat Kassidy like one of his boys because he didn't want to send her mixed messages. Sadly, it didn't work, and she was still wanting them to be more than just friends. She never came right out and said it, but RJ was no fool. No matter how many times he tried to play dumb, he knew what it was.

"What are you about to get into?" Kassidy asked when they pulled up to her office building.

He took her to bring her car to the dealership to be serviced and gave her a ride to work as well. Stopping to get Marlee breakfast was a spur of the moment thing that she could have done without.

"I'm meeting up with Raven to see a few houses and then I have to bring Marlee some lunch," he replied.

"Wow, so bringing her breakfast and lunch is a part of your daily routine now?" Kassidy asked.

"Let me know if you need a ride to get your car later," RJ said, ignoring her comment.

"Yes, I will." Kassidy smiled as she prepared to get out of his car.

"Cool, I'll tell Murk to swing by and bring you," RJ replied, wiping the smile from her lips.

"Never mind. I'll get somebody here to bring me," Kassidy said, making him laugh.

She got out of the truck and waved, as RJ pulled away. Kassidy walked into her office with a heavy heart as her thoughts wandered back to the other woman that she'd just seen. She could front all she wanted to, but RJ was right. Marlee was beautiful and she could see why her best friend was attracted to her. She was short and sexy, and her hair was to die for. Kassidy had a sew-in that reached the middle of her back. She alternated between wearing it curly and straight, just like Aspen often did. She assumed that was what RJ liked, but that obviously wasn't true. She grabbed a mirror from her desk drawer and raised it up to her face.

"Too damn plain," Kassidy said as she looked at her reflection.

After powering her computer on, she searched a few websites until she came across something that caught her eye. Kassidy printed up a few pictures and stuffed them into her purse. Hopefully, she would have enough courage to go through with what she had planned. She was a simple girl, but maybe she needed to spice things up a little bit. RJ liked different and different was what she was about to become.

Chapter 16

"Yanni though, bruh. The fuck made you even deal with her nasty again?" Jerry asked Tyson as they rode around.

"Man, I don't even know, but I hate that bitch," Tyson fumed.

"Now you got two cousins about to have your seeds," Jerry said, shaking his head.

He worked offshore, but he was shocked when he came home and learned that his boy had fathered two kids with two cousins. He always knew that Yanni was a hoe, especially after she gave him head while he and Desi were still together. He regretted it the moment it happened, and he shut her down every time she came at him after that. Obviously, Tyson didn't have as much restraint. Marlee was his girl though, and Tyson was a fool to lose her over Yanni's rat ass.

"Yeah, but Marlee is on some bullshit right now. She claims the baby ain't mine, but she don't want to take the test to prove it," Tyson fussed.

He was tired of playing games with her though. He was ready to drag her stubborn ass to the clinic to have the test done, if she wasn't willing to go on her own. He tried reaching out to her cousins, but they were no help. He knew that Desi was team Marlee, but Kallie was usually the talker. Apparently, they hadn't been talking to her too much because she swore that she didn't know what was up. His sister's boyfriend, Craig, had just seen Marlee and Desi sitting on Desi's porch, so Tyson headed straight over there to confront her once again.

"That shit is ass backwards though, bruh. I never heard of a nigga claiming a baby that a female said ain't his," Jerry noted.

"She's only doing that shit because Yanni is pregnant by a nigga. I know the situation is embarrassing, but it is what it is. She'll be five months soon and I don't even know what we're having. She won't even let me come with her to her doctor's appointments," Tyson replied.

"Yanni's having a girl, right?" Jerry asked.

"Yeah, that bum bitch is having a girl. I gotta get my head on straight with that hoe. I can't have my innocent child suffering because I hate the mama. I just don't even want to be in her presence if I don't have to."

"Why were you still fucking her then?" Jerry questioned.

"Being stupid and not thinking I would get caught. Fucked up my whole damn life behind some loose pussy and some fire ass head," Tyson said as he and Jerry laughed.

"Yeah, her head game is something serious. I can't even front," Jerry replied.

"Yeah, but it wasn't worth losing my baby though," Tyson said, getting serious again.

"Man, I wish you would have told me where we were going before I got in the car with you. You know Desi hates the ground I walk on. And I damn sure don't need to run into Dionne's crazy ass again," Jerry said nervously.

At one time, Desi was Jerry's heart until he did her dirty. It was bad enough that he cheated on her, but getting another woman pregnant was unforgiveable. He knew all about Desi's past and pregnancy was a touchy subject for her. He hid his secret for as long as he could, until his daughter's mother got in her feelings and put him on child support. Jerry took very good care of his daughter, but she still wasn't satisfied. She wanted him to be with her, but he refused to leave Desi. Once she found out where they lived, she had him served with papers and that was the end of his and Desi's relationship. Her mother, Dionne, was so furious that Jerry ended up with a knife in his shoulder blade when he went to get the rest of his things when Desi kicked him out of the house. Everybody knew that Dionne didn't play about her one and only daughter, and Jerry had been warned. She didn't want Desi to move out of the house, but Jerry promised to take care of her when she did.

She was overprotective of Desi and she didn't mind going to war over her baby. Jerry still called Desi from time to time, trying to clear his conscious and beg her to forgive him.

"That shit with you and Desi is old news bruh. I'm sure she's moved on by now," Tyson said as he and Jerry pulled up to the fourplex apartments that Desi lived in.

They spotted Desi and Marlee sitting on the steps with a pillow underneath for cushion.

"I know this fat muthafucka did not show up to my house with Jerry. I knew Craig's ole bumpy faced ass was calling him when he saw us sitting out here," Desi said to Marlee as they looked at the two men approaching them.

"A bitch can't even enjoy a snowball on a warm sunny day without being interrupted," Marlee complained, right as Tyson and Jerry walked up.

"What's up with you, baby mama?" Tyson smirked as he rubbed Marlee's thigh.

"Keep your hands to yourself and keep it moving Tyson," Marlee said calmly.

She was tired of having the same discussion with him and she was over it. There was a disconnect somewhere and Tyson didn't seem to comprehend what she kept telling him.

"Get the fuck away from my house, Tyson, and take your dog with you!" Desi yelled as she pointed to Jerry.

"Chill out Desi. This don't have shit to do with you," Tyson replied.

"It has everything to do with me when you bring the shit to my house. How many times does she have to tell you that her baby is not yours?" Desi yelled as she stood to her feet.

"Why is she so scared to prove it then?" Tyson challenged.

"I don't have to prove shit to you. As long as the real father knows, that's all that matters," Marlee said as she held the railing and pulled herself up.

Tyson looked at her cute little baby bump poking out from under her sundress and smiled. He'd always dreamed of Marlee giving him a little one and it had finally happened. He just hated that they were no longer together when it did. As much as he tried to resist, he just couldn't. He reached out and touched her belly and all hell broke loose after that.

"Didn't I tell you to keep your grimy ass hands to yourself?" Marlee yelled as she slapped him hard across his face.

"Yo Marlee! Are you losing your fucking mind out here or something? You better be lucky that your ass is pregnant," Tyson fumed.

"Chill out bruh," Jerry said, trying to calm his friend down.

Tyson was tripping, and he didn't understand why. There was no way in hell he would be trying to claim a baby that a woman swore wasn't his. Jerry knew that his boy loved Marlee, but it wasn't that real.

"Let his fat ass go Jerry. I bet I slice him up like a watermelon if he even tries to put his hands on me," Marlee swore as she flipped her box cutter open.

She and Desi were notorious for carrying them and Tyson knew better. He was still arguing with Marlee, never noticing that someone had walked up on their conversation.

***

"Damn man. How do you tell your baby mama that you want to fuck her, even though you have a girl?" RJ asked out loud as he rode with Murk.

"Shit, tell her ass the same way you told me just now." Murk shrugged like it was simple.

"No man. I can't go at her on no disrespectful bullshit like that. I know she need it too. She might as well give it to the father of her child."

"How do you know she ain't getting it already?" Murk questioned.

"Man, Marlee better not be fucking another nigga while she's pregnant with my baby," RJ fussed.

"The fuck did that girl do to you in Vegas? You been trying to hit it again since we came back home."

"I'm losing it cuz. The shit was good and, now, I can't stop thinking about it," RJ admitted.

"If it was that good before she got pregnant, you gon' lose your mind if you get it now," Murk warned him.

"Damn cuz, it be like that? I never had it from a pregnant woman before."

"Aspen bout to lose her nigga," Murk laughed.

"What's up with you and Desi? You trying to make her baby mama number five?" RJ asked.

"Nah man. It ain't even like that with us. Desi is like the sister that I never had. I love her lil bald head ass. She tries to keep my head on straight and shit. She fusses at a nigga all day, but I need that sometimes," Murk laughed.

"That's what's up. I guess it's a no on her giving you baby number six then," RJ replied.

"Nah, I would never try to cross that line with her and she would never let me. She can't even have kids anyway," Murk noted sadly.

His heart went out to Desi when she told him about what happened to her as a child. He swore that if her mother hadn't already killed her boyfriend, he would have gladly done it for her. He had daughters and he didn't respect a man who violated kids in any way. They had too much free pussy walking around for anybody to do that to an innocent child. It had only been a few months since he'd known her, but he could no longer imagine his life without Desi being in it. She was the true definition of a good friend.

"Damn bruh. I'm sorry to hear that," RJ said somberly.

"Yeah, but she can always adopt if she wants to. I'll be her baby's play daddy. Shit, I got enough experience," Murk replied.

"I didn't think I was ready for kids at first, but I'm excited now. Aspen used to always tell me that my feelings would change once it happened and she was right. I'm sure she was expecting to be the one carrying the baby, but shit happens."

"Aspen just don't know," Murk laughed as he drove towards Desi's house.

He stayed the night at her apartment, but he left his wallet over there. He was driving with no license and that wasn't a good look. RJ never rode with him anywhere because Murk always had weed in his car. He knew that the only reason he was with him now was because he told him that Marlee was there. His cousin was feeling his baby mama more than he cared to admit. He made it seem like it was all about sex, but Murk knew better. It had been a while since he'd seen RJ look at another woman the way he looked at Marlee.

"She just don't know what? Me and my girl are good. I might think about smashing Marlee, but I'm not going there again," RJ swore.

"I hear you, cuz," Murk chuckled.

"So what, you're team Marlee now? Just fuck Aspen, huh?" RJ questioned.

"Never that. Aspen is still my girl, but I like Marlee too. I'm team whoever makes you happy. I just know what I know," Murk replied.

"Here you go talking in riddles and shit," RJ said, waving him off.

"Ain't no riddles fam. I'm just saying," Murk said as he pulled up to Desi's house.

He frowned when he saw Desi and Marlee standing outside arguing with two men. Murk grabbed his gun from under his seat right as he and RJ jumped out of the car. RJ rushed over to Marlee since she seemed to be the center of the argument. One of the men was holding the other back, like he was trying to do something.

"What's wrong Marlee?" RJ asked as he pulled her close to his body.

"The fuck is these niggas Desi?" Murk asked as he looked Tyson and Jerry over.

Recognition set in the moment he got a good look at Tyson and he remembered where he knew him from. Murk was locked up with him a few years before and they got into in there too. He remembered knocking Tyson out and being sent to the hole for an entire week. Tyson promised to pay him back once they were released, but he hadn't done shit to him yet. Murk had seen him in a few clubs that he went to, but Tyson never made good on his promise.

"They ain't nobody for you to be worried about friend," Desi spoke up.

"Man Desi, fuck you!" Tyson yelled angrily.

"Nigga what?" Murk said as he walked up on him.

"Let it go Murk. Too many people are out here," Desi said as she held him back.

"Is everything okay cousin?" Kallie asked as she walked over and stood next to Desi and the unknown man.

She had just walked out of her apartment to go to her car when she saw all the drama unfolding. Kallie knew who Tyson and Jerry were, but she had never met the other two men before.

"Everybody and their mama will know what happened now," Marlee fussed, directing her comment at Kallie.

"Really Marlee? I was just coming to make sure that y'all were straight," Kallie said, taking offense to what she'd just said.

"Yes, really, with your undercover messy ass. A dog that will fetch a bone will carry one too," Marlee replied.

"I didn't even do anything," Kallie said as tears welled up in her eyes.

"Girl, bye. Desi might fall for your 'we are family' bullshit, but not me. The same bitch that gossips to you will gossip about you. I can't stand muthafuckas who straddle the fence!" Marlee yelled as she and Kallie went back and forth for a while.

"Calm down Marlee. Don't even stress my baby out with this bullshit," RJ said while rubbing her belly.

"Your baby!" Tyson yelled angrily.

"That's what the fuck I said," RJ barked just as heated.

"How do y'all even know this nigga?" Murk questioned.

"He's Marlee ex who can't seem to let go," Desi replied, embarrassing Tyson with her comment.

RJ looked at him and tried his best not to laugh. Marlee was a certified bad bitch to anyone who had eyes. To know that the fat mess that stood before him was her ex had him baffled. He knew all about her catching him in their bed with another woman and that was what landed her in Vegas. He didn't look at Marlee as a hoe and he understood why she slept with him on the first night. She was heartbroken, and he helped to alleviate some of the pain, if only temporarily.

"The fuck you mean? I don't have a problem letting go. Marlee can be with whoever she wants, but ain't no other nigga raising my child," Tyson swore.

"This is not your baby and I'm tired of telling you that. My baby's father is right here," Marlee said as she pointed to RJ.

"Prove it then. What's so hard about backing up what you say?" Tyson yelled.

"She don't have to prove shit to you, nigga. As long as we know is all that matters," RJ snapped.

"Mind your muthafucking business!" Tyson fumed.

"Her and my baby are my business. And I'm not about to stand out here and argue with a nigga who look like he wears a bra. Get the fuck on with that bullshit," RJ said, waving him off.

Tyson was heated when he saw Marlee turn and walk away holding the other man's hand. He started shouting obscenities to them, but they ignored him. Jerry was holding his boy back, but he was pissed that he was even put in that position. Marlee said that he wasn't the father and he should have left that shit alone.

"You trying to do something nigga? What's up?" Murk asked as he lifted his shirt to reveal his weapon.

"Nah man, we're leaving. It don't even have to be all that," Jerry said as he pulled Tyson away and back to his car.

Tyson was still going off, but he was no fool. He didn't have a weapon on him, so leaving was the smart thing to do. He would see Murk again and that he was sure of. The car that he drove guaranteed that with its unique mirror-like paint job.

"That was Jerry," Desi said once she saw the men pull away from her house.

"The fuck you just now saying something for Desi? I should have put a bullet in him and his fat ass friend!" Murk yelled.

"It ain't even that serious. Fuck them," Desi spat.

"Are you okay cousin?" Kallie asked, making her presence known once again.

Desi felt bad for how Marlee snapped on her, but she understood her frustration. Kallie talked all over herself and never even realized it. She really didn't mean any harm though.

"Yeah cousin. I'm good. I'll call you later to explain everything and I'll talk to Marlee for you too," Desi promised.

"Okay," Kallie said as she walked away.

"Life, huh?" Desi asked while looking at Murk.

"What about me?" he questioned.

"Huh?" Desi asked in confusion.

"Nothing," he replied dismissively.

They walked up to her apartment and heard Marlee and RJ arguing as soon as they walked in.

"I hope you ain't still fucking that fat ass nigga while you're pregnant with my baby," RJ fussed.

"I wouldn't fuck him even if I wasn't pregnant with your baby. Don't worry about what I do. This baby is your concern, not me," Marlee replied.

"You're my concern too until my baby gets here safely. I don't give a damn what you do after that. I don't want another nigga dicking you down and shooting his nut on my child," RJ said, making Murk and Desi laugh.

"You sound stupid as fuck. Come bring me home Desi. I'm tired of looking in this nigga's face already," Marlee fussed.

"Big gorilla looking ass nigga talking about his baby. Let's go Murk. I'm pissed the fuck off," RJ fumed as he walked out of the apartment and slammed the door.

Desi handed Murk his wallet and walked him out. Marlee was sitting on her sofa eating ice cream when she walked back inside.

"Damn cousin. Why that nigga gotta be so fine? I'm trying to get some dick. Fuck all this arguing and shit. A bitch is sexually frustrated," Marlee complained.

"You do know that he has a girlfriend, right?" Desi reminded her.

"I know, and I feel bad about trying to fuck her man. I can't just give it up to anybody while I'm pregnant though. My baby daddy is the only one who can get it right now."

"Or you could join me and be celibate." Desi smiled.

"Shoot me now," Marlee sighed dramatically.

"Stop being so dramatic. It's not all that bad," Desi shrugged.

"I thought you would have given it up to Murk by now."

"Are you crazy? Murk and I are only friends and that's all we'll ever be. That nigga got more hoes than my closet got clothes. I would never," Desi replied.

"What's his real name?" Marlee asked.

"That nigga refuses to tell me," Desi replied.

"You just had his wallet. Why didn't you look?" Marlee asked, as Desi kicked herself for not thinking of it first.

She and Desi sat on the sofa and watched a movie and pigged out on snacks. Not even an hour after RJ left, he was calling Marlee to apologize. Desi laughed as she watched her cousin on the phone blushing as they talked. A few hours later, Marlee was grabbing her things to leave and RJ was outside waiting on her. Desi saw her out, just as

Murk was walking up carrying his overnight bag. He damn near moved into her spare bedroom without asking, but Desi didn't mind. She loved his company, and anything was better than sleeping in the house alone.

Chapter 17

"Just see what he wants Marlee," RJ said when she told him to hit ignore on another call from her father, since he was holding her phone.

"I already did, and I don't want to hear it again," Marlee replied in aggravation as she tried to get comfortable in the small hospital bed.

After months of not hearing from him, Matthew finally decided to reach out to his daughter. Marlee told him how she felt about being blocked from calling and, of course, he had a lame ass excuse. He claimed that it was all Cara's doing and not his. Marlee still didn't buy it and she told him so. He never even tried to reach out to her and her feelings were hurt. Now that he and Cara had broken up, he wanted things to go back to the way they were, but she wasn't having it. He was pissed that he had to hear from one of his cousins that she was pregnant, but she didn't care. He was foul for how he handled things and she didn't respect him for it.

Marlee jumped slightly when the cool gel touched her stomach. She and RJ's eyes immediately went to the screen, but they couldn't make out what they were seeing. Dr. Boudreaux was telling them about how the baby was positioned and all the other things that he looked for in the ultrasound. He never mentioned anything about the sex and that's what they really wanted to know. Marlee was now five months into her pregnancy and her stomach seemed to have almost doubled in size. RJ said it's because her appetite picked up, but she didn't know if that was the reason. She was barely showing before, but it was obvious that she was with child now.

"Okay Ms. Davis, everything looks good. You can get dressed and get your next appointment from the front desk," Dr. Boudreaux said.

"Thank you," Marlee replied with a smile.

She was just about to ask about the sex of the baby, but the doctor's next words gave her the answer.

"I might want to start seeing you biweekly around the seventh month mark, just make sure all is well. It looks like he's going to be a big little fellow," the doctor smiled.

"It's a boy?" RJ asked excitedly.

"Yes, a healthy baby boy. Lay back for a minute Ms. Davis. I'll print you up a few pictures for your scrap book," the doctor said as he put a little more gel on her belly.

Once he was done, he gave them a few pictures and they were on their way soon after.

"Ryker, ugh," Marlee said as she made the gagging sound.

"Why you said it like that? What's wrong with my name?" RJ asked as he opened the door for her to get into the car.

"I gotta come up with a cute nickname or something," Marlee replied.

"Tre. He's the third, so we can call him Tre," RJ replied.

"Perfect!" Marlee agreed. "If anybody ask, we'll say that his name is Tre."

"Don't play with me, girl. His name is Ryker Dakari Banks III," RJ replied.

"Dakari!" Marlee yelled.

"Yes, it's African and it means filled with joy," RJ replied proudly.

"I guess." Marlee frowned.

"What do you have to do today besides complain?" RJ asked her.

"Nothing really, why?" Marlee countered.

"I wanna swing by my job right quick. I need to tell my pops the good news," he replied with a smile.

"Okay, but I need to eat first," Marlee replied.

"We can pick you up something and you can eat in the break room or my office."

"My baby daddy is fancy. Nigga got his own office and shit," Marlee joked.

"Goofy ass. What do you feel like eating?" he asked.

Marlee wanted to say that she had a taste for him, but she settled on a local restaurant in the area instead. Once she got her food, they headed to his job to talk to his father. Marlee had been to their building several times to pick Yanni up, but having a baby with one of the owners was something that she would have never imagined.

"You know I'm going to Atlanta in a few weeks, right?" Marlee asked once RJ parked in his assigned parking spot.

"For what?" he asked with a frown.

"Work. One of my sister's best friends is getting married and I have to do their makeup. This was planned long before I met you," Marlee replied.

"Who are you going out there with?" he asked as he grabbed her food and opened the door for her to get out.

"My sister and Sierra are in the wedding and Desi is coming too."

"Your sister is in a wedding? It must be two dudes," RJ assumed.

"It's two women, but why does that even matter? If you have a problem with gay people, then I'm going to have a problem with you. My sister is my heart and I don't play about her," Marlee snapped.

"What are you even talking about Marlee? I don't have a problem with nobody and their sexuality. Mat just doesn't seem like the type to dress up. Stop being so defensive about everything. I like your sister and Sierra too," RJ assured her.

RJ had met her entire immediate family and they welcomed him with open arms. Mat, Tiffany, and Alvin were happy that he wasn't a deadbeat and was taking responsibility for his baby.

"You better," Marlee said, making him smile.

"Where are you staying at out there?" RJ asked.

"I don't know. Mat and Sierra are staying with their friends, so me and Desi have to get us a room," Marlee replied.

"Book us at the Four Seasons. I'll foot the bill," RJ said.

"Us?" Marlee questioned with raised brows.

"Yeah, me and Murk can use a weekend getaway," he replied.

"Murk, I can understand, but how do you plan to pull that off?" Marlee quizzed.

"You let me worry about that," RJ smirked with a wink.

He looked over at her in her cute maternity outfit and licked his lips lustfully. RJ grabbed her hand and led her into the building. Joy was sitting at her desk, but she frowned when she saw him walk in with another woman.

"Just like daddy," she mumbled when he passed by her desk.

They all knew that he had a baby on the way, but that was her first time seeing the other woman. Aspen was a fool to still be with him, but her mother was just as foolish.

"Pops!" RJ called out while knocking on his father's locked office door.

Banks' door was never locked, and he usually just walked right in.

"Coming RJ!" Banks yelled out before he pulled the door open for him.

"Marlee!" Ivy smiled as she got up from the sofa in the office and rushed to greet her grandchild's mother.

"The hell was going on in here? What y'all had the door locked for?" RJ questioned as he looked at his parents.

"Hey sweetheart. How are you?" Banks smiled as he gave Marlee a hug.

"I'm fine," Marlee replied.

"Your stomach has gotten so big," Ivy beamed as she rubbed her belly.

"Stop changing the subject. What were y'all doing in here?" RJ asked again.

"We're grown Ryker. We don't ask you what you do when we're not around, although I already know," Ivy said as she pointed to Marlee's stomach.

"How did everything go at the doctor? Here baby, have a seat," Banks said as he pulled the chair from behind his desk for Marlee to sit down.

Marlee thought he was mean at first, but Banks turned out to be sweet. He had RJ spoiled rotten and he catered to her when she came around too. She only saw him at Ivy's house because she had never gone to his.

"That's why we're here. Look," RJ said as he handed them the ultrasound pictures.

Dr. Boudreaux had typed in 'it's a boy' in blue, just in case it was hard for anyone to tell.

"'n ander erfgenaam," Banks beamed as he pulled RJ into his embrace.

Ivy had tears in her eyes as she held the pictures close to her heart. Banks rocked his son from side to side as he engulfed him in a tight hug that lasted for about three long minutes. When he pulled away, he held RJ's face in his big hands and kissed his cheeks.

"Come on pops. I hate when you do that," he complained as he wiped his cheeks with his palm.

"Marlee." Banks smiled as he pulled her up to hug her.

"Not too tight honey," Ivy warned, knowing how emotional he was.

"What did you just say a moment ago? I didn't understand," Marlee said once he let her go.

"'n ander erfgenaam means another heir. My first grandson and all of this will be his one day," Banks said as he motioned around the room with his arms opened wide.

"Yeah pops and she didn't even want him to have our name," RJ smirked as he looked at the horrified look on Marlee's face.

"What?" Banks quizzed as he looked at Marlee seriously.

"Yeah, she said that our name was ugly and everything," RJ laughed.

"I did not say that. I'll be happy for him to have your name Mr. Banks," Marlee said as she frowned at RJ.

"Don't make my heart skip like that son. You know how important that is to me. And Marlee, whatever you need, no matter if it's for you or the baby, don't hesitate to ask," Banks replied.

"Thanks, but I'm good. I'll be working until it's time for me to push him out," she noted.

"Why, when you don't have to work at all?" Banks questioned, confusing her.

"Leave her alone baby. Maybe she likes her job," Ivy interrupted.

"Or maybe my son is not doing his job. We need to have a talk RJ," his father said, seemingly angry.

"Uh, where's the break room RJ? I'm going to eat my food," Marlee said, sensing the tension in the room.

"Here Marlee. Make the reservations," RJ said while handing her his credit card.

He was serious about going with her and he knew that Murk wouldn't mind. Aspen never questioned him about his weekend getaways with his cousin because that was not out of the ordinary for him. He and Murk did the same thing before he got with her and nothing had changed.

"Come on Marlee, I'll show you to the break room on my way out," Ivy offered. She gave Banks a peck on the lips before walking out of his office with Marlee.

"Is he upset about something?" Marlee asked Ivy as they walked down the hall.

"Banks is a man in every sense of the word honey. You're having a son by his only son and you're like precious cargo to him now. In his mind, all your needs should be met, and you shouldn't be working at nobody's job. But, do what you feel is best for you, Marlee. I let him talk me out of going to college and living my dreams and look at me now. I sit in that big ass house praying that someone will come over to keep me company. If I could do it all over again, I definitely would," Ivy said.

"I'm not RJ's responsibility though, Ivy. This baby is the only person that he's obligated to take care of," Marlee replied.

"Tell that to his father." Ivy smiled as she showed her to the break room and left.

Marlee was confused, but she didn't think on it too much. She sat down at the table and ate her food while watching tv. A few employees came and went, but they didn't mind her. That was, until her trifling, pregnant cousin walked in. Yanni's baby was doing a number on her appearance and she looked miserable. She was a little over two months further along in her pregnancy than Marlee, but she looked like she was ready to explode. Her nose was swollen, and she appeared to be a shade darker than her normal caramel color. She was shocked to see Marlee sitting in their break room eating, but she didn't say anything to her. Yanni got her food from the fridge and warmed it before sitting down to eat. Marlee got some change from her purse and got up to get a drink from the machine. Marlee was always the trendy one and Yanni admired the cuffed shorts that she paired with some rose gold combat boots. Not many people could have pulled the look off, but Marlee did it well. Her mohawk had a fresh cut and it was colored pink with hints of purple. She looked cute pregnant and that was something else that Yanni hated her for. She watched her until she got back to her seat, frowning the entire time. When RJ walked in a few minutes later, she perked up and plastered a smile on her face.

"Hey RJ," Yanni cooed as he stopped in front of Marlee's table.

"What's up?" he spoke just like always, never bothering to even look her way.

Her smile faded, and confusion took over when RJ sat next to her cousin and started eating off her plate. As far as she knew, Marlee and RJ didn't know each other and that was proven all those months ago when they saw them in the mall.

"Are you in trouble? Your father looked upset," Marlee said.

"Nah, he's good. We'll talk about it later," he replied as he opened her drink and took a sip.

"Did you book the rooms?" RJ asked.

"Yeah, but that damn place is high," Marlee said as she gave him his card back.

"It's worth it though. Besides, you can't take the money with you when you go. Might as well enjoy it while you're alive." RJ shrugged.

Yanni's mouth hung open in shock as she watched them interacting with each other. RJ was rubbing Marlee's stomach as they talked and ate like old friends. She remembered Kallie telling her about the altercation that happened between Marlee and Tyson a few weeks ago and she needed to ask her a few questions. Kallie said that Marlee's baby daddy and Tyson had passed words, but it couldn't be. RJ had a girlfriend, so he couldn't be the baby daddy in question.

"Where are we going after this?" Marlee asked as she closed the empty Styrofoam plate.

"Why? Are you getting tired of hanging with me?" RJ asked while putting their trash in the bag.

"No, I'm just asking," she replied.

"You wanna go see the house? You can pick out which room you want for the baby," RJ offered.

He hadn't officially moved into the house yet, but he planned to soon. He was having some of the floors changed out and two of the rooms painted. Raven and his mother were helping him decorate, but he still didn't have any furniture.

"Okay, that's cool," Marlee agreed.

"I want my son to have a Bentley crib or some fly shit like that," RJ said as he walked over to the trash can to get rid of their garbage.

"There is no such thing," Marlee laughed.

Yanni had eavesdropped enough and she was done once everything was confirmed. Marlee was having RJ's baby and, by the looks of things, they were together too. Yanni felt like her lunch wanted to come back up as she rushed out of the break room. That bitch Marlee just kept winning, no matter how much Yanni tried to cheat in the game.

"Isn't that the same chick that y'all were in the mall with a while ago? I remember her speaking to me and you and Desi were with her," RJ pointed out.

"Yep, that's my cousin," Marlee confessed.

"Why didn't y'all say shit to each other then?" he questioned.

"You remember me telling you that I caught my ex in bed with another woman?" Marlee asked.

"Yeah," RJ answered.

"She was the woman," Marlee noted.

"Your cousin!" RJ yelled in shock.

"My first cousin." Marlee nodded.

"Please don't tell me that's who her baby is for," RJ said.

"Sure is," Marlee replied.

"That's fucked up," RJ acknowledged.

"Yep. Bitch hated my guts, but stayed up in my face," Marlee said, shaking her head.

"What's up baby mama? You want me to fire her or what?" RJ asked seriously.

"Boy, no!" Marlee yelled as she laughed.

"I'm just saying. You say the word and she'll have her pink slip in the morning," RJ swore.

"No, it's not even that serious. I don't hate her. I just can't fuck with her no more." Marlee shrugged as they walked out of the building to RJ's truck.

Yanni watched them with envy, as RJ placed his hand at the small of Marlee's back as they walked. They talked and smiled before he opened the door to his truck and helped her get in. Marlee hit the jackpot once again, while Yanni got stuck with Tyson's fat stingy ass. He had no problem spending money on Marlee, but he was penny pinching when it came down to his own child. Yanni asked him to help her mother finance her baby shower and that was a waste. He sent his sister over with two hundred dollars and that wasn't even enough to cover the cake that she wanted. Yanni had stabbed one of her favorite cousins in the back and it wasn't even worth it. To see that Marlee was still on top had her more regretful now than ever. She thought that losing Tyson would break her, but it seemed to have made her stronger. Yanni had caused a strain in her family and it was all for nothing. Tyson showed her firsthand that everything that glittered was not gold.

Chapter 18

"Yes RJ! Don't stop! Make me come again!" Aspen yelled out in ecstasy as the water cascaded down their bodies.

"Shit," RJ grunted, "I got you, baby."

He had one of Aspen's legs in the crook of his arm as he held her up with the other. They were in the walk-in shower at her house going at it for the third time that day.

"Yes baby. Just like that," Aspen coached as she felt another release building up.

RJ's movements quickened, and his breathing became labored. She knew that he was almost done and so was she. Aspen's eyes rolled up to the celling as her screams of pleasure bounced off the shower walls. Her body went limp and she was thankful that her man was holding her up.

"Fuck!" RJ bellowed a short time later.

He pulled out of her just in time to spill his seeds on the floor of the shower. Aspen watched as the kids that she so desperately wanted with him blended in with the water and went down the drain. RJ put her leg down and tried hard to catch his breath.

"Maybe we should really try to take a shower this time," Aspen smirked as she lathered the towel with soap and began to clean him up.

"Maybe we should before I fall asleep. After busting that big one, I feel like I need a nap," RJ replied.

Once he was done with his shower, he got out, leaving Aspen to her own thoughts. A son. Aspen just couldn't believe it. There were only one of two things that RJ could have had, but she was hoping for a girl. He never really discussed anything about his unborn child with her because he didn't want to hurt her feelings. That ended up happening anyway earlier that day when he took her to see the house. The six-bedroom, three bath home that overlooked the lake was beautiful and she could just see herself growing old in it. She was all smiles, as Raven walked her around the massive dwelling until they came up to a room that was right next to the master suite. That was the room that Raven identified as her nephew's room. She even said that the baby's mama picked it out, letting Aspen know that the other woman had seen the house before she did. She did a great job of holding her emotions in all day, but she cried her heart out as soon as RJ was out of the bathroom. Thankfully, the steam from the hot shower helped with the puffiness because she didn't want RJ to know how emotional she had been.

Their relationship in and out of the bedroom had been great and she didn't want that to change. RJ still spent lots of time with her and their date nights still went on without a hitch. She didn't know how often he saw his child's mother and she never asked. She knew that they had gone to his job recently because Joy was pissed when she called to tell her. He respected his relationship with her and that was all that Aspen cared about.

"Did you get your auntie a card or do we need to stop and get one?" RJ asked when Aspen walked out of the bedroom.

It was Aspen's auntie's sixtieth birthday and she was having a small dinner at her house. Aspen's aunt, Patrice, was the one who raised her when her mother died. Her sisters, Anisa and Blythe, were ten and fourteen years older than her, but they helped in making sure that their little sister stayed on the right path too. Aspen loved her family, so RJ made sure to clear his schedule to accompany her to the gathering.

"No, I need to stop and get one. I hope she likes her gifts," Aspen said worriedly.

"You know Patrice is not hard to please. We can put some money in the card for her too, if you want to," RJ suggested.

"You're so sweet baby. Yeah, we can do that," Aspen smiled.

"Are you ready?" RJ asked as he stood up.

"Just let me grab my purse and I will be," Aspen replied.

RJ grabbed the three gift bags from the sofa and walked out the front door. Once Aspen locked up, she met him in his truck. After stopping to get a card, RJ gave her two crisp one hundred-dollar bills to put inside. Aspen was all smiles as she talked to her man, until they pulled up to her auntie's house. Her smile dropped when she saw Aaron's all-black Jeep parked out front. Aspen felt like she was about to start hyperventilating as she wiped her sweaty palms on her jeans. RJ and Aaron had never been in each other's presence and she wanted it to stay that way. Aaron had seen pictures of RJ in her phone, but that was about as close as it got. Aaron knew that they were coming to the dinner and he wasn't supposed to be there. He was doing too much, and Aspen was pissed. He knew the rules and he broke one of them.

"I'm hungry as fuck. Don't even ask me what I want to eat. Just pile everything on my plate," RJ said as they got out of the car.

Aspen was busy texting her sister, so she wasn't even paying attention to what he was saying. She was taking baby steps trying to prolong going into the house. RJ was oblivious to her stalling as he pulled her along like a child. He had the gifts in one hand as he held Aspen's sweaty hand in the other. When they walked inside, all eyes fell on them, including Aaron's. Aspen frowned at him and he only smirked in return.

"Happy Birthday," Aspen and RJ said as they hugged Patrice and handed her the gift bags.

"Aww, thank y'all so much. Go wash your hands and help yourselves to some food and drinks. There's plenty to go around." Patrice smiled.

Aspen went around the room introducing RJ to some of their family and friends that he'd never met. A few people she didn't know, so she didn't even bother with introductions. She skipped right over Aaron and proceeded to the kitchen to fix their food. Patrice saw the wounded look on Aaron's face and gave him a reassuring smile. Aaron was like family and he had been around since he was a teenager. They were the only family he had, and she didn't appreciate Aspen treating him the way she did. She understood that RJ was her boyfriend, but that was even more of a reason for her to leave Aaron alone for good.

Stringing him along wasn't fair and neither was leading him on. Once RJ sat with some of the other people in the room to eat, Patrice pulled her niece into another room to talk to her. Aspen's sister, Anisa, slipped into the room with them to address the text message that her sister had sent her.

"Who invited him here? I did say that I was coming with RJ. Are y'all trying to ruin my relationship?" Aspen whispered harshly.

"No, you're doing a great job of that all by yourself," her auntie replied.

"What is that supposed to mean?" Aspen questioned.

"Relax Aspen. No one invited Aaron here, he came on his own. You know he's never missed a birthday for any of us, unless he was away. He came to bring auntie her gift and decided to hang around for a while," Anisa noted.

"Well, y'all should have made him leave before I got here," Aspen fumed.

"You know I would never do that to him. We're all the family that he has Aspen. It's your own guilt that's making you feel this way. You need to stop playing with his feelings and just let him go. He's not a placeholder. You can't keep him around just in case RJ doesn't act right. It's not fair," Patrice chastised.

"It's not like that auntie. I do love him, I just love RJ more," Aspen said as her gaze fell to the floor.

"And that's fine Aspen, but don't keep leading him on. He deserves to move on and be happy with somebody else too," Anisa reasoned.

"That's not what he wants," Aspen said angrily.

"How do you know that Aspen? Aaron loves hard and you're using that to your advantage. You know that if he really puts his time and attention into someone else, it'll be all over for you. The thought of that alone scares you because he's always been like your little puppy," Patrice said, calling her niece out.

"What's going on in here?" Blythe asked when she walked into the room and found her aunt and sisters whispering amongst themselves.

"Nothing," Aspen quickly spoke up.

Unlike Anisa and Patrice, Blythe wasn't as nice. She didn't sugarcoat anything or try to spare Aspen's feelings. She was an attorney and Aspen desperately wanted to follow in her footsteps. Blythe was a bitch in and out of the court room, but that was how she'd made a name for herself.

"I'm an attorney baby sis. I can spot a liar from a mile away," Blythe said with a smirk.

"Don't start with me, Blythe. I'm not in the mood. I already have to deal with looking in Aaron's pitiful face," Aspen sighed.

"You might not have known mama, but you are just like her in every way. Just selfish and self-serving," Blythe spat angrily.

"Not now Blythe. This is not the right time," Patrice stopped her.

"No auntie, this is the perfect time. I was young, but I remember mama doing my daddy the same way she's doing Aaron. She loved him so much until she found someone who she started loving more. My daddy wasn't good enough after that. The only difference is, unlike mama, RJ is the one who made a baby on her instead," Blythe said, as Aspen looked at her in shock.

"What baby?" Anisa questioned.

"Oh, baby sis didn't tell y'all that RJ had a baby on the way with a one-night stand that he had in Vegas?" Blythe asked, shocking everyone.

"Who told you that?" Patrice asked.

"Y'all might want to talk to uncle Keith a little more than you do," Blythe replied.

"I talk to him all the time but only about his upcoming release next week. He never told me anything else," Patrice replied.

Patrice's brother, Keith, was in jail, but they didn't talk to him that much. Well, no one but her and Blythe. He was good friends with Lauren and Banks as well, and they kept in contact. Patrice and Keith were the first two in the family who befriended Lauren and that was years ago. Keith had been their gardener for years, but his occasional drug use kept him in jail quite often. Lauren told him all about her step son and the baby that he was expecting with another woman. She often vented to anyone who would listen, since she couldn't talk to her husband.

"RJ cheated?" Anisa asked loudly.

"No, we weren't together at the time," Aspen replied.

"Yeah, one weekend was all it took," Blythe sarcastically replied.

"This is all too much. I just feel so bad for poor Aaron," Patrice said while shaking her head.

"So do I," Anisa agreed.

"Well, that's too bad. RJ is my man, not Aaron," Aspen said as she folded her arms across her chest.

"That's perfect because one of my co-worker's daughters is out there and she's very interested. Your trash just might be her treasure," Blythe smirked knowingly.

"Let her try. She's only gonna waste her time." Aspen shrugged.

"Only one way to find out." Blythe smiled as she turned and walked out of the room.

"Ughh! I hate her. She's always trying to provoke me," Aspen groaned.

"Look, it's my special day and I want to have fun. Let's just put all of this behind us and enjoy ourselves. I'll keep Aaron occupied and you entertain RJ. We'll discuss this another time," Patrice said as she led her nieces back into the front of the house.

Aspen smiled when she saw RJ engaged in sports talk with some of the other men. He stood up and walked over to her when she got back into the room. They both fixed a drink and she took a seat on his lap when he sat down. She looked up and saw Aaron's eyes on them the entire time, but she ignored him. His expression was a mixture of anger and hurt as he watched her kissing another man. Her sister kept sneaking peeks at her too, but Aspen didn't care.

Just to piss Blythe off, she was a little overly friendly with RJ, who was oblivious to what was going on. Her auntie and some of her other family members were in the middle of the floor dancing, so Aspen decided to give RJ a personal lap dance. Her little show seemed to work for a while, until Blythe walked another woman over and introduced her to Aaron. To Aspen's dismay, Aaron smiled at the woman and immediately started talking to her. The smile on his face was genuine and Aspen wanted to scream.

"Are you ready to go baby?" Aspen asked RJ once she'd seen Aaron and the other woman flirting long enough.

"You're ready to go already? I thought we would be here for another few hours," RJ said as he checked the time on his watch.

"We can stay if you want to, but I'm kind of tired," Aspen replied as she faked a yawn.

"It's up to you. I'm good either way." RJ shrugged as he sipped from his drink.

Unfortunately, their stay was prolonged when some of her other cousins walked in late and started talking to her. RJ ended up shooting pool with some of the men, while Aspen helped her aunt cut and pass out the cake. She was furious when Aaron walked outside with the woman that he'd been talking to. Aspen went to look out of the window to see exactly what they were doing.

"Looking for someone baby sis?" Blythe came up behind her and asked.

"Real funny Blythe. Who is that you're trying to hook Aaron up with?" Aspen asked.

"Why does that matter Aspen? RJ's your man, not Aaron," her sister said, repeating what she'd said earlier.

"I don't know why you're wasting that poor girl's time Blythe. You know it'll never last. He'll drop her just like he did all the others. What can I say? I just have that effect on men," Aspen smiled triumphantly.

"Look Aspen, I know we clash often, but I'm not coming to you to start an argument. I'm not even coming to you as an attorney. I'm talking to you from one sister to another. I don't doubt that you have love for Aaron, but you obviously love RJ more. Playing with his heart the way you are is a recipe for disaster. I've seen cases like this hundreds of times and they never turn out good. If you've never listened to me before, listen to me now. Either fully commit to Aaron or leave him alone. Love him enough to do that much," Blythe said, giving her little sister something to think about.

Aspen backed away from the window and took a seat on the unoccupied sofa. She was deep in thought as her sister's words resonated with her. As much as she hated to admit it, Blythe was right. She was being selfish trying to keep Aaron at arm's length while she continued to be with RJ. After so many years of heartache and pain, he deserved to be happy too. Sometimes you had to love something enough to let it go. Aspen just didn't know if she was ready to do it.

Chapter 19

"Come on bruh. One of y'all do this for me. I swear I got y'all when I come back," Murk swore to his little brothers, Legend and Legacy.

"Fuck no, so don't even look at me," twenty-four-year-old Legacy said as he blew smoke from his nose.

"Come on Legend. Do that for that man." RJ begged his twenty-year-old cousin.

"Nah pop. I can barely stay inside for three hours and y'all want me to stay in here for three days. Fuck that," Legend said, waving him off.

"Dog, I swear on everything, y'all better not ask me for shit," Murk fussed as he pointed to them.

"Where are you trying to go this time Murk?" his mother, Iris, asked as she grabbed the blunt that his brother was smoking and started puffing on it.

"Me and RJ are going to ATL next weekend," Murk replied.

Murk was trying to go with RJ, Desi, and Marlee to Atlanta for the weekend, but nobody wanted to wear his ankle bracelet for him. He wasn't trying to get locked up, but he wasn't missing out on a weekend getaway either.

"Oh yeah, Ivy told me that your baby mama was going out there. She told me that she does hair or something," Iris said.

"That lady talks too damn much. That's why I hate telling her shit," RJ fussed.

"Don't talk about my sister, nigga. You know I play about a lot of shit, but Ivy ain't one of them," Iris warned.

Of all her brothers and sisters, Ivy was her heart. Iris was always rough growing up and she was always getting into trouble. She had been in and out of jail since she was fourteen and not much had changed since then. She and Ivy were only a year apart, but she could always count on her sister when she couldn't count on anybody else.

When she got pregnant with Murk, she got into some trouble that landed her in jail. Iris thought that she would never see the light of day, but Ivy hired her the best attorney that money could buy. She ended up having her first child while being shackled to a hospital bed, but her sister was there to claim him and take him home. Iris ended up doing four years, and Ivy took care of Murk like he was her own the entire time. She had her son there to see her at every visit and made sure that he knew who Iris was. Even when she came home, Ivy let her stay with her until she got back on her feet.

The only regret Iris had was not letting her sister continue to raise her son. She didn't know the first thing about raising kids and Murk turned out to be the male version of her. RJ graduated from high school and college and she knew that her sister would have done the same for her son. It was too late now, and her two younger sons were no better. Every policeman in town knew them and many people feared them.

"You know your sister can't keep nothing to herself. And she don't do hair, she do makeup," RJ corrected.

"Come on Legend, bruh. I'll pay you. How much do you want?" Murk asked, starting up his begging again.

"I don't want your money pop. I can't do it. Put that shit on Killa again," Legend replied.

"Hell no! Y'all left the damn dog outside all night and almost got me locked up. I can't trust that shit again," Murk fussed.

"I would do it for you, son, but I got my own anklet to wear," Iris said as she lifted her leg to show her own house arrest monitor.

"This shit gon' kill me, but alright bruh. I'll let you have my car for the entire day when I get back," Murk offered his youngest brother.

"Nah pop, I need the entire weekend if you expect me to stay inside for three whole days," Legend bargained.

RJ saw the veins pop out of Murk's forehead as he mulled over his brother's request. He really didn't see what the big deal was because he hated his cousin's car. Murk had a Camaro that was painted in a silver mirror tint. It was the ugliest shit that RJ had ever seen, but Murk loved it just as much as he loved his kids. He never let anybody drive it, not even for special occasions. RJ hated riding with him because his car caused too much unwanted attention. Everybody in New Orleans knew who it belonged to, including the police.

"Alright bruh, one weekend and it's all yours, but you better guard my shit with your life. Don't bring your punk ass home if my shit even got a scratch on it," Murk warned.

"I got you, pop. I'll stay inside this weekend, so I can floss in your shit all next weekend." Legend nodded as his brother and cousin walked out of the house.

"Why that nigga Legend always calling everybody pop?" RJ questioned.

"Retarded muthafucka got daddy issues," Murk said as they hopped in RJ's truck and pulled off.

"Who is his daddy?" RJ asked.

"Nigga, I don't even know who my own daddy is. How the fuck should I know who his pappy is?" Murk shrugged.

"Damn," RJ said, laughing at his cousin's comment.

"Where are we going?" Murk asked as he turned on the radio.

"I gotta bring baby mama some lunch. Them cravings been kicking her ass," RJ chuckled.

"You ready to keep it real with me now or what?" Murk quizzed.

"Nigga, I always keep it real. Fuck you mean," RJ snapped.

"You never lie to nobody else, but you don't have a problem lying to yourself. You fell in love with that girl and it's killing you to admit it," Murk pointed out.

"I'm not in love with her, but I do have feelings for her. I can't explain it, bruh. Something about her just pulls me in. Her smell, her smile, just simple shit like that," RJ admitted.

"The fuck are you smelling the girl for?" Murk asked with a frown.

"I don't sniff her or no shit like that. Her perfume just lingers whenever she's around me. It's only been five months and I feel like it's been five years. I can't explain the connection that we have. It's like she was the only one who I saw in the club that night in Vegas. Out of all the other women, I spotted her in the crowd. The shit is scary," RJ said, shaking his head.

"I keep telling you that love at first sight is real. I know I joke around a lot, but I really believe in that shit. I haven't experienced it yet, but I know it exist. You're in love with your baby mama and you're trying to fight it," Murk pointed out.

"Nah, it's not that," RJ denied.

"Stop lying to yourself bruh. I ain't never heard you say no shit like that about Aspen or none of your other girlfriends. You've had sex with lots of other women, but none of them had you feigning for more like Marlee did. That's all you talked about, even before you found out that she was pregnant," RJ noted.

"That don't mean I'm in love. That just means I want some pussy," RJ pointed out.

"Dog, think about it. You're loving the way she smell and smile, and all that other shit. Ain't no nigga who just after the pussy gon' say no shit like that. I don't give a fuck about a bitch and her smile. She don't even have to have teeth and I'll still hit it," Murk said, making his cousin laugh.

"Man, you say the dumbest shit. I see why Desi is always fussing at you," RJ replied.

"Forget Desi ole golf ball head ass. Bitch ain't speak to me in two days and I'm lowkey pissed. I miss her lil nagging ass," Murk admitted.

"Nigga what? I ain't never heard you say no shit like that about nobody. You sure you ain't the one in love," RJ said, giving him the side eye.

"I keep telling you that it's not like that with us. That's my sister from another mister, but she ain't feeling me right now."

"Why not? What did you do?" RJ asked.

"She's mad because I won't tell her my real name. I told her that besides family, nobody but the police and the hospitals know that classified info."

"You must not trust her as much as you say you do," RJ pointed out.

"I tell her just about everything, so trust ain't the issue. You know I don't tell nobody my real name. I don't know why Ivy let my mama name me that fucked up shit. She know my mama listens to everything she say. She should have stepped in," Murk fussed.

"My mama likes your name though," RJ replied.

"I don't know why." Murk frowned.

"So, that's it? You just gon' let your best friend go behind something so stupid? It's not even that serious bruh," RJ noted.

"Desi ain't going nowhere. I been sleeping by her house every night for a month. I know she's missing a nigga just as much as I miss her," Murk replied.

Once he checked in with his probation officer for the night, Murk usually hooked up with one of his many freaks and headed to chill with Desi soon after. A few times he almost got busted for putting his anklet on his dog, but he usually made it back home early enough, just in case he had a pop-up visit.

"Damn man. You're scaring me talking about missing people and shit. Now I know for sure it ain't nothing going on between y'all. You would never say no shit like that about somebody that you were smashing."

"You know you were my only friend for years. It ain't too many muthafuckas that I like. Her lil bald head ass is cool though. We'll talk once we get to ATL this weekend," Murk assured him.

"Y'all might be sleeping in the same room again," RJ replied.

"Aww shit. I told you, nigga. That pregnant pussy gon' have your head gone," Murk laughed.

"I was gone from day one, but we ain't do nothing since Vegas," RJ admitted.

"What! All the time y'all spend together and ain't nothing happened yet," Murk said in shock.

"It ain't like I don't want it to. I just don't know how to approach the topic. Knowing her crazy ass, she might curse me out and bring up my relationship with Aspen."

"What's up with y'all? Is she cool with you spending so much time with Marlee?" Murk asked.

"We don't really talk about it too much. I know me having a baby with someone else is a touchy subject for her, so I don't really bring it up. She don't nag me or trip, and I appreciate that shit more than she knows," RJ answered.

"What did she say about you going to ATL this weekend?" Murk questioned.

"She didn't say nothing. It ain't like we don't always go out of town by ourselves." RJ shrugged.

"So, I'm guessing you didn't tell her that we were going with your baby mama."

"Do I look stupid to you?" RJ asked with a frown.

"See, in the court of law, this would be called premeditation," Murk said, sounding like a lawyer.

"What?" RJ asked in confusion.

"Premeditation nigga. That's when you plan to do something before you actually do it," Murk explained.

"I know what it means, but what does that have to do with me and Aspen?" RJ asked.

"You're planning to cheat on Aspen this weekend. That's why you left out the part about us going to Atlanta with Marlee. That's premeditation," Murk said, like he was teaching his cousin something.

"Man, get the fuck out of here," RJ said as he fell out laughing.

"Am I lying?" Murk asked.

"Hell yeah, you're lying. She's almost six months pregnant with my son. I'm just making sure she gets there and back safely. It ain't no premeditation or nothing else. I'm just doing what any concerned father would do."

"For a baby who ain't even here yet, though. But okay, cuz. I got your back, so I'll say whatever you want me to say," Murk swore.

"I'm still responsible for him," RJ replied, trying to justify his actions.

"I hope Aspen ain't looking forward to moving in that big ass house with you. Marlee is about to be the woman of that house," Murk joked.

"Chill out bruh. I'm hearing enough of that shit from my pops," RJ replied as they pulled up to the restaurant to get Marlee's lunch.

"What that nigga Banks on now? I know he ain't trying to get you to break up with Aspen. You know I'm just fucking with you, but he's probably serious."

"Nah, that's not it. He just feels like I'm not doing enough for Marlee, but I'm doing all that she allows me to do. He wants to know why she's still working and shit like that, but I can't make her quit her job. I keep telling him that shit is not like it was back in the day. Marlee ain't like my mama and Lauren. I have no problem putting her up in her own place, but she's content where she's at. I don't want my son living under her mama's roof, but I can't force her to do something that she's not ready to do. He's talking like she don't have a choice and I don't agree."

"Did you ask her how she felt about getting her own spot?" Murk questioned.

"We talked about it briefly, but we didn't go into any details. She made it known that she was good living with her mama for now. Don't get me wrong, the house is nice and it's spacious. I would just prefer it if she had her own."

"Yeah, I feel that, but the decision is hers to make," Murk agreed.

"My pops just don't understand shit. My mama and Lauren are cool with sharing him, but every woman is not like that," RJ noted.

"Man, your pops is a fucking pimp. He don't even try to lie about the shit either. Nigga be telling his wife that he'll see her in a few days, so he can go spend time with his girlfriend. I love that nigga," Murk said excitedly.

"That shit ain't cute though, bruh. I hate to see how my mama be looking sometimes when that nigga be out of town with his wife and shit. He got her scared to even look at another man. She be in that big ass house by herself trying to find stuff to do. Him and Lauren take a trip every year on their anniversary and I hate to see how depressed she be. As fucked up as it is, she allowed it," RJ replied.

"Damn man. I guess I never looked at it like that. You know Ivy is like my second mama. I don't want to see my auntie hurting like that," Murk said solemnly.

"You won't because she never complains. It's been going on for years, so I'm sure she's use to it by now." RJ shrugged as they got out of the car.

His father made it known that he loved Ivy way more than he loved his wife. RJ really wasn't sure if he loved his wife at all. He treated her well and spoiled her the same as he spoiled Ivy, but it wasn't the same. RJ didn't see the same look of love in his father's eyes when he looked at his wife that he had when he looked at Ivy. He took Lauren wherever she wanted to go every year on their anniversary, but that was the only time that they went anywhere. Loyalty was what kept him with Lauren and he took that seriously.

She chose him over her family and he just couldn't forget that.

RJ didn't want that to be him. He wanted to be in love with the woman he married and that was why he never took that next step. He knew without a doubt that he loved Aspen, but he wasn't in love with her. She knew that, and she told him that falling in love took time. RJ wasn't so sure about that because his feelings hadn't changed, and it had almost been five years. Yet, after only five months and a weekend in Vegas, RJ was feeling something for Marlee that he'd never felt before. He denied being in love with her because it was too soon for all that, in his opinion. Murk had him questioning if what he said was true. If he was, in fact, in love with Marlee, what did that mean for him and Aspen? He knew that only time would tell, starting with their weekend in Atlanta.

Chapter 20

"I'm not going to that bullshit and I don't give a damn about who doesn't like it," Desi said as she talked to Marlee on the phone.

"Well, I'm sure nobody is expecting me to go, but I'll get the baby a gift," Marlee replied.

"You're joking, right?" Desi asked as she looked at the phone as if Marlee could see her.

"No, I'm not. As wrong as Yanni was, it's not the baby's fault. Now, I'm not about to go sit up in her baby shower like it's all good, but I will get the baby a gift. Like it or not, her and her baby are still our cousins," Marlee reminded her.

"I guess," Desi replied.

"Aren't you the same one who's always preaching to me about letting go and moving on?" Marlee asked.

"Yeah, you're right. The baby is innocent, but I'm still not going to the baby shower. I don't even want to look in Yanni's face if I don't have to," Desi replied as she sat out the coffee for the meeting that was about to take place.

She was at the center getting ready to assist the therapist with grief counselling. Besides setting up and getting the names of all the attendees, Desi didn't really have to do much. A few times she was asked to tell her story if they had someone there who had gone through something similar. It took a while, but Desi was able to relive that horrific night without breaking down. Her experience had made her stronger and she was hoping to help someone else get through it too.

"I feel the same way. Are you all packed up for Atlanta?" Marlee asked, changing the subject.

"You know I am. I can't wait to get away for a few days. Did you tell your daddy that you were coming down?" Desi asked.

"No and I'm not sure that I want to," Marlee replied.

"Why not?" Desi asked.

"Because Desi, he hurt my feelings with that stunt he pulled. He can try to blame Cara all he wants, but he was a willing participant. He let months go by without even trying to reach out to me. He can't pay me to believe that she was around him twenty-four seven and he couldn't call to see how I was doing. I'm just in my feelings right now," Marlee admitted.

"I understand cousin. Matthew definitely lost some cool points with me for that," Desi replied.

"And I don't need him and Mat going at it and shit, making me choose sides. You already know I got my sister's back, no matter who she's into it with. And then RJ and Murk will be with us and I just don't think I want to be bothered with all that," Marlee rambled.

"Fuck Murk! Malnourished bastard," Desi spat angrily.

"You and Murk need to cut that out," Marlee laughed.

"Forget him. How can he say that I'm his best friend and he won't even tell me his real name? I tell that nigga everything and you know that's not easy for me. We've met each other's families and I've been around his kids. That nigga be at my house more than he's at his own," Desi fussed.

"I tried asking RJ, but he said to leave him out of it," Marlee replied.

"Fuck that. I don't need no friends who can't keep it all the way real with me. I wish I would have been thinking and searched his wallet when I had it."

"Girl, I can't wait to see what happens with y'all this weekend," Marlee chuckled.

"Not a damn thing. I'll be ignoring his skinny ass just like I've been doing for the past few days. But, I gotta go cousin. A few people just walked in," Desi said before she hung up the phone.

Desi jumped right into work mode and started greeting the people who walked through the door. She checked a few names off the list and gave them a pamphlet to read over. About twenty minutes later, all the chairs were almost filled, and Desi took a seat in the last row. As soon the therapist started talking, a man rushed in carrying a pink and gray car seat and took a seat on the same row that she was on. He nodded and smiled at Desi as he sat the baby carrier in the chair next to him. He had the diaper bag around his neck and it took him a minute to get situated. Once he did, he listened to the therapist talk and Desi did the same. Midway through the session, his baby girl started crying and he was having a hard time trying to calm her down. People looked to be getting irritated, so Desi walked over to offer her assistance.

"Can I hold her?" Desi asked as she smiled and walked up to him.

He kind of hesitated, but he handed the wailing baby over to her as he tried to fix her a bottle. Desi placed the small blanket on her shoulder as she cradled the baby and walked the floor with her. That seemed to do the trick because she calmed down and started looking around the room.

"I think she's hungry," the baby's father replied when he walked up to her with the baby's bottle.

"I can feed her if you don't mind. That way, you can focus on what's being said," Desi offered.

"Thanks. I'm Desmond by the way and that's Destini," he said, referring to his three-month-old daughter.

"I'm Desiree, or Desi, and I'm a volunteer counselor here," Desi said.

"It's nice to meet you and thanks for your help. This is all new to me," Desmond admitted.

Desi took the bottle from him and sat down to feed the baby. Desmond seemed to be engrossed in the therapy session and Desi was shocked when he agreed to tell why he was there. Desi's heart ached, as Desmond told everyone how his wife died unexpectantly while giving birth to their daughter. He became a single father overnight and he didn't know the first thing about raising a baby. Desmond admitted that he had help from his mother and the baby's maternal grandmother, but it wasn't the same as having his wife there with them. He had everyone in tears when he was done talking and Desi felt bad for him. Destini was a beautiful baby and it was sad that she would grow up without a mother.

"I'm so sorry for your loss," Desi said once the meeting was over.

"Thank you," Desmond said with a sincere smile.

"I know you don't know me, but I've been volunteering here for years. If you ever need any help with her or anything, I'll be happy to do it," Desi offered.

"I appreciate that. I'm learning as I go along, and I think I'm getting the hang of things," Desmond replied as he watched her rub his daughter's back lovingly.

"She's a sweetheart," Desi said as she smiled at the baby.

"You seem to be a natural. How many kids do you have?" he questioned.

"I um, I can't have kids," Desi said solemnly.

"Oh, damn, I'm sorry. I didn't mean to be insensitive," he apologized.

"No, it's okay. You didn't know. That's why I'm here. I started coming here as a teenager and I haven't left since," Desi replied. She took a few minutes and told him her story and his heart went out to her just the same.

"Wow, I'm sorry to hear that. I couldn't imagine Destini going through something like that. I admire your strength Desiree." He smiled.

"Thanks." She smiled back.

"Are you married?" he asked, making her blush.

"No, I'm not married. No husband or boyfriend," she replied, just in case he wanted to know.

Desi thought that he was going to ask her out, but he never did. Maybe he wasn't ready to start dating since he'd just lost his wife three months ago, and she understood that. They did exchange numbers and that was good enough for her. Once everyone left, Desi cleaned up the meeting area before she did the same.

***

"A little while longer and you'll be somebody's wife. Are you nervous?" Aspen asked her cousin, Rosalyn.

She and Anisa were bridesmaids in Rosalyn's wedding and they had just come from their final fitting. The wedding was in a few more months and Rosalyn was putting the final touches on everything. They had been running all day and had finally settled down to eat dinner at a local soul food restaurant.

"I'm not nervous, but I'm ready to get it over with. This shit is stressful," Rosalyn said as she picked up the menu that sat on the table in front of her.

"That's exactly why me and Donald are planning to do the beach thing whenever we get married. A few hundred dollars and we'll be done," Anisa said, referring to her boyfriend of three years.

"Girl, you know how big Carter's family is. Besides, his mama would have died if we didn't do something big," Rosalyn replied.

"I want my first time to be big too," Aspen spoke up.

"Yeah, but who's going to be the groom? Are you with RJ or Aaron now?" Rosalyn asked with a smirk.

"Very funny Rosalyn. You know that I'm with RJ," Aspen replied.

RJ was in Atlanta with Murk and she was missing him already. He had just left that morning and she didn't want him to go. Aspen refused to become the nagging girlfriend, so she smiled and saw her man off. The last time he went out of town, he made a baby, but she had to keep reminding herself that they weren't together then.

"I heard he got a baby on the way. How are you handling that?" Rosalyn asked once they placed their orders.

"Blythe needs to mind her fucking business," Aspen snapped angrily.

"It wasn't even like that Aspen. Auntie Patrice mentioned it, not Blythe," Rosalyn noted.

"Well, RJ and I are fine. We were broken up when the baby was conceived, but we got back together soon after. He didn't cheat on me," Aspen clarified.

"That's good to know, but how do you feel about him having a baby with another woman?" Rosalyn wanted to know.

"I'm fine with it and I plan to love his son as if he were my own," Aspen said, hoping to end the conversation.

"That's sweet cousin and I hope everything works out." Rosalyn smiled.

"Same here, but I don't know if I could do it. I understand what you're saying Aspen, but Donald better keep his dick in his pants if we ever split up for any reason. I can't do the baby mama drama," Anisa replied.

"We don't have any drama. I've never met her, and she doesn't cause any problems," Aspen said.

"Good, so she won't have to get her ass whipped," Rosalyn said, giving her cousin a high five.

"Exactly," Aspen agreed.

When their food came, they ate and drank as they talked about Rosalyn's upcoming wedding. She and Aspen were the same age, so Aspen was praying that she was next in line. Rosalyn and Carter already had two kids and a home, so marriage was the only thing left.

"I'm so full," Anisa sighed as she pushed her empty plate away.

"Me too. I'm ready to get the check so I can go home. I've been running all week and I'm tired." Rosalyn yawned.

"Give me a second to go the bathroom and I'll be ready too," Aspen said as she stood to her feet.

Once she got done in the bathroom, Aspen washed her hands and fixed her hair. She sent RJ a quick text saying that she loved him before she walked out to go back to her table. As soon as Aspen exited the bathroom, she was shocked to see Aaron following the hostess to a booth. She was equally shocked to see that he wasn't there alone. The same woman who Blythe had introduced him to at their aunt's party was trailing behind him. Aspen stood there and watched as Aaron let the other woman get into the booth right before sliding in right next to her. They were all smiles as they gave their drink orders to the waitress who had just walked up to them. When he lifted the woman's hand and kissed it, Aspen had seen enough. Aaron had been ignoring her since she saw him at the party and now she knew why. Aspen saw Anisa looking over at her shaking her head, but she wasn't trying to hear what she had to say. She marched right over to Aaron's booth and stood there with her arms folded. Aaron looked up at her like she was interrupting something.

"Did you need something?" Aaron had the nerve to ask.

"Really Aaron? So, this is why you can't answer the phone or reply to messages?" Aspen snapped.

"I'm not your man, so I don't have to respond to you at all," Aaron replied nonchalantly.

"Who is this?" Aspen asked while pointing to the other woman.

"Hi, I'm Meagan. Your Blythe's sister, right?" the woman smiled and asked. She remembered being introduced to Aspen at her aunt's party a few weeks ago.

"Don't talk to me. This has nothing to do with you," Aspen angrily replied.

"Don't talk to her like that. Move away from our table, please. You're causing a scene," Aaron demanded.

"You're taking her side now Aaron? A bitch that you've only known for a few weeks. Does she know about me? Huh? Did you tell her how long we've been together?" Aspen asked, as people stared and whispered.

"We aren't together, and we haven't been for years. You have a man, remember?" Aaron reminded her, just as Anisa came over to pull her little sister away.

"Aspen, stop this. You're causing a scene. Let's just go," Anisa begged as she pulled her away.

Aspen was still yelling obscenities at Aaron and his female companion, as her sister and cousin dragged her away. She was happy that she was in her own car because she was not in the mood to entertain whatever they had to say. Anisa and Rosalyn were trying to talk to her, but she stormed off to her car and ignored them. She couldn't believe Aaron had the nerve to embarrass her like that in front of another woman. Aspen was losing her grip on him and she had to find a way to get it back. Just then, a thought came to mind. She still had the key to Aaron's apartment and she was about to put it to use.

After getting on the bridge, it took Aspen about fifteen minutes to get to where she needed to be. She didn't want Aaron to suspect anything, so she parked in a different building from his and walked to his apartment. When she entered his home, Aspen smiled at how neat and clean it was. Aaron was a military man and he liked everything in order. His front room lamp was on and Aspen left it alone. She wanted everything to be just as he left it when he finally decided to come back home. She made herself comfortable like always and waited for him to arrive.

Aspen was pissed because he didn't come back until almost one that morning and he wasn't alone. She was lying on his sofa dressed down in one of his t-shirts when Aaron and his female companion entered the apartment. He stopped dead in his tracks when he saw her and so did the other woman.

"What the fuck are you doing in my apartment Aspen?" Aaron barked angrily.

"Waiting for you, what else?" Aspen smirked.

"Get out before I drag you out," he fumed as he walked over to her.

"Uh, maybe I should go," Meagan said as she looked back and forth between Aaron and Aspen.

She didn't know what was going on between the two of them, but she didn't want to be put in the middle. They obviously had some unfinished business and she wasn't going any further with Aaron until it was resolved. She liked him, but it had only been a few weeks. She would get over it.

"That's a good idea Meagan. Leave me and my man alone to talk," Aspen smirked.

"I'm not your man and you don't have to leave Meagan. Just give me a minute to get rid of her," Aaron pleaded.

"You can't get rid of me and you know it. These other women are just something for you to do when you're upset with me. She's not the first and she won't be the last. If it's over like you said, why do I still have the key to your apartment?" Aspen asked.

Meagan didn't comment, but she was thinking the exact same thing. She didn't have time for games and Aaron seemed to be playing lots of them.

"I'm leaving Aaron and lose my number. I'm too old for the drama," Megan said as she turned and walked away.

"Bye Meagan. Drive safely!" Aspen called out to her departing back.

"Do you think this shit is funny Aspen? Get the fuck out and don't think about coming back. I'll have my locks changed as soon as I can, so you can keep the key," Aaron snapped.

"Why are you doing this to me, Aaron?" Aspen asked sadly.

"I'm not doing shit. This is all you. I'm tired of being your fool and I'm done. You showed me what it was at your aunt's party and I'm good on you."

"I'm sorry baby. I didn't even know that you were going to be there. Do you know how uncomfortable I was?" Aspen asked.

"I don't care Aspen. I'm done. I can't keep loving you more than I love myself. You love that other nigga, so that's who you need to be with."

"I love you, Aaron, and you know that. What happened to all the plans that we made? We're supposed to get married and start a family."

"That's bullshit Aspen. You say shit that you know I want to hear. I've never had a real family and you know how much that means to me. You hate to see me with anybody else, but you don't want me. This shit is driving me crazy and I can't take it no more," Aaron raged as he paced his floor and slapped his head repeatedly.

No one knew Aaron like she did, and she knew how to control his rage. He had a horrible temper and it was hard for anyone else to calm him down. Aspen was the exception because she always knew just what to do. It was nothing for Aaron to put his fist through a wall or break something when he was upset. When he was younger, he used to bang his head on the floor until it bled. Years of being in the service didn't help much either. Aaron was supposed to be seeing a psychiatrist, but he'd convinced himself that Aspen was all that he needed to get better.

"Stop it and calm down. I do want you, Aaron, but you have to be patient with me," Aspen said as she grabbed his hands to make him stop hitting himself.

"I'm done being patient Aspen. I barely get to see you anymore. You used to make time to stay the night at least once a week, but you don't even do that anymore."

"I know baby and I promise to do better. And to show you how serious I am, you can have me all weekend," Aspen cooed as she lifted his shirt and kissed his chest.

"Yeah right," Aaron said skeptically.

"I promise baby. This weekend is all about you. We can do whatever you want," Aspen promised.

"And what about your man?" Aaron asked.

"Let me worry about RJ. This weekend is all about me pleasing you," she said as she dropped down to her knees.

He didn't need to know that RJ was in Atlanta all weekend and she didn't bother telling him. She needed Aaron to think that she was making a sacrifice to be with him, and he was buying right into it. Once Aspen freed his erection from his slacks, she licked her lips and took him into her warm mouth. When he grabbed the back of her head and started telling her how much he loved her, she knew that she had him under her spell once again. It was selfish, but Aspen didn't care. Aaron had been hers for years and nothing was going to change that. Until she became Mrs. Ryker Bank Jr., she wasn't giving him up to another woman.

Chapter 21

RJ stood there with a smile as he watched Marlee do her thing. She was in her element and he could tell that she loved what she did. She had a determined look on her face as she made her clients beautiful for the special occasion.

"What?" Marlee asked as she looked at him and smiled.

"Nothing, I'm just watching you do your thing," RJ said, amazed at her skills.

They had got there the day before, but they didn't really do anything. Sierra and Mat flew in, but Murk, Desi, RJ, and Marlee drove in the SUV that RJ had rented. Once they checked into their rooms, Marlee got a few new makeup brushes and they all went to see a movie. After a late dinner, they all went their separate ways until it was time for Marlee to be at the hotel to do the bridal party's makeup. RJ and Murk's room was two doors down from theirs and he wanted Marlee to sleep with him. Since Murk and Desi still weren't speaking, that wasn't happening. RJ still ended up sleeping alone because Murk hooked up with a chick that he used to mess with in New Orleans who now lived there. He came back the next morning and went right to sleep. He didn't accompany them to the hotel, and Desi was happy. RJ helped her and Marlee set up, so he wasn't needed.

"Thank you so much. I love it." The woman smiled once Marlee handed her the mirror.

"You're welcome," Marlee replied, happy that her customer was satisfied.

She had done eight bridesmaids, including Sierra, and now she only had the bride left. The wedding and reception was in two hours in the hotel's banquet area and she and Desi had their changing clothes with them. RJ didn't want to stay, but the bride told him that he could.

Once Marlee finished with the bride, she and Desi got dressed and went downstairs until it was time for the ceremony. RJ decided to join them, and he was happy that he did. The wedding and reception turned out nice and Marlee was happy that it was over. They all headed back to the hotel to rest up before they hit the club that night. Mat and Sierra were flying back home on Monday, but everybody else was leaving Sunday.

"Yes cousin. I love it," Desi said as she looked at her makeup in the bathroom mirror. Marlee did a great job, as usual, and she was ready to hit the club.

"Are you and Murk still not speaking?" Marlee asked as she got dressed to go out.

"Nope and he better not say shit to me either," Desi replied.

"What about the other man that you met at the counseling center?" Marlee questioned, making her cousin smile.

"We've talk on the phone a few times, but I don't think he's ready to get into anything right now. I can't blame him, seeing as how he just lost his wife three months ago. He's sweet though. I don't mind us being just friends," Desi replied.

"That's good. Maybe he just needs someone to talk to," Marlee said.

"I definitely understand that." Desi nodded.

"Girl, I forgot to tell you that I finally met Murk's mama and brothers. All of them are crazy. Iris and Ivy are nothing alike," Marlee laughed.

"I told you. She's like the female version of Murk. She swears that she knows me from somewhere, but I've never seen her before in my life. Trust me, I would have remembered her crazy ass," Desi chuckled.

"You should have asked her Murk's real name," Marlee said.

"I asked her and his brothers. They said that snitching is not in their blood. His brother's names are cute though, so his can't be that bad."

"Yeah, Legend and Legacy are cute and unique. Unlike my poor baby's name. What the fuck is a Ryker? I just can't get with that ugly ass name." Marlee frowned.

"I think it's cute," Desi replied.

"You better not call my baby that shit. His name is going to be Tre. He gon' be just like Murk and don't want nobody to know his real name," Marlee said, making her cousin laugh.

"Bitch, you're killing the maternity game. You be dressing too cute," Desi complimented as she looked at her cousin's outfit choice for the night.

Marlee had on her ripped maternity jeans with a red off the shoulder shirt. The black Louboutin booties with the red flower on the side set the outfit off and so did the matching clutch.

"Thanks cousin. Let me tell them that we're ready," Marlee said as she dialed RJ's number.

He and Murk had been ready for over an hour, so they were standing in the hall when Marlee and Desi walked out of the room.

"Damn baby mama," RJ said when he laid eyes on Marlee.

Pregnant and all, Marlee was killing it. He didn't give a damn about Murk and Desi beefing. Marlee was going straight to his room when they got back.

"The fuck your bald head ass got on makeup for," Murk said as he looked Desi up and down.

He was trying to get a reaction out of her, but she didn't give him one. She only pointed her middle finger at him and kept walking down the hall. Murk followed her talking shit, as RJ grabbed Marlee's hand and followed them. Mat and Sierra were already at the club and they said that it was lit. RJ dropped Marlee and Desi off in front, as he and Murk went to find a parking spot. Marlee was still out front waiting on them, but Desi had gone inside. As soon as they walked into the overly crowded area, Marlee started looking around for her sister and best friend. She saw Mat standing on a bar stool waving at them, so they made their way over to where they were.

"Help yourselves to something to drink fam," Mat told RJ and Murk, as she motioned to the bottles that she had set up on the table.

The bar stools were kind of high, so RJ picked Marlee up and sat her down on one of them. She used to fuss at him for picking her up like she was a child, but she was used to it now. He was way taller than her, so he didn't see it as a problem.

"This bitch act like she's an invalid when her baby daddy is around," Sierra laughed.

RJ filled one of the glasses on the table with Coke and handed it to Marlee before fixing a drink for himself. Murk fixed himself one as well, as they watched all the people around them.

"Let's hit the dance floor cousin," Desi said while looking at Marlee.

Marlee made a move to hop down from the stool until RJ stood in between her legs.

"She's good," he replied, never once making eye contact with her.

"I'll come with you," Sierra said as she gulped down the rest of her drink.

"Don't get nobody fucked up in here Sierra," Mat warned as she looked at her seriously.

Sierra was wild when she got liquor in her system and she was always getting into it with somebody. Either that or she was always dancing a little too close to somebody else. As soon as Desi got on the dance floor, a man walked up to her and they started dancing. She was feeling herself in her bodycon bandage dress, so she turned around and started grinding on him. Sierra was in a world of her own, so she turned down his friend when he approached her. She wasn't trying to have it out with Mat over some dumb shit.

"Look at Desi ole hot bowling ball head ass," Murk said as he watched the other man feeling her up.

"Desi gon' knock your stupid ass out. Keep playing with her if you want to," RJ laughed.

Hours passed, and they were still enjoying the club scene. Besides going to the bathroom, Marlee and RJ stayed glued to the same spot they were in when they first got there. Sierra and Desi came back to the table a few times, but they didn't stay for long. They stayed on the dance floor and Marlee was happy to see her cousin enjoying herself. Her dance partner wasn't on the floor with her, but she knew that he would be back.

"I gotta piss," Murk said as he sat his glass down and walked away.

He squeezed through the tight crowd and made his way to one of the bathrooms. There was a short line for the ladies' rooms, but he walked right into the men's bathroom. As soon as he opened the door, Murk jumped slightly when he saw two men standing there wrapped up in each other's arms. It wasn't his business, so he continued to one of the empty stalls. Once he emptied his bladder, he walked out, preparing to wash his hands. The same two men were standing there, but they were in a heated lip lock that time. Murk continued to mind his business until they came up for air. He recognized one of the men and smirked as he walked out of the bathroom.

"Aye Mat, is this a gay bar?" Murk asked her over the loud music.

"Nah, why?" Mat countered.

"I was just asking," Murk chuckled.

He was falling out laughing as he watched Desi cutting up on the dance floor. Her male friend was back, and Desi was really putting on a show for the crowd. When she finally got tired and wanted to take a break, the man that she was dancing with asked for her number. She happily called it out to him before sitting down at the table once again.

"Bitch, I'm so tired. I need a break," Desi said as she fanned her sweaty face.

"Here cousin, drink some water. You should be all danced out by now," Marlee said while handing her a bottle of water.

"I am. That nigga got too much energy for me," she replied while referring to her dance partner.

The club was thinning out and Marlee was ready to go. The bottles were almost empty, and she was hungry again. They all agreed that they were ready to leave, until the DJ played a song that Sierra and Desi just had to dance to. Marlee stood up because she was leaving as soon as they were done. She was happy that she did stand because chaos erupted in the club soon after. A fight broke out and Sierra and Desi were right in the middle of it.

"Fuck!" Mat yelled as she jumped over the table and ran to see what was going on.

Marlee tried to run behind her sister, but RJ stopped her. "You buggin' my baby. You must have forgotten about my son that you're carrying," he fussed as he held her back.

Murk ran over to assist Mat and the lights came on a short time later. Marlee saw Murk pick Desi up and throw her over his shoulder, as Mat stood in front of Sierra.

"They're leaving," Marlee said when she saw her sister and everybody else walk out of the club.

The club was chaotic as people ran in every direction trying to get out. Usually, shots rang out after fights in New Orleans, so Marlee didn't blame them.

"Hold on tight," RJ instructed as he picked Marlee up and carried her outside.

He didn't want to chance her falling in her heels, so he didn't care if she got mad. He put her down as soon as they got outside and walked over to everyone else. Sierra and Desi were still going off and Marlee wanted to know what happened. The two paid security guards were holding another woman back and that's when Marlee figured it out.

"Is that Cara?" Marlee asked, referring to her father's ex-girlfriend.

"Yeah, that's that nappy headed bitch. That's why me and Sierra tagged that ass," Desi fumed.

"Who the fuck is Cara? We're all the way in Atlanta and y'all still don't know how to act," Mat fussed.

"That's daddy's ex who I got into it with," Marlee replied.

"Yeah?" Mat questioned as she studied the other woman.

Cara was still going off and it only got worse when she spotted Marlee.

"Bitch, you couldn't handle me. That's why you sent somebody else to do your dirty work for you. You know I would have knocked that baby right up out of your ass," Cara snapped.

"Bitch, what? I dare you to even try," RJ fumed as he looked at her.

"Fuck you too, nigga. I'll call my cousins to come around here and do you dirty," Cara threatened.

The security guards moved away from her trying to get RJ and his crew to leave, and that was a big mistake on their part. Mat walked over to her and delivered a punch so vicious, Cara went down to the ground and never got back up.

"Shut the fuck up bitch," Mat spat as she looked down at her and frowned.

"Oh shit! Mat got them money Mayweather hands!" Murk yelled as he fell out laughing.

"Let's go before you be going to jail," Sierra fussed as she grabbed Mat's hand and walked away.

"Call me when y'all get back to the room Marlee. And don't go nowhere else," Mat said as she and Sierra walked to their rental car.

RJ's rental was kind of far from the club, but he didn't trust leaving Marlee and Desi out there alone. Murk took the keys and ran to get it as they started walking in that direction. Once they were back in the car, they stopped for food before going back to their room. Their trip to Atlanta was an eventful one, but they still had a good time.

"Damn, this nigga is thirsty as fuck. He just got my number and he's texting already." Desi frowned as she looked at the message that the man from the club sent her.

"That's because your hot ass was dry humping him on the dance floor," Murk replied.

"You sound like you're mad," Desi replied.

"Nah, my baby, I'm good, but his boyfriend might be pissed," Murk laughed as he thought about the man that Desi's dance partner was kissing in the bathroom.

Desi didn't reply, but the wheels in her head were spinning. Sierra kept saying that he looked kind of feminine, but Desi brushed it off. She was good either way because she blocked him the moment he texted her.

"I'm tired as hell." Marlee yawned as they took the elevators up to their room.

RJ wanted to ask her to come back to the room with him, but he didn't know how. Instead, he saw to it that Marlee and Desi got into their room safely before going two doors down to his own. As soon as she got into the room, Marlee stripped and went straight to the shower. Once she was done, she slipped into her comfortable night gown and furry slippers. She talked on the phone with Mat for a while until Desi took her shower. Their father had been blowing her phone up and Marlee already knew why. She already knew that his ex was going to call and fill him in on what happened. Matthew probably didn't even care about what happened to Cara. He probably wanted to know why Marlee was there and didn't tell him. Once she got off the phone with Mat, Marlee uploaded some of her work to Instagram and got comfortable in her bed.

"What a night. I had fun though," Desi laughed as she put on her pajamas and climbed into the bed.

"I did too," Marlee agreed, right as someone knocked on their door.

"Who the hell is that?" Marlee asked out loud while making her way to the door.

"Let me get my box cutter out before we go see," Desi said as she grabbed the weapon from her purse.

"Who is it?" Marlee yelled from the other side of the door.

"Murk!" he yelled back groggily.

"Open it, so I can cut his thin ass," Desi snapped angrily.

When Marlee opened the door, Murk walked into the room carrying his pillow and duffle bag. He went straight to her bed and pulled the covers over his head. RJ was standing there shirtless in a pair of basketball shorts, staring at her.

"What's going on?" Marlee asked in confusion.

"We're trading roommates for the night," he replied as he picked Marlee up and carried her to his room.

"Aww, hell no!" Desi yelled as she flopped down in her bed.

"Wait! My phone!" Marlee yelled, not wanting to leave her phone behind.

"You don't need it," RJ replied as he walked her into the room and held her up against the wall.

He crashed his lips into hers, exploring her mouth with his tongue. His hands caressed her body as he pulled her night gown off and tossed it to the floor. Marlee didn't have on anything underneath and that was perfect for him. RJ never broke their kiss as he pulled off his shorts and boxers. He walked over to the chair in the room and sat Marlee down in it. Before she could say anything, RJ moved his head between her thighs. He rested the back of her knees on his shoulders and buried his face between her legs.

"Oh shit!" Marlee gasped loudly as she grabbed the back of his head.

His tongue did a sweeping motion up and down her folds, instantly driving her crazy. Marlee's mouth was opened wide, but no sound seemed to escape her. She was on an orgasmic high and she didn't know if she would ever come down. When the feeling got too much for her to bear, she tried to push him away, but he didn't let her. RJ pinned her wrists down to her sides and went in for a kill. He flicked his tongue up and down rapidly, making her eyes roll up to the ceiling.

"Fuck! RJ please! Wait!" Marlee screamed as her body shook violently.

She hadn't had a drink in months, but she felt like she was intoxicated when she came. RJ was like an animal attacking their prey and he still didn't let up. He went in on her some more until she cried out in a weak little voice, letting him know that she couldn't take anymore. Her entire body went limp and she felt herself sliding down to the floor, but he caught her before she did. Picking her up again, RJ put her back against the wall right before lowering her onto his erection.

"Fuck Marlee," RJ grunted as he bounced her up and down his shaft.

He had one hand on the wall while the other was used to hold her up. He sucked on her neck hard, branding what he considered to be his. He wanted her, and it didn't make sense to keep lying to himself. It was more than just sex, but he didn't quite know how much more. It was like she was made just for him and they fit like a glove. Murk had warned him about how it would feel, but there were no words to describe it. If he could live inside of her, he would until his son was ready to come out.

"Yes baby, don't stop," Marlee panted as she matched his thrusts.

She hadn't had sex since she was with him in Vegas and she was enjoying the feeling. As bad as it sounded, she didn't care about his girlfriend back at home. All she cared about was how he was making her feel. She knew that the guilt would eat away at her later, but she would deal with it when the time came.

"Don't make me fall in love with you, Marlee. I can't fall in love with you," RJ kept repeating over and over as he continued to stroke her.

Marlee didn't know what he meant by that, and she really didn't care. She had an itch and RJ made sure to scratch it all night. By the time they got done, the sun was coming up and they had a few hours left until it was time to check out. Just when she rolled over to get some sleep, he started kissing on her neck and down her body. Marlee lost count of how many times they went at it, but one more wouldn't hurt anything.

Chapter 22

"Get your ass up nigga. Do you see the time?" Murk yelled at RJ over the phone.

"Damn man. I'm tired as fuck. I can't drive us back home like this bruh. I'll fuck around and fall asleep behind the wheel," RJ replied groggily.

He and Marlee had only gone to bed about two hours ago and it was almost eleven. Check out was at noon, so they had to get moving.

"I'll drive, but y'all gotta get up," Murk fussed.

"Alright man," RJ groaned right before he hung up the phone.

Murk and Desi were showered, packed, and dressed to go. RJ knocked on the door a few minutes later for Marlee's bag, and he promised that they would be ready to go in twenty minutes. Marlee's work items were still in the car from the day before, so their duffel bags were all that they had to take.

"You wanna go get some get breakfast right quick?" Murk asked Desi.

"Not with you," Desi replied.

"Come on Desi. It's been days and you still won't say shit to a nigga. I miss your blow pop head ass," Murk confessed.

"I don't care Murk. I tell you everything. I've told you shit that I was too embarrassed to tell anybody else. You claim I'm your best friend, but you won't even tell me your real name. What kind of one sided shit is that?" Desi asked.

"Man, it's not even like that Desi. I don't tell nobody my real name. I got babies with muthafuckas who don't know my government," Murk replied.

"That's bullshit, and you know it. What name did you sign on the birth certificate?" Desi questioned.

"Murk Mitchell," he replied with a straight face.

It took everything in Desi not to laugh, but she didn't want him to see. She had to let him know how serious she was. Marlee was her best friend as well and they knew everything about each other. If Murk couldn't keep it all the way real, she was good on him as a friend.

"Stop talking to me, Murk," Desi said as she continued to play on her phone.

"Man fuck!" Murk yelled as he jumped up and paced the room.

"Don't make me get my box cutter for your crazy ass," Desi warned.

"Man, I'm gonna tell you, but I swear on my kids, you better not repeat that shit to nobody," Murk said.

"Okay, I won't say anything. Tell me," Desi said excitedly.

"I'm not playing with you, Desi. Your Mr. Clean looking ass gon' come up missing if you fuck with me," Murk threatened.

"I gave you my word. I promise not to say anything," Desi swore.

Murk paced the floor a while longer before he turned to face her.

"It's Lyfe," he replied.

"What about life?" Desi asked.

"That's my name. Lyfe with a Y," Murk replied.

"Bye Murk," Desi said, waving him off.

"I'm not playing Desi. That's my name, Lyfe Darnell Mitchell. Look at my license," Murk said as he pulled them out to show her.

"Like the singer? That's so cute." She smiled.

"That shit ain't cute man. I hate that name and the reason behind it." Murk frowned while putting his license back in his wallet.

"What's the reason behind it?" Desi pried.

"My mama said she thought they were gonna give her life in jail when she was pregnant with me. Illiterate ass was spelling it just like the regular word too. My auntie Ivy convinced her to use the Y instead of I," Murk said, shaking his head.

"That's why you're always responding when I say stuff about life. You thought I was talking about your crazy ass," Desi said as she doubled over in laughter.

"Ha ha ha," Murk mocked. "You just better remember what the fuck I said and keep your mouth closed."

"My lips are sealed. I missed you, bestie. If you weren't so stubborn, we could have been got pass this," Desi said as she pulled him into a hug.

"Get off me, man," Murk smirked as he pushed her away.

"Stop acting like you didn't miss me. RJ told me how you were whining to him all the time." Desi smiled.

"Stop with all that mushy shit and let's go. I'm hungry as fuck," Murk said as he got up from the bed.

More than twenty minutes had passed and RJ and Marlee should have been ready by now. He and Desi checked the room again to make sure they weren't leaving anything. Once they saw that they had everything, they got their duffel bags and headed two doors down to get RJ and Marlee. As soon as they got ready to knock, the door swung open and they both walked out.

"Y'all look bad as fuck," Desi remarked as she looked them up and down.

"Thanks bitch," Marlee replied.

She had shades on to cover her eyes, but her hair was all over her head. She threw on a pair of sweats with a maternity shirt and her combat boots. She felt like the walking dead and her stomach was growling something serious.

"We gotta stop somewhere and get Marlee something to eat," RJ said as he picked up their duffel bags.

"Marlee ain't the only one hungry nigga," Murk pointed out.

"No, but she's the only one who I'm worried about feeding," RJ replied.

"Me and my bestie are hungry too," Desi noted.

"Oh God, they're best friends again," Marlee groaned as she headed down the hall, with RJ following behind her.

They stopped and sat down to eat before getting on the road to head home. Murk drove and Desi sat upfront, while RJ and Marlee slept most of the way. When they were about an hour away from home, they stopped to get something else to eat before Murk pulled up to Desi's house.

"This is my stop too cuz. You can take over the driving from here," Murk said as he got out of the car with Desi.

He was going into her spare bedroom to take a nap before he hit the streets later that night. He needed to get his money right to take his kids shopping. One of his chicks had been blowing him up, so he would probably give her some time too. Once they got out of the car, RJ took over the driving and Marlee sat up front. When he got to her house, he took all her work supplies out and put them in the garage where she kept it. Marlee was on the phone with Mat, but she got off right after he was done.

"You think your mama and step daddy will mind if you have company?" RJ asked her.

"Really RJ? Do they ever mind when you come over here?" Marlee quizzed.

"No, but I've never spent the night before," RJ replied while looking at her. He wasn't ready to leave her, and she didn't want him to go.

"Come on," Marlee said as she got out of the truck and went inside.

RJ followed Marlee upstairs to her bedroom and didn't come out until it was time for her to go to work the following morning.

***

"I told you, nigga! You thought it was a game, but I told you!" Murk yelled.

"I know man, but I can't help it," RJ replied.

"That pregnant pussy got you gone," Murk laughed.

"It's not just about sex though, bruh. It's just... everything about her. I tried not to fall, but the shit was too hard," RJ confessed.

Marlee was now in her sixth month of pregnancy and he couldn't get enough of her. It wasn't just about the sex because they didn't always have sex when they were together. He just loved being around her, even if she was sleeping. Marlee had started staying some nights at Ivy's house because he didn't want to wear out his welcome at hers. He still saw Aspen just about every day, but he rarely stayed the night at her house anymore. He had about two more weeks before he moved into his own house and he couldn't wait.

"What's the plan nigga? You can try to have Marlee and Aspen, but I doubt if they'll go for that shit," Murk said.

"I don't want them both. I only want Marlee," RJ admitted, shocking his cousin.

"The fuck did that girl do to you?" Murk asked while looking at him sideways.

"Stop asking me that shit, bruh. I keep telling you that I can't explain it. I'm tired of trying to figure it out. I just know how I feel."

"Did you ever tell Aspen who Marlee was?" Murk asked.

"No man. They extended her therapy, so she's still going to Marlee's job every other week. She went there this morning," RJ replied.

"What does that have to do with anything?" Murk questioned.

"I know Aspen, bruh. She'll go in there with all that dumb shit and I don't have time for it. She's always throwing shade and Marlee ain't the one for her to play that shit with. Kassidy will argue with her all day, but Marlee be ready to swing. I can't have her fighting while she's pregnant with my son. I don't want it to come down to that at all," RJ reasoned.

"What's been up with Kassidy lately? She ain't been around too much," Murk pointed out.

"She came by my mama's house the other day because she saw my truck outside. My mama, with her big mouth ass, told her that me and Marlee were inside sleeping."

"Maaaan," Murk drawled. "I know she went home and cried her heart out."

"I don't know why. I never fucked with her on nothing but the friendship level. I barely answer the phone for her now because she be pissing me off. She always got something to say about Marlee and they haven't even officially met yet."

"If she can't have the dick, she don't want nobody else to have it either," Murk noted.

"That'll never happen. She better get her mind right when it comes to Marlee, though. I would hate to cut her off, but I will," RJ said.

"Fuck that bitch. She didn't let me hit, so I don't care about her feelings," Murk replied.

"Man, I'm all fucked up in the head right now," RJ sighed.

"Aspen gon' be fucked up too. You know she got it in her head that y'all are gonna be married with kids and shit."

"Yeah, but she put that in her own head. I never agreed to that shit. I just listened when she talked, but I never confirmed anything."

"You didn't tell her anything different though. She probably assumed that you wanted the same thing since you never said otherwise," Murk pointed out.

"You can't just be assuming that a nigga wants to spend the rest of his life with you. That's some serious shit," RJ replied.

"I wish I could help you, cuz, but relationships ain't my thing. If I were you, I would fuck with both of them and just see how it goes," Murk suggested.

"Nah man. Marlee ain't having that. We haven't made anything official yet, but I really want us to. I can't go at her like that until I end shit with Aspen though," RJ said as he pulled up to Murk's house to drop him off.

"Do what I do and let your dick make the decision for you," Murk said.

"Nigga what!" RJ laughed.

"I'm serious though, bruh. You keep laughing, but that's some real shit. Why do you think I have so many kids? Your dick got a mind of its own," Murk replied seriously.

Once his cousin got out of the car, RJ pulled off and got on the bridge. He had to pick Marlee up from work and they were going back to his mother's house. He and Aspen had lunch earlier, but she was helping her cousin with the final details of her wedding now. She had been on him about spending the night at her house and he promised her that he would soon. He had to run a few things by Marlee first.

"Hello," Marlee said when she answered the phone for RJ.

"I'm on my way to get you," RJ replied.

"You don't have to. Sierra is bringing me home. I was about to call and tell you," Marlee said, making him frown.

"Home?" RJ questioned angrily.

"Yes, home," Marlee countered.

"What's with the attitude?" RJ questioned.

"I don't have an attitude RJ," Marlee snapped angrily.

Truthfully, she was not in the best mood and she hadn't been all day. After looking online and seeing pictures of her cousin's baby shower, her mood turned sour for some reason. She was over Tyson and his betrayal, but Yanni was still her first cousin. Some of his people were at the shower, but Tyson didn't bother showing up, not that Marlee was surprised. Just about her entire family was there too and that put Marlee in a bad mood. Under different circumstances, she and Desi would have been right there by their cousin's side, making sure that her and her baby were straight. Yanni looked so pitiful, but that was her own fault. She caused a division in their family with her actions and things were all fucked up now.

Then, there was Aspen. She had come into the clinic earlier that day for an appointment and Marlee had to be the one to assist her. Sharon was out sick and everybody else had patients of their own. Marlee felt like shit sitting there answering questions about her pregnancy that the father of her child's girlfriend was asking. Guilt consumed her, and she didn't like how it made her feel. She had been cheated on and had her heart broken. She was foul for turning around and doing it to someone else. Her conscious had been bothering her all day and she couldn't do it anymore. As much as she liked RJ, she had to end their little fling and go back to her own house. No matter if it was at her mother's house or his, she had been sleeping in the same bed with him since they got back from Atlanta. It was time for her to do the right thing and put a stop to it. As much as Marlee liked Ivy, she couldn't see herself ending up like her in the long run. She wasn't cut out to be the other woman.

"Come outside," RJ said, pulling her out of her thoughts.

"I just told you that I had a ride," Marlee fumed.

"I heard you but come out here. We need to talk," RJ said before hanging up.

"Stick to the plan Marlee. Mean what you say," she whispered to herself as she made her way out of the building.

After a little over six months of knowing him, it felt like RJ had some kind of hold on her. Marlee was supposed to back away from him a week ago but, when she saw him, she changed her mind. The way he looked at her always had her melting like ice on a hot summer day. It was hard, but it had to be done. She wasn't a number and she kept reminding herself of that fact. She would gladly be his woman if he wanted her to, as long as she was the only one.

"What's up with you? You say you don't have an attitude, but that's not what it looks like to me," RJ said when Marlee walked up to him.

She had her arms folded on top of her belly and her posture screamed angry. And if her body language wasn't enough, the frown on her face confirmed it.

"I don't have an attitude. I just told you that I had a ride home," Marlee countered.

"Are you hungry? Do you need anything?" RJ asked as he rubbed her belly.

Marlee tried to hold her breath, praying that she didn't get a whiff of his cologne. His scent was intoxicating, and she was sure to fall back under his spell if she smelled him.

"No, I'm good," Marlee replied.

"Have you thought about what we discussed? Raven said that she's ready whenever you are," RJ said.

"I'm not ready to buy a house yet RJ. I have money saved up, but not enough to buy and furnish an entire house."

"You don't need to do anything Marlee. I told you that I got the financial side of it," RJ pointed out.

"I don't know what you thought, but I'm not your mama. I don't need you to buy me a house that's in your name, so you can come and go as you please. When I'm ready to get a house, I'll do it on my own. I'm not cut out to be the side chick," Marlee snapped.

"The fuck did that even come from Marlee? I never told you nothing about putting no house in my name. I'm not trying to have my son living up under nobody else's roof, when I have enough money to make sure he's straight. You were fine when I dropped you off this morning, but I don't know what your problem is now," RJ fumed.

"Get my stuff from by your mama's house when you get a chance," she replied as she turned to go back inside the building.

"Fuck that stuff! Get it your damn self!" RJ yelled to her departing back.

He didn't know what was wrong with Marlee and he wasn't trying to figure it out. She came at him sideways on some dumb shit and he wasn't feeling that. The comment that she made about his mother was uncalled for, even though it was true. Marlee was all smiles when he dropped her off that morning, but something was obviously wrong. She gave him some before she went to work that morning, but it didn't seem like he would be getting it again any time soon. RJ was having withdrawals already and it hadn't even been a full day yet. He was in need of a drink and he needed it to be strong.

Chapter 23

"Maybe you can go see a doctor and make sure that it's not something serious," Aspen said as she laid on RJ's chest and ran her fingers across his tattoos.

"I'm not going to no doctor about that shit Aspen," RJ snapped in disgust.

"I just think you should be sure baby. This has never happened before, but it's been a reoccurring thing over the past three weeks," Aspen noted.

Three weeks. The last time RJ and Marlee had sex and the shit was still fucking with him. It was so bad that his dick didn't even get hard anymore. It just laid there like a big log of ground meat. Murk was right. His dick had a mind of its own and Aspen wasn't what it wanted.

Marlee was in her seventh month of pregnancy and she was acting bad with the pussy. RJ never did find out what her sudden attitude was about, but she had come around since then. Well, she was almost back to her old self. She still wasn't having sex with him, but they still spent time together. Her baby shower was coming up, so she was always at Ivy's house going over the details with her. Her mother came over a few times too, but that was the extent of their relationship. RJ had made the decision to tell Aspen who she was in the next few days because she only had one more appointment at the clinic before she got released. That was bound to be a disaster, but it had to be done. Marlee wanted him to do it a long time ago, but he was trying to avoid the unnecessary headache. He knew that Marlee could handle herself, but he didn't want it to come down to that. "It's nothing to be ashamed of RJ. A lot of men experience erectile dysfunction," Aspen said, pulling him away from his thoughts.

"What!" RJ screeched. "Ain't a damn thing wrong with my dick!"

He wanted to tell her that it got hard as a brick whenever Marlee was around, but he kept that part to himself.

"We haven't had sex in weeks RJ. There's obviously something wrong," Aspen said, pissing him off.

RJ got out of the bed and started to get dressed. He stayed the night with Aspen and she had been trying to get him hard since then. Nothing that she did worked, and he already knew why. His heart was with another woman and, apparently, so was his dick.

"I gotta make a few moves," RJ announced as he stood in the mirror and brushed his hair.

"When are we gonna sleep at your house? I haven't seen it since you had it decorated. You didn't even get my input," Aspen said.

"I didn't get nobody's input. That's exactly why I hired someone to decorate for me. I wasn't feeling nothing that Raven and my mama wanted to do," RJ replied.

"Okay, but Raven and your mama are not your girlfriend; I am," Aspen pointed out.

"Where are my keys?" RJ asked, ignoring everything else that she'd said.

Aspen got up in all her naked glory and walked over to him. RJ had to admit that she was sexy as hell. He just wasn't as interested in her as he was before. It wasn't anything that she had done wrong. His feelings just weren't the same as they were in the beginning.

"Are you free to do lunch today?" Aspen asked as she stood on the tips of her toes and kissed him.

"I don't know. I need to go see my pops and I think we have to do some last-minute stuff for the baby shower," RJ replied, making her move away from him and sit on the foot of the bed.

"Next month, right?" Aspen asked solemnly.

"Yeah," RJ replied.

"Do you need me to do anything?" Aspen asked, even though she didn't want to.

She was trying to be a supportive girlfriend, but she didn't want no parts of the one thing that another woman had over her. Still, if her man needed her to be there, she would do it in a heartbeat.

"Nah, I got it covered but thanks." RJ smiled.

"I'm sure I'm not invited, but where is it going to be? Maybe I can bring my gifts ahead of time," Aspen said, trying to be nosey.

RJ looked at her like she was crazy, but she missed his expression. Of course, she wasn't invited, and he didn't know why she thought she would be. RJ didn't tell her anything when it came down to his son and that drove her crazy. She didn't even know the baby's mother and that was ridiculous.

"It's gonna be at my house," RJ replied, making her heart drop.

"Your house!" Aspen yelled.

"Yes, my house," RJ confirmed.

He knew that she was about to have a fit, but he wasn't gonna lie to her. Ivy loved the huge grassy area and the lake scenery behind his house. She wanted to have the baby shower there and RJ agreed. There was really nothing to think about when it came to his son.

"Why there? I've only been to the damn house once and you're gonna have a bunch of strangers running in and out of it for a baby shower!" Aspen fumed. Playing the good girlfriend was getting too hard and she was getting tired of it already.

"That's my house and my son. The fuck you mean?" RJ snapped angrily.

He spotted his keys on the dresser and quickly snatched them up. He wasn't in the mood to argue because nothing that she said was going to change his mind. Aspen was never the nagging type, so he couldn't give her that charge. He knew that she was in her feelings about the birth of his son, but there was nothing that he could do about that.

"I'm sorry baby and I don't want to argue. This is just hard for me. Your son is a part of you and I'll love him for that reason alone," Aspen swore as she wrapped her arms around him.

"I'll call you when I'm done. Maybe we can do dinner instead of lunch," RJ said as he kissed her cheek and walked away.

As soon as he got to his truck, he dialed Murk's number and waited for him to pick up.

"What's up fam?" Murk asked when he answered the phone.

"You were right bruh. My dick broke down like a fifty-seven Chevy," RJ sighed into the phone.

"The fuck is you on right now dog? What does that even mean?" Murk asked in confusion.

"My shit don't work no more bruh. Aspen been trying to get it up for weeks and ain't shit poppin'," RJ confessed.

"Your shit still work nigga. It just don't work for her," Murk replied.

"I need a blunt," RJ blurted out.

"The fuck! You don't even smoke," Murk laughed.

"Yeah, well, fuck it. I'm about to start. I'm stressed bruh. Marlee is holding out on the pussy. Aspen's trying to give it to me, but my dick is acting bipolar. I'm just all fucked up," RJ rambled.

"Damn cuz. I'm out here making money, but I'll close up shop for a little while. You need a few drinks. It don't matter that it's still early. It's happy hour somewhere," Murk replied.

"You ain't never lied, but I gotta go see what my pops want first. Marlee is off today and we gotta do some last-minute stuff for this baby shower too," RJ noted.

He talked to Murk the entire time until he pulled up to their building. Once he hung up the phone, he headed to his father's office and walked right in. Banks had a bunch of papers spread out on his desk. He had his glasses on, looking hard at something that had his undivided attention. RJ had been standing there for almost five minutes before he even acknowledged him.

"Hey son," Banks said as he removed his glasses and massaged his temples.

"What's up? You good?" RJ questioned skeptically.

"Yeah, I was just looking over some of my bank statements," Banks replied.

"Everything good with your money? Let me know if you want to make a loan or something," RJ joked, making his father laugh.

"Yeah, I know you got enough to get me right too," Banks chuckled.

"But, seriously pops. Let me know if you need me to look over anything for you. That's what I'm certified to do. I catch shit that other people might look over," RJ replied.

"I will son, but I just wanted to talk to see how everything is coming along. I'm sure you're enjoying that nice new house. And let's not forget that a king will be born in two more months," Banks beamed proudly while referring to his grandson.

"Yeah, everything is all good," RJ said with a forced smile.

"Why is it that I don't believe you?" Banks asked skeptically.

"Cause I'm lying like a muthafucka. Shit is all fucked up pops. Marlee is driving me crazy with her stubborn ass. She won't let me help her get a house and she made it clear that she's never quitting her job. She cut me off from sex and now my dick won't even get hard for nobody else," RJ rambled, happy that he could be himself with his father.

"Whoa," Banks said as he held up his hands to stop him.

"Yeah, that's my life right now." RJ shrugged.

"And where does Aspen fit into this equation? I haven't heard you mention her name once," his father smirked knowingly.

"That's another question that I don't have the answer to," RJ sighed.

"Marlee is a different type of woman than I've ever dealt with. She's stubborn, but not in a bad way. With Lauren and your mother, they were both young when I met them, so it was a little easier for me. They weren't like Marlee with a college degree and all that other stuff that she got going on. She's not easily swayed, so you have to take a different approach with her."

"She can't be swayed at all," RJ argued.

"Anybody can be persuaded son. You just have to know how to do it." Banks smiled.

"Shit, I got lots of time on my hands. I'm listening," RJ said as he got comfortable and listened to everything that his father had to say. Marlee was not like most women and she was headstrong. Unless his father planned to teach him voodoo, he didn't see how he was going to get her to come around.

Chapter 24

"Bitch, I'm about to cry. I'm so happy for you, cousin," Marlee said as she talked on the phone with Desi.

"Sit your over emotional ass down somewhere," Desi laughed.

After weeks of talking on the phone and seeing him at the center, Desmond had finally asked Desi out on a date. They had gone to dinner two nights in a row and to a movie on the third night. His mother was happy to see him get out of the house, so she had no problem keeping his daughter for him. He told Desi that the pain from his wife's untimely death was still fresh, so he couldn't make her any promises on a relationship. She understood his position and she assured him that she was in no rush. She had fallen in love with Destini and she held her the entire time that Desmond came to the center. She would be okay with a friendship, just as long as she could see her.

"I'm serious though, cousin. I know you said that y'all were taking it slow, but I have a good feeling about him. He seems so right for you. I can't wait to meet him," Marlee replied.

"I'm happy you said that because I wanted to invite him to your baby shower. I know it's at RJ's house and I understand if you're not comfortable with that," Desi hurriedly added.

"No, it's fine. He can come," Marlee replied.

"Thanks cousin. That way I can let him meet the family on the slick," Desi laughed.

"Yeah, but you better warn your bestie about him first," Marlee snickered.

"Girl, Murk better not fuck with me. I'll tell him about it long before the time comes. I don't know why he thinks he's my protector. I've been doing fine all these years without him."

"He swears he's your big brother. Nigga was about to cry when you stopped speaking to him. And his name ain't even all that bad. Lyfe, Legend, and Legacy. That is so cute."

"Bitch! Didn't I tell you not to say anything? I swore your ass to secrecy Marlee," Desi fussed.

"Girl, I'm in the room by myself. Ivy is downstairs, and I don't know where RJ went. I just woke up and he's not in the bed anymore." Marlee yawned as she stretched out in Ivy's bed.

"You finally stopped acting bad and gave it up again, huh?" Desi asked.

"Hell no, I did not. I'm not even going there with him again as long as he has a girlfriend. We just came over here for a little while after we left all the stores that we went to. I came upstairs to take a nap and his annoying ass followed me."

Ivy had gone with her and RJ to a few stores to do the baby registry. Marlee would be eight months in two more weeks and her shower was the day after she hit her eight-month mark.

"I saw a picture of Yanni's baby on Instagram," Desi said, changing the subject.

"I did too. She is so cute," Marlee replied.

"Were we looking at the same baby?" Desi questioned.

"I saw a picture of her with a pink jumper and matching socks," Marlee said.

"That's the same one that I saw, but ain't nothing cute about it. She looks like Tyson," Desi replied.

"No, she does not Desi. She's cute. She looks like Yanni to me. I hate her name though, but I don't have room to talk with a name like Ryker," Marlee said.

"What the fuck possessed her to name that baby Ty'Yanni? That shit is ugly and ghetto. And after the way Tyson did her throughout her entire pregnancy, my baby's name wouldn't be nothing even close to his," Desi fussed.

"I just don't understand why she needed two Y's in the baby's name. And Tyson ain't shit, but that's what she gets," Marlee replied.

Just like for the entire pregnancy, Tyson wasn't there when his daughter was born. At least he had a valid excuse this time though. The fat fucker got locked up two weeks before the baby was born and, go figure, Yanni was the first person that he called. Marlee hoped she wasn't dumb enough to fall for his games but, knowing her, she probably did. And if that wasn't bad enough, his ex-wife, Taj, was posting pictures all over social media saying how they were back together. Yanni was sick when she found out and the day of her baby shower was when it came to light. He didn't show up to support Yanni and his unborn child, but he was posing for pictures with another woman. He was a sad ass man and an even worse father. Tyson was still bugging Marlee for a DNA test up until the day he got locked up. He even had his mother and sister calling her and they were just as dumb as he was.

"Are y'all done with the registry yet?" Desi asked, shaking Marlee out of her daydream.

"I didn't really have much to put on there. RJ and Ivy got just about everything already. My mama was so mad that they didn't leave anything for her to get. I told her to just get a gift card or something, but you know how she is."

"That's Tiffany's first grandchild and it's a boy. Damn a gift card. She's trying to do it big. Ivy better not play with my auntie. You know Tiffany will snap in a minute. She's almost as bad as my mama," Desi laughed.

"Ain't nobody as bad as your mama. She's the reason why we don't leave home without a box cutter," Marlee laughed.

"You know my mama is paranoid as fuck. She cried for a whole week when I moved into my own apartment. I'm so scared for her to meet Desmond. I don't want her to run him off before we can really get together," Desi replied.

"You know how Dionne is, Desi. You can't just spring shit on her the same day. You have to start talking to her about him now and ease her into it," Marlee noted.

"I already did. She asked me if I'm sure that his wife died in child birth or did he kill her," Desi said, making Marlee scream with laughter.

"Girl, I'm weak. Let me go before I pee on myself. I'll call you later," Marlee said as she hung up the phone and got up from the bed.

Ivy opened the door a few seconds later with a worried look on her face. "Are you okay? I heard you in here screaming and got scared," Ivy said.

"I was laughing at Desi with her crazy self. I was about to pee on myself," Marlee said as she disappeared into Ivy's master bathroom.

"RJ went to get food. He should be back in a minute," Ivy said, right as someone rang her doorbell.

She figured RJ's hands must have been full, so she rushed downstairs to let him in. When she opened the door, she was pleasantly surprised to see Aspen standing there.

"Hey Ivy. Is this a bad time?" Aspen asked while pointing to Marlee's silver Charger that was parked in her driveway.

"No, it's fine honey. My grandson's mother is here, but come on in." Ivy smiled as she stepped to the side and allowed her to enter.

Aspen wanted to jump for joy when she said that. Finally, after months of wondering, she would finally get a chance to lay eyes on the woman who was having her man's first son. A task that she'd hoped to complete one day. When she walked in, she expected to see the other woman sitting on the sofa, but she wasn't. She was nowhere on the bottom level of the house because Aspen was looking. She felt some kind of way knowing that the woman was upstairs. She was a little too comfortable in her opinion, but she kept those thoughts to herself.

"Where's RJ? I know he said that y'all had to finish doing the registry today," Aspen said as she took a seat on the sofa.

"Yeah, we finished doing everything, but he went to get something to eat," Ivy replied.

"Oh okay. How is the planning for the shower coming along? RJ told me that it was at his house," Aspen said, fishing for more information.

Ivy usually spilled all the tea, but she wasn't messy about it. She just loved company and she loved to talk even more. She never came from a bad place when she said things. She just didn't realize that she said too much most times.

"Yes, and I can't wait. I've always wanted to have an outdoors event, and this is the perfect one. RJ has the perfect lot and the lake behind the house sets it off just right." Ivy smiled.

Aspen smiled too, but she was dying inside. She just sat there, as Ivy went on and on about her grandson and how she couldn't wait for his arrival. She didn't mean any harm, but she was driving Aspen crazy. Everything was Tre this or Tre that and she was over it already. RJ never said much about it, but Ivy made up for what he didn't say. Aspen heard movement on the top level of the house. A few seconds later, someone was walking down the stairs. She was anxious to see who the other woman was, but she wasn't prepared when she finally laid eyes on her.

"Marlee?" she quizzed as she stood to her feet.

"Oh, you two already know each other?" Ivy asked in confusion.

"Are you fucking serious right now? You're the baby's mother? All the times I've been around you and you didn't think to tell me that?" Aspen fumed.

"It wasn't my place to tell you anything. You're in a relationship with RJ, not me," Marlee replied.

She'd wanted RJ to tell her from the beginning, but he was the one who wanted to wait. Marlee didn't have anything to hide and she didn't appreciate how Aspen was coming at her.

"That's bullshit! You had multiple chances to tell me what was up, but you chose not to," Aspen fumed as she walked over to her.

"I didn't have to tell you shit. I don't owe you no explanation or nothing else. Your man will be back in a few minutes. Talk to that nigga!" Marlee yelled as she closed the small gap that separated them.

Pregnant or not, she would have laid Aspen the fuck out right there in Ivy's living room.

"Ladies, please. Let's not do this. Think of my grandson Marlee, please," Ivy begged.

She stood in the middle, as the two women argued back and forth. She didn't know how they knew each other, but there was no way that she was letting them fight. Ivy didn't care if she had to take most of the licks herself. That was a small price to pay for the safety of her grandson. When the front door flew open a few minutes later, she was so thankful to see her son walk in. RJ immediately sat the bags of food down and sprang into action. He saw Aspen's car when he first pulled up and he had a feeling that some shit was going to pop off. Marlee was still asleep when he left to go get food, but she was wide awake now. He heard them arguing as soon as he walked up, and he already knew what the argument was about.

"Marlee, calm down. You keep forgetting that you're pregnant. Stop getting so worked up. Sit down and relax," RJ said as he walked her over to the sofa.

Marlee was breathing hard as hell, so he gave her one of the drinks that he'd just purchased. Ivy was rubbing her back trying to calm her down as much as she could. Seeing how they were catering to her had Aspen ready to blow a gasket.

"Really RJ? All this time you had me around this bitch and you knew that it was your baby that she was carrying?" Aspen snapped angrily.

"I got your bitch!" Marlee yelled.

"I didn't have you around nobody. You were the one who had to go to the clinic. I didn't even know that she worked there," RJ replied.

"You're a fucking liar!" Aspen raged, making RJ frown at her comment.

"I admit that I was wrong for not telling you, but I've never lied to you or anyone else," RJ swore.

"Omitting information is the same thing RJ. Y'all both pretended to be meeting for the first time when I made the introductions. Now I see why you never wanted to come back with me after the first time. I must look like a damn fool to you," Aspen spat.

"You look like a clown with that cheap ass makeup on," Marlee chimed in, angering the other woman.

Aspen didn't think twice before charging at Marlee, but she didn't get very far. RJ grabbed her and pulled her away before any licks could be thrown.

"Let me go! I'm gonna kill that bitch! Let me go!" Aspen screamed as she fought to get out of his hold.

"I'm sorry Aspen, but you have to go," Ivy said, making Aspen stop her struggle to look at her in shock.

She and Ivy had always gotten along great and she was always over there. Now, Ivy was asking her to leave for a woman that she barely knew. If her feelings weren't hurt before, they were now.

"Seriously Ivy? That's how you feel?" Aspen asked sadly.

"It's nothing personal Aspen, but I have to think about my grandson. I don't need Marlee to be stressed out right now. It's obvious that you two can't be in the same room without wanting to fight," Ivy replied.

"It's cool Ivy, I'm gone," Aspen said as she grabbed her purse and rushed out of the house.

She hoped, no, she prayed that RJ came after her and she slowed her steps, just in case he did. After making it to her car and sitting there for a while, the door to Ivy's house never opened, and all her questions were answered from there. RJ obviously cared more about how the other woman was feeling.

"Are you okay Marlee?" Ivy asked her.

"I'm good, but I'm about to go home. I have a headache," Marlee said as she stood up and headed for the steps.

"Do you want to eat your food first?" Ivy asked.

"I'll take it to go," Marlee replied as she walked up the steps.

"Go make sure she's okay RJ," Ivy said, but he was already walking up the stairs behind her.

He couldn't even be mad with anyone because it was his own fault that things played out the way they did. He was trying his best to keep confusion down between the two women, but he seemed to have made things worse. When he walked into his mother's room, Marlee was grabbing her purse and keys from the dresser. When she tried to walk pass him, he grabbed her arm to stop her.

"Don't leave," RJ begged as he looked into her eyes.

"Before I curse you out, leaving is the best thing for me to do right now," Marlee replied as she went around him and walked out of the room.

"Curse me out for what. What did I do?" RJ asked as he stopped her again.

He pulled Marlee into the spare bedroom that he used whenever he stayed the night at his mother's house. She folded her arms on top of her belly as she glared at him angrily. She looked like she was ready to leave, so RJ locked the door and stood in front of it to prevent it.

"It's not what you did, it's what you didn't do. I told you from day one to tell her who I was. I can't even blame her for being mad because the shit was foul. I didn't owe her an explanation but, as her man, you did," Marlee replied.

"You're right Marlee, but I told you why I waited. My plan was to talk to her this weekend, but this happened before I could. I was trying to avoid her bringing the drama to your job, but I take the blame for that. Just don't leave," RJ said as he backed her up and sat her down on the bed.

He took her keys and purse out of her hands before kneeling to remove her shoes. Once he was done, he removed his own shoes and pulled Marlee down on the bed. They laid there facing each other while RJ rubbed her back. Her stomach didn't allow him to get as close as he wanted to, but he was satisfied with just looking into her beautiful face. After staying that way for about twenty minutes, Marlee was tired of the staring contest.

"What RJ? Just say what you have to say. I can tell that something is on your mind," Marlee noted.

"I want you," RJ said honestly.

"Move, let me up," Marlee said as she tried to get out of the bed.

"No, Marlee, I'm serious," he replied as he pulled her back down.

"And so was I when I said that I wasn't fucking another woman's man. I shouldn't have done it in the first place, but that was my mistake. I hate how I felt when I got cheated on and I was wrong for doing it to somebody else," Marlee replied.

"I'm not just talking about sex Marlee. I mean, I want that too, but that's not all. I'm talking about a friendship, a baby mama, a wife, a family. I want all of that with you. And don't say that we're moving too fast because I don't want to hear that shit. We fucked on the first day we met and didn't know a damn thing about each other," RJ pointed out.

As crazy as it sounded, RJ felt like he had a deeper connection with Marlee after only seven months than he did with Aspen after five years. He couldn't explain it and he didn't even try. Still, it baffled him how he was never in love with Aspen, but he fell madly in love with Marlee after only a few months. He wasn't big on the love at first sight theory, but maybe Murk was on to something.

"All that sounds good RJ, but you seem to be forgetting that you already have a girlfriend. Being your baby mama, wife, friend and all that other stuff is fine, just as long as I'm the only one. I'm not good at sharing, especially men," Marlee noted.

"I would never ask you to share me because I'm not sharing you. I just don't want to know what my life would be like without you in it," RJ replied honestly as he pulled her in for a kiss.

"I hear what you're saying RJ, but you're still in a relationship. I'm not getting into anything with you until you get out of what you're already in," Marlee swore.

"That's not where I want to be though, Marlee. I haven't wanted to be there for a while. It just took me meeting you to realize it," RJ admitted.

"I hear you, but I'm not the one who you should be telling it to," Marlee countered.

"I have no problem ending things right now. Where's my phone?" RJ asked.

"No RJ. You can't tell her something like that over the phone. After five years, you owe her a face to face explanation."

"Yeah, you're right," RJ sighed solemnly.

"Are you sure about this RJ? I mean, I don't want you to do this just because we have a baby on the way. Honestly, I want to be with you too, but I don't want us to be together just for Tre."

"This has nothing to do with us having a baby Marlee. I lost count of how many times I told Murk to ask Desi about you once we left Vegas. He kept telling me that if it was meant to be that I would see you again on my own. You don't know how happy I was when I saw you in that clinic, even though I was with Aspen. I was shocked to hear that you were pregnant, but that was all the confirmation that I needed. I was coming back to see you whether you were pregnant or not," he confessed.

"A bitch must have really put it on you in Vegas," Marlee said, laughing.

"Yeah, you put it on me and that's why I put him in you," RJ said while burying his face in her neck and inhaling.

"Why are you always smelling me?" Marlee giggled.

"I can't help it. What's the name of that perfume that you always wear?" RJ asked.

"Flowerbomb," Marlee replied.

"I gotta go buy you some more of that shit. That scent is addictive," RJ said as he kissed her neck and lips.

When he started going down lower, Marlee grabbed his shoulders and stopped him. “No playboy. Ain’t nothing happening until you’re officially a single man,” she noted.

“How can I be single if I’m your man?” RJ asked her.

He took off his jeans, boxers, and shirt, right before undressing Marlee. Aspen was trying to get him to see a doctor, but he didn’t have a problem. He was hard as a brick now and ready to slide up in Marlee. Murk said that his dick would make the decision for him. It obviously agreed with his heart and chose Marlee.

Chapter 25

After going to poetry night and dinner with Desmond, Desi talked on the phone with him for hours before finally going to sleep. Not even an hour into her peaceful slumber, she was awakened by someone banging on her front door. Desi stayed in bed, listening, just to see if it was her door or the neighbor's. Once she was sure that it was her house that they wanted, she grabbed her box cutter and tiptoed through the house. She tried looking through the peephole, but it was too dark for her to see. Desi had three locks on her door and a chain, but she was still paranoid.

"Who is it?" she yelled out, trying to make her voice sound deeper than it was.

"Open the door with your scary ass!" Murk yelled back.

"Murk? What the hell are you doing here this late? It's almost one in the morning," Desi fussed as she undid all the locks to let him in.

"I'm happy that nobody was after me. The fuck you got all these locks on the door for? Just get you a gun. I offered to give you one of mine," Murk said as he walked in and locked the door behind him.

"I'll pass. Ain't no telling how many bodies are attached to it. I thought you were staying the night by one of your little freaks," Desi said as she yawned.

"Did you wash the clothes that I left here Desi? I need a shower," Murk said as he walked into the spare bedroom that he usually occupied, with Desi following behind him.

"Yeah, look in the top drawer," Desi replied.

Murk had been there so much lately that he'd paid Desi's rent and all her bills for the month. She never really cooked, but he gave her money to get some food too, since he always ate whatever she did have in there.

"What you got to eat in here?" he asked as he rummaged through the drawers.

"Same shit as always. Sandwiches and microwaveable stuff. What happened to you sleeping by ole girl?" Desi asked.

"Fix me two sandwiches Desi, please. A nigga hungry as fuck," Murk replied.

"Stop ignoring me and answer my question. What happened to the bitch who was supposed to wine and dine you tonight? Bitch was talking about cooking steak and shrimp and all that other shit. Don't tell me she lied." Desi frowned.

"The bitch didn't lie, but she couldn't pay me to even drink a glass of water out of that nasty ass house," Murk replied.

"Her stupid ass invited you over there and didn't even try to clean up?" Desi asked.

"She can't clean that nasty ass house up man. She gotta move. Just throw the whole fucking house away and get another one. Bitch had roaches chillin' up in that muthafucka like they go half on the bills. You know it's bad when the roaches don't even run from you. Muthafuckas looking at me like I was interrupting some shit. I feel dirty as fuck after being over there for just five minutes. I need a shower," Murk fussed as he disappeared into the bathroom.

Desi laughed as she went into the kitchen and fixed him two sandwiches. She got out a bag of chips and a coke before cleaning up her mess. She sat at the dining room table scrolling on her phone until Murk walked in a few minutes later. He had his dreads pulled up into a high ponytail with some joggers and a t-shirt hanging off his scrawny body. Murk ate enough to feed an army, but Desi didn't know where the food went.

"Say your grace heathen," Desi fussed when he sat down and was about to start eating his food.

Murk bowed his head and said a few words before he picked up one of his sandwiches and dug in. "Thanks sis," he mumbled through a mouth full of food.

"You're welcome," Desi replied.

"What are you still doing up?" Murk asked.

"I have to tell you something," Desi replied.

"What's wrong?" Murk asked, his face full of concern.

"Nothing is wrong, but I met somebody," Desi replied.

"I don't like him," Murk blurted out as he bit into his sandwich again.

"You didn't even let me finish," Desi laughed.

"I don't care Desi. I don't like the nigga. End of discussion," Murk mumbled.

"You don't even know him Murk. I like him, and we've gone on a few dates. He's coming to Marlee's baby shower and you better be on your best behavior," Desi warned.

"What dates? I never knew that you went out with nobody." Murk frowned.

"I didn't tell you because you do too much. His name is Desmond and I really like him," Desi noted as she proceeded to tell him everything that she knew about Desmond so far.

"That nigga is lying Desi. He probably killed his wife and wants somebody to help him raise his baby. Fuck him," Murk said, waving her off.

"Oh, my God! What is it with you and my mama?" Desi groaned in frustration.

"Dionne is my girl. She knows what's up. You don't need a man right now Desi. You just broke up with that other fuck boy who made a baby on you."

"That was two years ago Murk. How long am I supposed to stay single?" Desi shouted.

"Wait about two more years before you just jump into something else," Murk replied.

"Are you crazy? You fuck a different bitch almost every night and you expect me to stay single for two more years?" Desi quizzed.

"Fucking different people don't mean that I'm in a relationship with them. I know how you think though, Desi. You be into all that fantasy and fairytale bullshit. You gon' fall in love all fast and be trying to move the nigga in with us and shit," Murk fussed.

"Us!" Desi yelled. "You don't even live here your damn self!"

"Fuck outta here girl. You can't even remember the last time I didn't sleep here because I damn sure can't," Murk said while shaking his head.

"Whatever Murk. Can you just meet him? That's all that I ask of you and my mama. If y'all still don't like him once you meet, then that's fine. It won't change how I feel, but at least give him a chance," Desi begged.

It was crazy how it felt like she'd known Murk all her life. He was like her big brother, best friend, and bodyguard all rolled up into one skinny package. He had a good heart underneath his tough exterior, but not too many people saw that side of him. He meant well, but he took everything to the extreme.

"Alright sis. I'll meet the nigga and give him a chance since you seem to like him. But, on God, Desi, the minute you shed one tear over this fuck boy, it's lights out for his ass. He gon' be laid up right next to his wife that he killed," Murk warned.

"Stop being so insensitive. He did not kill his wife," Desi said as she got up and stretched.

"I'll see when I meet him. I can't spot some bullshit from a mile away," Murk replied.

Desi went back to her bedroom, as Murk threw his trash away and turned off the lights. Desi thought he was playing, but he was about to get all in her male friend's business. Desi was fragile to him and he didn't want anybody to hurt her. After all the pain that she endured when she was younger, he didn't want her to feel anything but happiness now.

Desi didn't know it, but he'd even gone to confront her ex-boyfriend, Jerry, recently. Stupid ass nigga was still calling her trying to plead his case two years after doing her dirty. He claimed that he only wanted Desi to forgive him, but Murk wasn't trying to hear his excuses. Once Murk slapped him across the face with his gun a few times, the message was received. He hadn't called Desi in a minute and she was happy for that. She always told Murk that she didn't need a bodyguard, but that was too damn bad because she already had one.

***

"The nigga might turn out to be alright," RJ said as he talked on the phone to Murk.

His cousin was in his feelings about Desi's new man. RJ knew all about Desi's childhood incident, so he understood why Murk wanted to protect his best friend. Desi wasn't the type to make stupid decisions, so he knew that whoever she chose to be with would be okay.

"Fuck that nigga. He gon' get shot and dumped in the lake right behind your house if he's on some bullshit," Murk swore.

"Damn bruh. Don't make my house a crime scene yet. I never even got a chance to enjoy the place," RJ laughed.

"Speaking of crime scenes, I hope you got your gun with you, boy. Fucking with Aspen is the quickest way for you to meet your maker," Murk said.

Two days had passed since Aspen and Marlee had it out, and RJ hadn't seen or talked to her yet. She called him multiple times, but he never answered the phone for her. He was too busy making up with Marlee, but he couldn't put it off forever. He planned to swing by her house after he went to see his father about a few things.

"I'm just going to get whatever I left over there and hopefully have an adult conversation about our relationship," RJ replied.

"So, you're basically just going over there to break up with her," Murk commented.

"Basically, but what other choice do I have?" RJ questioned.

"Are you gonna tell her that you're with Marlee now?" Murk asked.

"I'm not gonna lie to her," RJ replied.

"You and your pops are some savages with that honesty shit. I'll lie to a bitch in a heartbeat. Nigga be shedding tears and all, just to make her believe me," Murk laughed.

"Like my pops always told me, either you tell the truth or somebody else will tell it for you. The truth may hurt for a little while, but a lie hurts forever. I don't have time to be trying to remember what I told a muthafucka the day before. Telling the truth makes sure that I never have to," RJ replied.

"I respect that cuz, but I'm not at that point in my life just yet. If I can lie under oath, another bitch don't stand a chance," Murk noted.

"You know how my pops is about that. He feels like a real man should be honest, no matter how painful the truth is. He didn't just preach it, he lived by it. Even though I hate how things are between him and my mama, she knew what it was from day one and so did Lauren."

"Yeah, you're right about that. Aye nigga, sit your bad ass down!" Murk yelled at one of his kids.

"Damn bruh. How do you deal with all five of them at the same time? I would probably lose my mind."

"I got this belt for their bad asses and I ain't scared to use it. They did me dirty in the mall just now. I don't know how many times I had to stop for somebody to use the bathroom. I lost my baby girl for thirty whole minutes before security paged me. My oldest son swiped a shirt out of Foot Locker when I turned my back to pay for their shoes. Now all five of them are hungry. I'm getting a fucking vasectomy," Murk fussed, making his cousin laugh.

"I thought Desi was supposed to be going with you. What happened?" RJ asked.

"See, that's exactly why I don't need her to have no man. Bald head bitch cancelled on me at the last minute when that nigga called and invited her out to lunch. That nigga cutting into our time already. That's just why I don't like his ass," Murk fumed.

"Stop being selfish nigga. Let that girl be happy. Dude seems like he's cool. He got a good job and shit," RJ replied.

"Hold up!" Murk yelled angrily. "You met the nigga already?"

"Aww shit," RJ groaned.

"The fuck did you meet that clown and why didn't you tell me?" Murk questioned.

"Me and Marlee saw them last night when we went to get something to eat," RJ admitted.

"Oh, so y'all doing double dates and shit now?" Murk quizzed.

"No man. Me and Marlee went to get food and we saw them in the restaurant. Desi introduced us to him and we talked to him for a few minutes before we left. Just give the man a chance before you decide that you don't like him."

"I'll see. I just don't want a nigga to do her wrong. She's already been through enough. I want her to be happy, but who's to say that he's the one that will get the job done. That nigga gotta prove to me that he deserves her. You know I can spot a fuck boy from a mile away," Murk replied.

"It seems like he's been through a lot too. They might be good for each other. Just wait and see. If shit don't work out, just be a good friend and be there for her if she needs you," RJ reasoned.

"I'll be there for her, right after I put a bullet in his head and make his daughter an orphan," Murk threatened.

"Bye bruh. I just pulled up to Aspen's house and I'm ready to get this shit over with," RJ replied.

"Take your gun in there with you, nigga. Don't trust her ass. I like Aspen and all, but she looks like one of them Fatal Attraction bitches," Murk said.

"I don't even think she's here. Her car is not in the driveway. I'll get up with you later. Let me call and see where she's at," RJ said as he hung up with Murk and dialed Aspen's number.

He hoped she wasn't far because he wasn't trying to prolong the inevitable any longer. He didn't want to give Aspen false hope about where they stood. He also didn't want Marlee to leave him because he didn't handle his business with the other woman like he was supposed to. RJ sighed as he listened to the phone ringing in his ear, hoping that Aspen answered his call.

Chapter 26

Lauren washed the dishes from the meal she had prepared as she fought back tears. She'd slaved over a hot stove for hours preparing all of her husband's favorite foods, but he didn't eat any of it. That wasn't the first time that it happened, but it was getting harder to appear unaffected by it. Her daughters, Hope and Faith, were in the living room talking to Aspen, while her baby girl Joy dried and put the dishes away. Joy was livid as she listened to her father talk on the phone right there in the presence of her mother. Lauren looked like she was ready to break down at any moment and that only infuriated her more.

"You need to say something and stop acting like it's okay. You cooked all this damn food for him, but he'd rather go by his other woman to eat with her instead," Joy whispered angrily.

"Stop it Joy. Just leave it alone. I'm okay," Lauren replied in a hushed tone.

"You are not okay, and you need to stop pretending like you are," Joy fumed.

Lauren never got a chance to reply because Banks walked into the kitchen a short time later. He stood behind his wife and placed both of his huge hands on her shoulders.

"I'll see you in a few days. Call me if you need anything," he said while placing a soft kiss on the top of her head.

Joy threw the towel that she'd been drying the dishes with on the counter and stormed off when she saw her mother nod her head in acceptance. Banks was oblivious to her anger, just like always. He said a few more words to his wife before grabbing his keys and leaving to go spend a few days with Ivy. As soon as he left, Lauren went into the living room and joined the other women.

"Are you okay mom?" Faith asked as she grabbed Lauren's hand.

She saw the saddened look in her mother's eyes and her heart went out to her. As much as she wanted to blame her father for the pain that her mother was in, she couldn't. It was Lauren's own fault that she was hurting, and she couldn't blame it on anyone else. For years, they had watched their father divide his time up between two houses and not once did their mother say anything. She cried to them a lot, but she never confronted him about it.

"I'm fine honey," Lauren said with a forced smile.

"You are not fine, and you need to stop pretending like you are. God! How can you let him treat you like a doormat while he parades his whore all over New Orleans?" Joy fumed.

"Just shut up Joy," Lauren said while shaking her head.

"She's always at the job, and he has lunch with her every single day. Not to mention the luxury car and house that he put her in. Her clothes are top of line and I'm sure her bank account is just as big as yours, if not bigger. Hell, I'm surprised he didn't put her on y'all joint account," Joy continued.

"Stop it Joy. You're not making her feel any better," Faith said as she saw the expression on her mother's face.

"You're his wife, but she gets treated better, just because she has a son," Joy said.

"That's enough!" Lauren yelled, silencing her youngest daughter.

She got it, Joy was upset, but she didn't need a constant reminder of what was going on in her life. She had to live with it every day and it was miserable. She wasn't in denial, but there was nothing that she could do. With no education or work experience, she was stuck. She'd only been a flight attendant for a few months when she and her husband met, but that was the only job that she'd ever had. Lauren regretted getting too comfortable with him taking care of her because now, she was dependent. Leaving wasn't an option because the prenup that he had her sign before they got married guaranteed that she would leave with nothing. The prenup was his father's idea because he never trusted Lauren, for some reason. Banks was young at the time, so he did whatever his father requested. The old man went to his grave not liking her, but she never knew why. He made sure that if things didn't work out with his son, Lauren would be on her own. She was in it until the end and she had come to accept that a long time ago. She didn't like it, but her hands were tied.

"I'm sorry mom, but I'm just so angry. The same way he puts Ivy before you is the same way that he puts RJ before us," Joy ranted.

"But, I though your father was good to y'all," Aspen said in confusion.

"Yeah, but he's better to RJ," Hope chimed in.

"How?" Aspen wanted to know.

"He just is. RJ barely comes to work, and nothing is ever said. The minute I ask for a day off, I have to go through the hassle of filling out paperwork and all that other crap. RJ wanted a Bentley truck and he got it the very next day. Never mind that he already had a brand-new truck. I asked for a Beamer and I had to wait for a week. And I'm sure that RJ didn't spend a dime on that big beautiful house that he lives in," Joy said, as her sisters nodded in agreement.

"But, didn't your father buy y'all a house too?" Aspen asked.

"Yeah, but I'm sure his is better," Joy said bitterly.

To Aspen, they sounded like a bunch of ungrateful fools. She wished she had a parent to do half as much for her as Banks did for his daughters. She didn't see the differences that they spoke of because their father had all of them spoiled, including Raven. She remembered them telling Banks that they wanted to go to Dubai and he sent them on an all-expense paid vacation the following month. He even gave them spending money and took them shopping for vacation attire. Joy was making six figures at his company, just for answering the phones and renewing parking contracts. The only reason why all three of them didn't have their own house was because they preferred to live together. And the house that their father purchased them was something straight out of a magazine. Aspen got her first house on her own, but RJ paid her down payment. She didn't get an elaborate mansion, but she wasn't complaining. From what she could see, they had nothing to complain about either.

"What about Raven's mother? Where is she?" Aspen questioned.

That was something that she'd always wanted to know but never asked. Raven and her husband and daughter always came around, but Aspen had never seen her mother.

"She didn't have a son, so she got discarded like yesterday's trash. At least she got a house out of the deal though," Joy, who was always the most vocal, replied.

"Wow," was all that Aspen could think to say.

"I hate to say it, but RJ is no better. I know you said that y'all were broken up when he made his son, but he's just like my daddy. And from what I saw when his son's mother came to the job, there's more than just a baby between the two of them," Joy said while looking at Aspen.

"And I can't believe that bitch Ivy put you out of the house for her. After being with her bastard son for five years and that's how she treats you," Lauren argued.

"She claimed that it was nothing personal, but that's not how I took it," Aspen replied.

"Bullshit! It was very personal. You're a fool if you go anywhere near her house again," Lauren countered.

"That was just so unlike her. Ivy and I have always gotten along great. She wasn't mean about it, but my feelings were still hurt," Aspen admitted.

"Ugh! And we have to go to RJ's house for this baby shower," Joy groaned.

"I'm not going to that mess. I've already told daddy that I have to work. I refuse to be a part of anything that Ivy does," Hope replied.

"I'm not going either and Joy is only going to be nosey. I'll send a gift, but that's about it," Faith spoke up.

"Well, I'm not going there all by myself. I'll just make up something to tell daddy. I won't even know anybody there," Joy replied.

"I'm just shocked that it's at RJ's house, but that was Ivy's decision. I know she didn't do it to be malicious, but I still felt some kind of way about it." Aspen shrugged.

"Don't be fooled by her, Aspen. Ivy has spent years being the other woman and she's probably grooming her grandson's mother to do the same. She's having his son, so she already has a huge advantage over you," Lauren pointed out.

"So, Banks has been with RJ's mother for almost thirty years? Is that what you're telling me?" Aspen asked in shock.

It was no secret that they messed around, but she just assumed that they hooked back up years down the line. She didn't want to believe that Ivy had been the side chick for all those years. RJ had just turned twenty-nine and that was a long time to be someone's mistress.

"Basically." Lauren shrugged.

"Did he ever try to hide it from you or did you just assume that they were still messing around?" Aspen asked.

"As you probably already know, my husband is a very honest man, Aspen. He's always been honest with me about his feelings for her. He's in love with another woman and he's never tried to hide it." Lauren shrugged sadly.

"I don't mean to be intrusive, but I'm just asking. Did he ever have any other women besides her?" Aspen questioned.

"Besides Raven's mother, none that I know of. That's the part that hurts the most. If he would have had multiple women, I would have assumed that it was just him being a dog. But to only have one other woman besides me lets me know that some deep feelings are involved," Lauren said somberly.

"And I hate to break the news to you, Aspen, but I can guarantee you that RJ is gonna be the same way," Joy countered.

"I don't think so honey. I have no problem with him taking care of his son, but I refuse to sit back and let his child's mother reap the same benefits as me. No offense Lauren, but I'm not taking a back seat to RJ's mistress. I don't want to be his number one; I want to be his only one," Aspen spat angrily.

"You might not want to admit it, but it's already happening. You haven't seen or spoken to RJ in two days. Who do you think he's been with?" Lauren questioned, giving Aspen something to think about.

Lauren and her daughters were looking to her for answers that she didn't have. She had been blowing RJ's phone up with calls and text messages, but he had yet to answer or reply. Aaron had been calling her like crazy, but he wasn't who she wanted to talk to. Aspen was deep in thought wondering what was up with her man when her phone rang, displaying his number.

"Speak of the devil and he will appear," Aspen said as she showed them her phone.

"Answer it and see what that dog wants," Joy replied, but she didn't have to tell Aspen twice.

"Hello," Aspen answered calmly, trying not to sound as excited as she felt.

"Hey, I'm at your house. Are you coming back any time soon? If not, I can come back tomorrow," RJ said.

"No, I'll be there in a few minutes," Aspen said, refraining from screaming for him not to leave.

She hated the state that their relationship was in and she desperately wanted to fix it. RJ sounded like he had a lot on his mind and so did she. Aspen had a lot to say after listening to Lauren and his sisters. RJ had some decisions to make because she couldn't see herself being in his stepmother's shoes. Once she hung up with RJ, she grabbed her keys from her purse and stood up. She needed to get some things off her chest and there was no time like the present.

"Don't accept something now that you'll live to regret later. Remember Aspen, old fools were young fools at one time. Don't say yes today because it'll be too late to say no tomorrow. Trust me, I know," Lauren said, as Aspen walked out of her house.

***

RJ paced the sidewalk waiting for Aspen to pull up. He wasn't heartless and hurting her was not a part of his plan. He did love her at one point in time, but things had changed over the years. His feelings for her had changed and that was long before Marlee entered the picture. When he saw Aspen pull into her driveway a short time later, RJ walked up on her porch and waited for her to let him in.

"You could have used your key to go inside," Aspen said when she got out of the car and joined him on her porch.

RJ had a key to her house but, under the circumstances, he didn't feel right using it. He had already removed it from his key ring because he was prepared to give it back to her.

"I was good standing out here," he replied, as she opened the door and they both walked inside.

Aspen dropped her keys and purse on her living room table and took a seat on her sofa. RJ sat in the recliner right next to her and thought about what he wanted to say first. Before he even had a chance to get it out, Aspen started going off on him.

"I really don't know what you thought RJ, but I'm nothing like Lauren. If you think for a minute that I'm gonna sit back and knowingly let you cheat on me, you got another thing coming. I haven't seen or spoken to you in two days, but I'm sure that your son's mother has," Aspen hissed.

"I can see that you've been talking to my stepmother and sisters," RJ replied as he shook his head.

"Yes, I have, and we need to get some things clear before we go any further. Now, I want you to be a great father and, as I've always said, I'll love your son as if he were my very own. But, what I won't do is be disrespected by you and his mother. I'm not a number RJ. Either I'm your only one or nothing at all. I'm not sharing you," Aspen noted.

"I never asked you to and that's not what I want," RJ said, making her smile.

"Good," Aspen replied triumphantly.

"I think it's best that we end things on a good note and just go our separate ways," RJ said, removing the smile of victory from her lips.

"What?" Aspen questioned in shock.

"I'm sorry Aspen, but I'm not happy being with you anymore," RJ replied honestly.

"Since when RJ? You were happy a year ago. Hell, you were happy just a few months ago until you went to Vegas. Is that why you want to end things? Because of her?" Aspen asked.

"Let's not do this Aspen. You know just as well as I do that I haven't been happy for a while. When you asked me, I was honest and told you that I wasn't. You wanted me to give us another try, and I did. I didn't come here to argue, but you deserved to know how I feel," RJ countered.

"I also deserve the truth!" Aspen yelled as she jumped up from her place on the sofa.

"Yes, you do, and I have no problem giving you that. I'll tell you whatever you want to know," RJ replied.

"Are you planning to be with her?" Aspen asked while looking at him.

"Yes," RJ replied, his gaze never faltering.

"Did you know her before you went to Vegas?" Aspen wanted to know.

That was a question that had been on her mind since she found out that Marlee was the mystery woman. She just didn't want to believe that a one-night stand in Vegas had the power to end her five-year relationship.

"No, we met for the first time in Vegas," RJ replied honestly.

"God, RJ! Five years and you want to end it all for a one-night stand that just so happened to get pregnant with your child. You don't even know her!" Aspen yelled.

"I know all that I need to know about her. You can't put a time frame on feelings," RJ countered.

"What feelings RJ? It hasn't even been a year yet. Are you standing here telling me that you're in love with a woman that you haven't even known that long?" Aspen asked.

"Yes," RJ answered truthfully.

"I knew it! I knew that you were still messing around with her," Aspen said as tears fell from her eyes.

She was hoping that RJ would deny it, but he never did. He just looked at her sadly as he ran his hand through his waves.

"So, that's it RJ? Our relationship is over just like that? You don't even want to try to work it out?" Aspen asked, grasping at invisible straws.

"Why would you want to Aspen? You just said that you're nothing like Lauren. I seriously doubt if I'll ever be able to leave Marlee alone, so why even bother?" RJ replied, hammering the final nail into the coffin.

He and Aspen just stared at each other for a while until RJ walked off towards her bedroom. He grabbed his Nike duffel bag from her closet and started gathering the items that he'd left there when he stayed over. Aspen tried to give him space in her drawers and closet, but he always declined. Most times, he packed a bag and took it with him when he left. He accidentally left his bag there when he spent the night last time, but there wasn't much for him to pack. She could toss out whatever he left behind because it wasn't too important anyway. When RJ walked back into the living room, Aspen was pacing the floor mumbling something under her breath. When she looked at him, she frowned and started going in on him once again.

"You try so hard to be different, but you're just like your father. Both of y'all think just because you're honest, that makes what you do right. Lauren might be okay with being treated like second best, but I would never allow that to happen to me. You and your father don't want real women. Y'all prefer to wife the side bitches instead," Aspen spat, angering RJ with her words.

He didn't go there for all the extras, but she had him fucked up for real.

"Was I supposed to say fuck my feelings and put yours first Aspen? You always ask for honesty, but you can't even handle it. If I would have stayed with you and cheated with another woman, I would have been called a dog. When I'm honest and tell you straight up that I want to be with somebody else, I'm still wrong. A nigga can't win for fucking losing," RJ snapped angrily.

"Just leave RJ. Get the fuck out of my house. Go be with your side bitch, just like your daddy always does," Aspen replied bitterly.

"She ain't no side bitch my baby, that's wifey. And just so you know, I'm good on going to see a doctor. My dick stays hard whenever I'm around her," RJ smirked, as Aspen gasped at his choice of words.

He threw her house key on her coffee table right before he walked out of her house and out of her life. Once RJ got into his car, he sighed in contentment as he closed one chapter in his book of life and prepared to start a new one. He pulled away from Aspen's house with a smile on his face, never noticing Aspen's ex-boyfriend, Aaron, who pulled off right behind him.

"Lying ass bitch," Aaron fumed as he trailed behind RJ to see where he was going.

It was his first time seeing where Aspen lived, since she never bothered to show him the house that she'd purchased two years ago. Aaron was tired of the games that she kept playing and all the lies that she constantly told. Aspen had spent the last two nights with him screwing his brains out and professing her undying love. She claimed to be so ready to do right and make their relationship work, but she was full of shit. Aaron had been following her around every time she left, just to see what was up for himself.

RJ hadn't been around once but, on day number three, he seemed to have appeared out of thin air and was back on the scene. Aaron saw him leaving Aspen's house with a duffle bag and he followed right behind him. He didn't quite know what his plan of action was just yet, but he needed to come up with something. He had so many questions, but he had no one else to go to for the answers. His first thought was to put a bullet in RJ's head and be done with it, but that wasn't the answer. Aspen would probably have another nigga by the end of the month. And, truthfully, RJ wasn't the person who he had a problem with. Aspen was responsible for how he felt. She was always trying to ruin his relationships and he was ready to take a page from her book and do the same to her.

Chapter 27

"Keep your nervous ass still before you be looking like a clown," Marlee fussed at Desi as she did her makeup.

Desi, Marlee, Ivy, and Murk had stayed the night at RJ's house to prepare for her baby shower. The day had finally arrived, and Desi was going crazy about Desmond meeting her friends and family. He told her that he could handle himself around anyone, but Desi wasn't so sure.

"I'm sorry cousin, but you know my nerves are shot. I just want everything to be perfect for Desmond's first time meeting everybody," Desi replied.

"Murk and your mama are the only two that you have to worry about. Everybody else will be fine," Marlee replied.

"Tiffany said that she talked to my mama and she promised to behave. I told RJ to talk to Murk, but that's like talking to a brick wall. Sometimes I regret ever befriending his ass," Desi fussed, as Marlee looked at what color lipstick she wanted to put on her.

Desi tried to warn Desmond about the possible craziness that he would encounter. He assured her that he would be fine, and she hoped that he was. He was bringing Destini with him and Desi couldn't wait to see her. Desmond hadn't had a babysitter the last few times they went out, so Destini ended up tagging along. Since Desi was around her so much, Destini knew her well. It warmed her heart whenever the six-month-old beauty reached for her and that made Desmond smile too.

"Don't worry Desi, it's fate," Marlee replied.

"What's fate?" Desi questioned.

"You and Desmond being together is fate. Just think about it. You're unable to have kids, but you meet a single father who's raising his daughter all alone. It was fate that put both of you in the same place at the exact same time. And look, even your names are almost alike. Desiree, Destini, and Desmond. Sounds like one big happy family if you ask me," Marlee said, making Desi blush and smile.

"He asked me to be in a relationship with him," Desi confessed.

"Really? And what did you say?" Marlee asked her.

"I told him that if he can survive today, then we must be meant to be," Desi laughed.

"I think you should go for it. You just never know when and where your happiness will come from, but you have to take chances. Look at me. A one-night stand in Vegas got me a fine ass man and a son on the way," Marlee joked.

"You play too much, but I agree. I'm willing to take a chance and see where it goes. He even invited me to his family picnic next Saturday." Desi smiled.

"Bitch, you were supposed to be helping me with a wedding next Saturday," Marlee fussed.

"Oh shit! I'm so sorry cousin. I completely forgot. I'll be there to help you. I'll cancel my plans with Desmond," Desi replied.

"Oh no, bitch! It took you too long to find a decent man. Don't worry about me. I'll get Sierra to help me with the wedding," Marlee maintained.

"What wedding?" RJ asked when he walked into the room.

"The wedding that I'm doing next weekend," Marlee replied.

"C'mon now Marlee, damn. You're eight months pregnant and you're trying to do too much," RJ fussed.

"No, I'm not, but I already got paid to do this months ago. This is my last job and then I'm taking a few months off," Marlee promised.

"A few years," RJ countered, making her roll her eyes behind his back.

RJ didn't mean any harm, but Marlee had to get used to his controlling ways. RJ was all about a man being a man, and he and his father believed in taking care of their women. He had been in Marlee's ear about being a stay at home mother, but she wasn't trying to hear it. Ivy had already agreed to babysit, and she was going back to work just as soon as she was cleared by her doctor.

"Everything is so nice." Marlee smiled as she looked out of the window at the finished product.

Ivy and Tiffany had done a great job of putting her baby shower together and the water backdrop was perfect. They had about an hour before people started to arrive, but there was nothing else that needed to be done. Marlee just had to slip into her maternity dress and shoes and she was done. She'd already applied a little makeup and she had her hair colored the day before. She was now rocking a frosted blue color that RJ loved. Since she was natural, she was able to change up her color a lot without worrying about the chemicals pulling her hair out.

"Yeah, it is," RJ said as he came up and hugged her from behind.

"Aww, y'all are so cute together," Desi cooed as she watched them standing there.

Their special moment was interrupted the moment Murk walked into the room and opened his mouth. His dreads were freshly twisted and styled, and he was wearing Ralph Lauren from top to bottom. He looked handsome, even though his clothes hung off his thin body just like always.

"The fuck you got on makeup for? That nigga ain't that special." Murk frowned when he looked at Desi.

"Chill out bruh. Didn't we just talk about this shit?" RJ asked.

"Don't tell him nothing RJ. I swear if you embarrass me today, I'm done with you for the rest of my life," Desi threatened.

"That nigga means that much to you, Desi?" Murk asked, getting upset by her comment.

"No, but I should mean that much to you. I've met all four of your baby mamas and about ten other bitches that you introduced as your girlfriend. Even though I know that you're a lying man whore, I still didn't do anything to embarrass you or make you uncomfortable. All I ask is that you give me the same respect," Desi said sternly.

Murk saw the seriousness in her eyes and decided to relax a little. In such a short period of time, Desi had become a very important part of his life. His mother and brothers loved her and that was almost impossible for them. They looked at everybody sideways and they didn't trust a soul. When they took an instant liking to Desi, Murk knew that she truly was destined to be his best friend. Although he wanted to protect her, he couldn't run the risk of losing her.

"Alright man, I'll behave. But, I'm warning you right now Desi. If that nigga fuck over you in any kind of way, don't tell me about it. If you don't want me to kill him and his entire family, keep that shit to yourself," Murk argued.

"What kind of friendship have I gotten myself into?" Desi questioned out loud.

"One that your bald head ass can't get out of," Murk replied.

"How do I look?" Desi asked him as she stood up and showed off her outfit.

"You straight," Murk replied, meaning that she looked good.

It took Desi a while, but she learned how to read through what he said. He wasn't the mushy type, so she understood him like no one else.

"Are your kids coming Murk?" Marlee asked.

"Do you want your baby shower ruined?" he asked, making them all laugh.

"They can't be that bad," Marlee replied.

"Even the girls," Desi noted while shaking her head.

"Are any of them named after you?" Marlee questioned.

"No, but you shouldn't even know my real name," Murk said while looking at RJ and Desi.

"I don't. That's why I asked if one of your kids was named after you, so I could figure it out," Marlee said, quickly covering her tracks.

"Nah, I wouldn't even do my kids like that," Murk replied.

"I don't blame you," Marlee said while looking at RJ.

"I don't know what the hell you're looking at me for. That's on him if he don't want his kids to have his name. Don't make me mad Marlee." RJ frowned.

"You need to get dressed cousin. Come on Murk. Let's go outside," Desi said as she pulled him out of the room.

Marlee and RJ got dressed and went outside a few minutes before the shower was scheduled to start. Ivy rented two huge white chairs trimmed in gold especially for them. Once people started arriving, the servers passed around the appetizers as Sierra, Raven, and Tiffany started the games. Marlee was happy to see that Murk and Desmond seemed to be getting along, and even Dionne was behaving. She played with Destini as she talked to Desmond about him and Desi's relationship.

Once Murk found out that Desmond owned a bails bonds company, he was ready for Desi to marry him. That was like music to his ears as much as he went to jail. Desi walked around holding Destini as she introduced her boyfriend, as she referred to him, to her family. Desmond was a natural and he fit in with them perfectly. Desi couldn't stop smiling and Marlee was happy for her. The lawn was packed, and everything was going great. Her cousin Kallie was there, but Marlee didn't really say much to her. They spoke, and she thanked her for coming, even though she didn't invite her. She knew that it was her mother's doing, but she didn't trip. Her day was going too good for her to even worry about it. Kallie was probably going to report everything to Yanni and she had a lot to report. At Desi's urging, she and Kallie talked and made up, but Marlee's feelings remained the same. Kallie talked entirely too much, but they had to take some of the blame for that too. She wouldn't know anything unless they told her and Marlee knew not to talk around her anymore. She knew that Kallie wasn't coming from a bad place and that was the only reason why she hadn't cut her off completely.

"I thought your pops was supposed to be coming," RJ said while looking at Marlee.

Marlee finally gave in and started talking to Matthew again. He swore that he was coming to her baby shower, but he stopped answering his phone again a few days before the event. Marlee's feelings were hurt, but she didn't know why. Alvin had been more of a father to her than her own and she was happy that he was there. Matthew was selfish, but Marlee couldn't help that she loved him. Mat kept telling her to let him be, but she was having a hard time doing it. No matter how many times he disappointed her, Marlee always forgave him like nothing ever happened.

"I already told you how he is. I don't even know why I keep expecting him to change," Marlee replied, as RJ grabbed her hand and kissed it.

"The fuck," RJ said when a female walked up in the middle of one of the games.

She was walking right over to them, and Marlee was trying to figure out who she was. She looked familiar, but she couldn't quite remember when or where she'd seen her before.

"Man, do you see this shit? I told you, cuz. That bitch is on her single black female shit," Murk said as he fell out laughing.

"The fuck is Kassidy on bruh?" RJ said as he watched his best friend stop to give his mother a hug.

He and Kassidy hadn't talked much since she voiced her opinion about Marlee a few months before. It was nothing personal with RJ, but he had a lot going on with him since then. He knew that she stayed in touch with Ivy, so it was no surprise that she was there. What did surprise him was the short, blonde colored mohawk that she was now sporting. She even had lines cut into the sides of it, but they were crooked as fuck. The entire look was a mess and didn't fit her at all. Even the distressed jeans, off the shoulder shirt, and combat boots were out of character for her. Kassidy was a basic chick and that just didn't go with her personality.

"Just the bitch I wanted to see," Marlee said once she realized that the woman was RJ's best friend.

"I told you to leave that shit alone Marlee. I already handled it," RJ said as he kissed her hand again.

"Fire the stylist," Marlee said when she got a good look at Kassidy's attire.

It was crazy because her outfit looked almost identical to the one that Marlee had on a few days ago. She and RJ took a picture when they went out to eat and he posted it on his Instagram. Kassidy obviously tried to mimic her look, but it was an epic fail. Marlee was pissed because Kassidy commented under the picture asking RJ where Aspen was, as if they were good friends or something. RJ clearly referred to Marlee as his girl in the caption, so Marlee knew that the bitch was being messy. RJ went off on her under the post, but that wasn't good enough for Marlee. She had a few words for Kassidy herself, but RJ told her to let it go.

"Who the fuck is that disaster?" Desi asked when she walked over holding Destini.

"RJ's best friend who's secretly in love with him," Marlee snickered.

"Stop playing Marlee," RJ fussed as he frowned at her.

"Shit, it's true." Murk shrugged as he took Destini out of Desi's arms.

"I'm so proud of you, bestie. You actually behaved like a human being today," Desi said as she kissed Murk on the cheek.

"I'll admit that I was wrong. The nigga is cool, but he can still get this heat if he fucks over you. But, on another note, your step daughter is bald headed just like you," Murk said as he looked down at Destini and made her smile.

"Shut up and give her back," Desi said as she took the baby from him.

"Here comes your future stalker RJ. I got my gun on me if you need it," Murk said when they saw Kassidy walking over to them.

"Hug her and die," Marlee threatened when she saw RJ stand up to greet her.

"Hey bestie. The new house is beautiful. Well, it is from the outside," Kassidy said as she tried to hug him.

"What's up Kassidy?" RJ said as he quickly grabbed her hand and shook it.

"Oh shit. Marlee got that nigga trained already," Murk said as he and Desi fell out laughing.

"Kassidy, this is my wifey, Marlee. I know y'all saw each other before, but we never did do the introductions," RJ said, trying to ignore what Murk had just said.

"Hi Marlee," Kassidy said with a fake smile.

She didn't like hearing RJ refer to her as his wifey, but she had to keep her game face on. She was still baffled as to where Aspen was and when RJ and Marlee made things official. She felt so out of the loop and she missed talking to her best friend every day.

"Hey," Marlee spoke back dryly. She saw right through Kassidy and she wasn't buying into the best friend act. RJ told her what Kassidy said when they first met, but she already knew what was up. Kassidy reminded her of her cousin Yanni with that fake smile and Marlee didn't like her already. She was tempted to give her the name of her barber so that he could fix the crooked lines that someone had cut into her head.

"I didn't even know that you had moved into the house already RJ. When can I get a grand tour?" Kassidy asked, turning her attention back to the man that she secretly loved.

"You can't. The baby shower is an outdoors event. No one is allowed inside. Food and drinks are over there, and the bathroom is in the pool house if you need to use it," Marlee said, pointing to everything as she spoke like she lived there.

"Oh God. My stomach hurts. That bitch is crazy," Desi said as she and Murk laughed out loud at Marlee's comment like some damn fools.

"Um, here you go RJ. I got a gift card for the baby. I know you probably got everything that he needed already," Kassidy said, feeling uncomfortable.

"Thanks, I appreciate it. Here baby," RJ said while handing the card to Marlee.

"No problem. I guess I'll go back over here and talk to Ivy," Kassidy said as she turned to walk away.

"Yeah, you do that," Marlee said, dismissing her.

"Your pregnant ass is mean as fuck," RJ laughed once Kassidy was gone.

"I'm not mean, but I can spot a fake bitch when I see one. I would hate to lay hands on your best friend, but I will. She played that shit with Aspen and you let it slide. Please warn that bitch and tell her that I'm not the one," Marlee threatened.

"You got that baby," RJ replied as he gave her a peck on the lips.

Marlee was feisty as hell and he loved it. Aspen always told him when Kassidy pissed her off, but Marlee handled shit herself. The rest of the day went on smoothly. Marlee and RJ opened all the gifts and took a few pictures with their guests. Of course, the grandfather to be had to show out. Banks started the baby a bank account and deposited fifty thousand dollars in it. He was big on education and he wanted his first grandson to go to the best schools.

"Aww shit. Here comes Iris," RJ said, referring to Murk's mother.

Iris had sent her gifts with Murk because she wasn't feeling well. She didn't want to disappoint her sister, so she forced herself out of bed just to show her face for a little while. Ivy would do anything for her and she wanted to help her celebrate her first grandson.

"Hey, my beautiful sister. How are you feeling?" Ivy asked when she walked up and hugged her.

"Like shit, but you know I had to come show my face. I'll be on my death bed, but I'm coming if you need me," Iris replied as she kissed her sister's cheek.

"Are you hungry? I can fix you something to eat. We have plenty of food left," Ivy said as they walked over to where RJ and Marlee were.

"I'll probably get something to take home," Iris said as something else got her attention.

Ivy saw her sister staring at someone, but she didn't know why. She grabbed Iris's hand and gave it a little squeeze, which was how they communicated without words. She didn't want her sister trying to act a fool at her son's house. The shower had come to an end, but there were a few people still hanging around.

"I'm okay sister, but I think I know her," Iris said, pointing to a woman who was seated at the table that they were walking up to.

"From where?" Ivy asked her.

"Is that you, Dionne?" Iris asked with her eyes squinted to get a better look at the woman.

"Iris! Bitch! Come give me a hug!" Dionne yelled as she jumped up from the table.

Murk and Desi looked at each other quizzically as they watched their mothers scream and hug like they were long lost friends. Everyone just stood around watching until both women calmed down and took a seat.

"What are you doing here?" Iris asked Dionne.

"Marlee is my niece," Dionne replied.

"RJ is my nephew. This is my oldest son, Murk," Iris said as she pointed to him.

"Yes indeed. I knew I liked his ass for a reason. Desi is my baby," Dionne replied.

"Didn't I tell you that I knew your lil ass from somewhere?" Iris said while pointing to Desi.

"Yeah, you did, but how do y'all know each other?" Desi asked.

"Me and Iris were locked up together. That was my fucking girl," Dionne said as she hugged her again.

"This is a small damn world. Who would have thought that our kids would have ended up being friends? I'm happy I got my ass out of bed and came over here." Iris smiled.

Desi was older now, but Iris remembered all the pictures that Dionne had of her when they were in jail. The two women sat there and played catch up as RJ, Murk, and Desmond took all the gifts inside.

"I bet your mama was my mama's bitch while they were in jail. My mama look like she had them hoes when she was locked up," Murk said while looking at Desi.

"You are one retarded muthafucka," Desi said as they all laughed.

Only Murk would say something so stupid. No one but him even thought of that kind of shit. Desmond was holding his stomach laughing at her best friend.

"I'm getting ready to go Marlee. Everything is cleaned up outside and Ivy is waiting for the event company to pick up the stuff that we rented. Do you need me to take any of the baby's stuff home with me?" Tiffany asked.

"No, we got it Tiffany. Thanks for everything," RJ said as he stepped up and hugged her.

"You're welcome baby." Tiffany smiled before she left.

"Why didn't you let her take some of this stuff home with her, RJ?" Marlee asked.

"All his stuff is staying here. You ain't putting my son's stuff in the garage next to your makeup equipment," RJ fussed.

"I wasn't putting his stuff in the garage, but you already have enough stuff over here. I need to have some stuff at my house too," Marlee replied pissing him off.

He wasn't in the mood to argue, so he didn't bother replying. Marlee knew that he wanted her there with him, but she was always being difficult. The only reason she stayed the night before was because of the baby shower. He had to damn near beg her to stay again. RJ tried not to pressure her, especially since he and Marlee were still getting to know each other. Instead of getting into it with her, he went outside to find his father. Banks was sitting in a lounge chair by himself, as Ivy and Kassidy stood a few feet away talking. RJ didn't know why Kassidy was still there, but he wasn't going anywhere near her. He didn't need Marlee going off on him about nothing.

"Your sisters are going to hear from me. I didn't expect Lauren to show up, but the three of them should have been here," Banks fumed when RJ sat down next to him.

"I don't know why you were looking for them to show up either. I know you see it pops. They don't fuck with me and they never did. Raven is the only one that I've ever had a relationship with and I'm good with that," RJ replied.

"Of course, I see it RJ, but that's nothing but a little sibling rivalry. You're my only son and, yes, I do favor you over my daughters sometimes. It's just a lot of jealousy there, especially with Joy. That doesn't mean that I love them any less though. Our bond is just different, and they should understand that," Banks pointed out.

"I don't say too much because I would never want you to choose sides for any reason. I never wanted to make you feel uncomfortable and I still don't," RJ spoke up.

"Make me feel uncomfortable about what son?" Banks asked as he sat up in his chair.

"It ain't just no jealously or no sibling rivalry. Your wife and her daughters hate me, and they don't try very hard to hide it. The only reason I still step foot in your house is because of you. That's why I'm so happy that I got my own, so we can spend time together over here. I respected Lauren as your wife and that's why I never told her some of the things that I wanted to say. But, I'm done going over there and I'm done holding my tongue. She even told Aspen a bunch of bullshit about me and my mama, and I'm over being nice. Joy got one more time to say something slick and she gon' get the fuck slapped out of her too," RJ rambled angrily.

"Why am I just now hearing about this RJ? We talk every single day and you never said anything to me," Banks countered.

"I just told you why. I tried to keep the peace for your sake, but I'm tired of it now," RJ said, right as he heard yelling coming from the back entrance of his house.

He and his father jumped up and rushed over to see what was going on. Kassidy was holding her mouth, as Ivy stood in between her and Marlee.

"What happened baby?" RJ asked as he rushed over to Marlee.

"That crazy bitch punched me in the face!" Kassidy yelled.

"You better watch your muthafucking mouth!" RJ fumed as he pointed at her.

"RJ!" Ivy scolded, shocked to hear him speaking to his best friend that way.

He was happy when his father pulled her away and walked off because he was not in the mood to be watching what he said in her presence. Banks let him speak freely, but Ivy wasn't having it. He tried his best to refrain from using bad language around her, but it didn't always work.

"Are you serious right now RJ? I've been your friend for years and you talk to me like that over somebody that you've only known for a few months," Kassidy said sadly.

"I don't give a fuck how long I've known her, you're not about to stand here and disrespect her. This is my girlfriend and the mother of my son. You really got this friendship shit twisted," RJ replied.

"I told the bitch when she first got here that she couldn't come inside. I guess she thought that shit was sweet because she was with Ivy," Marlee noted.

"You don't even live here. This is RJ's house, not yours!" Kassidy yelled.

"There he is. Go ahead, ask him if you can come in. I dare you," Marlee smirked.

"Just go home Kassidy. I didn't invite you here for a reason," RJ said, making her eyes fill with tears that soon fell.

"We've been best friends for years RJ. Why are you letting her do this to us?" Kassidy cried.

"Bitch! There is no us. It's me, him, and in one more month, our son. You've spent years hiding behind the best friend title because you knew that he didn't want your stupid ass. He's had numerous girlfriends during your friendship and you've never been one of them. That should have told you a lot right there. And if that wasn't enough, you stooped even lower and tried to become someone who you're obviously not. No matter how many fucked up haircuts you try to get, you will never be Marlee. Delusional ass hoe," Marlee spat angrily before walking away.

RJ only shook his head in pity right before closing the door in her face. Kassidy felt like a fool as she turned around and headed back to her car. Ivy was standing there looking at her, but she never made a move to comfort her. She really did like Kassidy, but she didn't want to interfere in her son's business. Kassidy had obviously overstepped her boundaries and she didn't want to get in the middle.

Kassidy asked Ivy if she wanted her to help her bring a box of cupcakes in the house. Ivy told her that she had it covered, but Kassidy followed behind her anyway. As soon as Marlee saw her walking in behind Ivy, she jumped up from the table and blocked her path. Ivy didn't know what was said after that, but Marlee punched Kassidy so hard that Ivy had to help her up from the ground. She hurriedly jumped in between them, making sure that they didn't fight.

"You can't be fighting people while you're pregnant Marlee. That shit ain't a good look," RJ said once they saw Desi, Murk, and Desmond off. His parents were still there, but they were about to leave too.

"I didn't fight that bitch. I hit her, and she hit the ground," Marlee clarified with a shrug.

"Just chill out Marlee. At least give our son a chance to get here in one piece. You don't have to entertain every situation," RJ replied.

"Was I supposed to let that bitch play with me and come in here after I told her that she couldn't?" Marlee asked.

"That's not what I'm saying, but you didn't have to hit her. I just want you to think about our son in every situation before you react," RJ reasoned.

"Okay RJ. I'll give everybody a pass for the sake of our son," Marlee swore.

"That's all that I ask. You know I love you, right?" RJ asked, saying what he'd felt since the first night they spent together.

"I love you too." Marlee smiled and blushed. "But as soon as I drop this load and heal up, your best friend gon' get these hands."

"Fuck Kassidy and everybody else. I'm trying to get some," RJ said as he pulled her dress down over her shoulders and started kissing her neck.

"Ooh, my baby daddy is nasty," Marlee said as she tugged at his belt buckle.

He wasted no time helping her out of her clothes, right before she turned around and put her palms flat on the dresser. RJ came up behind her and kissed her neck while entering her at the same time.

"Shit. I swear, this shit gets better every time," he hissed as he stoked her long and slow.

RJ didn't know when or if his parents left because he and Marlee stayed locked up in the bedroom until the next afternoon. Kassidy tried calling his phone a few times, but he blocked her number. He didn't have time for the drama and he wasn't losing his girl over a friendship that was built on lies. He was good on her and anybody else who tried to come in between them.

Chapter 28

"Does she live there with him?" Yanni asked Kallie as they spoke over the phone.

Kallie didn't tell her that she'd gone to Marlee's baby shower, but she was on a lot of the pictures. She had been following RJ since she started working for him and his father. He had posted tons of pictures and videos from the shower and Yanni was shocked when she found out that it was held at his house. She was still having a hard time trying to figure out how Marlee and RJ knew each other at all. When they saw him in the mall a while ago, they didn't let on that they were familiar with each other, so she was baffled.

"I don't know, but he has a beautiful home. The shower was nice too," Kallie replied.

"I can't believe that you went after how you said she talked to you," Yanni instigated.

"I know she said some things out of anger, but we're good now," Kallie noted.

She didn't bother telling Yanni that Marlee didn't invite her. She wasn't in the mood to hear the negativity. It was getting old and she was over it.

"Are they together or just having a baby together?" Yanni was curious to know.

"They're in a relationship. It says so on their Instagram. They make a really cute couple too," Kallie acknowledged.

"I'm trying to see how though. RJ was just in a relationship with somebody else. She used to come to the job all the time. They were together for years," Yanni said.

"I don't know Yanni. Maybe they broke up and he got with Marlee," Kallie reasoned.

"Marlee is eight months pregnant and I know for a fact that it hasn't been that long since his girlfriend has been to the office. That bitch was talking about me, but she must have been fucking somebody else's man too."

Yanni knew without a doubt that RJ's girlfriend was at her job at least three months ago because she talked to her. She remembered the other woman asking her how many months she was and what she was having. Two weeks later was when she saw Marlee in their break room and that's why she was shocked to know that RJ was her baby's father. That bitch Marlee had managed to snag one of the hottest niggas in New Orleans. And if that wasn't enough, she was having his first son. She just kept winning and Yanni didn't know how or why.

"I don't think so. You know Marlee is not like that," Kallie said, interrupting Yanni's hate filled thoughts.

"Girl please. Marlee ain't fooling nobody. She's not as perfect as y'all think she is," Yanni replied.

"I really don't care. I just want our family to go back to the way it was. I hated that you and Marlee weren't at each other's baby showers," Kallie replied.

"Girl bye. You were dumb as hell for going to that shit after the way you said she talked to you," Yanni snapped.

"I didn't hold that against her because she was upset. She was arguing with Tyson and she just snapped. We talked about it and moved on. I hope y'all can do the same one day."

"Don't hold your breath boo. You'll die before that happens," Yanni laughed sarcastically.

"Would you be open to it if she wanted to?" Kallie asked.

"Seriously Kallie? Do you honestly think that things will ever go back to the way they were? You can't possibly be that dumb. My baby will always be a constant reminder of what happened between us. Every time she sees my daughter, she'll see Tyson," Yanni noted.

"Did that fat dog ever get out of jail?" Kallie asked.

"No, but things are looking good for him. He was only caught with a small amount of marijuana. They probably just assumed he smokes it and not sell it," Yanni replied.

"I can't believe that you're even talking to him, especially since he hasn't done shit for your daughter," Kallie said.

"He was in jail when our daughter was born Kallie. How could he do anything?" Yanni questioned.

"That nigga didn't do shit when he was out, and you were pregnant. I bet if he was still free, you wouldn't even hear from him. Isn't he back with his ex-wife? Why can't he call her?" Kallie countered.

"He's not back with her and he said he doesn't know why she was telling people that," Yanni defended.

"I guess you don't know then. And you called me dumb?" Kallie giggled.

"Don't know what?" Yanni questioned.

"His ex-wife got locked up with him. That's probably the only reason why he was calling you. I'm sure he asked you to do something for him. I know his sad ass wasn't calling you just to talk," Kallie answered.

"Who told you that?" Yanni asked.

"More than one person. Everybody has been talking about it," Kallie replied, making Yanni mad.

She should have known that Tyson was on some bullshit. He up and called her out the blue and apologized for not being there like he was supposed to. He swore that he wanted to be a good father to their daughter and that was all that Yanni ever wanted. She wasn't dumb enough to think that her and Tyson would be together, but her daughter deserved a father. He told her everything that he thought she wanted to hear before getting to the real reason for his call. Kallie was right, and he did want something. One of his boys had some money for him and he needed Yanni to pick it up and drop it off to his lawyer. Yanni was pissed to know that she was probably helping to not only get him out of jail, but his ex-wife too. She was in a foul mood and no longer wanted to talk to Kallie.

"I'll talk to you later Kallie. I want to take a nap before my baby wakes up," Yanni said before she hung up the phone.

She scrolled through her phone until she came across Craig's number. He was the male version of Kallie and he told everything that he heard. Yanni and Craig used to kick it a few years back and they'd recently hooked up again. She knew that he was Tyson's sister's man, but she didn't give a damn. Trinity couldn't stand her, so she had fun fucking her man while pregnant with her brother's baby.

"What's up sexy? You trying to see me or what?" Craig asked when he answered the phone.

"No, nigga. Did you forget that I just had a baby not too long ago?" Yanni asked.

"That ain't got shit to do with your mouth," Craig replied.

"Tell me something good and I just might," Yanni cooed seductively.

"Tell you something like what?" Craig asked.

Yanni didn't want to come right out and say what she wanted to say, so she took a different approach, knowing that Craig would correct her if she was wrong.

"How did you get out of jail so fast? I heard that you and Tyson got locked up together. Let me find out you a snitch," Yanni said.

"You got me fucked up. I'll do a life sentence before I snitch on somebody. I don't know who told you that, but they got it wrong my baby. Tyson got locked up with Taj. She's out now, but that nigga got a probation hold on him," Craig clarified.

"Oh okay. I knew they had you wrong. I said my boo ain't no damn snitch," Yanni said, trying to butter him up.

"You already know that my baby. But, what's up with it. I'm trying to see what that mouth do," Craig replied.

"I got you, boo. We'll talk later," Yanni said before she hung up the phone.

She had no intentions on calling him back or hooking up with him. He told her what she needed to know, and she had no more use for him. Admittedly, Yanni felt like a fool. Tyson had her believing that he was ready to man up and do right by his daughter, but he was just playing her for a fool. Yanni didn't know all the details about his relationship with Marlee, but he surely had her fooled. The way he treated Marlee was what made her want Tyson for herself. When she got pregnant, she really thought she'd hit the jackpot. As it turned out, she'd taken a gamble and lost.

***

RJ drove in silence, ignoring the many times that Marlee looked over at him. He had just picked her up from her mother's house and the frown on his face let her know exactly how he felt. She and RJ had their first real argument as a couple the night before and he was clearly still upset about it. Marlee had said some things that she shouldn't have said, and she knew that she owed him an apology. After telling Desi some of the things that she had told him, her cousin agreed that an apology was needed. Still, being the stubborn bitch that she was sometimes known to be, Marlee hadn't given it yet. Instead, she got mad about the attitude that he was displaying.

"You didn't have to come with me you know. Sierra was willing to come help me set up," Marlee said.

"I don't have a problem coming to help you set up," RJ replied flatly.

"Well, you need to lose the attitude because I don't have time for it," Marlee replied.

"And I don't have time for my eight months pregnant girlfriend to be trying to work two jobs like I'm a broke ass nigga who can't provide for her," RJ snapped.

"Where did that even come from? I never said that you couldn't provide for me. I told you that this lady booked and paid for her wedding months ago," Marlee replied.

Usually, she'd require half down if she was doing a wedding. The bride who she was going to service now had paid her entire fee upfront. Marlee wasn't one to play games, so she was on her way to do what she was already paid to do. She couldn't imagine standing a bride up on her wedding day. She had worked too hard to make a good name for herself.

"I get that Marlee, but that's not my only issue. On some real shit, I'm still pissed about our conversation from last night. I need you to understand that this baby that you're carrying is not just yours and you can't make decisions for him by yourself. We're gonna have some serious problems if you're not willing to compromise," RJ fussed.

"I know that he's not just mine and I don't have a problem with compromising. You never even gave me a chance to say anything before you went off," Marlee replied.

"Yeah, I went off because you go too far. Whatever we discussed had nothing to do with my mama and daddy and you should have left them out of it. I wanna do for you because I'm your man and you're about to have my first son next month. It has nothing to do with me trying to make you a kept bitch and you were wrong for even saying that shit," RJ argued.

"I know and I apologize," Marlee said, giving him the apology that he was due.

She was wrong, and she could admit that. When he kept talking about buying her a house, she got mad and told him that she wasn't his mother and she didn't want to be his kept bitch. That was unnecessary, and she regretted the words as soon as they left her mouth.

"I was raised to be a man, Marlee. I don't care how many jobs you have, I'm still gonna take care of you. That's what my pops taught me to do and I'm not apologizing for that."

"I know baby and I didn't mean it that way. I have no problem with moving into my own house once the baby is born. I'm just not in the mood to go through the whole looking for a house and moving thing right now."

"I understand that," RJ said, nodding his head in agreement.

"This is my last makeup job for a while and I'll take maternity leave from work too. I just don't want to argue anymore," Marlee said, agreeing to everything that he asked her to do.

"Me either. I couldn't even sleep last night," RJ admitted.

"Well, I won't lie and say that. I slept good as fuck," Marlee said, making him laugh.

"I love you, baby," RJ said as he leaned over the seat and kissed her.

"I love you too, boo." Marlee smiled as they continued to their destination.

She had a total of six ladies to do, including the bride, and then she was putting her equipment away for a while. Hopefully, she would be in her own house by the time she went back to work, and she would have a permanent place to store her work supplies. She agreed to stay with RJ for two weeks after she had the baby and then they were going back home.

"I got everything. Just get your purse," RJ said when they pulled up to the building next to the church

According to the bride, the building next door was used for them to relax and get themselves together before the wedding. There was an area that connected the building to the church so that they didn't have to walk outside.

"Okay, let me go look for the bride," Marlee said as she wobbled away.

She was comfortable in a black maternity jumper with some black flats. She had on a makeup smock with her name on the front and her business card printed on the back. Marlee walked up to the door and got ready to knock, but it opened before she had a chance to.

"Can I help you?" an older woman smiled and asked.

"Yes, I'm Marlee, the makeup artist," Marlee replied with a smile of her own.

"Oh, yes, I'm Mary, the mother of the bride. She's right in here waiting on you," Mary replied as she ushered her inside.

"Oh, my boyfriend is right behind me with my supplies," Marlee noted.

"Okay, I'll leave the door open for him," Mary replied.

She walked Marlee over to her daughter and watched as they spoke and talked briefly. She showed Marlee where she could set up at as she went to get her bridesmaids. A few minutes later, RJ walked in with her chair and light. He went back out to get her cosmetic cases and started to help her set up. When the bride walked back in a few minutes later with two other women, time seemed to have stood still.

"Hey RJ. How are you?" Aspen's cousin, Rosalyn, asked, making Marlee turn to look at him.

"What's up?" RJ spoke as he looked at Marlee with questioning eyes.

Aspen's sisters, Blythe and Anisa, spoke to him too, right as Aspen walked in with her other two cousins.

"Is this a fucking joke?" Aspen asked when she walked in and saw RJ and Marlee standing there.

Aspen could have screamed when she saw her ex with his new girlfriend, standing there surrounded by her family. She hadn't even told them about her and RJ's breakup yet, but it was all out in the open now.

"Who's going first?" Marlee asked, trying to remain professional and ignore the tension in the room.

"I will," one of Aspen's cousins said as she stepped up.

Marlee instructed her to have a seat as she positioned her makeup light right where she needed it to be.

"She's not doing my makeup. I'm sorry cousin, but I'll run to the Mac counter in Dillard's before I let her touch me!" Aspen yelled.

"She don't have to do none of y'all if its gon' be a problem. We can pack up and get the fuck on," RJ replied angrily.

"RJ, no, please. Aspen, stop it. This is my wedding day," Rosalyn pleaded.

"Fuck that! I just won't wear any makeup. You need to make her leave," Aspen replied childishly.

"Fuck this shit. Let's go Marlee. I'll pay you double what you paid her for your trouble Rosalyn, but we're done," RJ fumed.

"Baby, stop. I'm fine," Marlee assured him.

"I'm not about to stand here and let nobody talk crazy to you, Marlee. You ain't hurting for no money," RJ countered.

Rosalyn was having a full-blown panic attack and Marlee felt bad for her. It wasn't even about the money. She didn't want to ruin her wedding day, so she was willing to ignore Aspen and do her job. Rosalyn's mother saw everything unfold, so she pulled Aspen out of the room and into the hall. Rosalyn and Aspen's sisters followed them to see what was going on.

"I'm guessing that's RJ's baby mama," Anisa said, speaking up first.

"She's more than the baby mama honey. She's the girlfriend. Question is, when did you and RJ break up for that to happen?" Blythe asked her.

"None of the matters, just know that we did. I can't believe that you hired her, of all people, to do our makeup for the wedding," Aspen spat angrily as she looked at Rosalyn.

"You were the one who gave me her card," Rosalyn pointed out.

"What? When?" Aspen questioned.

"You gave it to me months ago. You said that you met her when you went to physical therapy and you gave me her card. I looked at some of her work on Instagram and hired her the same day," Rosalyn replied.

"Oh God! How could I have been so stupid?" Aspen questioned as he slapped her forehead.

She remembered the first day that she and Marlee met and she told her about her side job as a makeup artist. She gave Aspen some cards and, like a fool, she passed them out. She knew that her cousin was getting married soon, so she was the first one who she gave one too. Of course, that was before she knew who Marlee was.

"Look, I don't give a flying fuck whose baby mama or girlfriend she is. She's here to do a job that she's been paid to do and she's doing it. You better put your personal feelings to the side Aspen, especially on today. We've spent too much time and money to make this day perfect. You will not ruin it because you're in your feelings," Aspen's aunt, Mary, fussed.

"Aspen, please, just do this for me. This is one of the most important days of my life," Rosalyn begged.

"Ugh!" Aspen groaned in frustration. "Fine, let's just get this over with."

They all walked back into the room and watched as Marlee started on the first bridesmaid. Her work spoke for itself and Rosalyn was pleased with the outcome. She was sure that Marlee would never work with her again after Aspen's stupidity. Even if she wanted to, she was positive that RJ wouldn't let her. Rosalyn thought it was cute how he pulled up a chair right next to her and watched her work. Aspen had a frown on her face the entire time, but no one seemed to care.

"You are very talented," Mary said as she complimented Marlee's work.

She was almost done with the third bridesmaid and they all looked beautiful.

"Thank you," Marlee said, smiling at the compliment.

"What are you having?" Blythe asked her.

"A boy," Marlee replied as she continued to work.

"From a one-night stand," Aspen mumbled loud enough for everyone to hear.

"Bitch-" RJ started before Marlee cut him off.

"RJ, relax. You just told me that every situation doesn't need to be entertained. Ignore her," she said, whispering in his ear.

RJ nodded his head as his jaws clenched in anger. He wasn't one to disrespect a woman, but he was ready to curse his ex-girlfriend out. He was regretting Sierra not being with them because she would have probably knocked Aspen the fuck out and he would have let her do it. RJ's leg bounced in anger as he tried to take the advice that he'd given to Marlee.

"Who's next?" Marlee asked after a little while.

She had done four bridesmaids and Aspen was next. She was dreading having to even touch the other woman, but she really had no choice. Aspen was a pretty girl, but it was hard to tell with the permanent scowl that seemed to be etched on her face.

"Don't make me look like a clown," Aspen snapped once Marlee had cleaned her face.

"Too late. Goofy looking muthafucka," RJ mumbled.

"Baby stop," Marlee scolded once again as she looked at him with pleading eyes.

She started working on Aspen's makeup as everyone stood around and talked. Aspen hated that Marlee's stomach kept touching her arm, but it was too big not to. She cringed as she listened to her and RJ talk like they were so in love. They kept calling each other baby and Aspen wanted to vomit. When Marlee was finally finished, she tried to hand Aspen the mirror to see the finished product, but she declined. Instead, she went to a mirror that was on the wall to look at her reflection instead.

"You look beautiful cousin," Rosalyn complimented as she got into the chair.

"It looks okay," Aspen spat as she sat down next to her sister.

Marlee started on Rosalyn's makeup as everyone else stood around and watched. She made small talk with the bride, but she was happy that it was almost time for them to leave. RJ was still angry, and she had to calm him down before he snapped on somebody.

"It's almost that time for two to be joined as one," Mary said when she walked back into the room and saw that everyone's makeup was done. Rosalyn was getting lashes put on and her lipstick was the only thing left.

"Yes, and I can't wait," Rosalyn replied.

"Be careful of who you trust cousin. Some of these bitches be quick to try to knock somebody else out of the picture, just so they can be in the frame," Aspen spat bitterly.

"I don't know what you mean by that, but Carter and I are good. We've had problems in the past, but cheating was never the cause of them," Rosalyn said.

"Well, that's good, even though I can't relate. A relationship is meant for two people, but some of these hoes can't count," Aspen replied with a wicked smirk.

"That's enough Aspen," her auntie warned.

"I'm just saying auntie. You can't expect to get treated like number one when you're so comfortable playing the role of number two." Aspen shrugged, directing all of her comments towards Marlee, who only chuckled.

RJ was about to comment, but he was happy that Marlee beat him to it. He was proud of her for remaining professional, but she was obviously tired of Aspen too.

"Stop watering dead plants my love. If he wanted you in his life, he would have made room for you to stay there. Maybe he got tired of the rhinestones and decided to get a diamond instead. And I don't do numbers baby. I'm not his number one, I'm his only one," Marlee replied in her own defense.

She was done with work, so professionalism went out the window. She didn't care if Rosalyn or none of the other ladies ever wanted to use her again. She was good either way. Aspen had her fucked up, eighth month pregnant belly and all.

"Bitch!" Aspen said as she jumped up and tried to get at her.

Her aunt was right there to hold her back and make her behave.

"Please let her go so she can do it. I'll forget everything that I was ever taught about never hitting a woman and knock her the fuck out," RJ threatened.

"Fuck you, RJ! After all the years we were together and that's how you do me. You don't even know her!" Aspen screamed as tears rolled down her cheeks.

She was ruining her makeup, but that was all on her. Marlee wouldn't have fixed it, even if they paid her to.

"Aspen, stop this. You're ruining your makeup and making a fool of yourself," her auntie scolded.

"I didn't deserve that, and you know it! Five fucking years of my life wasted and that's how you do me!" Aspen screamed, never noticing that Aaron had walked in and was watching.

RJ locked eyes with the other man, but he couldn't figure out where he knew him from. Aaron was an hour early for Rosalyn's wedding, but he wanted to drop off the flowers that he'd just purchased for Aspen. He never expected to walk down on her crying and acting a fool over her ex. She was just swearing that they were no longer together the night before. Seeing as how RJ had his arm wrapped around a pregnant woman's waist, he believed that to be true.

"I'm so done with you after today Aspen. I swear on my kids that we're through," Rosalyn said, trying hard to fight back her tears.

She didn't know the entire story behind her and RJ's breakup and she really didn't care. Aspen should have respected her enough to let that shit go for her sake, if nothing else.

"Do you need help? I can help you carry your things out," Aspen's cousin, Nikki, offered.

She needed RJ and Marlee to leave before her cousin's wedding day got ruined even more than it was. Aspen was dead ass wrong for behaving the way she was on Rosalyn's special day.

"No, we're good," RJ said as he sat some stuff outside by the door.

"Thanks for everything and I'm so sorry about what happened," Rosalyn apologized as she walked them out.

"You're welcome and it's okay. Here, you can tell her to pat her face dry with this and she won't mess up her makeup or smear it," Marlee said as she handed her a sponge for Aspen to use.

If there was anyone that she felt sorry for, it was Rosalyn. She was innocent, and she didn't deserve to have her wedding day ruined by RJ's bitter ex. Marlee was willing to put her feelings to the side and help Aspen on the strength of the bride. RJ was looking at her like she was crazy, but she didn't expect him to understand. That was one of the most important days of a woman's life.

"Thank you so much. And despite what happened today, I would love to do business with you in the future," Rosalyn replied.

"You know the number. And congrats again," Marlee said as she and RJ walked away.

"Fuck them! You better not deal with none their asses no more. I don't even want you around Aspen's people. They're guilty by association and I don't trust nobody in that family," RJ fussed when they got into the car.

"I was only being nice, but I'm done with it. I did what I was paid to do, but I'll never do it again," Marlee swore.

"Bitch pissed me off. Talking reckless like I won't pay somebody to beat the fuck out of her," RJ fumed.

All the years that he spent with Aspen meant nothing when it came to her coming for Marlee. Hurting her meant hurting his son, since she was still carrying him.

"That's not even necessary boo. You can just add her name to my list, right next to your bestie's name," Marlee replied.

"What list?" RJ questioned.

"The list of bitches who gon' catch these hands after I have my son," Marlee replied, making him laugh.

Neither of them was ready to go home, so they decided to go out for a bite to eat before going to catch a movie. Marlee couldn't wait to tell Desi and Sierra about her day. She knew that they were gonna be mad that they missed it, but everything happened for a reason. Had her cousin or best friend would have been there, Rosalyn probably wouldn't have even had a wedding. She was hoping that things worked out for her, but she had Aspen to blame if they didn't.

Chapter 29

It took Kassidy forever, but she was finally able to find a place to park. The nail salon that she went to was always crowded and it seemed as if that Saturday was no exception. They never took long, so she didn't mind waiting a little while. It wasn't like she had anything better to do. She hadn't talked to RJ in weeks, but she still followed him on social media. Apparently, Marlee was due to have their son any day now and he was doing a countdown. RJ posted a picture of Marlee every day with a caption saying how he couldn't wait until the big day arrived. He showed pictures of his son's nursery, as well as a lot of other things that he'd purchased for him. Kassidy's feelings were still hurt about how he treated her, but it was her own fault. She would do anything to get her best friend back, but she knew that Marlee would never allow that.

"Hi, I need a full set and a pedicure," Kassidy said when she walked into the salon. All the pedicure chairs were full, but she did notice that a few people were getting polished.

It took about fifteen minutes before three chairs became available. Kassidy was led to the very last chair, where she was instructed to sit and soak her feet. The nail techs were all busy, but she didn't mind letting her feet relax in the warm water. She closed her eyes and relaxed in the oversized plush seats. When another woman walked in and asked for a pedicure a few minutes later, Kassidy never even opened her eyes to see who it was. That was, until she heard a man's voice close by.

"I'm going to get some gas and some money from the ATM. I'll be back in a minute," the man said before placing a kiss on Aspen's lips.

She frowned when he pulled away, but he obviously didn't see her. Aaron was becoming an even bigger pain in her ass and she was over him already. Since her cousin's wedding a few weeks ago, he had been on some bullshit about her and RJ. Aspen had enough to worry about with her entire family being mad with her. She wasn't trying to get into it with Aaron too.

"Hi Aspen," Kassidy spoke when Aspen was put into the chair next to hers.

"Girl, bye. Since when did you start speaking to me?" Aspen questioned with her lips turned up.

"Well, excuse me for trying to be friendly," Kassidy replied.

"Newsflash sweetie, we were never friends. RJ is your friend, even though you wanted him to be more," Aspen smirked.

"He was my friend," Kassidy said, putting emphasis on the word was.

"What do you mean was?" Aspen asked while turning slightly in her chair to face the other woman.

She'd wanted RJ to end his friendship with Kassidy years ago, but he never did. He was either a great actor or he was oblivious to the feelings that she had for him. Kassidy used to look at RJ like a love-sick puppy, but he never paid her any mind.

"Me and his new girlfriend had it out and he took her side. That crazy bitch hit me, and he told me to leave," Kassidy said as she ran the entire story down to her.

"When?" Aspen questioned.

"At her baby shower," Kassidy replied.

"I would have knocked that bitch the fuck out, baby and all," Aspen fumed.

"Girl, he probably would have killed me. I've been friends with RJ for years and I've never seen him look at me like that before. I don't doubt that he would have hit me over her," Kassidy replied.

Aspen knew all too well what she meant because she felt the exact same way. RJ looked like he was ready to lay her out when she tried to get at Marlee. That was what hurt her the most. The hateful look in his eyes was enough to let her know how he really felt. She didn't see any of the love that she saw when they were together. Granted, RJ was honest and told her that he wasn't in love with her. She just never imagined that it would take less than a year for him to fall in love with another woman.

"What did Ivy do? Isn't she the one who invited you?" Aspen asked.

"Yeah, but she didn't really do anything. She just stayed out of it." Kassidy shrugged.

"That bitch ain't no good. She put me out of her house talking about it was nothing personal. Fuck her and her son. She's the president of the side bitches club. I don't know why I expected anything different from her," Aspen ranted.

"What happened with you and RJ?" Kassidy asked.

"His baby mama is what happened," she replied, refusing to elaborate.

She would never give Kassidy the satisfaction of knowing that RJ left her for another woman. That bitch would have been all too happy to hear that.

"I just can't believe that he let a woman that he barely knows turn his life upside down like that. She ruined his relationship with you and his friendship with me. Bitch standing there like she's the woman of the house," Kassidy argued.

"Does she live there?" Aspen wanted to know.

"She must live there if she's calling the shots like that. I mean, he didn't even try to see what happened before he went off. He basically said fuck me and our friendship. I was so hurt," Kassidy replied.

"I know you were, especially since you're in love with him," Aspen snickered.

"He was my best friend, Aspen. Of course, I love him. If you're trying to insinuate something more than that, then you're sadly mistaken," Kassidy replied.

"Yeah okay. And I guess that haircut has nothing to do with you trying to look like his girlfriend. No need to lie to me, sweetie. You're Marlee's problem now," Aspen noted, as Kassidy patted her hair.

She couldn't even lie; Marlee's mohawk was the shit, but Kassidy's was a disaster. If she was trying to mimic another bitch, the least she could have done was get it right. The color didn't fit her complexion and the cut was uneven. The shit was just a mess on too many levels. As much as

Aspen loved RJ, she wasn't changing who she was just to please him.

"Yeah right. You can pretend all you want, but you still love RJ. You surely don't seem to be into your new man as much," Kassidy pointed out as she pulled Aspen away from her thoughts.

"Ain't nothing new about Aaron, honey. He was there before, during, and after RJ," Aspen clarified.

"You were cheating on RJ?" Kassidy asked with wide eyes.

"And? His dog ass was obviously cheating on me too. I'm not the one with a baby on the way. And to think that I was willing to give it all up for him. If a one-night stand in Vegas can break us up, then there wasn't all that much there to begin with," Aspen surmised.

"A what! Please tell me that's not how he met her," Kassidy gasped.

"What kind of best friend were you? You don't know shit." Aspen frowned.

"God! What the hell was RJ thinking? Now I see why she seemed to have appeared out of thin air," Kassidy said.

"That's exactly why I keep Aaron in my back pocket. These niggas play too many games. At least I know that I can depend on him and he's not going anywhere. I can have a million niggas, but Aaron will always be the last one standing," Aspen replied.

"How did you find out about Marlee and the baby?" Kassidy asked.

"He told me. They did a test while she was pregnant, just to be sure. You know Banks wasn't letting him claim nothing unless he knew for sure."

"I'm sure he's happy just because it's a boy. To say he wasn't raised in Africa, he sure adapted to some of their customs," Kassidy pointed out.

"He's a sad ass excuse for a man. I never expected him to give RJ any good advice on our relationship, when he treats his side bitch better than his own wife. Lauren is doing the right thing and I hope his face gets cracked in the end," Aspen spat angrily.

"What do you mean?" Kassidy asked.

Aspen hesitated for a minute, but she shrugged it off and proceeded to tell Kassidy what she knew. She and RJ weren't friends anymore, so she wasn't worried about her saying anything. Kassidy sat there with her mouth agape as she listened to what Aspen was saying. To say that she was shocked was an understatement. Apparently, Lauren was fed up with her husband's antics and she should have been a long time ago. Kassidy was surprised that Aspen was talking so freely, but she soaked up her words like a sponge. She was wondering how she could get back in RJ's good graces and Aspen had just given it to her. Once she told him what was going on, their friendship would be stronger than ever. She was even willing to get along with Marlee, if that meant getting her friend back.

***

"I'm stopping to get gas and then I'll be on my way once I drop Murk off," RJ said over the phone to Marlee.

"Okay, let me find some sweats to throw on. Does she know that we're coming over there?" Marlee asked, speaking of Ivy.

"Nah, I didn't tell her. I wanted her to be surprised," RJ replied.

"That's so sweet baby. She's gonna be so happy," Marlee said.

"That's my goal," RJ said as he noticed that someone was watching him.

He talked to Marlee for a few more minutes before he hung up and told his cousin what he noticed. It finally came to RJ where he knew the man from. He was at Aspen's auntie's house for her birthday and he had showed up to the church building the day of Rosalyn's wedding. The nigga looked crazy as fuck and he was creeping RJ out with the way he was staring. Niggas didn't do no shit like that, so that was a red flag. Murk was staring right back at him, but he wasn't with the bullshit. He threw his hands up like he was asking him what was up.

"Do we know you, my nigga?" Murk asked the other man.

He blinked a few times and seemed to have come out of the trance that he was in.

"The fuck. This nigga is crazy," RJ mumbled, as the man shook his head like he was trying to shake away his thoughts.

"You're RJ, right?" the man asked as he looked at him.

"Who wants to know?" RJ asked.

"I already know who you are. Do you know who I am?" the man asked as he fidgeted nervously.

"No, my dude. Who are you?" RJ asked.

"This nigga is off his shit cuz. Look at him. Muthafucka standing there looking like Cuba Gooding when he played Radio," Murk said as he gripped his gun.

"I'm Aaron," the other man said, like RJ was supposed to know.

"Aaron who?" RJ asked, clearly making the other man upset.

"So, she's never told you anything about me?" Aaron questioned.

"Who is she?" RJ asked as he put a calming hand on Murk's shoulder.

His cousin was ready to snap, and he didn't need that. They were at a semi-crowded gas station with witnesses and cameras.

"Oh, my fault. I'm Aspen's fiancé," Aaron said as he extended his hand out for RJ to shake.

"What's up bruh? If you're coming at me on some bullshit about your girl, you can kill that noise right now. I'm in a relationship with somebody else and we're expecting a baby any day now. Aspen and I are done, and we always will be. I'm very happy with my girl and I don't want nothing else to do with yours," RJ assured him.

For the first time since he'd seen him, RJ saw some normalcy in Aaron. The crazed looked in his eyes had disappeared and was replaced with a genuine smile.

"I knew you were a good man when I first saw you. Thank you for clearing that up. Have a good day and congrats on the baby," Aaron said as he grabbed his hand and shook it.

Aaron was happy as hell to know that RJ was all the way out of the picture. In his mind, he was the only thing stopping him and Aspen from being happy. He thought that he was going to have to get rid of RJ, but there was no need for that now. He saw him with the pregnant girl the day of Rosalyn's wedding and he was happy to know that RJ had moved on. He was building a life with someone else and that was music to Aaron's ears. Now, he and Aspen could get married and start the family that he'd always wanted.

Aaron wanted to be a great father, especially since he didn't have one. He wanted to give his kids the life that he wasn't fortunate enough to live, with a mother and father under the same roof.

RJ and Murk watched as he hopped in a Jeep and sped away. That was weird as hell and RJ didn't know how to take the encounter. He didn't say anything, but he knew exactly who Aaron was. Aspen told him all about her family basically raising him and all the years that they spent together as a couple. RJ wanted to hear what he had to say, so he pretended not to know him. The fact that he introduced himself as Aspen's fiancé was hilarious. Aspen must have really been desperate for a husband to be marrying his crazy ass. That nigga was unstable, and it didn't take a genius to figure that out.

"You know I gotta kill that nigga, right?" Murk questioned when they got back into the car and pulled off.

"For what? Being crazy? A lot of muthafuckas should be dead in that case," RJ replied.

"Dog, that nigga is a different kind of crazy. Did you see the way he was looking at you? Then, he snapped out of it and started acting normal. That nigga is possessed. I might need a silver bullet to take him out!" Murk yelled.

"You watch too much tv nigga. Now, I admit that dude ain't right, but it ain't nothing that a little medicine can't fix." RJ shrugged as he drove Murk back to his car.

Murk was still going off about killing Aaron when RJ dropped him off to his car that was parked at Desi's apartment complex. Once his cousin was gone, RJ headed to Marlee's house to get her. He went inside to get the bag that she had, before they left to go to his mother's house. He told Marlee all about the strange encounter with Aspen's man. Just like him, Marlee thought that it was strange, but she didn't know what to make of it. She did feel like Aspen was probably dealing with them at the same time, and RJ agreed. There was no way Aaron would be doing so much if she wasn't. She was going crazy about him dealing with Marlee and she was probably doing the same thing. He really didn't care because he had who he wanted, and it wasn't Aspen.

"I hope Ivy got some food in here," Marlee said when they pulled up to Ivy's house.

"Why didn't you say something? I can go get you something to eat right quick," RJ offered.

"No, that's okay. I don't want y'all to be late. I'll get something later," Marlee replied.

She waited until RJ came around and opened her door. He didn't bother knocking or ringing the doorbell. He used his key and they both entered his mother's home. Ivy was sprawled out on the sofa with a bunch of junk food on the table in front of her.

"Hey. What are y'all doing here?" Ivy asked as she sat up and smiled.

"Are you sharing?" Marlee asked as she picked up the bag of chips and started eating.

"I can kiss my snacks goodbye now," Ivy chuckled.

"You already know," RJ agreed while shaking his head.

"When is my grandson coming? I'm ready to spoil him," Ivy said.

"Me too," RJ admitted.

"I wish he would come today. I feel like I've been pregnant for a year," Marlee said.

"It won't be much longer. Your stomach has really dropped," Ivy pointed out.

"That's what my mama said too," Marlee replied.

"You look nice baby. Where are you going all dressed up and stuff?" Ivy asked as she admired the Ralph Lauren slacks, sweater, and loafers that her son was wearing.

"On a date," RJ replied with a smile.

"Well, why is Marlee sitting here wearing sweats and pigging out on junk food and not dressed to go?" Ivy asked.

"Marlee is not my date," RJ answered.

"Excuse me? If she's not your date, then who is?" Ivy asked.

"You are," RJ smirked.

"What?" Ivy asked in confusion.

"Get up and get yourself together. Marlee is here to do your makeup. I made dinner reservations," RJ answered.

"Are you serious?" Ivy asked as her heart swelled with joy and her eyes filled with tears.

"Yes. Just me and you and a night out on the town," RJ replied.

"Oh baby. This is so sweet of you. I have the perfect dress too. Give me a minute to take a quick shower and put it on," Ivy said as she raced up the stairs to her bedroom.

"Aww, she's so happy. You're so sweet RJ," Marlee said as she planted a sloppy kiss on his lips.

"I try." RJ smiled.

It was his father and Lauren's anniversary and they had taken their annual vacation. They were in Hawaii and weren't due back for three more days. RJ knew that his mother was bored out of her mind and he wanted to do something special for her. He came up with a mother-son date night, and Ivy seemed to be happy with the idea. Marlee offered to help make her beautiful and he appreciated her help.

"How do I look?" Ivy asked when she walked downstairs a little while later wearing a dark grey bodycon dress that she paired with red shoes and accessories.

"You look so cute Ivy. Come sit down so I can do your face," Marlee said as she stood to her feet.

"You had me scared for a minute boy. Talking about Marlee wasn't your date," Ivy laughed.

"I don't want to cut your only son, but I will," Marlee threatened, making RJ laugh.

"I'm a one-woman man and you're it," RJ said as he kissed her cheek and made her blush.

Once Ivy's makeup was done, Marlee took a few pictures of them before they all left. RJ stopped to get her something to eat before bringing her back home. Ivy looked beautiful and she couldn't stop smiling. She was really going to be excited when she saw that RJ had purchased front row tickets to the Motown review. Ivy loved her old school music, so she was guaranteed to have a good time. Marlee's mother and stepfather had gone the night before and they really enjoyed themselves. Ivy wasn't perfect, but she was a great mother. RJ didn't agree with some of the decisions that she made, but he didn't have to. She was grown and did whatever she wanted to do. He just wanted to put a smile on her face, the same as she'd always done for him. His mother deserved that and so much more.

Chapter 30

RJ parked his truck in his assigned spot and killed the engine. He had a bunch of paperwork in his hand that he needed to go over with his father. Banks had come back from his trip the day before, but RJ didn't want to bother him. His father had him going over some discrepancies in a few of his bank accounts and some things just weren't adding up. RJ sighed deeply and proceeded to get out and get the dreadful conversation over with.

"Hey RJ?" Yanni smiled as she looked at him like he was her favorite dessert.

He tried hard not to frown at her, but he couldn't stand her nasty ass. After what she did to Marlee, he was ready to fire her, just so he didn't have to look in her face again. Marlee told him to let it go and that was the only reason why she was still there.

"What's up?" RJ said, giving her his signature two-word greeting.

He didn't have anything more to say, so he kept walking. He was shocked but annoyed when Yanni said something else to him.

"Did Marlee have her baby yet?" Yanni asked.

"Why do you even care?" RJ asked as he turned around to face her.

"You do know that we're cousins, right?" Yanni had the nerve to ask, like that was supposed to mean something to him.

"And? Being her cousin didn't stop you from getting pregnant by her nigga, did it? Don't ask me shit about my girl because she don't fuck with you and neither do I. You're here to do a job and nothing more. Keep that friendly shit away from the work place," RJ said, shocking her with his tone.

Aside from speaking when she spoke first, RJ had never uttered a single word to her. She wasn't even surprised that Marlee told him what transpired between them. She pretended like she didn't care, but she was still a bitter bitch. She had a fine ass nigga with money, but she was still in her feelings about Tyson.

"Fuck him," Yanni mumbled as she walked back outside to her booth.

RJ continued down the hall and straight to his father's office. Banks was sitting behind his desk with his focus on the computer screen. When he looked up and saw his son, he removed his glasses and stood to his feet. He had a huge smile covering his face as he opened his arms and pulled RJ into a bone crushing hug.

"Damn pops. You must have really missed a nigga. What was that for?" RJ asked once he released him.

"I did miss you, but that wasn't what the hug was for. Your mother told me what you and Marlee did for her, and I appreciate it. You know I love to see her happy and y'all made it happen. She sent me the pictures that y'all took and she can't stop talking about it. She said that Marlee made her look ten years younger," Banks laughed.

"Yeah, she had a good time and she deserved it," RJ replied.

"I couldn't agree more." Banks nodded.

"Did you have fun?" RJ asked with a smirk.

"Do I ever?" Banks grumbled.

"I might be out of line, but I just don't get it. You claim that you're so in love with my mama, but you're still married to Lauren. I just couldn't see myself being miserable with Aspen, knowing that Marlee was who I wanted."

"It's not that simple for me though, son. No, I don't love Lauren nearly as much as I love your mother. Honestly, I don't love her at all and that's no secret. I just can't repay her loyalty with betrayal. She went against her family and came here with only the shirt on her back, just to be with me. Some things you just don't forget. I never dreamed that I would meet and fall in love with another woman while I was married, but it happened. I would have loved to walk down the aisle with your mother, but it just didn't happen that way," Banks said with a far-off look in his eyes.

"Yeah, that's life." RJ shrugged.

"I see my grandson is still not ready to meet me yet. Today would have been the perfect day too." Banks smiled as he stared off.

"No, man, and I wish he hurry his ass up. My girl is miserable as hell. All she wants to do is lay around the house now," RJ replied.

"Whose house?" Banks asked with raised brows.

"It damn sure ain't mine, with her stubborn ass," RJ frowned.

Marlee was unlike any other woman that he'd ever been with. Anybody else would have been happy to share space with him, but not her. She refused to move in with him and she barely spent the night. She was content with living with her mother and he just didn't get that.

"I see you still haven't taken my advice," Banks pointed out.

"I don't even want to talk about that right now. I got a few things to run by you," RJ said as he pulled the paperwork from the folder that he had and laid it out on the desk.

"This doesn't sound too good," Banks said as he put his glasses back on.

"That depends on what you call good. I looked into all four of your accounts and only one of them seemed to be off," RJ noted.

"How off?" Banks questioned.

"Like seventy-five grand," RJ replied, dreading his father's response.

"Seventy-five thousand dollars!" Banks shouted as he stood to his feet.

"Calm down pops," RJ urged.

"A few dollars is off, but seventy-five grand is a big fucking problem. A problem that I need to be fixed now. I knew that something looked strange, but that's crazy. Which account is it?" Banks asked.

That was the question that RJ wasn't prepared to answer. He knew that his father was about to have a fit and he didn't blame him.

"It's the account that you share with my mother," RJ replied as his father looked at him in shock.

"What? No, that must be some kind of mistake. Ivy would never do something like that. I give her whatever she wants, whenever she wants it. She wouldn't need to take that kind of money out of our account."

"I agree, but that's what it says right here in black and white. I drove myself crazy trying to figure the shit out," RJ sighed.

He was up all night and most of the morning going through his father's financial records. Banks had joint accounts with Lauren and Ivy, but his other two accounts were his alone. The one that he had with Ivy had the most money and that's why his father didn't catch the mistake as fast. Ivy probably figured that Banks wouldn't notice since it was so much money in there, but he did. He couldn't figure out what was going on at first, but that was his own fault. Banks had so much money and he just spent it without care. RJ was always on him about managing his accounts, but he never listened. It took something happening for him to finally take heed. RJ just didn't know what to make of it all. He didn't understand what Ivy needed that kind of money for.

"I don't care that she spent it. I just want to know what she spent it on," Banks replied.

"Yeah, that's what I want to know too," RJ admitted.

"Does it show that on the statements?" Banks asked.

That was yet another issue that RJ wasn't prepared to address. Ivy had been writing out checks to people that he'd never heard of before. The checks ranged from five hundred to fifteen hundred and had dated back a few months. That was probably why it took his father so long to notice it. The latest check was for five thousand and that's what had his father questioning things. RJ accompanied Banks to his banks and had a rep to pull up statements dating back to six months ago. Something just wasn't right, and he needed to get to the bottom of it.

"Yeah, but I don't know any of these people that the checks were made out to," RJ said, answering his father's question after a long uncomfortable pause.

He handed his father the manila envelope with copies of the cashed checks inside.

"Checks!" Banks yelled. "Ivy doesn't even use checks. She hates them. And who the hell are these people that she's giving my money to?"

"I don't know pops. I've never heard of any of them. This shit is crazy and not like my mama at all," RJ noted.

"I need to get out of here and go talk to your mother. She better have a damn good reason as to why she's giving strange people so much money. I don't mind her helping people out, but seventy-five thousand is a lot of damn help," Banks said as he shut his computer down and prepared to leave.

"Yeah, I need to get back to Marlee. I don't like to leave her alone for too long since she's so close," RJ said as he followed him out.

They both walked down the hall, but RJ stopped when he saw Kassidy standing there talking to Joy.

"There he is," Joy said with her usual attitude when she saw RJ coming from the back. She had the phone in her hand preparing to buzz her father's office for her brother, but she didn't have to.

"What are you doing here Kassidy?" RJ asked with a scowl.

"I um, I needed to talk to you about something," Kassidy said as she nervously played with the hem of her shirt.

"We don't have anything to talk about and make this your last time coming here," RJ snapped angrily.

He wasn't for the bullshit with Kassidy and she needed to keep it pushing. She had been on some shady shit lately and he didn't have time for it. When she made the comment under his picture on Instagram, he started to embarrass her and curse her out. Instead, he took a different route and put her in her place the right way.

"It's really important RJ. I need your father to hear it too," Kassidy replied.

"What do you need me to hear?" Banks asked curiously.

"It's kind of personal," Kassidy replied.

Kassidy looked over at Joy, and Banks understood her hesitation. She knew that Joy was close with Aspen and she didn't want her to run back and tell her what she was saying. Joy had answered the phone, so she missed the look that the other woman was giving her.

"Come on back to my office," Banks said as he turned around and led the way.

Kassidy was right behind him, as RJ brought up the rear. He really wasn't interested in what Kassidy had to say but, obviously, his father was. When they walked into his office, Banks offered her a seat as he sat behind his desk. RJ opted to stand because he didn't plan to stay very long.

"What is it that you think I need to hear?" Banks asked as he leaned forward and steepled his fingers.

"Well, I was in the nail salon with Aspen and she told me some interesting things," Kassidy started.

"Man, I know damn well you didn't come here on no gossiping shit. Who gives a fuck about what Aspen said? I'm sure she wasn't talking by herself," RJ snapped.

"Calm down and let her talk son," Banks said as he held up his hand to silence RJ.

"It's not gossip RJ. It's important and I think your father should know," Kassidy spoke up.

"I'm listening. What's going on?" Banks asked.

RJ took a seat and listened as Kassidy told them everything that Aspen had told her. A few times, he and his father made eye contact, shocked at what they were hearing. A few things were made clear, while some other stuff was just unbelievable. RJ saw the look of anger that flashed across his father's face and he understood his frustration.

"How do we know that what you're saying is true?" RJ asked.

"How would I know any of this RJ? I don't know any of these people. Hell, I barely know Aspen. We've never been friends and you know that," Kassidy replied.

"Exactly. And that's why I don't understand why she felt comfortable enough to tell you all that she told you," he said, looking at her skeptically.

"I really don't know, but she did," Kassidy replied.

"That's bullshit Kassidy. I was with Aspen for years and I know her just as well as I know you. You can't pay me to believe that she confided in you just because y'all were at the same place at the same time. More than likely, you told her what happened at the baby shower and Marlee became the topic of conversation. Nothing unites muthafuckas better than having a mutual enemy," RJ smirked while shaking his head.

RJ didn't doubt that what Kassidy said what true. His issue was why she felt the need to say it. If she thought for a second that their friendship had a fighting chance, then she was sadly mistaken. Kassidy couldn't be trusted, and he saw that for himself. She was an undercover snake, and he was mad at himself for taking so many years to see it. Marlee saw something in her from the very first day and she was right. Kassidy was the type to put a knife in your back, pull it out, and help you nurse your wounds. She was the kind of friend who would cause trouble and then help you out of it. The worst kind, in RJ's opinion, and he could do without it. Even if he did want to give her another chance at friendship, Marlee wasn't having it.

Kassidy lowered her head, not wanting RJ to see the look of guilt that covered her face. She and Aspen did bond over their mutual enemy, but that shouldn't have mattered. What mattered was that she was being a good friend and telling him what was up. Anything else was irrelevant.

"That's not true RJ. Believe it or not, I still consider you to be my best friend. I'm sure that Marlee will never like me, but that shouldn't come between our friendship," Kassidy tried to reason.

"I guess I should just say fuck the mother of my child just to be your friend, huh?" RJ chuckled sarcastically.

"Is there anything else that you have to say Kassidy?" Banks asked her.

"No, that was it," she replied.

"Well, thank you. I appreciate you coming to see us," Banks said as he stood to his feet.

He was conflicted about a lot of things and he didn't know where to start. He'd just learned a lot in just a short period of time and it was too much to take in. His head was pounding, and he needed a stiff drink or two.

"You're welcome Mr. Banks. Can we talk RJ?" Kassidy asked as she stood up and looked at him.

"I'm good on you, Kassidy. I can't be friends with somebody that I can't trust. And my girl ain't letting me be friends with somebody who wants to fuck. It just ain't looking good for you, my baby," RJ replied.

"So, you don't trust me now?" Kassidy questioned, right as RJ's phone rang.

Marlee was calling and her timing was perfect. He was done with his conversation with Kassidy and he was ready for her to bounce.

"What's up baby?" RJ asked when he answered the phone.

"Where are you RJ? I think I need to go to the hospital. My back is killing me," Marlee replied.

"Are you in pain anywhere else?" he asked as he hurried out of the building.

"Just my back. It usually doesn't hurt this long though," Marlee groaned.

"Okay baby. Stay on the phone with me. I'm on my way," RJ promised.

"What's wrong son?" his father asked.

"I think Marlee is in labor or close to it," RJ replied.

"Let me call your mother. I'll be right behind you," his father said.

"Do you need me to do anything RJ?" Kassidy asked louder than she needed to.

"Who the fuck is that?" Marlee yelled through the pain.

"Keep it pushing Kassidy," RJ snapped angrily.

She knew that he didn't need a damn thing from her. Her sneaky ass just wanted Marlee to know that she was there. That's exactly why RJ couldn't fuck with her anymore. She was too shady, and she tried to be slick with it.

"Are you trying to get cut RJ? The fuck is that bitch doing around you?" Marlee questioned. She tried to sit up in bed and winced in pain.

"Seriously Marlee? You're probably in labor and talking about cutting somebody," RJ laughed as he got in his truck and sped away, with his father following close behind him.

"Ooh, I can't wait until I have this baby. I'm fucking you up. Oh shit. I think I'm starting to have contractions," Marlee panted.

"Calm down with all that gangster talk and relax. Just breathe baby. I'm getting there as fast as I can," RJ said as he increased his speed.

A drive that usually took fifteen minutes only took him six. He ran red lights and all trying to get to her. He'd lost his father a long time ago, but he sent Banks a text and told him to meet them at the hospital. He stayed on the phone with Marlee until he pulled up to her house. She was home alone, but the door opened as soon as he ran up the stairs. Marlee looked like she was in pain and she was sweating like crazy. RJ grabbed her bags, locked the door, and rushed her to the hospital. He spotted Tiffany and her husband as soon as he pulled up and his parents were already inside. Tiffany had a wheelchair for Marlee and she was rushed to labor and delivery.

"Did anybody call Mat and Desi?" RJ asked, while Marlee was in the room getting an epidural.

"Desi is on the way and Mat is getting Sierra and they're coming too," Tiffany replied.

"My boy is smart already. He waited until his grandpa came back home to make his grand entrance. And today would have been my father's eightieth birthday," Banks beamed proudly.

"Really? Today is your father's birthday?" Tiffany asked with a smile.

"It sure is," Banks replied happily.

All the issues that he'd had faded into the background once he entered that hospital. His grandson was his top priority and nothing else mattered. He kept looking at Ivy, but he knew it wasn't the right time to talk to her.

"Hey everybody," Raven spoke when she and her daughter, Paris, walked up.

Everybody spoke back, as Paris ran over to her grandpa.

"Hey baby. Are you ready to meet your little cousin?" Banks asked as he picked her up and kissed her cheeks.

Mat, Sierra, Murk, and Desi finally arrived, and the hallway was packed. They were supposed to be in the waiting room, but no one had said anything to them yet. When the door finally opened, the doctor's eyes widened in surprise when he saw so many people littering the hall. He was sure that security would be coming to break it up soon, so he didn't even bother.

"Can I go in?" RJ asked when the nurse came out of the room.

"You sure can," she replied with a smile.

"Look, we're not supposed to be in the hallway like this and we can't all go in the room. Let's just speak to Marlee and leave her and RJ alone," Tiffany suggested.

RJ went in and sat on the bed next to Marlee and grabbed her hand. Everyone came in and spoke before going back out into the hall.

"I'm gonna be in labor forever. I'm only four centimeters," Marlee complained.

"It's okay baby. As long as you're not in any pain," RJ replied as he kissed her lips.

"I would have been. He was trying to make me wait until I was five centimeters to get pain medicine. I was about to cut up," Marlee said, making RJ laugh.

He and Marlee talked and watched tv as the doctors and nurses kept coming in and out of the room. Marlee was only five centimeters and almost three hours had passed.

"Are they still out in the hall? I don't think they can do that." Marlee yawned.

"Security must be sleep or just don't give a fuck," RJ said, right as a nurse walked back into the room.

"I need you to try turning on your side a little more for me, Marlee," the nurse instructed as she looked at the monitor.

"Okay," Marlee replied.

RJ helped her turn on her side and get comfortable, but he didn't like the look on the nurse's face.

"That doesn't seem to be working," she said as she continued to look at the monitor.

"What's wrong?" Marlee asked as she tried not to panic.

"Something's not right," the nurse said as she ran out of the room.

A few seconds later, two doctors and two more nurses came running back in with her. RJ heard their families asking what was going on, but no one answered. One of the doctors looked at the monitor and started talking in medical codes.

"Get her prepped for surgery!" he yelled, as everyone else sprang into action.

"Surgery! What the hell is going on? Y'all not even telling us nothing!" RJ yelled.

"The baby's heart rate dropped, and we need to prepare for an emergency C-Section," the doctor said as they started to wheel Marlee out of the room.

They put an oxygen mask on her face and that only made it seem worse. RJ felt like his world was falling apart right before his eyes, but he had to stay strong for Marlee. She was scared enough, and he didn't want to make it worse.

"Oh God!" Marlee said and she burst in tears.

Her first baby and she was having complications. The way they were moving made it seem like her baby possibly wouldn't even make it. As soon as the door opened, everyone wanted to know what was going on, but RJ had no answers.

"You can't come into the operating room sir. She'll be fine, trust me," one of the nurses said when she saw RJ following them.

"That's bullshit! I'm going wherever she goes!" he barked.

"Let them do their jobs RJ. She's in good hands," Banks reasoned.

"Yes, we've seen this happen a million times. Everything will be fine," the nurse said with a reassuring smile.

"Fuck that! She's not having no surgery without me being there! That's my girl and my son!" RJ bellowed.

The nurse tried to calm him down, but he wasn't hearing it. When the doctor saw how much of a scene they were causing, he intervened and put a stop to it.

"Let him come. It's fine!" the doctor yelled.

Every hospital set their own rules and he had no problem with the child's father being there. RJ wasn't having it any other way. While Marlee was being prepped for surgery, RJ had to wash up and change into scrubs. When he got into the room, he sat next to her bed and held her hand.

"I love you, baby. Everything will be okay," RJ assured her, and he prayed that he was right.

Marlee nodded her head as she gripped his hand. RJ kept talking to her until his voice started to sound muffled. Marlee felt her grip on his hand loosen until everything faded to black.

Chapter 31

Marlee struggled for a while, but she finally found the strength to open her eyes. It took her a minute to focus but, when she did, she smiled at RJ sitting in the recliner next to her bed holding their son. Desi and Murk were there as well, and she was happy to see them. Marlee remembered being a nervous wreck earlier when they said that her baby's heart rate had dropped, but she was thankful that they were both okay. At least, she hoped they were.

"Your mommy is finally up," RJ said as he got up and walked over to her bed and handed the baby to her.

"Happy birthday Tre." Marlee smiled down at him. He was too new to see who he looked like, but he had a head full of silky hair.

"His birthday was yesterday," RJ pointed out.

"Yesterday?" Marlee gasped. "I slept that long?"

"Yep and everybody has been up here. You got up long enough to drink some water, but you went right back out," RJ answered.

"And you were talking crazy as hell," Desi laughed.

"I don't remember nothing," Marlee said.

"They gave you the good shit fam. Ask them if they got some more," Murk replied.

"This damn crackhead," Desi mumbled as she shook her head.

"What's up Vegas baby?" Murk asked as he rubbed the baby's hand.

"Nigga, I told you to stop calling my baby that dumb shit," RJ fussed.

"I can't wait to tell him all about how his mama and daddy met," Murk joked.

"And I can't wait to cut your crazy ass if you do," Marlee threatened.

"Are you hungry, cousin? We can go get you something to eat," Desi offered.

"I'm starving, but I don't want nothing too heavy. My diet starts today. You can get me a salad or some soup," Marlee replied.

"Okay. What do you want RJ?" Desi asked.

He gave her his order, right before her and Murk left to go get them something to eat.

"How do you feel baby?" RJ asked before planting a kiss on her chapped lips.

"I'm good, but what the hell happened? I remembered them saying something about his heart rate and then wheeling me off to surgery."

"They thought he was in distress and they didn't want him to lose any oxygen. Everything is fine though. All his tests came back good and yours did too," RJ replied happily.

"How big is he? I feel like I missed out on his birth and everything else." Marlee frowned.

"Nine pounds even," RJ said.

"Damn. He doesn't even look that big," Marlee noted as she looked down at him.

"All the weight is in his diaper. That's my son for sure," RJ said, making her laugh.

"You would say that," Marlee chuckled, right as her room door was pushed open.

"How do you feel Ms. Davis?" the nurse asked when she walked in.

"I feel fine." Marlee smiled.

"I just need to check your vitals," the nurse informed her as she got right to work.

RJ took the baby and sat down, as Marlee got her temperature and blood pressure checked.

"I want his first party to be like a big ass circus. I want real animals and everything," RJ spoke up.

"Really RJ? He's not even a week old yet," Marlee laughed.

"I don't care. We're planning it early," he replied.

"Can we at least get out of the hospital first?" Marlee asked.

She went back and forth with him for a while, as the nurse laughed at their friendly banter.

"Y'all are so cute. How long have y'all known each other?" the nurse asked.

"Let's see. It took Tre nine months to get here, so it's been about nine months," Marlee replied, making RJ laugh.

The nurse was laughing like it was a joke, but they were dead ass serious.

"Where did y'all meet?" she questioned nosily.

"In Vegas," RJ replied.

"Oh okay. What happens in Vegas stays in Vegas, right?" she joked.

"Apparently not," Marlee said as she looked at her son and fell out laughing.

"Quit playing girl," RJ said as he laughed with her.

"Where's the lie? Not a damn thing stayed in Vegas," Marlee replied.

The nurse didn't get the joke, so she just left it alone. Once she made sure that all Marlee's vitals were good, she updated her charts and left.

"Why you told that lady that shit? I know she's probably wondering how we've only known each other for nine months and got a newborn," RJ laughed.

"Isn't it obvious?" Marlee asked with raised brows.

"Everybody don't need to know that you got pregnant during a weekend in Vegas by a stranger," RJ chuckled.

"It sounds even worse when you say it out loud," Marlee said as she covered her eyes with her hands.

"Who gives a damn Marlee?" RJ said, waving her off.

"We gotta come up with a good story to tell people when they ask how we met. We have to make sure that our stories match though. We can't get caught up in a lie."

"You must be crazy. I'm not lying about nothing. I'll tell a muthafucka to mind their business and be done with it," RJ replied with a frown.

"I'm just playing baby. Calm down," Marlee giggled.

"You're still coming by me when you get released, right?" RJ asked.

"Yes, for two weeks only," Marlee replied.

"Why not a month?" he countered.

"I don't know RJ, maybe." Marlee shrugged.

"You can stay forever if you want to," RJ noted.

"You told me, but are you ready to tell me what your best friend with the bad haircut was doing at your job? My box cutter still works you know," Marlee threatened.

"You and Desi need to chill out with them rusty ass box cutters," RJ said, making her laugh.

"I'm listening," Marlee said while looking at him expectantly.

"It's a lot to tell Marlee, but I'll tell you everything later tonight when it's just the two of us," RJ promised, right as the door opened again.

"Hey guys. The lady is coming around to get the baby's legal name for his birth certificate and social security card," the nurse stuck her head in and said.

"Okay, thank you," RJ replied.

"So, are we still going with the same name? No changes while I was doped up, right?" Marlee asked.

"Do you want me to be a single father Marlee? I can put that pillow over your face and make it happen," RJ threatened.

"No need for violence. I was just asking." Marlee shrugged.

When the lady came in to fill out the paperwork for the baby's name, Marlee wanted to punch her in the throat. She was going on and on about how cute RJ and the baby's name was, but Marlee disagreed. To her displeasure, Ryker Dakari Banks III was named but, to her and everyone else, he would always be Tre.

***

After months of being locked up, Tyson was finally a free man. His boy, Jerry, was waiting out front for him and he almost ran to get into his car.

"Damn bruh, you just don't know how much I appreciate you," Tyson said as he gave his friend dap.

Jerry was one of the realest niggas that he knew, and he was like the brother that Tyson never had. Not only did he get his car out of the impound, but he put his furniture in storage for him too. Tyson had lost his apartment, but it would be nothing to get another one. Taj was crazy if she thought that he was coming to stay with her. She was good for sex when he was out, but he didn't want her like that. She was running around posting shit online like shit was all good, but none of it was real. Tyson was riding around with her smoking when he got pulled over, so she went to jail too. He didn't know how long she stayed in there, but she had been out for a while. He had a probation hold on him, but he was thankful that his lawyer talked on his behalf. One of his boys loaned him the money and Yanni's rat ass paid the lawyer for him. She was another one who he wasn't trying to see. She sent him pictures of his daughter and she was the only one who he cared about. Yanni could get the fuck on because her services were no longer needed. Tyson told her what she wanted to hear and, as usual, she fell for his lines.

"You know I got you, bruh. I'm just happy I wasn't on the boat when all this happened," Jerry said, referring to his offshore job.

"As soon as I get cleaned up, I'm going to my stash spot, so I can pay you and everybody else their money back. I really gotta get out here and grind to get my money up," Tyson replied.

He had a nice bit of money stashed away, but he owed a few people. As much as he liked Jerry, he didn't trust anyone knowing where he kept his cash. Money turned friends into enemies and he didn't want that to happen.

"Yeah, because I know you ain't trying to be living up in your mama's house too long. She was fussing when I had to bring all your clothes over there," Jerry laughed, pulling Tyson away from his thoughts.

"That's all she do is fuss. That's exactly why I didn't ask her to do nothing for me when I got locked up. Nigga don't need to keep hearing all that shit. Going to her house is better than being bothered with Taj every day though."

"Taj is trying to get her husband back," Jerry laughed.

"That bitch don't have no husband." Tyson frowned.

"You know Marlee had her lil boy," Jerry informed him.

"When?" Tyson asked.

"A few weeks ago, I guess. I saw the pictures on Instagram. I still follow some of her people, but her page ain't private since she do makeup and shit," Jerry answered.

"Who does he look like?" Tyson asked.

"I don't know nigga," Jerry replied, trying to spare his boy's feelings.

Marlee's baby didn't look a damn thing like Tyson, but Yanni's did. He was worried about another nigga's baby and not enough about his own. Marlee had posted pictures of her son and his father, and that baby was the other man's twin. Everything including his complexion was that of his father and he had nothing for Marlee.

"Let me see. Pull it up on your phone," Tyson requested.

Jerry pulled up his Instagram account as he tried to watch the road. He went straight to Marlee's page and noticed that she'd added more pictures. He handed Tyson the phone and watched as he looked through all of them.

"That's me all day bruh," Tyson said, making Jerry almost swerve off the road.

That nigga had to be legally blind for him to think that Marlee's son looked anything like him. Jerry was trying to spare his friend's feeling, but he couldn't let him go out like that. Being a good friend meant keeping it real and that's exactly what he had to do.

"Where he look like you at dog? Because I don't see it. That lil nigga look just like his daddy," Jerry replied honestly.

"We don't even know who his daddy is," Tyson replied.

"The same nigga who he's on most of the pictures with!" Jerry yelled in frustration.

"Man, look at his nose," Tyson said while pointing to the picture.

Jerry squinted his eyes, but he couldn't see what his boy was seeing. He scrolled through the phone that Tyson was holding and went to a picture of Marlee's boyfriend holding their son.

"Dog, look at this picture. That lil nigga look just like his daddy. Eyes, nose, mouth, and complexion. Shit, his whole fucking face. They even got the same ears. He don't even look like his mama," Jerry added.

"I don't see it," Tyson replied as he shoved the phone back in Jerry's hand.

"You can't be serious right now. Do you need to borrow my glasses? I know you still got love for Marlee but damn," Jerry said, shaking his head.

"I still want some blood work," Tyson noted.

"For fucking what!" Jerry yelled, getting angry.

Tyson was dumb as fuck and he was getting on his nerves. He knew for a fact that Yanni's baby was his, but he didn't ask about her once.

"I'm just saying bruh. If she don't have nothing to hide, she shouldn't have a problem with proving it." Tyson shrugged.

"I hear you, man," Jerry said, deciding to leave the entire conversation alone.

There was no reasoning with Tyson and he saw that for himself. He had in his mind that he could be the father of Marlee's baby and nothing that Jerry said was changing his mind. He had Tyson's car parked in his garage, so he drove him over there to get it. Tyson was Jerry's boy, but he didn't want to get caught up in the mess that he was creating with Marlee. He had a feeling that it was going to turn out bad and he didn't need the drama.

"Good looking out fam. I got you as soon as I get cleaned up and get my hair cut," Tyson said before he got into his own car and pulled away.

He had a lot of business to handle and he planned to do most of it that day. His car insurance had lapsed on his car, so that was one of his top priorities. He also wanted to see his kids and he needed his sister to make that happen. She didn't mind picking them up for him because he didn't want to be around none of his baby mamas. Kim was never an issue because she was married now. Taj thought she was an exception, but she was in the category right with Yanni's hoe ass. He also planned to get with Marlee because he was tired of playing games with her. She swore that he wasn't the baby's father, but she had yet to prove it. She had Tyson fucked up if she thought that another man was going to raise his son. She was happy and smiling now, but she was going to see him real soon.

Chapter 32

Lauren was all smiles when she walked into her home. She was surprised to see that her husband was home, especially since it was the weekend. That was usually his time with Ivy and she barely talked to him. The thought of him possibly being tired of his mistress made her happy, but that was just wishful thinking. If she didn't know anything else, Lauren knew that her husband loved his son's mother. He never denied it, nor did he try to hide it. That thought alone was enough to make her physically sick.

Being in a loveless marriage was not how she envisioned her life. She still loved Banks with all her heart, but the feelings weren't mutual. Several times she'd contemplated going back to Denver to be near her family, but her pride just wouldn't let her. They begged her not to move to New Orleans with Banks when she got pregnant, but she did it anyway. Her family had basically disowned her for years, minus an occasional phone call or greeting card during the holidays. After years of being estranged from them, they finally started to come around. They were proud of the way Banks had her living, never knowing how miserable she was.

She always smiled, but that was only to mask the pain. She just couldn't go back home because then they would know the truth. They would know that they were right all along, and Lauren couldn't give them that satisfaction. They would really ridicule her if they knew that she'd signed a prenup. Miserable and all, that was one of the things that made her stay as long as she did. Instead of moping around the house being sad all the time, Lauren started taking steps to make herself happy.

"Hey honey. I'm surprised you're home," Lauren said when she saw her husband lounging on the sofa watching tv.

"Yeah, I'll be leaving soon, but I just wanted to run a few things by you," Banks replied.

"Okay. What's going on?" Lauren asked.

"Sit down," Banks ordered.

She took a seat, while Banks stood up and paced the floor. He had so much to say and he didn't quite know where to start. After pacing for a while, he handed her some papers that she immediately started to read over.

"I left you twenty-five thousand dollars in the bank. The house and the car is also yours to keep. I'm really being generous because the prenup said that you weren't entitled to anything," Banks said, as Lauren's hand started to shake uncontrollably.

"What are you talking about? You're leaving me? After all these years and you're leaving me with practically nothing," Lauren said as tears rapidly fell from her eyes.

"As I just stated, I'm being generous," Banks repeated.

"But why, Ryker? I've been the perfect wife and stood by your side for all these years," Lauren cried.

"I know that I haven't been the perfect husband to you, but I've always been honest about my feelings. Right or wrong, I've never kept you in the dark about what I was doing or who I was doing it with. You asked for it and you got it, no matter what it was," Banks replied.

"I didn't want all that stuff! I only wanted you!" Lauren shouted.

"I hate a liar. A liar and a thief have no place in my life and you've turned out to be both," Banks scowled as he threw some papers at her feet.

Lauren picked everything up and flipped through the pages. She had a perplexed look on her face, but Banks wasn't buying the act.

"What the hell is this and what does it have to do with me? These things clearly have Ivy's name on them," Lauren said as she threw the copies of the cashed checks on the floor.

What Joy said about Ivy having a bigger bank account than hers was hurtful because it was true. Lauren had seen the statements a long time ago and she was sick to her stomach when she did. Banks had a lock box where he kept all his important papers. He forgot to lock it when he took a shower one night and that was how she found out.

"I said the same thing when my son first presented everything to me. I was baffled as to why a woman who hasn't written a check in over ten years or more decided to write up to seventy-five thousand worth," Banks replied.

"Maybe you need to ask her that. I'm sure she's who you're leaving me for," Lauren sniffled.

"She seemed just as baffled as I was. I wonder why," Banks smirked.

"She's a liar, that's why. It's right there in black and white Ryker," Lauren said as she pointed to the documents that were thrown all over the floor.

"That's the same thing I said until an unexpected visitor told me otherwise," Banks chuckled.

"What unexpected visitor?" Lauren questioned.

"The same one who told me about the checks that you took out of my lock box. The same checks that you just threw to the floor. The ones that you wrote for other people to cash and signed Ivy's name to them," Banks answered.

"That's a lie!" Lauren jumped up and shouted.

"You were smart as hell too and you almost got away with it. But, just like every other criminal, you couldn't keep your mouth shut," Banks replied.

"That is not true baby. I don't even know any of these people," Lauren said as she picked up some of the papers and read the names off to him.

"No, you don't, but Keith does," Banks said, referring to Aspen's uncle who had just been released from prison.

The look on Lauren's face showed her guilt, but she refused to tell the truth. "What does Keith have to do with this?" Lauren asked.

"Don't insult my intelligence Lauren. I'm no fool, so don't try to play me like one. You've been fucking him for three years and I've been knowing that. Thing is, I really didn't care about you having a man on the side. Hell, I haven't touched you in seven years, so I don't blame you. What I have a problem with was you using my money to take care of the bum."

"Who told you all this mess? Someone is lying on me and you're buying right into it," Lauren cried.

"The only person who's lying here is you. I was wondering how a man who goes around begging to cut people's grass just to get by could afford a nice new truck like the one he started driving. He can't even stay clean long enough to pass a fucking drug test and that's who you spent my hard-earned money on. Every check that was written was made out to one of his low life friends to cash. Y'all got greedy and started doing it too much and that's how you got caught," Banks said.

Banks was thankful for Kassidy because she helped to put the pieces together. RJ would have never figured that out and he would have probably drove himself crazy trying. Sure enough, when Banks checked his checkbook that he kept in his lock box, some of the checks were missing. Lauren was slick with her shit, but she was a dumb criminal. Banks knew that was her sick way of trying to drive a wedge in between him and Ivy, and it would have worked too. He would have surely looked at Ivy sideways and thought that she was lying if she said she didn't know what was going on. He was happy that things played out the way they did, and he didn't do or say anything to her that he would later regret.

"I didn't do anything. Someone is feeding you lies and you're eating it up," Lauren swore.

"I knew you would say that and I was prepared. Keith is waiting for my call. Let's see what he has to say about all this," Banks said as he pulled his phone from his back pocket and started dialing a number.

"No!" Lauren screamed as she knocked the phone out of his hands and onto the floor.

"Relax baby. I don't even know his number," Banks chuckled while retrieving his phone.

Lauren felt like a fool, but she was angry too. The nerve of him to scold her for having an affair, when she'd never had him all to herself. At least he still fucked her even though he was with Ivy, but that had long ago stopped too. Then, when she asked him if he still loved her, he looked her in her eyes and said no. A thousand knives being plunged into her heart had to feel better than the pain she felt after that. Banks never lied, but that was one time that Lauren wanted him to.

Keith and his sister, Patrice, had always been good friends of hers but, a few years ago, he started to be more. Once he entered the picture, it didn't hurt as much when her husband spent the weekends with his other woman. Keith gave her the love and attention that she wasn't getting at home, and she craved it. The only down side was his financial status. He didn't have money or anything to offer her, but that wasn't what Lauren wanted. She already had that with her husband. She wanted someone to make her feel beautiful again, since her husband didn't anymore.

It started out with her giving Keith a few dollars here and there, but he would always ask for more. Even when he was locked up, he needed things, and she always tried to provide it. Lauren was scared that her husband was going to find out, so she came up with another plan. She waited until Banks was occupied with RJ one day and took the key to the lockbox. She took some of the checks out of his and Ivy's joint account checkbook and had been using them since then. In her mind, she was killing two birds with one stone. She was getting the money that Keith asked her for, while throwing Ivy under the bus at the same time. She thought sure that her husband would have confronted his other woman when she first started doing it, but it took longer than she thought it would.

"I didn't deserve this Ryker. I'm your wife. The mother of your first child and you treated me like shit. And for what? Because I didn't have your son," Lauren cried.

"You think me loving Ivy has anything to do with her having my son? She could have given me a daughter and I would still feel the same way. Yes, I wanted a son, but that didn't make me magically fall in love with her. You're really delusional," Banks fumed.

"That's bullshit! If that was true, why didn't you stay with Raven's mother?" Lauren asked.

"Raven's mother was passing time with me until her man came home from the military. The shit wasn't even that deep. Had she given me a son, I still wouldn't have been with her because I didn't love her. You just couldn't accept the fact that I had fallen in love with another woman. You had to make yourself feel better by creating stories in your own head and telling them to other people. Saying that I fell in love with Ivy because she had my son made you feel better. You had to have a reason, so you made one up," Banks ranted.

"I still deserved better," Lauren cried as she rocked back and forth in her chair.

"What else did you want? You have a beautiful home, a brand-new car, and a wardrobe fit for a queen," Banks replied.

"Yeah, but I didn't have you. Don't you understand Ryker? I didn't need material things to make me happy. I only needed you."

"Have I ever lied to you, Lauren?" Banks questioned.

"No, never," Lauren admitted.

"When I came to you and told you how I felt about Ivy, what did you say?" Banks asked her.

"I know I said that I could handle it, but it got to be too much. I thought you would mess around with her and get tired, the same as you did with Raven's mother. I didn't expect her to be afforded the same luxuries as me. I had three of your kids and took your last name. I turned against my family for you," Lauren shrieked.

"And that's exactly why I promised to stay, even though I wanted out of this marriage years ago," Banks noted.

"And now you're breaking that promise. That makes you a liar in my book," Lauren replied.

"You can miss me with your pathetic attempt at using reverse psychology. I promised to take care of you, not that pitiful excuse of a man that you've been sleeping with. What kind of man allows a woman to take care of him? He's just as pathetic as you are," Banks scowled.

"What's the difference between what I did and what you've been doing for years? You've always taken care of Ivy and I never said anything about it," Lauren pointed out.

"Are you really that delusional?" Banks questioned as he stared at her like she was crazy.

"Well, it's true," she stupidly replied.

"Whatever I did, I did it with my money! You expect me to be okay with you giving another man money that you didn't even earn? What kind of fucking loser even allows that? The very thought of a woman providing for a man sickens me. There's no way for you to justify that, so don't even try," Banks fumed.

His entire life, he'd been taught that a man should provide for his woman, and he raised his son the exact same way. When he first learned that Marlee was pregnant, the first thing he wanted his son to do was buy her a house. Although she declined, RJ's responsibility was still to take care of her and his son. All of Banks' kids were grown, but he still gave them whatever they wanted.

"I know that what I did was wrong, but it doesn't warrant divorce. I stayed with you through two babies and another woman that you've been seeing for almost our entire marriage," Lauren sniffled.

"Don't insult my intelligence Lauren. You've never accepted my other kids and it took my son pointing it out to me for me to realize it. Honestly, the money is only a small part of why I'm ending this marriage. Your hate for my son is what really sealed your fate," Banks noted.

"What are you even talking about? RJ has always been welcomed here. He never did say much to me, but I think of him and Raven as my own."

"The bastard children that you wish you never had to see again. Especially RJ because he's so much like his father. I hate the day that he ever took his first breath. Isn't that what you said?" Banks asked, noting the shocked expression on Lauren's face.

"I didn't mean that. I was angry at the time and I said some things that I shouldn't have," Lauren replied.

"At least you have the decency to be honest about it," Banks said as he headed for the door.

"Please don't do this Ryker. Don't leave me over one stupid mistake," Lauren begged.

"No reason to stay is a good reason to go," Banks replied.

"How am I supposed to survive with twenty-five thousand dollars? Is that all I'm worth to you?" Lauren asked as she chased after him.

"I always said that if we ever parted ways, I wanted to leave you with at least one hundred grand to keep your head above water. Since you've already spend seventy-five of that, enjoy your other twenty-five," Banks said calmly, right before walking out of the house.

"Fuck you, Ryker! I regret the day you ever got on that plane and crossed my path! My life has been miserable ever since! Fuck you and your bitch! And fuck that bastard son that you love so much!" Lauren yelled as she stood on the porch.

Banks didn't even bother with a reply. He calmly got into his truck and backed out of their driveway. Lauren went back into the house and raced up the stairs. She wanted to see if he had taken all of his things and her heart broke when she saw that he did. She then grabbed her laptop and logged into their bank account to check the balance. Lauren's heart dropped when she saw that what he said was true. After all the changes that he had taken her through, twenty-five thousand dollars was all that she had to show for it. And sadly, she couldn't do a damn thing about it. Although he told her that she could keep the house, it was still in his name. He could come back and snatch it right from up under her any time he wanted to. Even if he didn't, she wouldn't be able to maintain it for very long on her own.

Lauren was so confused about a lot of stuff. Banks knew things that she planned to take to her grave. Besides her daughters, she didn't talk to very many people. She didn't have a lot of females that she considered friends. Patrice and Aspen were the only non-family members that she'd ever confided it. Then, as if being hit by a ton of bricks, Lauren figured it out. Aspen! She was the only one who had access to both Banks and RJ. Patrice never really saw them unless there was a function that they were invited to. Aspen knew way more than her aunt did, like how Lauren really felt about RJ. She was a damn fool for telling her ex-boyfriend anything after he'd left her for another woman. Lauren was heated as she headed back down the stairs to get her phone. She wanted to tell her daughters what happened, but she also had a few things to say to Aspen as well. That bitch crossed the wrong one and whatever friendship they had was through.

Chapter 33

"That wasn't your place Aspen. Lauren confided in you and you should have kept whatever she said to yourself. Now, look at what you've done. Lauren's husband left her with barely enough money to survive. She might have to move in with her daughters now," Patrice said as she scolded her niece.

"Not to mention you fucked everything up for me. I was trying to get me a motorcycle," her uncle Keith argued.

Keith was a known user, and Lauren was dumb enough to fall for his games. He was pissed with Aspen because she had ruined a good thing, as he so begrudgingly put it. Lauren was his personal piggy bank, but his funds were cut off since Banks had left her with next to nothing. Keith had been living it up with Lauren's help, but things had ended almost as quickly as they started. He didn't have anymore use for Lauren now and he barely answered the phone when she called. Keith didn't know that all of the money belonged to her husband. He thought that Lauren had a little something to live on without Banks. She was just as broke as he was without her husband, so that was a waste.

"I apologized to her already, but I'm not kissing her ass. If it was that much of a secret, she should have kept it to herself," Aspen spat angrily.

It had been days since everything happened and she was tired of hearing about it. Lauren had called her a few days ago going off and phone calls from her daughters came soon after. Aspen was a fool for confiding in Kassidy, knowing that they had never been friends. Kassidy was so in love with RJ that she would have done anything to get back in his good graces. Joy told her that she'd seen her at the job, but Aspen didn't think her snitching was the reason why. She'd given Kassidy way more credit than she deserved and ended up looking like a fool. The fact that she'd told RJ everything that Aspen had told her was lower than low. Aspen couldn't blame anyone but herself because she shouldn't have repeated what was told to her. The conversation between her and Kassidy was flowing so good that she ended up talking all over herself. They had both been wronged by RJ, and they both hated Marlee. In her mind, that was good enough. Now, thanks to her big ass mouth, everybody, including her auntie, was mad with her.

"The nerve of you to get mad when all of this is your fault. All this behind RJ and his new woman and it's not even that serious. He's moved on and you need to do the same. You got a man who worships the ground you walk on, but you're still moping around over the one who could care less about you. I don't understand y'all young girls these days," Patrice argued.

"I've already moved on and none of this has anything to do with RJ. Like I just said, if it was so secretive, she shouldn't have said anything at all. I'm sorry that her husband left her, but let's keep it real. He didn't really want to be there anyway," Aspen said, right as her phone rang.

She blew out a breath of frustration when she saw that it was Aaron calling once again. Aspen's aunt and uncle were still fussing, but she was done entertaining it. She walked out of the house and sat in her car. Her thoughts were all over the place, but she was so angry. Kassidy took her to play with and she had been doing that since Aspen and RJ were together. She had the right one and she was about to find that out the hard way.

When Aspen's phone rang again, she picked it up and finally answered Aaron's call as she drove. Just like everyone else, he was spitting some bullshit that she was not in the mood to hear. It took about ten minutes, but Aspen pulled up in front of the building as she talked on the phone with Aaron. She was already pissed off and his constant nagging wasn't helping the situation.

"Are you even listening to me, Aspen?" Aaron yelled.

"No, because I'm not in the mood for an argument," Aspen replied.

"There's nothing to argue about. You have a key to my damn house and I've never even stepped foot in yours. I can't even entertain a woman without you ruining shit, but you had another nigga damn near living with you," Aaron fumed.

"Stop overexaggerating. RJ did not live with me, but he did spend nights there. Who do you think gave me the money for the down payment?" Aspen questioned.

"It's not like I couldn't do it, but you never asked. But, it's all good Aspen. I'm tired of chasing you. I thought it was because of that nigga, but it's you. He's out of the picture and you still be on that bullshit. I'm telling you now, if I find somebody else, ain't no coming back for you. I'm getting sick of doing the same shit and expecting different results. There's only so much more that I can take. A lot of women would be happy to call me their man, but there's just no satisfying you," Aaron ranted.

Aspen rolled her eyes to the heavens and sighed. Aaron was talking that moving on bullshit again and she wasn't in the mood to hear it. His ass wasn't going nowhere and they both knew it. All she had to do was sweet talk him and she was prepared to do just that.

"You also told me that you would give me time since I'm just coming out of a relationship," Aspen reminded him.

"How much time do you need Aspen? It's been months. That man has moved on and has a family. I'm trying to do the same thing with you, but I'm done begging!" Aaron yelled.

Aspen was tired of everybody reminding her that RJ had moved on. She knew that better than anyone else. She was the one who was still nursing her broken heart. She was the one who cried herself to sleep some nights because like a fool, she went to his and Marlee's Instagram pages multiple times a day. Their baby was a constant reminder of the love she had and lost. To say that RJ wasn't ready for kids, he jumped into the fatherhood role like a pro. He had the biggest smile on his face in every picture and Aspen's heart broke a little more each time.

"I just need you to be patient with me, Aaron," Aspen mumbled.

"Fuck that Aspen! I have no more patience to give. You keep stalling me and the shit is driving me crazy!" Aaron yelled.

He was mumbling something under his breath and, then, Aspen heard a loud crash in the background. He was further proving her point that he wasn't stable enough for them to be together.

"Aaron, stop it. Stop throwing things and calm down. Just take a few deep breaths and relax," Aspen coached, trying to calm him down.

"Stop talking to me like I'm a fucking child!" Aaron barked, making her jump.

"Baby, just relax and listen to me," Aspen said softly, knowing that she was the only one who could calm him down.

She heard Aaron inhale and exhale a few times before he started talking again.

"I'm listening," he said in a leveled voice.

"Have you been taking your medicine?" Aspen asked him, right as Kassidy walked out of the IRS building and got into her car.

Aspen waited until she pulled off before she slowly trailed behind her. She made sure to stay at least two cars behind so that she wouldn't be noticed. Kassidy had the entire game fucked up if she thought that Aspen was going to let what she did slide. She didn't want to fight her. She just wanted to bat that bitch in her mouth for talking so much. She would have done it when she first walked out of the building, but she didn't need to be caught on camera.

"I told you that I don't need that medicine," Aaron replied.

Aspen begged to differ, but she had to take another approach with him. Aaron didn't like to feel like he was being treated like a crazy person, but that's how he behaved sometimes. He suffered from PTSD, but he didn't like to take his medicine that was prescribed for him. The side effects were too much for him to handle. Aspen hated staying the night at his house because he often had nightmares about some of the things that he had seen. Either that or he couldn't sleep at all. His moods ranged from hostile to anxious and sometimes depressed. She didn't know who she was getting most days and things seemed to be getting worse. The medicine made him feel nauseous and dizzy, or so he claimed. He was much better when he took it, but Aspen couldn't convince him of that. They lived together for a while and she was scared to go to sleep most nights. She didn't want Aaron coming to her house and then never wanting to leave. She couldn't go through the headache of living with him again, which was why she always went to his house.

"Yes, you do baby. They gave it to you for a reason. It calms down your anxiety and mellows you out," Aspen tried to reason.

"It also gives me the shits and makes my mouth feel like cotton," Aaron replied.

"Just take the medicine Aaron. You keep saying that you want to be married and start a family, but we can't do it like this. How can you care for a child when you're always so angry and hostile?" Aspen asked him.

"Taking that bullshit ass medicine has nothing to do with the kind of father that I'll be. My kids are going to have the kind of life that I never had. They won't ever have to feel like they're in the world alone," Aaron said passionately.

"I know that you'll be a great father Aaron, but you still need to take your medicine. Can you do it for me, please?" Aspen begged.

"I'll do anything for you. You know that," Aaron replied.

"Good, now I have to make a few runs and I'll see you later," Aspen promised.

"Okay. I love you, baby," Aaron said, but she had already hung up.

Aspen was annoyed with following Kassidy around because she made too many stops. She'd gone to the dollar store, a grocery store, and a food place. Everywhere that she went had a crowd and Aspen didn't want to take any chances. She had too much going for herself to ruin it all for bitch slapping Kassidy.

Aspen was ready to abandon her mission, until Kassidy pulled into the parking lot of the shopping center by Dillard's. It was getting dark and the area was nice and isolated. Aspen smiled to herself when she saw Kassidy park her car. Dumb bitch had the nerve to be looking in the mirror finger combing that ugly ass hairdo. She was so preoccupied with her appearance that she never noticed Aspen, who'd parked three cars over from hers. As soon as Kassidy opened her car door, Aspen pulled her out.

"Ahh! What the hell are you doing!" Kassidy yelled when she saw that it was Aspen who had yanked her from the car.

"I'm helping you keep your mouth closed since you can't seem to do it on your own. Stupid bitch begging a nigga for a friendship that he no longer wants," Aspen said as she slammed her closed fist into Kassidy's mouth.

The ring that Aspen wore split her lip and had blood pouring out like a faucet. Kassidy used one hand to cover her bloody lip while she tried to swing with the other. Neither woman was much of a fighter, so hair pulling, and slapping was all that they were doing. Kassidy found the strength to kick Aspen and sent her flying to the concrete.

"You're the stupid bitch for confiding in somebody who never fucked with you. Don't get mad with me because you couldn't keep your mouth closed," Kassidy replied.

She tried to hurry back into her car, but Aspen was too fast for her. They started slapping and hair pulling again until they both landed on the ground. No one was really around to break them up and the few people who were kept going and minded their own business. It wasn't until both women heard their names being called that they stopped and stood to their feet.

"Dog, I swear. Kassidy and Aspen are out here fighting in the parking lot by Dillard's. Desi is recording the shit," Murk said, laughing uncontrollably.

Another woman with a blonde colored fade was standing there with her phone out, recording them. Aspen was so embarrassed because she knew that it was RJ who he was on the phone talking to. She was too old to be getting out there making a fool of herself and, now, she had been recorded. Without uttering a word, Aspen got into her car and pulled off.

"The fuck was you and Aspen out here fighting for Kassidy?" Murk asked as he watched her trying to fix herself up.

He and Desi had gone to the mall to get his kids some more shoes and they had just walked out when Aspen pulled up behind Kassidy. They already knew that something was about to go down and Desi started recording the entire act. She couldn't wait to show Marlee how stupid they looked. She was sure her cousin was going to laugh, just as much as she and Murk did.

"Mind your own business," Kassidy snapped angrily.

"See, I was trying to be nice to your dusty ass, but now you're going on WorldStar. Send me that video, Desi," Murk requested as he and the other woman walked away.

Kassidy hurriedly got into her car and sped out of the parking lot soon after. She was already embarrassed and knowing that RJ would probably see the video didn't help all that much. After all she'd done to help him and his father out, he still didn't want anything to do with her. Kassidy still kept up with him on social media and that was how she saw his son. She never imagined that she wouldn't have RJ in her life as a friend, but that was her reality. Still, after so many years of being around him, Kassidy was having a hard time accepting it. She knew that if she could get him alone to hear her sincere apology, he would feel differently. That would probably be the hardest part. From the pictures that he posted on Instagram, Marlee seemed to always be around.

Chapter 34

"Bitch, that ain't no fight. All they're doing is slapping and pulling hair," Sierra laughed as she looked at the video on Desi's phone.

"That's the same thing I said," Marlee replied.

Desi had showed the video to her and RJ a few days ago, and they fell out laughing when they saw it. RJ didn't even need to ask what the fight was about because he already knew. Kassidy had started a war when she told them everything that Aspen had told her, and he expected things to get ugly. His father had left Lauren and filed for divorce and was now living in the house with his mother. That was always what he wanted anyway, and Lauren had given him a good reason to do it. RJ was shocked when Kassidy told him what Lauren was doing, but it made perfect sense. Lauren was trying to cause confusion, but things didn't work out quite how she had planned them to. Instead, she pushed her husband into the arms of the woman he loved, while she was left with nothing. The entire situation was a mess and things at the office were tense. Joy was in her feelings and her attitude was ridiculous.

"Imagine how shocked we were when we walked out of the mall and saw the shit," Desi laughed.

She and Marlee were at Sierra and Mat's house enjoying their Saturday. Sierra had fried some seafood for them, and Mat had mixed some drinks. Marlee had pumped enough milk to last Tre for the entire day and he had formula whenever that ran out. She had gone to her six-week checkup the day before and she was ready to unwind.

RJ and the baby were at home, giving her a much-needed break. She was only supposed to be by him for two weeks, but she was still there six weeks later. Every time she mentioned something about going home, he came up with another reason for her to stay. Marlee was getting spoiled being over there because she didn't have to lift a finger. RJ did everything for her and so did Ivy whenever she was around.

"Y'all want some more to eat?" Sierra asked everybody.

No, I'm good. I cheated today, but I'm not even supposed to be eating that," Marlee replied.

She still hadn't lost all her baby weight, but it was slowly coming off. She couldn't work out too much since she got cut, but she did watch what she ate. RJ got her a treadmill and she got on it as often as she could. She was happy that she got cleared by her doctor to wear a girdle and she already had one on. It made a big difference in her clothes and made her look slimmer.

"That shit was good though. I'm taking a plate home," Desi replied.

"When is your ass going back home Marlee?" Sierra asked.

"I got cleared to go back to work, so I'll probably be doing both sometime next week," Marlee replied.

"Girl, bye. That bitch has been saying that for the past two weeks," Desi replied.

"I am going back home until I get my own place. We've been looking, but I haven't found one that I really like yet. I would have been good with an apartment, but RJ is too extra," Marlee replied.

"He's not being extra, he's being a real man. That's what wrong with y'all now," Mat argued.

"What are you even talking about?" Marlee asked her sister.

"A nigga offers to buy and not rent, and he's extra. If he would have offered to rent instead of buying, you would have said that he had enough money to buy. Just ain't never satisfied," Mat fussed.

"I am satisfied, and I would have been happy either way." Marlee shrugged.

"I don't even know why you're wasting that man's time with all that. As big as that house is, you can live there with him and be comfortable. I know he wants you to," Mat said.

"Yeah, he does, but I don't think we're ready for all that just yet," Marlee replied.

"You can't be serious," Mat said as she paused her game to look at her sister.

"I know what you're about to say, but just hear me out. Yes, RJ and I had sex the first day we met and I got pregnant, but it wasn't like we planned it. We have a baby together and we haven't even known each other a year yet. That's his house, not mine. I don't want to be in that kind of position where he can kick me out if things don't work out between us. We're still learning things about each other and we don't even know if we can live together on a permanent basis yet. Staying over there a few nights is one thing, but being there for good is something altogether different," Marlee rambled as she made her feelings known.

"I understand what you're saying cousin and I don't blame you," Desi said.

"Do y'all honestly think that RJ would do her dirty like that? The nigga is offering to buy you a house of your own," Mat tried to reason.

"I understand that Mat, but I can't help how I feel. Hell, Aspen was his girlfriend for five years and look how that turned out," Marlee noted.

"But, Aspen didn't have his first and only son either," Mat pointed out.

"Both of y'all make some good points, but the wrong people are discussing it. You need to tell RJ how you feel and y'all need to sit down and talk about it. Don't just have the man thinking that you don't want to live with him and not tell him why. I think he really loves you, Marlee, but he deserves to know what's up," Sierra spoke up.

"Now, that's some real shit," Mat replied.

"Yeah, that's true," Desi agreed.

Marlee was deep in thought, but she agreed with her best friend. RJ needed to know how she felt and they could take it from there. She would have loved to share space with him, but she wasn't comfortable with it being his place and not theirs. When she and Tyson had their apartment, the lease was in both their names. Marlee's name only came off five months after the breakup, when it was time for him to renew it.

"I'm going shoot some hoops," Mat said as she stood up and stretched. She went to grab her running shoes and sat down on the sofa to put them on.

"Let's go sit on the porch," Sierra suggested.

"I hope Tyson's big, fat chaffed ass ain't out there." Marlee frowned.

She was so aggravated when she and Desi pulled up and saw Tyson sitting on his mother's porch. He was trying his best to talk to Marlee, but she only ignored him. When Sierra informed her that he'd moved back in with his mother, that was even more of a disappointment. Marlee loved to spend time at her sister's house, but she didn't want to look in her ex-boyfriend's face every time she did.

"Fuck Tyson!" Desi spat when they walked out on the porch.

Marlee groaned because Tyson and Jerry were the first two who they laid eyes on. There were a few other dudes surrounding them but, when Mat came out, they all followed her to the basketball goal that they kept on the sidewalk.

"What's up baby mama?" Tyson spoke as he smiled at Marlee.

She looked behind her, trying to see who he was talking to. When he got up and made his way over to her, she was ready to get up and go back inside.

"Why didn't y'all stop me from messing with his ugly ass?" Marlee asked when she looked at him.

"We tried sis, but you didn't want to hear it," Sierra laughed.

"Where my son at?" Tyson asked.

"Fuck off Tyson. My baby is way too cute to be yours and you know it," Marlee replied.

"If he's not mine, then prove it." Tyson shrugged like it was simple.

"Girl, will you please give this alien a blood test, so he can get the fuck on?" Desi frowned.

"Really Desi? You know just like I do that my baby ain't his. My baby is with his father right now and it ain't this nigga," Marlee replied while pointing to Tyson.

"Prove it then, Marlee. What's so hard about backing up what you say? You won't ever have to worry about me again if he's not mine," Tyson swore.

"It's already been proven. The fuck you so pressed about my son for. You don't even be bothered with the ones you have!" Marlee yelled.

The door to Tyson's mother's house flew open and his sister, Trinity, and her boyfriend, Craig, came outside arguing.

"Don't even try to play me like that Marlee. You know better than anybody that I take care of my kids," Tyson replied.

"That's because I made your cheap ass do it. If it weren't for me, you would have never even seen them. The fuck out my face with that dumb shit," Marlee fumed.

"You can still be with that nigga, but ain't no other man raising a baby that has my blood flowing through his veins," Tyson swore.

"Oh, my God! What part are you not understanding?" Marlee yelled as she and Tyson went back and forth.

Jerry heard their entire conversation from across the street and all he could do was shake his head. The baby had another man's name and face, but Tyson was still on that dumb shit. He was happy that he worked offshore and didn't have to be around as often as he used to. He had a low tolerance for stupidity and his friend was very stupid. It was embarrassing listening to his boy arguing about a baby that wasn't even his. His oldest son was being raised by another man and he didn't have shit to say about that. His son's mother, Kim, had gotten remarried and her husband was more of a father than Tyson ever was. He didn't really see Ty at all since he and Marlee broke up because Kim never came around. She had just had another son for her husband and Tyson was the furthest thing from her mind.

"Look at this nasty bitch," Sierra said when they saw Yanni pull up in her mother's car.

Tyson frowned when he saw her because she came at the worst possible time. His mother was watching the baby, but he hated that Yanni pulled up while Marlee was outside. They weren't together anymore, but the shit just felt weird.

"See, fat boy, that's one of your baby mama's right there, not me," Marlee said, as Sierra and Desi laughed.

"We gon' do this shit or what? You want me out of the picture, but there's only one way to make that happen," Tyson smirked.

Marlee never did get a chance to answer because things went left soon after.

"Oh shit!" somebody yelled when Trinity walked up to Yanni and started punching her.

Yanni was barely out of the car before she hit her, and the first lick was loud as hell. She never even had a chance to get her baby out of her car seat before Trinity went into attack mode.

"Nasty ass bitch! Always fucking somebody else's man!" Trinity yelled as she continued to reign down blows on Yanni.

Yanni wasn't a slacker, so she was holding her own. She swung back, but she never got right after that first unexpected lick.

"Chill out Trinity," Craig said as he pulled his girlfriend off the other woman.

"Get the fuck off me! I'm done with your punk ass too. All y'all niggas better go get checked after messing with that mutt. And that goes for you too, Jerry," Trinity huffed angrily.

"This don't have shit to do with me," Jerry replied.

"Nigga, please. That hoe was sucking your dick at one time too and you were with her cousin at the time. Hell, I don't even know why I expected anything different. She got pregnant by my brother while he was with Marlee. Nasty bitch just don't have no respect for herself and nobody else!" Trinity yelled, spilling all the tea.

"Y'all niggas ain't shit," Desi said while shaking her head at Tyson in disgust.

Yanni really wasn't shit and that much was proven. Desi couldn't believe how she used to defend her against other people and she was doing her dirty the whole time. She and Marlee would get out there and go to war with other bitches over Yanni, and they were the main two that she fucked over. When Craig let Trinity go, she started swinging on Yanni again and her cousins just sat there and laughed. Jerry went into the car and got the baby, who had started screaming to the top of her lungs. He was the only one who seemed to care.

"I'm so happy that my son is being raised by a real man and not one of you fuck boys," Marlee said with a frown.

"What?" Tyson asked in confusion.

"You're pathetic, that's what. I can see you not helping Yanni, but you didn't even check on your baby," Marlee said while shaking her head.

"She straight," Tyson replied as he waved her off.

Jerry had knocked on the door to give Tracy the baby, and she came outside fussing when she saw what was going on.

"Y'all wrong for this shit. Stop standing there watching and break them up. Trinity, bring your ass in this house!" Tracy yelled.

Tyson walked across the street and helped Jerry break the fight up. Yanni and Trinity were still yelling at each other, until Tracy pulled her daughter inside. Craig tried to follow her, but Tyson stopped him before he could. He didn't need them tearing his mama's house up and he knew that Trinity would swing on him as soon as he walked in. He wasn't even surprised to learn that his sister's boyfriend was smashing Yanni. She fucked everybody, but he was the only one dumb enough to get her pregnant.

"I'm gone bruh. I don't have time for all this bullshit," Jerry said as he gave Tyson dap and headed to his car.

It was time for him to fall back from Tyson, just like he'd done once before. He was finally in a good place in his life and he didn't need anything happening to change that. He was in a relationship now and he didn't need the added drama. He was sorry that Desi was out there to hear what Trinity said about him and Yanni, but it was out in the open now. Jerry gave up on trying to make amends with her. The nigga that she was cool with was a different kind of crazy and he didn't want to be on the receiving end of the butt of his gun again.

He had to get over thirty stiches from the last time. He was good on everything that didn't mean him no good.

"The fuck you still standing out here for. Get the fuck on," Tyson said to Yanni, who was trying to reattach her mother's rearview mirror that she and Trinity had knocked off during the fight.

"Fuck your fat ass. I do what I want," Yanni snapped angrily.

She was so embarrassed for her cousins to have seen and heard everything that took place. Trinity already hated her, and she only made things worse when she slept with Craig. She was digging herself in a deeper hole and she didn't know how to get out of it. Kallie was the only one of her cousins who really talked to her and even she seemed to be distancing herself. Her boyfriend had recently moved in with her and she didn't invite Yanni over to visit anymore. She couldn't blame her cousin because she didn't have the best track record.

As much as Yanni loved her daughter, she hated her father equally as much. He wasn't shit, but that was her karma for doing her cousin dirty. All the shit he talked in jail was nothing but a bunch of lies. He had no intentions on doing right and that much was clear. He was too busy kissing Marlee's ass and she didn't even want him. With a fine ass nigga like RJ on her arm, Yanni didn't blame her.

"Girl, auntie Yvette is going to have a fit when she see her mirror hanging off like that," Marlee said when Yanni finally got into the car and pulled away.

"I know she is. She just got that car two months ago," Sierra replied.

"Knowing my auntie, she probably only let her use it because of the baby. Stupid bitch fucked just about every nigga in New Orleans and still catching the bus and the ferry. I wish the fuck I would," Marlee said, shaking her head.

"She better get some gorilla glue and put that shit back up. Or least do something to buy herself some time until she can get it fixed," Sierra replied.

"Girl, my auntie gon' murder her ass. She never let Yanni use her cars and now I see why. She better pray that she can do something before Yvette finds out," Marlee noted.

"Too late," Desi said as she put her phone up to her ear.

"Too late for what?" Marlee asked.

Desi didn't reply, but Marlee got her answer when she started talking.

"Hey auntie Yvette, this is Desi. I was calling to talk to you about what just happened," Desi said, as Marlee and Sierra fell out laughing.

They listened as Desi ran the entire story down to Yvette word for word. As expected, Yvette was livid as she waited for Yanni to return with her car. Marlee heard her yelling on the other end of the phone, while she and Sierra continued to laugh. Desi was petty as hell, but she didn't care. She wanted Yanni to confront her about anything, so she could knock her the fuck out.

Chapter 35

"What color are you wearing?" Marlee asked Ivy as she cleaned her face with a wipe.

"My dress is black, and my accessories are silver," Ivy replied.

Marlee nodded her head and got right to work on applying her makeup. Ivy and her siblings were throwing their mother a small dinner party, and she was trying to get herself together to go. She never really wore makeup, but she loved the way that Marlee applied it. She didn't do too much, and she always made her look natural.

"Why is my grandson not here?" Banks asked when he walked into the bedroom.

"Him and RJ were sleeping, so I left without them," Marlee replied.

"When can he stay the night with us? My son keeps saying soon, but maybe I can get a real answer out of you," Banks said.

"Y'all can come get him whenever you're ready. I live for a break and some free time," Marlee replied, right before he walked out of the room.

"How are things going with you and RJ?" Ivy asked.

"It's going." Marlee shrugged.

She had gone back home, but she and the baby were by RJ for the weekend. She had also gone back to work, and RJ wasn't pleased with any of her decisions.

"His feelings were hurt when you went back home. I overheard him and his father talking about it the other day," Ivy whispered, so Banks wouldn't hear her.

"Why were his feelings hurt?" Marlee asked.

"I think he feels like you don't really want to be with him or something. His father told him that he didn't think that was the issue, but he didn't sound too convinced. I guess he feels like that because you went back home," Ivy replied.

"Me going back home has nothing to do with me not wanting to be with him. Honestly, Ivy, my ex-boyfriend was the only man that I've ever lived with. I was comfortable when we got our condo because it wasn't his or mine, it was ours. I just don't like the idea of me moving into a home that doesn't belong to me at least partially."

"That's where quitclaim deeds come into play," Ivy replied.

"What is that?" Marlee questioned.

"A way to add your name to the deed of the house legally. That way, half of it will belong to you," Ivy answered.

"No Ivy. I couldn't ask him to do that. We have a baby, but we haven't even known each other long enough for that," Marlee noted.

"You can't put a clock on love Marlee. Sometimes the best moments are the ones that you didn't plan for. Tre is proof of that," Ivy said.

"That's true, but I just don't know Ivy. I can't expect RJ to alter his life for me, just because we have Tre. And I don't want him to feel obligated to take care of me."

"Do you know that I had only known Banks for one month before he got me my first car?" Ivy asked.

"Seriously?" Marlee asked in surprise.

"Yep and not just any old car either. Honey, he took me on the lot and got me a brand-new Benz. I didn't even have a driver's license, but I had a brand-new car. I mean, I had never even kissed him, and he got me a car. He told me that he didn't like the idea of me asking anyone else for a ride. And that car was only the beginning. I got this house when I was only five months pregnant with RJ. He told me that he wanted me to have my own place, and I agreed. I went out there looking for apartments and he laughed like it was the funniest joke ever. He told me that his son would never know what the inside of an apartment looked like if he could help it. He got a realtor and we started looking for houses."

"Damn," Marlee mumbled.

"I just need you to understand the kind of men that they are. They love hard and they're great providers. Whatever RJ does for you has nothing to do with Tre. It's because he loves you. His father told me something last night that I thought was hilarious," Ivy chuckled.

"What's that?" Marlee asked.

"He said that you were the first girl that RJ ever told him that he loved. Of all the girlfriends that he's had, you're the first one that he openly confessed to loving. Now, that might not mean much to you, but it says a lot to me," Ivy replied, giving Marlee something to think about.

"Can I ask you a personal question Ivy? I won't get upset if you don't answer and I don't want you to get upset about me asking," Marlee said.

"I already know what you're about to ask. No, I didn't know that Banks was married when we first got together. I was only seventeen years old being wined and dined by an older man. I mean, he used to rent these extravagant suites and have gifts there waiting for me. We would stay there the entire weekend, but we didn't have sex until my eighteenth birthday. First time and I got pregnant. Even then, he treated me like a queen. He got me this house and anything else that I wanted. He spent nights here and everything was all good. Imagine my surprise when RJ was about three months old and I bumped into his wife in the mall. A wife that I didn't even know he had," Ivy said, shaking her head.

"And what happened?" Marlee asked her, engrossed in their conversation.

"She knew who I was, but I had never heard of her. She told me that she prayed for my baby to die and she was sorry that her prayers weren't answered," Ivy said.

"That bitch was evil." Marlee frowned.

"She still is, but I whipped her ass in the mall that day with my baby sleeping right there in his stroller," Ivy replied.

"Y'all had a fight!" Marlee yelled in shock.

"Girl, that was just one of many. I was young and dumb back then. After a while, that shit got old. She used to be the one to initiate it though."

"What happened when you told Banks that you met his wife?" Marlee questioned.

"I was so hurt to know that I had fallen in love with someone else's husband. I didn't want to see him or talk to him. I was depressed and moping around here like somebody died. It wasn't until Iris gave birth to Murk did I snap out of it. I not only had my three-month-old baby, but I had another newborn that I had to care for. That's what got Banks back in my good graces. He helped me out so good with my nephew and I was so thankful for him. I would have lost my mind in here trying to take care of two babies by myself. Hell, I was still a baby my damn self," Ivy rambled.

"That sounds like a Tyler Perry movie," Marlee said, making her laugh.

"I need to call him and sell it. But, seriously Marlee. I think you and RJ need to have a serious conversation about how you feel. You have some very valid points and he needs to hear them," Ivy replied.

"I don't know Ivy. We'll see," Marlee said, feeling torn about what she wanted to do.

"Sometimes the words that we leave unspoken are the most important ones that should have been said. Don't be haunted by the things you didn't say," Ivy said, before getting up to look at her makeup in the mirror.

Marlee took a seat in the chair that she'd just vacated and thought about everything that she and Ivy had just discussed. Admittedly, she wanted everything that RJ was offering, but she was scared. After having three failed relationships before him, Marlee was afraid of that kind of commitment. Everything moved so fast with them and she just didn't want to make another mistake. She hated to feel like she was making RJ suffer for the men before him, but that was exactly what she was doing. It wasn't fair, and he deserved a chance just like all the others. If nothing else, RJ was honest. If he felt a certain way about something, he had no problem letting her know. Everyone kept telling her that they needed to talk, and they were right. She was telling other people how she felt, but she had never expressed it to him.

***

"Fuck!" Marlee screamed out hoarsely.

RJ lifted her up and put her legs on his shoulders while he bounced her up and down as hard as he could. Skin slapped against skin as their moans of pleasure filled the room. RJ moved them into different positions, trying his best to please her from different angles. Marlee held on tight as she bit and sucked on his neck to muffle her moans. RJ felt another orgasm building, but he wasn't about to be the first one to tap out. He put Marlee's legs down and pulled out before lying her down at the edge of the bed.

"Oh shit! Yesss!" Marlee yelled when he guided her dampness to his tongue.

He put his tongue inside of her as deep as he could while moving her up and down on it. Marlee pulled the sheets and grabbed at the covers as another orgasm caused her to lose control. She tried to push RJ away, but he didn't budge.

"RJ please. I can't do it no more," Marlee whimpered as she tried to move away from him.

She exhaled when he came up for air, but he still wasn't done with her. He flipped Marlee over on her stomach and entered her again. Instead of giving her long deep strokes like he usually did, he pushed her face down in the mattress and started beating it up.

"Damn Marlee," RJ mumbled as he bit his bottom lip.

Marlee was tired, but her hips rose as she met his hard thrusts. When she went hard, RJ went harder until Marlee started to scoot away. RJ kept pulling her back, but she scooted away again until she slipped off the bed headfirst. He grabbed her when she fell, but he never stopped stroking. He lost his grip again, letting Marlee's head slide until it touched the floor. RJ grabbed her thighs and held on tight while utilizing their new position.

"Fuck! Oh shit!" Marlee screamed, as RJ used her legs to pull her into him over and over while he stroked her.

Their legs were crisscrossed like a pair of scissors and neither of them had ever felt anything better. Marlee's hands found the floor, as RJ gripped her waist and stroked her into another orgasm.

"Shit baby. I'm almost there. It's coming!" RJ yelled out, right before he pumped a few more times and unloaded inside of her.

Marlee yelled out as another wave of pleasure overtook her and her entire body slid down to the floor. RJ reached down with one arm and pulled her up, lying her damp body on top of his.

"My new favorite position," Marlee panted as she rested her head on RJ's chest.

"I don't even know what position it was, but that shit was good as fuck," RJ replied as he slapped her ass cheek.

"Always." Marlee yawned.

"Don't even try to go to sleep. We're supposed to be moving the rest of your stuff in today," RJ reminded her.

"I know baby, but that can wait. Most of it is already here," Marlee replied.

"No, Marlee, get up. I don't want most of it here. I want all of it here. I did my part and you promised to do yours," RJ replied.

"It's not even that much RJ. It's only my makeup stuff," Marlee noted.

"Okay and the room is finished, so we need to go get it," he replied.

Marlee and RJ ended up having a long talk after she left Ivy's house two weeks before. She laid everything out for him, the same as she had done for his mother. RJ assured her that them having a baby had nothing to do with how he felt about her. He not only wanted to share his space with Marlee, he wanted to share his life with her too. Marlee was happy when he offered to add her name to the title of his house. She was even happier because she didn't have to ask. That made her feel like he really wanted her there and she wasn't pressuring him to make the decision. They went to a real estate attorney the following Monday and had the paperwork signed and filed with the courts. They were mailed a new deed, naming them both owners of the property. That gave Marlee the security she needed and RJ the family that he wanted.

He gave Marlee one of the rooms that he never used and turned it into a makeup studio for her. He had some shelves and drawers built into one wall and two huge lighted mirrors put up on the other. A long counter was put up in the area where she would work, and she had more than enough space for whatever she needed to sit on it. Marlee had someone airbrush her logo, a huge tube of lipstick, and a makeup brush on the wall and her work area looked like a real studio. She got a lot of new supplies and she and RJ spent an entire day putting it all away. The only thing left to do was get all the supplies from her mother's garage and add it to her collection.

"Okay. Just give me a few minutes. You just had me hanging halfway out the bed. Let a bitch get right for a few minutes," Marlee laughed.

"I'm hungry," RJ said, as Marlee nodded her head in agreement.

Instead of taking a nap, they decided to shower and go get something to eat. Tre was with Tiffany and they planned to get him when they got the rest of Marlee's things. Once they were dressed and ready to leave, Marlee's phone rang, displaying her mother's number. Thinking that something was wrong with her son, she quickly answered to make sure that everything was okay.

"Is my baby okay?" Marlee asked as soon as she answered.

"Yeah, he's fine, but did you know that Matthew was down here?" Tiffany asked, referring to Marlee's father.

"No, I haven't talked to him since he lied and said that he was coming to my baby shower. Hell, Tre is two months old now and he's just making his way down here." Marlee frowned.

"I guess, but he's sitting in my living room and I want him gone. Alvin let him in because I was leaving his ass standing on the porch. I told him that you don't live here anymore, and he started asking a bunch of questions. It's fine if you didn't plan to come here right now, but his ass gotta go if you're not. We ain't friends and I don't want him to think that we are," Tiffany ranted.

"No, I'll be there in a little while. I just finished getting dressed," Marlee replied, before she and her mother hung up.

"What's up baby?" RJ quizzed.

"My daddy finally showed his sad ass face. I don't know what he expects, but I'm still not fucking with him. It was one thing when he lied and got my hopes up when I was a child. I'm a grown ass woman now and I'm done playing games with him."

"Don't even let that shit stress you out baby. Just say what you have to say and be done with it. Come on, we can get some food to go once we get Tre," RJ replied as he held his hand out for her to grab.

"I guess," Marlee replied, as she grabbed his hand and walked out of the house.

He could see the change in Marlee's mood as he drove, and he didn't like that. She was good until she found out that her father was in town. Now, she looked aggravated and disgusted. She was looking out of the window and not saying too much. He knew all about her relationship with her father and he didn't like him already. RJ didn't really know how she felt because he'd always had his father in his life. He planned to always be there for his son as well. He wanted to do something to cheer Marlee up, so he decided to tell her what had been on his mind.

"I was thinking about going back to Vegas next month for a few days. What do you think about that?" RJ asked.

"Hell no, nigga. You must have forgotten what happened when you went to Vegas the last time," Marlee said as she frowned.

"What? No baby, not by myself. I'm talking about me and you. Maybe Murk and Desi will come too. You do know that next month will make a year since we first met. I want us to go back there. Maybe we can stay in the same hotel and shit," RJ replied with a smile.

"Aww baby. That's so sweet. Yeah, we can do that," Marlee said as her mood instantly changed.

RJ grabbed her hand and kissed it, while she smiled brightly. He was happy to make her feel better and he hoped that seeing her father wouldn't change that. When they pulled up to Tiffany's house, Marlee spotted her father's truck parked at the curb. She took a deep breath and prepared to face the man who she hadn't seen in months.

"There she is. Hey baby. You look beautiful," Matthew said as he stood up to hug her.

"Hey daddy, thanks." Marlee smiled and returned the greeting.

"I just got to hold my very first grandson," Matthew beamed proudly.

"Yeah and this is his father and my boyfriend, RJ. Baby, this is my father, Matthew," Marlee said as she introduced her father and her man for the very first time.

"It's nice to meet you, sir," RJ said as he shook Matthew's hand.

"You too, son. I was wondering who my grandson looked like, but now I see," Matthew replied.

"What are you doing down here daddy? Did something happen?" Marlee asked.

"No, nothing happened. Why is that the only time you think I come to visit? I wanted to see my first grandchild. I'm sorry that I couldn't make the baby shower, but I got him a lot of stuff from the Galleria before I came down," Matthew said as he gestured at a bunch of gift bags that sat next to the sofa.

"Thank you," Marlee replied emotionless.

"Can we step outside and talk for a minute Marlee?" her father asked.

She looked like she was thinking about it, until RJ nodded his head and spoke up.

"Go ahead baby. I'll get the rest of your stuff from the garage and put it in the truck," RJ said.

"I'll help you," Alvin offered, as Tiffany sat there holding her grandson.

Matthew followed his daughter outside and over to where his truck was parked. Marlee folded her arms across her chest and waited for him to speak. It was about to be a bunch of bullshit, but that was nothing new.

"I first want to apologize to you, baby girl. I was wrong for not calling you all those months when I was with Cara. I was just getting back to work, and she was paying all the bills in the house at the time. I just wanted to keep down confusion," Matthew lamely stated.

"So, calling your daughter was causing confusion?" Marlee questioned angrily.

"In her mind, it was. Y'all got off to a bad start and things just went downhill from there," Matthew replied.

"I'm sorry daddy, but I don't buy that. You could have snuck off to call me if you really wanted to talk. You never even tried to make sure that Desi and I got back home safely. Then, when I tried to call you, I found out that my number was blocked. Do you know how that made me feel?" Marlee asked.

"I know I was wrong for blocking your number, and I should have handled things a little better than I did," Matthew said, shocking Marlee with his confession.

He lied and told her that it was Cara who blocked her number, and she stupidly believed him. She just knew that it was Cara who was behind it and she defended him when Mat told her otherwise. To know that it was her father instead hurt her even more, even though it had happened months ago. Matthew must have forgotten what he told her, and she didn't remind him. For years, Tiffany had called him selfish and inconsiderate and she was right. Marlee used to take up for him, but that wouldn't happen again. Matthew didn't give a damn about anyone else and his actions always proved it. Marlee refused to even give him anymore of her time and energy. Matthew was good for telling people what they wanted to hear and Marlee wasn't opposed to doing the same.

"It's cool daddy. No hard feelings over here," Marlee said as she plastered on a big fake smile.

"Thank you, baby. You know I love you to the moon and back," Matthew said as he pulled her in for a hug.

"I love you too, daddy," Marlee replied and that was the truth.

Marlee watched, as RJ and Alvin went back and forth from the garage and packed the rest of her equipment in his truck. She stood outside and caught her father up on everything that had taken place in her life over the last couple of months. As far as he knew, she was still with Tyson, but that had been over with for a minute. He was shocked to know that Yanni now had a baby with his daughter's ex. He told her how his feelings were hurt when he learned that she'd come to Atlanta and didn't come to see him, but Marlee didn't care. She was done caring about his feelings because he obviously didn't care about hers. He told Marlee that his visit was a surprise, but he ended up being surprised when he learned that she had moved out a few weeks ago. Marlee promised to show him her new house, but that was another lie. She was done going out of her way for him and she swore that she never would again.

Once RJ was done, he got Tre and strapped him in the car. Matthew invited them to dinner the next day and they both agreed to it. When he left, Marlee got in the car with her family and went to go get something to eat.

"You good baby?" RJ asked as he gently squeezed her hand.

"Better than ever," Marlee replied as she smiled at him.

She wasn't about to let her father get her down because she had done that enough over the years. It wasn't just about her anymore. She had a good man and baby to worry about. Everything else took the back seat, especially her father.

Chapter 36

RJ was over the drama, but that seemed to be all that followed him lately. Crazy thing was, it wasn't his drama that he was dealing with. His father and his soon to be ex-wife were going to drive him crazy. Lauren had to be about the dumbest bitch on planet earth. It wasn't enough that she got busted stealing once before, but she was still at the foolishness. Once Banks had learned about what she'd done the first time, he got all of his and Ivy's banking information changed and made sure that they didn't send him any checks. He started a whole new bank account with the rest of the money that he'd taken from his and Lauren's joint account. If he hadn't, she probably would have got her other nigga a house by now. Her stupid ass tried to write a check at the Harley Davidson store and ended up getting arrested. The check was no good, of course, and she was dumb for thinking that it was.

"I just pulled up to the office baby. I'll see you in a little while for lunch," RJ said, before he hung up the phone with Marlee.

He'd just dropped their son off to Ivy and he was trying to see what was up with his father now. As soon as he got out of his car and headed into the building, he heard screaming and arguing. RJ hurried down the hall to his father's office where the noise was coming from.

"That's not fair daddy! She did the same thing that you did and you're trying to make her suffer for it!" Joy yelled as she stood in front of her father's desk and cried.

RJ made his presence known, but he didn't try to intervene. He really didn't have anything to do with it, so he stayed out of the conversation. He wanted to tell Joy that she sounded like a damn fool. Her mother hadn't worked in years, but she had the audacity to be dishing out money to another nigga. Money that wasn't even hers.

"I'm sorry about what's happening baby, but the best thing for you and your sisters to do is stay out of it," Banks tried to reason.

"How can I stay out of it when my mama is talking about moving back to Denver? How can you do this to her, daddy? She's your wife and she doesn't have any money. That chump change that you gave her is almost gone," Joy cried.

"I tried talking to your mother to offer my assistance, but she doesn't want it," Banks said calmly.

RJ was pissed at the way Joy was talking to their father, but Banks didn't seem to be bothered by it.

"You didn't offer her any assistance. You want to spoon feed her by paying all her bills. She deserves half of all the money that was in that joint account and you know it," Joy replied.

"If we're being honest, she wasn't entitled to a dime, but I would never do her like that. Even after I swore that I was done with her, I still went back on my word. I offered to keep the bills paid and get her whatever she needed. I'm not giving her any money, so she can turn around and hand it to another man," Banks pointed out.

"Why? Isn't that what you're doing with your whore?" Joy spat bitterly.

"You better watch your fucking mouth!" RJ barked angrily.

"Fuck you! You're just like him, so you have no room to talk!" Joy yelled.

"Bitch-" RJ started as he jumped up.

"RJ! Be respectful. That's your sister," Banks scolded as he stood up and put a calming hand on his son's chest.

"Fuck that bitch. I'm tired of holding my tongue for her stupid ass. I already told you how I felt about that shit. I'm done being nice. Let that bitch say some slick shit about me and my mama again, and I'm knocking her the fuck out," RJ swore.

"Son, please," Banks pleaded.

"Let him go. I dare him to put his hands on me. I'll put that illegitimate bastard in jail where he belongs," Joy threatened.

"Yeah and I'll be in a cell right next to your mammy. Dumb bitch trying to buy dick with bad checks," RJ taunted.

Keith drove Lauren to the store to purchase the bike, but he left once he saw that she was being cuffed and taken away. Joy was talking all that shit, but it was Banks who bailed her mother out and made sure that the charges were dropped. He wasn't obligated to give Lauren a dime, but he still tried to work out some financial arrangements with her. Her stupid ass was trying to bargain, when she wasn't even entitled to anything. When she told Banks that she wanted all her bills paid plus ten grand every month, he laughed at her and withdrew his initial offer. Now, Joy was mad because Lauren was packing up and planning to move back to Denver with the little money that she had left. Her daughters didn't want her to go, but RJ was willing to pay for her a one-way ticket to get the fuck on.

"Fuck you and fuck this job. I quit!" Joy fumed as she stormed out of the room.

"Joy!" Banks yelled as he went after her.

"Miserable ass bitch," RJ mumbled as he sat back down and massaged his temples.

He had a big headache now, thanks to his stupid ass sister. Honestly, he understood Joy's frustration. It had to be hard seeing their mother hurting all the time. He knew because he'd experienced that with Ivy a few times and it was never easy. He hated how things were between his parents too, but they were grown. There was nothing that he could do about it. He and his sisters never really had much of a relationship because they never gave him a chance. It wasn't his fault that their father was in love with his mother, but they always took it out on him. It took about twenty minutes, but Banks finally walked back into his office and took a seat behind his desk.

"This entire situation is a disaster," he sighed as he hung his head low.

"I'm sorry pops, but I already told you what it was," RJ replied.

"It's not your fault RJ. This is all on me," Banks admitted.

"Why do you feel like that?" RJ asked.

"Truthfully, I should have left Lauren years ago. I haven't loved her for a while and I shouldn't have stayed as long as I did. True, she gave up her family to be with me, but that was her choice. I shouldn't have let that affect my decision to stay with her. I've been looking for her to give me a reason to leave for years and I jumped at the first chance I got. That's why I was proud of you for being man enough to end things with Aspen before you got with Marlee," Banks admitted.

"I don't see how you did it for so many years. I couldn't juggle two relationships like that and not lose my mind. One relationship is hard enough," RJ replied.

"It's only hard if you're sneaking around. I was always upfront and honest about whatever I did," Banks pointed out.

"I guess we need to look into hiring some help for the front desk," RJ said, jumping to another subject.

"No, not yet. Joy is just upset. I'll give her a few days to calm down before I call her again. Her assistant can handle everything until then," Banks replied.

"So, now what? Is Lauren really moving back to Denver?" RJ asked.

"That's what she said, but who knows? It's not like she doesn't have a place to stay. I don't know what else they want from me, but I'm done offering. It's one thing for me to still support Lauren, but I'll be damned if I support her and her man too. A man that doesn't work, doesn't eat. It's been said since the beginning of time and nothing has changed," Banks noted.

"That nigga is a bum, straight up. What kind man even allows that shit?" RJ frowned as he stood up and prepared to go to his office.

He had some work to do before he went to get Marlee for lunch. He didn't have time to dwell on what just happened and he wasn't going to.

***

"Cousin, it was everything!" Desi yelled over the speaker phone to Marlee.

"Girl, I know you tried to kill his ass. It's been a minute since you had some," Marlee laughed as she gave her son a bath.

"You know I had no mercy on his ass. He was up fixing a bitch breakfast early this morning," Desi laughed.

"And where was Destini?" Marlee asked.

"In her crib knocked out just like her daddy was when I finished with him," Desi chuckled.

"I think it's so cute that she's spoiled behind you. I guess by her seeing you every day, she got attached," Marlee said.

"Yeah, it's been six months now. She's so sweet. It's hard not to spoil her. Even Murk wants to hold her when her and Desmond come to the house," Desi noted.

"As crazy as he is, he's good with kids," Marlee replied.

"He should be after having five of his own," Desi laughed.

"Is he done Marlee?" RJ yelled from the bedroom for the second time.

He was trying to play with Tre, but she was taking forever giving him a bath. He knew it was because she was on the phone gossiping with Desi. He knew she wasn't done, but that was his way of hurrying her along. It was early in the day, but Tre had thrown up all over his clothes after he ate, and Marlee went straight to the bathroom with him. For the first time in a while, RJ didn't have any plans and he wanted to spend the entire Sunday relaxing with his family. Marlee had cooked and cleaned up the kitchen once they ate.

"Let me call you back Desi. I've been having my baby in this tub for a minute and his daddy is having a fit," Marlee said.

"Okay, but did you put in your time at work for our Vegas trip in two weeks?" Desi asked.

"I only needed that Monday off, but it's already been approved," Marlee said before they disconnected. She finished bathing her baby and took him to the room to dress him.

"It's about time. My baby's water probably was cold as fuck while you were in there gossiping," RJ said as he moved her out of the way and dried his son off.

Tre was smiling, as RJ made baby talk and played with him. He would be three months old in two weeks and he was really filling out. They were thankful that he was a good baby and he slept for most of the night. RJ usually got up with him if he did get up since Marlee had to be to work so early.

"Where's his baby lotion?" Marlee asked as she searched Tre's diaper bag.

He was dressed, but she wanted to rub him down with some lotion. She loved the way it smelled, and she kept a bottle of it with her.

"I don't know. It should be in there," RJ replied.

"I don't see it," Marlee said as she dumped everything out onto the bed.

"Maybe it's in your purse. You keep everything in there," RJ noted, as she walked out of the room.

She went to go get a new bottle from Tre's nursery, while RJ grabbed her purse to see if it was in there. Marlee kept the worst purses that he'd ever seen, and they were all huge. RJ started pulling stuff out of it as he felt around for the bottle of lotion. Once he had his hand on it, he pulled it out and started throwing everything back inside. He picked up the last handful of papers, ready to stuff them back into her purse right as something else cause his eye. There was a letter from DNA solutions that instantly made him frown. He and Marlee didn't use that company when they did their test, but that wasn't the only problem. The date that was stamped on the front of the envelope showed that the test was done only two weeks ago.

RJ damn near ripped the envelope trying to get to the paper that was inside. He was heated when he saw Tyson's name, along with his son's and Marlee's. Of course, the test said there was a percentage of zero that Tre could be for the other man, but RJ was pissed that she had the test done at all. He and Marlee knew the truth and he didn't give a fuck about Tyson. The fact that Marlee had gone behind his back and had their son tested anyway had him heated.

"I had to get a new bottle from the top of the closet. I don't know where all of his lotion is disappearing to," Marlee said when she walked back into the bedroom.

"The fuck is this shit Marlee? You gave that nigga a blood test anyway after we talked about it!" RJ yelled.

"Yes, but let me explain," Marlee replied.

"Explain what Marlee? Huh? How you went against what I said just to please your ex?" RJ fumed.

"No RJ. It wasn't even like that. I was just tired of him assuming shit and I wanted to shut him the fuck up. I hate it when he calls Tre his son or say shit like our baby. The nigga came to my job twice since I've been back at work. I can barely go visit my sister and best friend since he lives across the street now. Me telling him that Tre wasn't his obviously meant nothing without proof," Marlee replied.

"You didn't have to prove a muthafucking thing to that nigga! That ain't your man!" RJ yelled.

Marlee wanted to tell him the first day that she agreed to give Tyson a blood test, but she was trying to avoid an argument. Since he found out about it on his own, that made it seem even worse. Tyson was going too far with claiming Marlee's son and he even had people on the block thinking that Tre was his. No matter how many times Marlee told him otherwise, he was still asking her to prove it. He came to her job twice trying to give her money for her son, and Marlee was over it.

She set an appointment up to have the test done and she met Tyson there with Tre two days later. She had the results mailed to her mother's house, even though she already knew what they would say. That was two weeks ago, and she hadn't heard a peep from Tyson since. That was her goal and she was happy that it was accomplished.

"Will you at least try to understand my point?" Marlee asked in frustration.

"Fuck that Marlee. The fuck you with me for if you still doing everything that your ex nigga tells you to do," RJ argued.

"I just told you what was up, but you obviously don't care enough to listen. Maybe you were okay with another nigga walking around claiming your son as his own, but he had me fucked up. When you're ready to sit down and have an adult conversation, you know where to find me," Marlee replied as she picked her son up and sat down on the bed.

"You got the nerve to get mad when you were the one who fucked up. You went behind my back and did some shit that I told you not to do. Fuck what that nigga thought. We knew the truth and that was all that mattered. How the fuck you go against what I say, just to please another nigga? You should have just stayed with his ass since he's the one calling all the shots. I'm done with this shit. Go be with that nigga if that's what you want!" RJ yelled as he grabbed his keys and walked out of the house.

As soon as the front door slammed, Marlee burst into tears. She was wrong and she could admit that, but RJ didn't even try to hear her out. Her wanting to get the test done had nothing to do with Tyson calling the shots. She wanted him out of her life and she succeeded with making that happen. RJ's reaction was what had her scared to even bring it up in the first place.

"Fuck him," Marlee sniffled as she laid her now sleeping son down in the middle of the bed.

She threw on some tights and a shirt before packing Tre's diaper bag. If he wanted it to be over, then Marlee wasn't kissing his ass or begging him to stay. Just like he added her name to the deed, he could have it removed just as easily. Whenever he decided to come back home, her and her son would be long gone. Alvin and some of his brothers would move her out just as quickly as they moved her in.

"That's exactly why I didn't want to move in with his stupid ass," Marlee fussed.

When she went to get her keys, they weren't where she last put them. She checked her son's diaper bag, her purse, and the key hook where she normally kept them. Without her keys, she couldn't lock up the house or get into her car to go anywhere.

Then, it hit her. That was the entire point. RJ had taken her keys to make sure that she stayed there until he returned, but he had her fucked up. Marlee grabbed her phone and was about to call Desi. She thought against it, since she knew that her cousin was spending time with her man. She would never want to interfere with that, so she abandoned that idea. Mat and Sierra were home and she was preparing to give one of them a call. She would just have to leave out of the side door and lock it behind her.

Marlee had just dialed the last digit of her sister's number when her phone rang displaying Ivy's picture. That was even better. Ivy had a key to lock up her son's house and she could drop Marlee off home until her stupid ass son decided to hand over her car keys.

Chapter 37

RJ didn't even have to think about where he was going. His mother's house was the first place that came to mind. He needed to talk to his father and get his input. RJ needed to know if he was overreacting or if he had a valid reason to be as upset as he was. He told Marlee that he was done with her, but he regretted the words just as quickly as he'd said them. He was in love with her and he couldn't see himself being without her. He sat in his car deep in thought until he finally got out and used his key to enter his mother's home. As soon as he walked in, Ivy was walking down the steps with his father right behind her. She was dressed with her keys and purse in her hand.

"What the hell is going on RJ? I just called Marlee to see what her and the baby were doing, and she begged me to come pick her up. I don't need my grandbaby in the middle of no mess," Ivy fussed.

"She's good. Don't go get her ass." RJ frowned.

"I have to RJ. I already told her that I was on my way," Ivy replied.

"Well, call her back and tell her that you're not coming. I took her keys for a reason. She better sit her ass down and stop playing with me," RJ fumed.

"I don't know what to do," Ivy sighed as she plopped down on her sofa.

"Just wait a minute before you do anything baby. Come up here and talk to me, RJ," his father requested as he turned and walked back up the stairs.

RJ followed him into his old room and threw his body onto the bed. His father stood there with his back against the wall and his legs crossed at the ankle. RJ covered his face with his arm, as his father patiently waited for him to start talking.

"Her hard headed ass snuck and had a DNA test done on my son. After I specifically told her not to worry about what that nigga was saying, she went and did the shit anyway. Then, she didn't even tell me about it. I found the shit out by accident," RJ barked angrily.

"What did the test results say?" his father asked, making him scrunch up his face while looking over at him.

"What do you think it said? Even if Tre didn't look just like me, I knew he was mine before he was even born," RJ replied.

"And that's my point son. Why keep up the unnecessary drama when you don't have to? If something as simple as a DNA test could eliminate a potential problem, what was the big deal?" Banks questioned.

"Man, fuck that nigga! We didn't owe his ass no explanations. Tre ain't his and she told him that even before she had him. The fuck is he supposed to be where niggas gotta jump through hoops for him?" RJ snapped.

"It's better to lose your pride for the one you love rather than lose the one you love for your pride," Banks said as he looked at his son.

"This has nothing to do with pride pops. I'm pissed at the fact that she went behind my back and did the shit," RJ replied.

"That's bullshit RJ. I know you better than anyone and I know what's really got you upset. You always did hate doing what you thought other people wanted you to do, and this time ain't no different. Marlee getting the test done ain't as big of an issue as you're trying to make it out to be. The thought of you doing what her ex wanted y'all to do is what's bothering you," Banks said, calling him out.

RJ sat there for a while, refusing to admit that his father was right. He could be stubborn at times and he hated being told what to do. He had no problem with authority but, when one of his peers tried to do it, was when it became an issue.

"Like I just said, fuck that nigga!" RJ hissed.

"I hear you, son. And exactly what did you tell Marlee?" Banks wanted to know.

"I told her that I was done. The fuck is she with me for if she's listening to the next nigga," RJ snapped angrily.

"Alright, well, I guess we need to go get your stuff out of the house until you can find you another one. That house now belongs to her and my grandson. Call Murk and see if he can come help us," Banks said as he pushed himself off the wall.

"Hold on pops. What you mean? I'm pissed, but I'm not leaving my family," RJ said as he jumped up from the bed.

"That's my point, so why are you here bitching about it to me?" Banks asked.

"Huh?" RJ asked in confusion.

"Huh, my ass. You're always complaining about being treated like a child, but that's exactly what you're acting like right now. If you can stand here and tell me that you can picture your life without Marlee being in it, then I'll be the first one to tell you to leave. If not, you need to man the fuck up and bring your spoiled ass home," Banks fussed.

"Damn pops. Ain't no more baby talk and shit, huh? Just straight gutta with it," RJ laughed.

"You got your own family now RJ. You can't run over here to me and your mama every time something doesn't go like you planned it. Your family is looking for you to lead them and I can't help you with that. If I didn't teach you anything else, I taught you how to be a man," Banks noted.

"Yeah, I know. I just need a minute to get my mind right. I have too much to lose, so I need to get my words right," RJ said as he fell back onto the bed.

"Stick to the plan son. Remember everything that we talked about a few weeks ago and stick to the plan," Banks replied.

"I will, and tell my mama to sit down and let me be. Marlee will be alright until I get there," RJ said as his father walked out of the room and left him to his thoughts.

Just like always when he was deep in thought, RJ closed his eyes and replayed things over in his head. His father used to always tell him to do that when he had to make a decision about something important. Banks used to always tell him that if the bad outweighed the good, then there was nothing to fight for or even think about. On the other hand, if the good outweighed the bad, then he needed to make the smart decision. When it came to his relationship with Marlee, there really wasn't much to think about. RJ loved her, and he loved her living under the same roof with him. They hadn't known each for a year, but his heart let him know that being with her was right. He knew that he could live with her. He just didn't know if he could live without her.

RJ was so deep in thought that he'd drifted off to sleep without even trying to. Three hours had passed, and it was dark when he finally opened his eyes.

"Shit," he hissed as he jumped up from the bed. He grabbed his keys and jogged down the stairs. His parents were cuddled up on the sofa watching tv, when he walked into the living room.

"It's about damn time. You got me lying telling Marlee that I was on my way and I never even left the house," Ivy fussed when she saw him.

"My fault ma. I fell asleep, but I'm going home now," RJ assured her.

He got into his truck and headed straight home. He knew how Marlee could get when she was mad, and that made him a little nervous. Marlee popped off something serious and he had seen that too many times to count. When RJ pulled up at home, he was happy to see that Marlee's car was still there. Although he had her keys, he wasn't sure if one of her family members had come to pick her up or not. He had her spare key on his ring, but that didn't mean anything if she got a ride.

Suddenly, the fear of Marlee and his son not being there started to choke him, and he regretted that he ever left. RJ had a lump in his throat the size of a baseball and his hands were damp with sweat. He entered the dark, quiet house and tiptoed up the stairs to his bedroom. When he opened the bedroom door, he exhaled, relieved to see Marlee and his son stretched out across the bed. Tre was on his round pillow sleeping and Marlee was right next to him. Her back was to the door, so RJ kicked off his shoes and got in behind her. He kissed the Fleur de Lis tattoo that she'd recently gotten on the back of her neck, and she stirred a bit. When he pulled her closer to him, her eyes popped open and she tried to move away.

"Get off me, RJ. Stupid, childish ass," Marlee huffed groggily.

She sounded sleepy as hell, but she was still mad at him. Ivy had told her that she was on her way hours ago and

Marlee had fallen asleep waiting for her. She was kind of happy that she didn't come because she wanted to patch things up with RJ. Marlee didn't want to leave things like they were, and she didn't want RJ to think that he couldn't trust her.

"I'm sorry baby. I shouldn't have overreacted like I did and I'm sorry," RJ apologized.

"I wasn't trying to sneak and do anything behind your back, but I knew how you were going to react if I told you. I didn't have the test done just for me. I did that for us. You know just as well as I do that Tyson would have been a problem in the long run. I didn't want that and that's why I agreed to do it," Marlee tried to reason.

"I know why you did it Marlee. I wish you would have told me first, but I'm happy that it's done. That's one less issue that we have to worry about. I just don't want us to start keeping secrets from each other. That's not the kind of relationship that I want us to have," RJ explained.

"Neither do I, but I was just trying to find the right time to tell you. I wanted to say something every day since I got the results, but there never seemed to be a good time," Marlee replied.

"I understand baby. It's all good. Now that that fat muthafucka knows what's up, he don't have a reason to say shit to you," RJ said with a frown.

"He hasn't. I haven't heard from him since we got the test results back," Marlee acknowledged.

"Good," RJ said as he ran his hand down her thigh.

"And why did you take my keys?" Marlee asked as she punched his leg.

"Because I didn't want you to leave," RJ admitted.

"Why not? You broke up with me before you left," Marlee said as she punched his leg again.

"Girl, you know I didn't mean that shit. I was mad and just talking stupid," RJ noted.

"I should hold you to it," Marlee taunted.

"You can't hold me to a damn thing. Ain't no breaking up," RJ said as he bit her neck.

"Well, stop saying shit that you don't mean. Once words are out, you can't put them back in. Consider my feelings too before you say anything," Marlee lectured.

"Point taken baby. I promise that it will never happen again," RJ swore as he pulled her closer to him.

Being with Marlee just felt right. He couldn't explain it and he wasn't going to try. He just knew that they were meant to be. There was no other way to say it. Some things didn't have to be forced. They just fit perfectly without having to try.

Chapter 38

Aspen's mouth hung open in shock as the doctor spoke what seemed like a foreign language. Pregnant. No. She couldn't be. That had to be a mistake. She prayed that it was a mistake. The one time that she agreed to let Aaron accompany her to the hospital and that was what she was hit with. After two days of having what she thought was a stomach bug, Aspen decided to go to the emergency room on day three. Her aunt was concerned that it was something more serious and she encouraged Aspen to go. Usually, she wouldn't want Aaron nowhere around her, but she was in no mood to drive. She was kicking herself for letting him come to the back with her because the news was delivered in his presence. He was smiling hard and all Aspen wanted to do was die. Of all the times that she'd tried to get pregnant by RJ on purpose, she never succeeded. Now, she was finally blessed with the baby that she'd always wanted, but she wasn't excited about it. Aaron thought he was ready to start a family, but Aspen knew better. He wasn't stable, no matter how hard he tried to pretend.

"Do you have any questions Ms. Connors?" the doctor asked, pulling Aspen back into the present.

"Um, no. Thank you," Aspen replied with a fake smile.

"Okay, well, sit tight and I'll get your discharge papers ready. I'll also write you out a few prescriptions to help with the nausea," the doctor replied.

He wasn't an OBGYN, so he couldn't tell her how far along she was or anything like that. Aspen had only missed one cycle, but she didn't think anything of it. Since she'd changed from the pills to the shots and back to the pills again, that had happened twice before. She couldn't be no more than five or six weeks and she wished she could go back in time to make it go away.

"I hope we have a girl who looks just like you. I'm gonna spoil her rotten. I can't wait to tell everybody that we're having a baby," Aaron beamed, as soon as the doctor was out of the room.

"I can't believe that this is happening to me," Aspen said as she hung her head low and sighed.

"What do you mean? This is a blessing Aspen. I mean, I know we didn't plan for it right now, but it happened anyway. That lets you know that it was meant to be," Aaron replied.

"This is not the right time for us to be having a baby, Aaron. I'm trying to get into law school. A baby will only complicate things."

"No, it won't baby. We can do this. It's the perfect time. Marcus and Jeremy just had kids and Johnathan is getting married soon. I was the only one who didn't have any good news to share, but now I do," Aaron said, speaking of three of his friends from the military.

He pissed Aspen off when he tried to keep up with them because their situations were different. The time in the military didn't affect the other men the same as it had done to him. Aaron's traumatic childhood coupled with some of the things he'd seen while serving his country had done a number on him. He didn't function like some of the others but, in his mind, he did.

"What's so good about it? I can barely get you to take your medicine. Now, I'll have another child to look after," Aspen snapped.

"I'll take my medicine every day, I swear. I'll do whatever I have to do to make this easier on you, baby. Even if I have to get another job to support us while you go to law school, I'll do it. Whatever it takes to make you happy," Aaron promised.

Aspen was happy when the nurse walked into the room with her paperwork because she was tired of hearing him talk. Between his frequent mood swings and a new baby, she was bound to lose her mind through it all. Truthfully, she didn't even know that she could trust Aaron to be alone with a child. He just wasn't right in the head.

"Go get the car," Aspen said when they walked out of the emergency room.

She was in a foul mood and she wanted to be away from him for a while. She was sure that everyone would know that she was pregnant by morning, thanks to Aaron. She was turning her phone off as soon as she got home to avoid the annoying calls. Aaron was starting to annoy her already. As soon as Aaron pulled up in the car, he jumped out of it and rushed to open the door for her like she was handicap.

"I got it!" Aspen snapped when he tried to buckle her seatbelt.

When he got back into the car, it took everything in Aspen not to cry. That was not how she envisioned her life and she wanted a do over. RJ seemed to be happy with his new baby boy and girlfriend, but she didn't share the same feelings.

"Are you hungry baby? I can stop and grab you something to eat," Aaron offered as he drove.

"No, just bring me to my car, so I can go home," Aspen sighed.

"Why are you going home? I think you should stay by me another night. What if you start feeling bad again?" Aaron asked her.

"I'll be fine Aaron. Just bring me to my car. I'll go fill my prescriptions before I go home," Aspen replied.

"I can come home with you and take care of you," Aaron said as he looked at her hopefully.

"No, I'm fine," Aspen replied.

As usual, Aaron did exactly what he wanted to do. Instead of bringing her straight to her car, he stopped at the pharmacy first. He went inside and filled her prescriptions and they were on their way again. Instead of being thankful, Aspen was annoyed. He was trying to prolong their time together and she wanted nothing more than to be away from him. As soon as he pulled up to his house, Aspen grabbed her prescriptions and hopped out of the car. Aaron was saying something to her, but she rushed to her car without even seeing what he had to say. She burned rubber getting away from him, even though she knew it wouldn't be for long. Aaron didn't go away easily and it would only get worse since she was carrying his child.

***

“Aww baby. This is so sweet. How did you manage to do all of this?” Marlee asked when she walked into their hotel room.

They had just arrived in Vegas and checked into their room. She didn’t know how RJ managed to get the same room that he had before, but he did it. He also had roses, fresh fruit, and champagne waiting for her. There was a gift bag sitting on the bed that Marlee peeked inside of. A big bottle of her favorite perfume was inside, and she wanted to cry at his thoughtfulness.

“Money talks baby. One phone call to the right person was all it took,” RJ replied.

“Thank you. I really appreciate this.” Marlee smiled.

“No thanks needed, baby. This is the room where it all started,” he acknowledged.

“Don’t even remind me.” Marlee blushed.

“Yep and tomorrow marks one year since we met,” RJ pointed out.

“I know, but it feels like it’s been much longer than that,” Marlee said.

“That’s how you know that it’s real,” he replied while kissing her lips.

It was early, but they were both tired from the long flight. Desi and Murk were in the room next door, but they dropped their bags and went straight to the casino as soon as they got there. Desmond wanted to come with them, but it was too last minute for him. He had to make arrangements at work and he needed a babysitter for Destini. Desi promised him that they could plan a trip soon, since he had never been before. After getting comfortable, Marlee and RJ took a nap and laid around for most of the day.

“Did you call to check on my son?” RJ asked Marlee when he walked back into the room.

He went to get them some food since they had slept for most of the day. Marlee hated room service, so he had something delivered and met the delivery man in the lobby.

“Twice and your daddy said not to call back again,” Marlee laughed.

“He must be crazy. This is our first time leaving him for more than a day. I’m calling every hour on the hour,” RJ replied as he dialed his mother's number and put the call on speaker.

"Tre is fine, just like he was when his mama called a few minutes ago," Ivy answered.

"That was an hour ago," Marlee corrected.

"What do you want boy?" Banks yelled.

"I'm calling to check on my son," RJ replied.

"Call on Facetime so you can see that your son is in one piece," Ivy suggested.

She didn't have to tell RJ twice. He hit his mother's contact on Facetime and his son's face appeared on the screen soon after.

"Hey baby. I miss you!" Marlee yelled as soon as she saw him.

"What's up Tre? You miss me?" RJ asked as if his son understood.

Tre was almost three months, so he wasn't really able to focus on the screen. RJ and Marlee were happy to see him, as if they hadn't seen him before leaving that morning.

"Leave him alone and go have fun. Bye," Ivy said before hanging up on them.

RJ and Marlee laughed, but they left them alone. Once they ate, they took a shower and got ready to hit up the club. Desi and Murk were already dressed and Marlee and RJ didn't take long to join them. They walked the old and new strips for a while before deciding to go to the club in their hotel. It was the same club where the four of them met a year before. It was crazy because the times almost matched up perfectly from when they met the year before.

"Let's hit the dance floor and fuck it up cousin!" Desi yelled as she grabbed Marlee's hand.

"I dare you," RJ said without even looking at her.

"Seriously RJ? What the hell did we come to a club for if I can't dance?" Marlee asked.

"For real. We could have stayed in the room if we just came here to sit down," Desi pouted.

"Sit your hot pussy down somewhere. Your bald head ass already got a man at home. You can fuck around with these lames if you want to. Stupid ass gon' end up losing a good nigga," Murk fussed.

"Aww, look at my bestie giving out good advice and shit. Hood as fuck, but I get it," Desi laughed.

"This is too damn boring. Bitch can't even dance," Marlee complained.

"You dancing is what got Tre here. I'll be damned if another nigga sees what I saw a year ago," RJ fussed.

"Had my boy gone from the first day too," Murk laughed.

"Exactly. I'm not trying to get locked up tonight. But happy one-year anniversary baby," RJ said as he tried to kiss her.

"Nigga please," Marlee said as she put her hand up to block it.

"Damn. It's like that," RJ smirked.

"I met you a year ago, but this ain't no damn anniversary. You had a whole bitch at home and I didn't see you again until I was three months pregnant," Marlee pointed out, as RJ got up and stood in between her legs.

"What that got to do with anything? Stop trying to kill my vibe," RJ fussed.

"Stop trying to be all mushy and shit like we were together a year ago. We fucked, you got me pregnant, and got back with your girlfriend. End of story," Marlee replied dismissively.

"Damn. So, I guess I shouldn't give you this then, huh? I mean, I don't want to be all mushy and shit," RJ said as she pulled out a black velvet box.

"Quit playing RJ," Marlee said with wide eyes when he opened the box to reveal the huge diamond ring.

"Nah, fuck it. You messed it up. I'm not even feeling romantic no more," RJ teased.

"Stop playing and start talking before I pull out my box cutter," Marlee threatened.

"You already know what it is baby. I don't need to make no long speeches to tell you how I feel because you already know. A year ago today, I saw you and my life hasn't been the same since. It's been a roller coaster ride of ups and downs, but I wouldn't change one thing about it. The only thing that you're missing is my last name and I'm trying to fix that too. You trying to marry a nigga or what?" RJ asked, as only he could.

It was the most ghetto proposal that Marlee had ever heard, but she loved it. RJ wasn't the get on one knee type of man and she loved that he stayed true to his personality. People in the club were oblivious to what was going on because he didn't make a big scene. Nobody even cared when Marlee jumped into his arms and wrapped her body around his.

"Yes baby!" Marlee screamed in his ear before crashing her lips into his.

"Aww, that was so sweet," Desi said, as they watched RJ slip the ring on Marlee's finger.

Just like they did a year ago, he carried Marlee out of the club and over to the elevators, with Murk and Desi following close behind. They were in a heated lip lock as they got onto the elevators and went up to their floor. Suddenly, Marlee broke their connection and jumped out of his arms.

"Hold up nigga. I know you ain't trying to play me cheap and get married in Vegas. This will be my first time getting married and I want to do it big," Marlee said as she put her hand on her hip and looked at him.

"I'm not trying to get married in no damn Vegas. That shit is tacky and played out. I'm not trying to wait forever to do it either. The way I see it, we can have everything planned and be married in six months or less," RJ replied.

"Why so soon?" Marlee questioned.

"Why do we need to wait Marlee? The money is good, so all we need to do is pick a date and start planning," RJ replied.

"Just hire a wedding planner. That's too stressful," Desi spoke up.

"Shit, that's even better," RJ agreed.

"Rose gold and mint. That's our wedding colors," Marlee smiled.

"Weird ass," RJ laughed.

He was only joking because Marlee had great taste. He loved the way she dressed and the way she dressed their son. It didn't matter to him what she wanted or how she wanted it. He was going to make it happen by any means necessary. The hardest part was over with and she said yes. He was nervous at first, but his father assured him that he didn't have anything to worry about. It was weird how a year ago, RJ came to Vegas just to have a good time after him and Aspen's breakup. He never imagined that a weekend getaway would lead to him meeting the mother of his child and future wife.

Chapter 39

"No RJ. The answer is no and I'm not changing my mind," Marlee fussed as they walked through the mall.

"Come on baby. We're gonna be married soon. We can make it a family thing," RJ pleaded as he pushed Tre in the stroller.

"Why can't you put an ad in the paper and find somebody else?" Marlee questioned.

"I don't want nobody else. I want you to do it. It pays more than what you make now," RJ noted.

"No, it doesn't RJ, but I'm sure you'll make sure that it does," Marlee laughed.

"You're fucking one of the bosses. You already know the pay gon' be straight," he joked.

"Shut up," Marlee laughed.

Joy was serious about quitting and she hadn't returned to work since the day she walked out. The girl who assisted her ended up leaving too, probably because Joy put some bullshit in her head. RJ was aggravated with trying to keep all the contracts renewed and putting together new ones. Ivy helped out as much as she could, but she kept Tre while RJ and Marlee worked. She didn't like bringing him to the office with her because she was always concerned about germs. Banks asked RJ if Marlee might have wanted the job and he had been damn near begging her to take it for the past week. Joy was making six figures for doing nothing and he would make sure that Marlee got the same or more.

"Y'all need to hire your step mammy. She needs the money more than anybody," Marlee replied.

"That bitch is crazy. You know my pops went over there and the entire house was empty," RJ informed her.

"Are you serious?" Marlee asked in shock.

"Yep. Her and my sisters got their numbers changed and everything," RJ replied.

"What did she do with all the furniture and stuff?" Marlee questioned.

"Who knows? My pops went to Aspen's auntie's house last night to see if she knew what was up. He ended up talking to her sister, Blythe, instead."

"And? What did she say?" Marlee inquired.

"She didn't know anything about the house, but that nigga Keith is back in jail. That ain't nothing new though. She told my pops about how her mama did her daddy and why he killed her. And you were right baby. Aspen and ole boy been fucking around since they were kids. Her sister said that she do him dirty just like their mama did her daddy. Said she been playing with his feelings and shit. Her auntie took him in when he was younger, so they're like his only family. Oh, and Aspen is supposed to be pregnant by him now," RJ said, trying to remember everything that his father had told him.

"I told you that she had to still be messing with him. Why else would he feel the need to come at you the way he did? And then it was crazy how you said he was staring at you at her auntie's party," Marlee replied.

"That nigga ain't right in the head baby. You only saw him for a second when you did their makeup, but you have to be around him for a few minutes to really see it. It's like he tries too hard to be normal and it makes it worse," RJ remarked.

"He sounds crazy. But, why did their daddy kill their mama?" Marlee asked.

"Aspen been told me that story a long time ago. She didn't even know if that was her real daddy or not though. She said that her mama was cheating on her husband and got pregnant for another man. The husband didn't even know that the baby wasn't his until the other man knocked on their door and wanted to see her. A few months of back and forth and the husband snapped. He killed his wife, her man on the side, and himself. Aspen was too young to even remember, but her sisters and auntie told her the story," RJ answered.

"Damn. That's fucked up. Her sister spilled all the tea. Aspen would probably die if she knew all what she told your daddy," Marlee replied.

"Blythe was always the realest one. She used to tell Aspen off all the time. But shit, that's what Aspen wanted. She's been trying to get pregnant for years, so she should be happy."

"Maybe she just wanted to get pregnant by you," Marlee pointed out.

"Yeah, but I made sure that shit didn't happen," RJ replied as they walked into Saks.

She and RJ were taking engagement pictures the following weekend and they were looking for something to wear. They still hadn't decided on a date, but they did agree on a wedding planner that they wanted to use.

"What is Banks doing with the house?" Marlee asked as she picked up a pair of shoes.

"I think he's gonna let Raven sell it. Lauren probably moved in with her stupid ass daughters. They all need to pack up and move back to Denver with their weird asses," RJ replied.

He and Marlee walked around for a while until they decided on the outfit and shoes that they wanted to wear. They picked up a few things for Tre and left soon after. They wanted to go out to eat, but Tre was not in the best mood. He slept most of the time that they were in the mall, but he was cranky now.

"Maybe we should get some food to go. He's not feeling being in that car seat no more," Marlee said as she turned around to the back seat and tried to give him his pacifier.

"You think he's hungry?" RJ asked.

"I don't know what his problem is. Maybe he needs to be changed," Marlee said as she felt his diaper.

"I'll bring y'all home and then go get us something to eat. He's making me think something is wrong with him. He never cries like that," RJ replied as he looked back at his son.

He headed straight home, while Marlee tried her best to comfort their crying baby. When they got to the house, RJ got the bags out while Marlee got the baby. She immediately undressed him and changed his diaper. RJ handed her a warm bottle and that seemed to do the trick. Tre closed his eyes as he drank the bottle and was sleeping soon after.

"Faking ass," Marlee laughed as she looked down at him.

"My baby wanted to come home," RJ replied.

He placed their food orders over the phone and left to go pick it up. RJ was happy to see that someone was coming out of a parking spot right as he pulled up. It wasn't too close to the door, but he was happy that he had one at all. He pulled into the spot and got out of his truck. He was almost up to the front door when it opened, and a familiar face came strolling out.

"Hey. RJ, right?" Aaron asked, as if he didn't already know.

"Yeah. What's up?" RJ greeted as he shook Aaron's free hand.

He looked to have picked up a food order too, but he wasn't in a hurry to leave.

"So, what did you have?" Aaron asked him.

"Huh?" RJ questioned in confusion.

"You said that you were expecting a baby any day now when we last saw each other," Aaron reminded him.

"Oh yeah. We had a boy. He's three months old now." RJ smiled.

"Congrats. I have a long way to go, but my girl is six weeks pregnant," Aaron beamed proudly.

"Congrats to you too. That's a wonderful feeling," RJ replied.

To a normal person, that would have been the end of their conversation. But, Aaron just stood there and looked at him. He was weird as fuck and he creeped RJ out. He had that crazy look in his eyes like he wanted to snap and go off the deep end.

"Are you and your son's mother still together?" Aaron asked him.

It was at that exact moment that RJ understood what Aaron was looking for. He wanted to be sure that RJ wasn't going to be a problem in his relationship. He needed confirmation from him that it was really over between him and Aspen, and RJ had no problem giving him what he wanted.

"Yeah, we're engaged to be married. We already got our house and our son. Marriage is the only thing left for us to do," RJ replied honestly.

And just like before, the crazed look on Aaron's face was replaced with a huge smile. He was bat shit crazy and RJ was ready to get away from him. The nigga made him uncomfortable and that didn't happen too often. Aspen's sister said that she was always playing with dude's feelings, but she needed to be careful with that.

"Congrats again. I wish you and your family all the best. You have a good night," Aaron said as he walked away excitedly.

Hearing RJ say that he was getting married was the best news that he'd heard since learning that Aspen was carrying his child. Aaron just couldn't seem to shake the feeling that RJ and Aspen would eventually get back together. It had happened several times before, but he was confident that they were officially done this time. It had been a while, but he was happy to finally have Aspen all to himself again.

"Crazy muthafucka," RJ mumbled when he saw Aaron pulling out of the parking lot.

He kept telling Murk that Aaron was harmless, but he was starting to rethink that. RJ wasn't a killer, but Murk's name definitely spoke for itself.

***

"His stupid ass. He don't even know her like that," Aspen fumed as she and her cousin looked at RJ and Marlee's engagement pictures.

She couldn't even lie if she wanted to. RJ and Marlee looked good as fuck with their Gucci attire and Rolex watches. They even took a few pictures with their son and they looked like one big happy family. Aaron told her that he'd seen RJ a few days ago when he went to get them something to eat. He said that RJ told him that he was getting married, but Aspen thought he was lying. He would say anything to make sure that she didn't go back to her ex, but it turned out that what he said was true. She was pissed when she learned that Aaron had told him about the baby. She and RJ had both moved on, but it felt weird with him knowing that she was pregnant by another man.

"Girl, fuck RJ. You got a good man and a baby on the way. He showed you what it was on Rosalyn's wedding day," her cousin, Nikki, replied as she lounged on Aspen's sofa.

"Oh, I'm done with him, but I'm just voicing my opinion. He's only known the bitch for a year and they're getting married already. And, truthfully, it wasn't even a full year. He didn't see her again until she was three months pregnant. She fucked him in Vegas and he didn't even call her afterwards. Like, seriously nigga. You're really turning a hoe into a housewife," Aspen spat bitterly.

"That hoe must have done something right. She's living in that big ass house and got that big ass ring on her finger," Nikki replied.

"The only thing she did right was get pregnant," Aspen noted.

"Why are you so focused on RJ? You have your own family now," Nikki pointed out.

"Girl, bye. The worst thing I could have ever done was let Aaron's annoying ass start coming over here. I knew it was a mistake, but I did it anyway. Now, he's acting like he doesn't want to leave," Aspen said as she rolled her eyes up to the ceiling.

"Bitch, you are too ungrateful. A lot of women wish they had a man who loved them as much as Aaron loves you. If you can get RJ off your mind for a minute, maybe you can take the time to appreciate what you have. I wish I had a man who catered to me like Aaron does with you," Nikki replied.

"If you want him, he's all yours." Aspen frowned.

Nikki only shook her head at her cousin. Aspen was a piece of work and had been that way her whole life. She and Nikki were the same age, but their personalities were total opposites. Aspen was spoiled, and her sisters and Patrice were the cause of that. She was much younger than her sisters, so they always did cater to her. Anisa and Patrice still did, but Blythe wasn't having it. She told Aspen how it was and didn't care about how she felt. It didn't help that Aaron had her just as spoiled. She dogged him out, but he didn't seem to mind. He loved her more than life and that much was clear. Aspen was the talk of the family after the way she behaved at Rosalyn's wedding. True to her word, Rosalyn hadn't seen or spoken to her since then.

"When is the baby due?" Nikki asked after being silent for a while.

"I don't know," Aspen replied with a frown.

"Didn't you have your first doctor's appointment?" Nikki asked.

"Yep and I didn't listen to nothing he said. Aaron was talking to him, so I'm sure he knows," Aspen answered nonchalantly.

"Why don't you seem happy?" Nikki asked her.

"Because I'm not. This pregnancy couldn't have come at a worst time. I'm studying for law school and I just can't be tied down like that," Aspen hissed.

"It'll all work out cousin. You know we're all here for you. I set my own schedule with Uber, so I can babysit whenever you need me to," Nikki offered.

"Thanks cousin." Aspen smiled.

When Aaron walked from the back room clad in nothing but sweat pants and socks, her smile turned upside down and her mood was ruined. He had been there for three days and he was getting too comfortable. It was time for him to go and, as soon as Nikki left, he was leaving too.

"Don't you see that I have company?" Aspen snapped.

Aaron had just woken up from a nap and he still looked tired. He didn't even see Nikki sitting there when he first walked in. He would have put a shirt on if he did.

"Oh, damn, I'm sorry baby. My fault Nikki. I didn't even see you sitting there," Aaron replied as he rushed off to the back.

He came back in with a t-shirt on and took a seat next to Aspen. She frowned when he rubbed her stomach because there was nothing there to rub.

"Aww," Nikki cooed, as Aspen gave her a disgusted look.

"I have to go do my final fitting for the wedding next month. I can't wait to see all my boys again." Aaron smiled as he stood up and stretched.

His friend Johnathan lived in Memphis and Aaron was going there for his wedding the following month. The place who was providing their tuxedos had a New Orleans location, so Aaron was doing all his fittings locally. He and Aspen were going to stay in Memphis for four days and he couldn't wait to see all of the men who he'd served in the military with. Besides Aspen's family, they were like the brothers that he never had.

When he walked away, Aspen rolled her eyes at his back. He was so excited about going to Memphis, but he was in for a big surprise. She wasn't going to the wedding, nor was she going to Memphis. She had her own plans and she needed him far away when she executed them.

Chapter 40

"That's fucked up. His fat ass is wrong for that shit." Marlee frowned as she looked at Craig sprawled out on the ground.

Craig and Trinity were no longer together, but he still hung out on the block with his friends. He was out there with Mat and some of the other men playing basketball, when Trinity came outside starting shit with him. She was trying to put on a show for her lil friends and ended up getting embarrassed when he cursed her out. She was calling Craig lil dick and broke, and he ignored her for a while. When she started talking about his mama and sisters, he'd finally had enough and went off on her. It was all good when she had people laughing at him, but she didn't like it when the tables were turned.

Trinity ran inside to tell Tyson what happened, and he rushed out of the house like the bad big brother he thought he was. He told Craig to get from around there, but the younger man refused. Tyson must have felt disrespected because he punched Craig in the face and knocked him out cold. Marlee, Desi, and Sierra were on the porch and they saw everything as it unfolded.

"He is wrong for that. He's way bigger than that boy in height and weight," Desi replied.

Mat and a few other dudes helped Craig up and made sure that he was okay. They placed cold, wet towels on his forehead and made him drink some water. Once they were sure that Craig was okay, one of the older men in the neighborhood gave him a ride home. They didn't even feel like playing ball no more, so Mat came and sat on the porch next to Marlee.

"He's always doing that boy dirty and embarrassing him in front of everybody. Trinity is wrong for that shit. Bitter bitch been picking with that boy since they broke up," Mat spat angrily.

"I wish Craig had some older brothers, so they could beat Tyson's fat ass." Sierra frowned.

"That's fucked up though. He handled him bad last week in front of everybody over some shit that Trinity told him," Mat pointed out.

"She needs to move the fuck on. The nigga cheated, get over it," Marlee snapped.

"The fuck is you feeding my nephew? He looks like a stuffed animal sitting in that car seat," Mat joked.

"Leave my baby alone. We put food in his bottles now," Marlee said as she looked over at her baby sucking on his pacifier.

Tre was four months old now and one of the best babies ever. If he wasn't hungry or needed to be changed, he rarely cried. Marlee thought for sure that he was going to be a crybaby because somebody was always holding him.

"Girl look. More drama," Desi said when they saw Taj pull up and get out of the car.

Her daughter got out of the back seat, and Marlee smiled when she saw her. Tyanna had gotten so big and Taj dressed her so cute. They walked up the steps to Tracy's house, but Tyson stepped outside before they had a chance to go in. Tyanna passed him up and went inside without even bothering to speak.

"That nigga is a sad ass pappy. That baby never speaks to him," Marlee laughed.

"Where is his son? I haven't seen him in a minute," Desi noted.

"Girl, Kim don't let her son go by him. I was the only reason that he used to come around at all. Tyson just don't care one way or the other. She had another lil boy for her husband not too long before I had Tre. She still hit me up sometimes," Marlee spoke up.

"He don't be bothered with Yanni's daughter either. He barely be home when that baby be over there. Yanni better be thankful for Tracy," Sierra spoke up.

"Girl, Tyson don't be bothered with none of his kids. He used to get mad at me when I wanted to get them for the weekend," Marlee admitted.

"Oh bitch! It looks like they're fussing," Desi said, not bothering to be discreet as she watched.

Taj was pointing her hand in Tyson's face and he kept slapping it away. They were quiet for a while, but she started getting loud.

"You better get your money up nigga! Baby number four will be here in seven more months!" Taj yelled.

"You better go find the daddy. You got me fucked up," Tyson replied.

"I bet your fat ass be in child support court. Fuck with me if you want to," Taj threatened as she opened Tracy's door and yelled for her daughter.

Tyanna came running out and straight into the car. She never acknowledged her father and he never bothered saying anything to her.

"That nigga ain't shit. I'm glad you got you a good one sis. I would have had to fuck his fat ass up for playing with you and my nephew," Mat said as she got up and went inside.

"So, how's the wedding planning coming along?" Sierra asked Marlee.

"It's going good. I tried to push the date back, but RJ ain't having it," Marlee laughed.

"Push it back for what? Three months is more than enough time to have everything done. It's not like y'all have anything to do. The wedding planner is doing all the work," Desi noted.

"I know. I was telling him to do it in the summer, instead of spring. But, it's fine either way. I just hope we get some good weather." Marlee shrugged.

"May is usually a nice month. I think you'll be fine," Sierra replied.

They all sat around and talked for a while, until Tyson decided to walk over there. He hadn't bothered Marlee in a while and she was not in the mood for him now.

"Why I gotta look on social media to find out that you're getting married?" Tyson asked as he looked at Marlee.

"You need to be worried less about me and my marriage and more about baby number four," Marlee replied while holding up four fingers.

"How long have you and dude been knowing each other?" Tyson questioned.

"Bye Tyson. The test said zero percent and I was done with you after that. Stop talking to me and act like you don't know me," Marlee answered dismissively.

"Damn. I'm just asking you a question. The fuck is you getting so defensive for?" Tyson frowned.

"I think that's my cue to bounce. Can you get my baby's diaper bag for me, Sierra?" Marlee asked as she stood to her feet.

Sierra and Desi stood up at the same time, but Sierra walked into the house. Mat must have been in the shower because she wasn't holding down her usual spot on the living room sofa. Desi had a feeling that something was about to pop off, so she sent Murk a text message. He and RJ were together, and she wanted to be prepared just in case. Tyson hadn't said anything to Marlee in a minute, but he was on some straight up bullshit now.

"You must have been fucking with that nigga while you were with me. That's the only way I can see you being pregnant by somebody else so soon after we broke up," Tyson ranted.

He was in his feelings and he didn't even try to hide it. The situation with Craig already had him heated and then Taj came over there with her bullshit. Tyson wanted to put a bullet in her head when she came at him on some pregnancy shit. He barely saw his other kids unless they came to his mother's house and she was trying to give him another one.

Once Taj left, Tyson went inside and grabbed a beer. He was on some relaxation shit and decided to go on Instagram. He was new to social media and his sister had only created him a page the week before. Everything seemed to be posted online and he wanted to stay in the know. He had Trinity to pull up Marlee's page and show him how to follow her. Tyson's heart dropped when he scrolled through her photos and saw her engagement pictures. He knew without a doubt that he and Marlee were through, but she was moving on fast as hell. Not only did she have a baby with somebody else, but she was marrying the nigga too. He couldn't even hide his anger and he wasn't going to try.

"So what if I was? You were fucking my first cousin in a bed that we shared for years!" Marlee yelled, drawing the attention of the some of the men on the block.

"You admitting to the shit Marlee. You standing here telling me that you were fucking another nigga while you were with me," Tyson fumed.

Desi took her box cutter from her purse and flipped it open. She walked down the stairs with Marlee and up to her car. Marlee unlocked the door to put Tre inside, right as Sierra came out with the baby's bag. She was sorry that Mat was in the shower because Tyson was standing too close to Marlee for her liking.

"Stop trying to put on a show and keep it moving Tyson. Nobody got time for that dumb shit," Desi argued.

"Fuck you, Desi. Mind your muthafucking business for once in your life!" Tyson barked angrily.

"Move Tyson. Get away from my car," Marlee ordered.

"Or what?" Tyson countered angrily.

He knew that he was wrong as hell for how he was acting, but he was hurt. He still loved Marlee and he couldn't help that. Granted, he'd messed up their relationship, but she didn't even try to give him another chance. She went right out and fucked another nigga, if she wasn't already doing it before. Even if she was, he still would have given her another chance. He loved her enough to forgive whatever wrong she'd ever done. It pissed him off to know that she didn't feel the same way.

"Chill out bruh. That's family," one of Mat's friends said as he walked over and inserted himself in between Tyson and Marlee.

Mat was cool with everybody on the block and they would never let Tyson put his hands on her sister. Marlee was far from scary, but she had to think about her son. It would have been nothing for her to gut Tyson like a fish, but her son's safety came first.

"Don't tell his fat ass nothing. His mammy gon' be looking for a plus sized coffin for him," Marlee warned.

That comment seemed to send Tyson over the edge. He reached around the other man and grabbed Marlee's shirt. She swung around the middle man and hit the side of Tyson's face with her closed fist. When the mirror painted car pulled up, Desi smiled, but nobody else seemed to be paying attention. RJ jumped out of the passenger's side and took his shirt off as he rushed over to Marlee. He pushed her and the other man to the side and started throwing jabs at Tyson. That nigga was like termites to wood. He just wouldn't go away. Marlee was yelling for him to stop, but RJ wasn't paying attention to nothing that she was saying.

Tyson got caught slipping. He was so busy trying to get at Marlee that he never noticed her man walking up on him. He couldn't even say that the nigga caught him off guard because he didn't come at him from behind. That ugly ass mirror tinted car was in his peripheral and he didn't know how he'd missed that.

"His fat ass is getting tired already," Murk joked as he watched RJ punishing Tyson.

Tyson was slow as hell, and RJ didn't even have to work hard before he had him down on the ground. When he kicked him twice, Marlee ran over and pulled him away. She didn't want her man going to jail behind something so stupid.

"Baby, stop, please," Marlee begged as she grabbed his hand and led him away.

"Where my son at?" RJ huffed, as Marlee walked him to her car.

She grabbed a wipe from Tre's bag and wiped the sweat from RJ's face. He had blood on his knuckles, so she cleaned them off too.

"He's good. He's sleeping," Marlee said as she pointed to Tre in his car seat.

"Are you alright baby? Did he hit you?" RJ asked as he inspected her face.

"No, I hit him," Marlee laughed.

"Chill out from coming around here for a while Marlee. Mat and Sierra are welcomed at our house anytime. At least until this shit dies down," RJ said.

"Okay baby," Marlee said, nodding her head in agreement.

"Get in the car so I can make sure y'all leave," RJ said as he kissed her cheek.

Tyson was back up on his feet and the shit talking started soon after. "Lame ass nigga. Your wife and son are riding around in the muthafucking car that I paid for nigga. You ain't no boss!" Tyson yelled enraging RJ.

Marlee was about to tell him not to worry about it, but he was back on Tyson in a flash. Tyson got in a fighting stance and was ready to throw down. He never had to throw a punch because RJ's first lick was his last. Marlee heard when his fist connected with Tyson's jaw, right before he went down to the ground. Just like Tyson had done Craig not too long ago, RJ had knocked him out cold.

"Oh shit!" Murk yelled, just as he'd done when Mat knocked Cara out in Atlanta.

RJ was breathing hard while he frowned down at Tyson's body. Once he saw that the other man was no longer a threat, he made sure that Desi and Marlee got into the car and pulled off. He and Murk got into the car and left soon after.

"I need a favor cuz. It's fucked up what I'm about to say, but I don't give a damn," RJ said.

"What's up fam? You know I got you, no matter how fucked up it is," Murk promised.

A sly smile spread across his face as he listened to what his cousin had to say. Murk loved to get his hands dirty, so RJ had the right man for the job.

Chapter 41

"Ha! That's so good for his fat ass," Yanni laughed as she handed Craig his phone back.

The entire block had been buzzing about Tyson getting knocked out by Marlee's man. After the way he'd done Craig, everybody was happy to see his karma come back to him so soon. Everybody was calling to tell Craig what happened and one of his boys sent him the video. They never really had no drama around that way until Tyson moved in with his mother. That nigga thought he was the Deebo of the block, always trying to handle people bad and talk crazy to everybody. He had done Craig dirty for the last time and he was done giving him passes. Craig wasn't really a street nigga, and Tyson knew that. He used that knowledge to his advantage and always treated him like a flunky because of it. Craig sold weed for his sister's boyfriend when he needed extra cash, but he wasn't out there like that.

"The video is good, but I wish I was there to see that shit," Craig replied as he passed her the blunt that they were smoking.

"That bitch Trinity was wrong too. Niggas cheat every day. The fuck made her think she was special?" Yanni frowned.

"I'm not saying that I was right, but I can't take back what happened. She broke up with a nigga and that should have been enough. She always gotta say something when she sees me, then she gets mad when I tell her ass something back," Craig argued.

"I hate that hoe and her mama. Shit, I hate the whole damn family," Yanni replied with a scowl.

"That's what you get for fucking your cousin's nigga," Craig laughed.

"The biggest mistake that I've ever made in my life. Like, seriously. I don't really have no friends, so my cousins were all that I had. Kallie still fuck with me sometimes when she's not all up under her man," Yanni replied.

"What about your other cousins? I know Desi and Mat are team Marlee, but you got a lot of other cousins," Craig noted.

"I guess they're team Marlee too. My cousin Nika comes around, but it's not the same. Apparently, I'm the cousin that nobody wants at their house." Yanni shrugged.

"Do you blame them? Nobody wants you around their niggas," Craig said as he fell out laughing.

"I didn't put a gun to nobody's head. It ain't my fault if their niggas can't say no," Yanni replied.

"Your cousin though? That shit was foul. And you don't even regret it," Craig said, shaking his head.

"I do have a lot of regrets, but what's done is done. I feel like shit ain't been right for me since then," Yanni admitted.

"You ever thought about apologizing to Marlee?" Craig asked.

"Nope. She probably wouldn't accept it anyway," Yanni assumed.

"She probably would. I heard that Marlee is living good as fuck now. The nigga she's marrying got long money and shit," Craig said, repeating something that he'd heard just like always.

"I can't believe he's marrying her so soon. They haven't even known each other that long," Yanni pointed out.

"Shit, that don't matter. Marlee be pushing that Bentley truck like a boss," Craig bragged.

"Enough about all that. What's up with what I asked you to get?" Yanni asked him.

"The fuck you need that much weed for though? You must be trying to sell it because you damn sure can't smoke it," Craig replied.

"As long as I pay for it, it doesn't matter what I do with it," Yanni countered.

"Yeah, that's true. Let me know when you get all the money and I'll hook it up with my brother-in-law," Craig said.

"Cool, but you can bring me home now. Big boy will probably be bringing my baby back soon," Yanni replied.

She and Craig were sitting in his sister's car that she let him use. They drove to the park around the corner from Yanni's house to talk and smoke. Tracy didn't want Yanni at her house anymore, so Tyson picked the baby up and dropped her off whenever his mother wanted to see her. Yanni was grateful for a break, so she didn't care how they worked it out.

"You got me fucked up Yanni. You sat here and smoked all my shit and now you're trying to go home. You better handle your business," Craig said as he pointed to his crotch area.

"Ugh," Yanni groaned.

"Quit playing girl. You know the deal," Craig said as he unbuckled his pants and freed his erection.

"Trinity must not know how to give head. All you ever want is somebody to slob on your knob," Yanni said as she gulped down some water to moisten her dry mouth.

She turned her body towards him slightly and buried her head in his lap.

***

"I'm so damn tired." Marlee yawned as she laid her head on the desk.

She was watching the clock, praying that the next forty-five minutes came soon, so she could go home. She was looking forward to relaxing in their oversized jacuzzi tub and climbing into their California king-sized bed. Tre had been cranky the night before, and she and RJ were up for hours trying to comfort him. His doctor said that he might be teething, but Marlee thought it was too soon.

"You look tired friend," Sierra replied.

"I feel like telling Ivy to let Tre stay over there." Marlee yawned.

"You should. You know she won't mind," Sierra said.

"I know, but I won't feel right leaving him with anybody else if he's not feeling good," Marlee noted.

"I understand that." Sierra nodded.

Marlee felt like she was dozing off, so she got up and busied herself to make the time pass faster. She refilled all the medical supply trays and straightened the desk. By the time she swept the floors and organized their appointment folders, it was time for them to go.

"Thank God," Marlee sighed as she and Sierra got their things and headed for the door.

"I agree," Sierra said as she watched Marlee set the alarm and lock up.

They were parked in the rear parking lot right next to each other, so they walked to their cars together. When Marlee got to where she'd parked that morning, she stopped and looked around the almost empty parking lot.

"Where's my car?" Marlee asked as she looked around frantically.

"Did you move it when you went to lunch?" Sierra asked.

"No, RJ picked me up for lunch. Oh, my God, Sierra! Somebody stole my car!" Marlee yelled.

"I'm calling the police," Sierra said as she dialed the three familiar digits.

While she was on the phone giving the dispatcher their location, Marlee called RJ.

"What's up baby? Are you on your way?" RJ asked her.

"Somebody stole my car!" Marlee yelled into the phone.

"Calm down baby. I'm on my way," RJ replied.

"I can't believe this. Somebody stole my damn car," Marlee repeated as she continued to look around the parking lot.

"It's okay baby. As long as you're alright. Everything else can be replaced," RJ assured her.

"I know baby, but this is so fucked up. My baby's car seat was in there and everything. I'm happy that you cleaned it out over the weekend or they would have had more than that. I'm always leaving money and shoes in there," Marlee replied.

"And this is one of the reasons why I told you to stop doing that. Who's there with you?" RJ asked.

"Just me and Sierra, but the police are on the way," Marlee replied, repeating what Sierra had just told her.

She and RJ talked on the phone until he pulled up, but the police hadn't showed up yet.

"You can leave since RJ is here," Marlee told her friend.

"Are you sure Marlee? I don't mind hanging around," Sierra replied.

"No, you can leave. There's really nothing that you can do anyway," Marlee said.

"Okay, but call me the minute you get home," Sierra said as she hugged her. She spoke to RJ when he walked up, before getting into her car and pulling off.

"You alright baby?" RJ asked as he kissed Marlee and pulled her in for a hug.

"Yeah, but I'm pissed. How the fuck can they steal my car without setting the alarm off? I would have heard it," Marlee fussed.

"These criminals are smart as fuck these days Marlee," RJ pointed out.

"I know baby, but they need the key to even get in without setting the alarm off. Where's your key?" Marlee asked him.

"It's right here," RJ replied as he held his keys up for her to see that her spare was on his keyring.

"See, mine is right here too. What kind of high tech shit are these niggas working with these days?" Marlee asked, making him laugh.

"The police are here," RJ said as he pointed to the cruiser that had just pulled into the parking lot.

He and Marlee walked over to the car and explained what happened. Of course, the police officer had the same questions as Marlee, and wondered how they didn't set her alarm off when they took the car. They had cameras around the building, but Marlee was parked out of the camera's view. She and RJ talked amongst themselves while the officer prepared a report for her to give to her insurance provider. He told Marlee that there was next to no chance that her car would be found in once piece and that was not what she wanted to hear.

"Thanks for everything" Marlee said as she smiled and shook the officer's hand.

She and RJ got into his truck and headed over to Ivy's house to get their son.

"Stop looking so sad baby. It's just a car. You can have another one tomorrow," RJ said as he grabbed her hand.

"I know RJ, but it's just annoying. I don't feel like dealing with the insurance claims and all that other mess. Then, I have to wait for them to cut the check and all that other bullshit before I can get another one," Marlee fussed.

"Is your man broke Marlee?" RJ asked while looking her.

"I know you're not broke RJ," Marlee said as she discreetly rolled her eyes.

"Well, act like you know then. And stop rolling your eyes before they cross up and you be looking like Biggie," RJ said, making her laugh.

"Stop playing RJ. This is serious," Marlee smirked.

"I'm serious too. You can take the Bentley truck tomorrow and I'll drive my other one," he suggested.

"I don't want to be riding around in that flashy truck. If they liked my car enough to take it, just imagine what they'll do with that one. That's why I'm happy that you keep it in the garage," Marlee replied.

"Fuck it then. Call off tomorrow and we'll go get you another car," RJ said.

"No RJ. I can wait on that. They might find my car. You never know." Marlee shrugged.

"Why do you always have to fight me on everything Marlee? We're about to be married soon and you don't even try to be submissive. You really don't like to compromise. If I tell you to let me handle it, then sit back and let me handle it," RJ argued.

"Okay baby, but why do I have to call off? I'm trying to build my time back up," Marlee said.

"See, if you were working with your man, you wouldn't have to go through all that. You could be off any time you wanted to," RJ noted.

"Can we do it when I'm off Friday?" Marlee questioned, ignoring what he said about her working with him.

"Friday it is. That'll give you some time to decide on what you want," RJ replied as he leaned over and kissed her.

They went to Ivy's house to get their son before going home. Marlee was tired, but she was too hyped up to sleep. She was mad that her car was stolen, but she was excited about the idea of getting a new one. Once she and RJ ate, they put Tre to bed and looked at cars online until they fell asleep too.

Chapter 42

"Thank you." Aspen smiled while handing her Uber driver a tip.

She got out of the car and walked into the building. She was thirty minutes early for her appointment, but she checked in with the receptionist and took a seat in the almost empty office. Her phone chimed with a message from Aaron, letting her know that he loved and missed her and wished she was there with him. Aaron had caught a flight to Memphis the night before for his good friend Johnathan's wedding. Aspen was supposed to accompany him, but plans changed at the last minute. Aspen never had any intentions on going with him, but Aaron didn't know that. She hated his friends, but that wasn't the reason why she stayed behind.

"God, please forgive me. I know that this is wrong, but I don't know what else to do. Please forgive me," Aspen mumbled as she clasped her hands in prayers.

"We're ready for you in the back Ms. Connors," the nurse walked up to her and said low enough for only Aspen to hear.

She had been so deep in thought that she never noticed that a few more people had walked into the waiting room. Aspen got up and followed the nurse to the back and into a cold all-white room. She was instructed to change her clothes and lie down on her back. When the doctor walked into the room, Aspen jumped at the sudden intrusion. He was talking to her as he got things in order, but Aspen wasn't really listening. She was scared and nervous but determined at the same time.

Aspen's heart beat a mile a minute as she sat back and thought about what she was about to do. While Aaron was in Memphis celebrating his friend's union, Aspen was back home terminating her pregnancy. She had been battling with herself since she found out about the pregnancy, until she finally made up her mind. She couldn't do it. She just couldn't see herself having a baby with Aaron, at least not right now. Aaron had the potential to be a good man, but he needed to get professional help first. He still had nightmares and his mood swings were unpredictable and frightening. Aspen couldn't bring a child into that madness and she wasn't. Aaron didn't think anything was wrong, so getting help was out of the question. Add that to her upcoming law school test and Aspen just wasn't ready.

Over the past week, she had started up her act and played the role up until the night before when Aaron left. Aspen started complaining of stomach aches and even went as far as going to the emergency room. They sent her home on bed rest and Aaron catered to her the entire time. When it was time for them to pack, she told him that she didn't think it would be a good idea for her to travel, and he reluctantly agreed. Now, when she faked a miscarriage, he would believe it because of the pains that she claimed to have before.

"Okay Ms. Connors, just relax as much as you can," the doctor said.

Aspen's legs were in the stirrups as if she was getting ready to push a baby out, instead of getting rid of one. She closed her eyes and said another prayer as she had the procedure done. It was painful, but it was also necessary. Once everything was done, Aspen was put into the recovery area for a while. She felt like shit when she got a text from Aaron saying that he missed her and their baby. Sadly, there was no longer a baby there for him to miss.

About an hour later, Aspen was given a prescription for pain and the okay to leave. While she was getting dressed, she pulled up the Uber app on her phone. There was a car about seven minutes away, so she moved a little faster. As soon as she was done, Aspen rushed outside and waited for her ride. It was sad that she didn't have anyone to accompany her, but she couldn't let her family know what she was doing. They wouldn't approve, and she didn't need to be judged. Aspen had her head down responding to Aaron's text when the honk of a horn startled her. She lifted her head and was frozen in place when she saw her cousin, Nikki, sitting behind the wheel of the car. Her Uber sticker was displayed up front and Aspen just wanted to die.

"Oh God. How careless could I be?" Aspen mumbled to herself.

The app clearly gave you the information on the driver and the car that was coming to get you. Aspen was in such a hurry to get dressed that she didn't even pay attention to it. If she did, she would have known that her cousin was the one who was coming to get her, and she would have canceled immediately.

"Are you just gonna stand there or are you coming?" Nikki rolled down the window and asked her.

"Oh yeah, sorry," Aspen replied as she snapped out of her daze and got into the back of her cousin's car.

"Really Aspen? We're family. You could have gotten into the front seat," Nikki giggled.

"I'm fine. Besides, you're at work," Aspen pointed out.

"Are you going home or somewhere else?" Nikki asked as she pulled away.

"Home," Aspen replied.

"Where is your car and what is that place that I just picked you up from?' Nikki questioned.

Aspen was happy that the building that did her procedure didn't have any signs or anything out front. They couldn't advertise for safety reasons and probably for privacy too. It was a huge white building that almost looked abandoned. If you didn't know exactly where you were going, it was easy to pass up.

"My car is at home," Aspen replied, ignoring Nikki's other question.

Nikki caught on quickly and decided not to press her for answers. She changed the subject and moved the conversation on to something else. She and Nikki talked the entire ride, but Aspen was happy when her cousin pulled up to her house. Her stomach had started to cramp a little and she was ready to relax.

"See you later cousin." Nikki smiled.

"Thanks Nikki. See you later and lunch is on me," Aspen replied as she handed her a twenty-dollar bill.

"Aww, thanks Aspen," Nikki said, before watching her cousin get out of the car.

She couldn't put her finger on it, but Aspen was up to something. Nikki had never known her to use Uber before, especially when her car was parked right in her driveway. And that building that Nikki picked her up from looked even more suspicious with no signs out front. Aspen was always the sneaky one, so there was no telling what she was up to. Only time would tell, but Nikki put it to the back of her mind for now.

***

Aaron grabbed his bags from the trunk of the cab and rushed up to Aspen's front door. He got the earliest flight home that he could find, trying to get to her as soon as he could. He was sorry that he couldn't spend more time with his friends, but his woman needed him more. Aspen and his friends didn't get along, but they felt his pain. Aaron's friends thought that Aspen was stringing him along, but he didn't agree with them. They all had wives now and he was trying to get to where they were. They were prepared to give him hell when he told them that he was leaving until he told them the reason why.

After getting over ten missed calls from Aspen the day before, Aaron called her back, only to be hit with some devastating news. Aspen had miscarried their unborn child and he was heartbroken. Guilt consumed him because he wasn't there with her, but he had no way of knowing that something bad was going to happen. As soon as Aaron walked up to the door, it opened, and Patrice was walking out with a trash bag.

"Hey Patrice," Aaron said as he took the bag from her and threw it in the trash can out front.

"Hey baby," Patrice said when he walked back up the steps that led into the house.

"Where is she?" Aaron asked as he dropped his luggage by the front door.

"She's in the bedroom. Nikki, Blythe, and Anisa are back there with her. I just feel so bad that this happened to y'all. I wish she would have called me instead of going to the hospital by herself," Patrice said sadly.

"I wish I was here with her too," Aaron said as he made his way to her bedroom.

Anisa was straightening up the room, while Blythe and Nikki just stood against the wall.

"Hey everybody," Aaron spoke as he rushed over to Aspen's side and grabbed her hand.

"Hey Aaron," they all spoke back.

"How are you feeling baby?" Aaron asked her.

"I feel okay," Aspen mumbled, making Blythe roll her eyes to the sky.

She wasn't trying to be insensitive, but she wasn't buying her baby sister's story. Something just wasn't adding up. Aspen claimed she was in so much pain and that's what prompted her to go to the hospital. It was crazy that she was hurting so much but managed to drive herself, instead of calling someone else to bring her. She supposedly stayed in the hospital for hours after having a complete miscarriage but, still, no call to none of her family members. Yet, she managed to call Aaron, who was all the way in Memphis. She knew that he wasn't going to answer because he was in a wedding. More than likely, he didn't even have his phone on him at all. She didn't call anyone else until she had made it back home.

Patrice and Anisa was eating it up, but the attorney in Blythe knew better. Aspen didn't look like she'd been anywhere near the hospital and she was a piss poor liar. Even if she did get rid of her hospital band, there was no paperwork or nothing else to back up her claims. Not to mention, the story that Nikki had told her about being her sister's Uber driver two days before. Something just wasn't adding up, but Blythe was going to get to the bottom of it.

"Are you hungry honey? I can whip up something before I leave," Patrice offered.

"No, I'm fine," Aspen said in a weak little voice.

"Okay. I'm gonna get out of here, but let me know if you need anything," Patrice said as she kissed Aspen's cheek.

"I'm leaving too sis, but call me if you need me," Anisa said as she squeezed her hand.

"I hope you feel better cousin," Nikki said as she followed them out.

Blythe wasn't with the bullshit, so she only glared at Aspen before grabbing her purse to leave. She had a huge caseload, but she wasn't giving up on finding out the truth. She had resources and she wasn't afraid to use them. Her paying clients came first though.

"I'm so sorry that I wasn't here with you, baby. You needed me, and I failed you," Aaron said as he buried his head in her chest and cried.

"It's okay Aaron. It wasn't your fault," Aspen said as a twinge of guilt hit her.

"I'm so fucking stupid. I'm so stupid," Aaron kept repeating while hitting himself in the head.

He jumped up from the bed and started pacing the floor like a crazy person. He kept hitting himself in the head and saying how stupid he was.

"Aaron, stop it. Please, stop hitting yourself," Aspen begged as she got out of bed and walked over to him.

He flinched when she touched him and dropped down to the floor. He put his knees up to his chest and buried his head in between them. When he started screaming, Aspen backed away and grabbed her phone. She had never seen him do that before and she was scared out of her mind. He sounded like a wounded animal and even she didn't know how to tame him. After he was tired of yelling, he did his breathing exercises before standing to his feet once again.

"You need to rest baby. Get back in bed and relax. Maybe I can give you a massage later," Aaron said, like he didn't just have a mental breakdown a moment ago.

Aspen was scared, but she allowed him to help her back to the bed. He kicked his shoes off and got in there with her. He grabbed the remote and put on a movie before pulling her closer to him. He seemed to be back to his normal self, and Aspen was happy for that. As hurt as he seemed to be about her no longer being pregnant, he'd also proven that she'd made the right decision.

Chapter 43

"Bitch, this truck is nice! RJ got his wife riding fly," Desi yelled when Marlee picked her up.

Before getting in, she walked around the canyon beige metallic colored Mercedes Benz truck and admired its beauty. The interior was a peanut butter color that matched the outside perfectly.

"Thanks cousin." Marlee smiled before pulling off.

It took her a little longer than she thought it would to get her car because she didn't really see anything she liked. When she started looking for cars online, she fell in love with the color of the Benz. Unfortunately, the dealership in New Orleans didn't have it, but the one in Houston did. Once RJ and his father pulled a few strings, her car was waiting for her in the driveway when she got home from work two weeks later.

"Where are we going first?" Desi asked.

Marlee had two months before she and RJ got married, but she didn't have much to do. She was looking for accessories for her girls and some shoes for Tre. She had her dress and everything else that she needed. RJ didn't really have many friends, so Murk and his two brothers were his only groomsmen. He had other cousins, but he was closer with them. Mat didn't want to wear a skirt, so Marlee made her an usher instead. Desi, Sierra, and Raven were her bridesmaids and Raven's daughter was her flower girl. One of Murk's sons was the ring bearer and Marlee found something else for the rest of his kids to do.

"I need to find Tre some shoes. I'm kinda scared to get them because I know he won't be in the same size two months from now," Marlee replied.

"Buy them a size up. He should be good," Desi said.

"That's what Ivy said," Marlee noted.

"Did you talk to your father yet?" Desi asked as she looked over at her cousin.

"No, but I will soon," Marlee replied.

"How soon Marlee? You're getting married in two more months," Desi reminded her.

"Exactly and I told him three days after RJ proposed. He hasn't asked me anything about it since then. My mind was made up from day one, so it would have been a waste anyway." Marlee shrugged.

"I know that his feelings are gonna be hurt, but he has nobody else to blame but himself," Desi replied.

"That's all on him. Alvin has been more of a father to me than he's ever been. He's always been good to me and Mat and that's who's walking me down the aisle. My daddy needs to realize that when he divorced my mama, he didn't divorce his kids. He basically said fuck his marriage and us too. If I wouldn't have made sure to keep in contact with him, I probably would have never seen or talked to him. I'm his child and that should have been the other way around. I'm just tired of being lied to and I'm tired of trying," Marlee rambled.

"I understand cousin. Even when Mat gave up on a relationship with him, you never did. He was wrong for how he handled that situation with Cara too. I don't even feel bad for him," Desi replied.

"Girl, forget that. What's up with you and your boo?" Marlee asked.

"We're good cousin. He's so sweet. I've been helping him plan for Destini's first birthday party next month." Desi smiled.

"Damn girl. That time passed fast," Marlee said.

"It really did. She was only three months old when I first met them. I think she called me mama the other day and I almost fainted. I went to the bathroom and cried like a baby, so nobody would see me," Desi said sadly.

"Aww cousin. I think that's so sweet," Marlee replied.

"Desmond said the same thing, but it scares me," Desi admitted.

"Why does it scare you?" Marlee quizzed.

"Because, Marlee. I love her like she's my own and I've already gotten attached. I just don't want nobody to think that I'm trying to take the place of her mother. And it would literally kill me if Desmond and I don't work out and I can't see her anymore. I guess I gotta get over my own fears and just see it through."

"Yes, you should. You make some very valid points, but you can't dwell on the negatives. I think Desmond is feeling you more than you know. He's hardly ever at his own house anymore. That should tell you something right there," Marlee pointed out.

"Him and Murk just took over my apartment. They got my shit looking like a man cave," Desi laughed.

Murk had basically moved in months ago without even asking if he could. He paid all of Desi's bills, but she wouldn't have complained if he didn't. She loved the company. A few weeks ago, Desmond and Destini stayed the night and he had been there since then. Unlike Murk, Desmond was very clean, and he was a great cook. He kept Desi's place spotless and there was always a hot meal on the stove. He gave her money for bills too, but she just put it in her account.

"Murk ain't going nowhere. You and Desmond will be married, and his crazy ass will be living in the spare bedroom," Marlee laughed.

"I already know. He kills me when he be saying our house," Desi giggled.

"He came over there with them bad ass kids the other day," Marlee said.

"Girl, they are bad as hell. They cut up so bad when we took them to the movies. I told Murk that I was done. I'm not going nowhere else with them ever again," Desi swore.

"I don't blame you," Marlee replied.

She and Desi walked around the mall and found the accessories that she was looking for. She ended up buying two pairs of shoes for Tre because she couldn't decide which ones she liked best. She got both a size up and she prayed that his fat feet could get into one of them. When her phone rang, Marlee stepped away from the counter where Desi was making a purchase and answered. She walked out of the store as she talked, and Desi was right behind her. Once Marlee was done, she and Desi headed back to the car.

"You okay cousin?" Desi asked.

"Yeah, I'm good. That was the detective calling me about my car," Marlee replied.

"Did they find it?" Desi asked.

"Yeah, burned to a crisp," Marlee chuckled.

"Aww damn, cousin. I'm sorry to hear that. But, it's all good. Hubby got you riding fly now," Desi acknowledged.

"I don't know Desi. I might be wrong, but I just feel like hubby is the one who's behind all this," Marlee replied.

"What! You can't be serious. You think RJ had something to do with your car being stolen?" Desi gasped.

"Yes, I do," Marlee admitted.

"Why do you think that?" Desi asked.

"He just never seemed surprised when I told him about it. He just said that he was on his way. And why didn't my alarm go off? I would have heard that shit, as loud as it was. The only thing he was worried about was getting me another car. He didn't care about them finding it or nothing. He had my spare key, so he had access to it. Now I see why he was so pressed about cleaning my car out. He wanted to make sure I didn't have anything of value in there when he had it stolen," Marlee noted.

"I just can't see him doing nothing like that," Desi said, shaking her head.

"I can. That comment that Tyson made about me and his son riding around in a car that he bought fucked with him and I know it did. The thought of somebody else doing something for me and Tre probably had him losing it," Marlee replied.

"Damn cousin. You might be right. Did you ask him?" Desi questioned.

"No, but I've been wanting to. I know he won't lie, so I'll get the truth out of him," Marlee answered.

"Does he still have the key, or did he mysteriously lose it?" Desi smirked.

"No, he still has it, but that don't mean nothing," Marlee noted.

"You should ask him. And call me the minute you do," Desi said, laughing with her.

Once they left the mall, Marlee dropped Desi off home before going to her own house. When she walked in, Tre was in his swing while RJ made him some more bottles.

"Did you find everything that you were looking for?" RJ asked after he kissed her.

"Yeah, I did," Marlee said as she washed her hands.

She had taken some steaks out earlier and she was about to cook them. RJ sat on the bar stool and talked to her as she moved around the kitchen. Simple things like that was what he loved the most. He and Marlee had intimacy in and out of the bedroom and that was important.

"Everything is paid for, so all we're doing is waiting for the big day now." RJ smiled.

"Yes, and then it's off to Paris for a week," Marlee replied.

"Baby number two," RJ winked.

"I just got back right from baby number one. I need to build my time up at work from all the time I've been taking off. Maternity leave and all those extra days for different reasons got me almost in the negative. I went from never taking off to barely having any time at all," Marlee complained.

"That wouldn't be happening if you worked with me. You wouldn't have to be at work so early in the mornings either. You can set your own schedule and everything," RJ said, trying to persuade her.

"Stop making shit up RJ. That job does not come with all those perks. You're only doing that because it's me," Marlee replied while rolling her eyes.

"Why can't you just try baby? Give me one day and, if you don't like it, I won't bring it up again. You can come one Friday when you're off," RJ suggested.

He saw Marlee contemplating his offer and got excited. "Come on baby. Just one day and I promise to never bother you again," RJ swore.

"One day?" Marlee asked with raised brows.

"That's it," RJ replied with hopeful eyes.

"Okay. My next Friday off, I'll come check it out. What am I supposed to wear? I see that just about everybody there wears a uniform, except you and your father," Marlee noted.

"You don't have to wear no damn uniform. You can wear whatever you want," RJ said.

"Why not? Your sister used to wear one. See, that's why I don't want to work there. I don't want special treatment just because I'll be your wife. And I got a feeling that this is all a setup anyway. I'll quit my job to come work for you and get fired. That'll be your way of getting me to stay at home like you want me to."

"Why don't you want to stay home? You can focus on just doing makeup," RJ replied.

"No, RJ. People don't wear makeup every day like that. I go days without clients sometimes and I won't have anything to do," Marlee pointed out.

"I'm all for you working if that's what you want to do. I'll never stand in the way of that," RJ promised.

"And I appreciate you for that." Marlee smiled.

"How are you liking your new truck?" RJ asked, moving on to a different subject.

"I love it. Oh, and I forgot to tell you that the detective called me today," Marlee informed him.

"What did he want?" RJ asked.

"They found my car in the middle of nowhere burned to a crisp," Marlee noted.

"Yeah," RJ replied, as if it was no big deal.

"You are not a good criminal," Marlee laughed.

"Huh?" RJ questioned in confusion.

"You could at least pretend to care," she replied.

"Overreacting is how niggas get caught. Be at the police station falling out when somebody die, and they be the one who killed them. You got a new car, so you're good. I'm not about to pretend to care about something when I really don't." RJ shrugged.

"I guess you don't care if you're the one who did it," Marlee said, calling him out.

"Did what?" RJ asked.

"Stop playing RJ. You had my car stolen because of that comment that Tyson made. And I'm sure that Murk was in on too. How did y'all do it?" Marlee questioned.

"How did we do what?" RJ asked, playing dumb.

"Tell the truth RJ. Did you have my car stolen or not?" Marlee quizzed as she turned to face him.

If she didn't know anything else about him, she knew that he wasn't a liar. RJ would tell the truth, even if it hurt.

"I'm trying to spend some time with my son. I don't feel like answering questions right now," he replied dismissively.

"You already did," Marlee smirked as she continued to cook.

She knew RJ better than he thought she did. If he didn't want to answer a question truthfully, he avoided it or just refused to answer at all. He basically admitted his guilt without verbally saying it.

"Fuck that burned up ass car and the nigga who paid for it," he replied as he got his son from the swing and went to the living room.

"Petty ass," Marlee laughed when he was gone.

RJ wasn't about to answer her question, but he knew that she would figure it out eventually. As soon as the words left Tyson's mouth, he already knew what he was going to do. He gave Murk his spare key and dropped him off to Marlee's job. RJ rented a car storage space for two weeks and had the car hidden there. After he felt that enough time had passed, Murk got the car out and doused it with gasoline before setting it on fire. Marlee had him fucked up if she thought her and his son were going to continue riding in a car that her ex had purchased while they were together. RJ didn't even think about it until Tyson opened his mouth and put it on his mind. It was all good though. Marlee had a new truck and the insurance would be sending her a check soon. The only loser in the entire game was Tyson and RJ could live with that.

Chapter 44

Banks pulled up to his daughter's house and killed his engine. He was on the phone with RJ, who had been trying to talk him out of going over there. Lauren had called him the day before out of the blue and asked him to come over. She gave him her new number and his daughters did the same. He was even surprised when Joy called and apologized to him. RJ thought it was a setup and he was worried about him going alone. There was no way that Banks would have asked his son to come with him. The tension between his kids was disheartening, but they were grown. There was nothing that he could do about it. He hated to see his kids divided like that, but that's just how it was. RJ and Raven had their own bond and his other three daughters had theirs.

"I'm telling you pops, it's a setup. That shit don't even sound right. Why they just up and called you out of the blue after they did their best to avoid you? They even changed their numbers, so you couldn't get in touch with them. How many times did you go to that house and didn't get an answer?" RJ questioned.

"It's fine RJ. Things just took a crazy turn, but they're my kids too," Banks replied.

"Don't even remind me," RJ said.

"I just wish that y'all could put the past behind and get along. That's all I've ever wanted," Banks sighed.

"Yeah and I want Trump out of the white house, but we can't all get what we want," RJ pointed out.

"Is Marlee still coming to the office Friday?" Banks asked.

"Yeah and I hope she likes it," RJ answered.

"That makes two of us. If not, it's time for us to hire someone else. We're probably losing out on money since we're not in the office as often as Joy was. The phones are going unanswered and that's not good for business," Banks noted.

"I agree, but enough about that. Leave pops. Don't got in there, I'm telling you," RJ started up again.

"I'll be fine son. You'll be able to say that you were the last person to talk to me if not," Banks chuckled.

"That ain't funny bruh. They're trying to collect on your will early and you're helping them. Joy ain't never apologize to nobody a day in her life. Something is up," RJ fussed.

"Let me go inside and get this over with. I'll call you when I come out. If I come out," Banks joked as he laughed heartily.

"Man, stop playing. Don't eat or drink nothing in there!" RJ yelled before his father hung up the phone.

Banks got out of the car and jogged up the steps. He rang the doorbell only once before Faith opened up and let him in.

"Hey baby." Banks smiled while hugging his daughter.

"Hey daddy. Come on in and sit down," Faith said as she led him into the living room where her sisters and mother were seated.

Joy and Hope stood up and hugged him, but Lauren stayed seated. She looked worn down or maybe she was just tired. Banks greeted her with a smile and she returned the gesture. He looked around the home that he'd purchased his daughters in admiration. They kept the place neat and clean and it was decorated nicely. The house was huge, but it was always strange to him how they all wanted to live together. Admittedly, his daughters were a little weird, but he had Lauren to thank for that. They had been doing everything together for so long that it was hard for them to break away. Even now, there was a lot of room for them to sit elsewhere, but they were all crammed up on the sofa next to their mother.

"So, what's going on?" Banks asked as he took a seat in the leather recliner.

His daughters turned to look at their mother, like they had been trained to do so. Three grown ass women who probably couldn't even think without their mother's help.

"Let me talk to your father," Lauren said as she looked at the three of them.

Just like robots, they all got up and walked to the back of the house together. RJ always said that they were strange, but Banks never paid any attention. It wasn't until now that he realized just how right his son was.

"What's going on Lauren?" Banks asked her.

"Well, first of all, I've decided not to go back to Denver. At least not right now. The girls want to stay here, and they want me to stay with them. They don't know Denver like I do. New Orleans has always been home to them," Lauren replied.

"Okay," Banks replied, sensing that there was more to the story.

"I'm sick Ryker. I just found out two weeks ago. Breast cancer," Lauren stated.

Banks just sat there and looked at her, not knowing what to say. He'd recently learned just how deceitful Lauren could be and he didn't know how to take what she'd just told him. Lauren saw the look in his eyes and she got up and grabbed something from her purse.

"God, Ryker. Do you think I'm that desperate for attention that I would lie about something so serious? Here, it's right there in black and white," Lauren said as she shoved the papers in his hands.

Banks looked over the papers carefully as a lump formed in his throat. He and Lauren weren't together anymore, but that didn't mean that he didn't care. She was his wife for years and the mother to his first child. He didn't love her romantically, but he did have love for her for those reasons alone.

"Damn," Banks said as he ran his hands down his face.

"Yeah, that's how I feel," Lauren chuckled nervously.

"What can I do Lauren? I'll do anything to help," Banks offered.

"That's why I asked you to come over here. I know that our divorce is pending, but I really need to stay on your insurance just a little while longer. I can't afford treatment without it. I'm blessed that they caught it so early and they're confident that I can beat it."

"Of course. That's not a problem at all. And listen, the house is for sale, but it hasn't sold yet. It's yours if you want it. I can have Raven pull it off the market right now," Banks said.

"Thank you, Ryker, but that won't be necessary. The girls want me to stay here and I feel better being around them," Lauren replied.

"Do you need any money or anything?" Banks asked as he grabbed her hand.

"No, I'm fine. I appreciate what you're doing for me. That's more than enough." Lauren smiled as she squeezed his hand.

She didn't know why, but she expected him to turn her down for some reason. Lauren had basically given him her ass to kiss once he bailed her out of jail. Keith had made a fool of her and used her for whatever she could give him. He was the reason why her house was empty. He had Lauren selling stuff out of there to support his growing drug habit. Before long, the only thing she had left were her clothes and shoes and he was back in jail facing ten years. And he had the nerve to call and beg her from behind bars. He was a real low life and his own sister made her see that. Keith was a user and Lauren had been thoroughly used.

"Let me know if you need anything Lauren. I'm so sorry that this is happening to you," Banks said somberly.

"It's okay Ryker, really. I have a positive attitude about it and I don't think of this as a death sentence. But while you're here, I do want to take the time to apologize for everything. I know that we didn't have the best marriage, but I didn't have to stay in it. I was wrong for giving Keith your money. He damn sure didn't deserve it. I'm sorry for turning our daughters against you too. They wanted to call you, but I made them choose. I was upset, and I said some things that I shouldn't have said," Lauren admitted.

"No hard feelings Lauren, but you should really encourage separation. At their ages, it's not healthy for them not to be on their own. No man, no kids. You don't think that's strange?" Banks inquired.

"They're close Ryker. You know that. And speaking of kids, I hear you have a healthy grandson now," Lauren said, changing the subject.

Banks caught on to what she was doing, and he decided to leave it alone. She had been using their daughters as a crutch for so long that she probably couldn't survive without them. While Banks was out wining and dining Ivy, Lauren had her daughters to keep her company. They had been so busy being her comfort zone that they didn't have a life of their own. No matter how weird it was to other people, it was perfectly normal to them.

"Yeah, and he's getting big," Banks said as he pulled up some pictures on his phone.

"He looks like you and RJ," Lauren smiled.

She and Banks had light conversation until her daughters walked back into the room. They talked to their father for a while and they were happy to see him and their mother getting along. Although they loved and appreciated their father, they favored their mother so much more. When she wasn't happy with him, neither were they.

"Any chance of you coming back to work at the parking garage?" Banks asked as he looked at Joy.

Banks would have loved for Marlee to take the position, but he knew that she didn't really want it. RJ was pressuring her to work with him and that was the only reason that she agreed to even give it a try.

"Not as long as your son is still there. And since he owns half the place, I guess that will never happen," Joy replied.

"RJ is not the enemy you know. You hate his mother and I understand why. But, it's not fair for you to take it out on him. If you want to be mad at anybody, be mad with me," Banks said.

"I was until mama told me not to be. If she's okay, then so am I." Joy shrugged, as her simple sisters nodded.

"Are you the spokesperson for everybody?" Banks asked jokingly.

"Haven't I always been daddy? I say the things that my mama and sisters are too afraid to say," Joy noted.

"Choose your words carefully baby. Not everybody will be as understanding as your mother and sisters," Banks replied.

"But anyway," Joy said dismissively, "I've already found another great job working from home."

"Doing what?' Banks asked.

"I'm working for a collection agency. It pays well, and I get commission." Joy smiled proudly.

"That's great baby. As long as you're happy. If you're sure that you're not coming back, maybe you need to come clean out the desk and get your personal belongings," Banks suggested.

"I will soon," Joy promised.

Since he'd been there much longer than he intended, Banks said his goodbyes and promised to keep in touch. He looked down at his phone and laughed when he saw that he had five missed calls and three text messages from RJ. He was threatening to send the police to his sister's house if Banks didn't call him soon. Banks didn't want him to worry, so he dialed his number and decided to put him out of his misery.

***

"I told you, baby. It's easy. We can get you an office if you don't want to sit out here in the open area," RJ said as he looked at Marlee.

She looked good as hell sitting behind that desk and that's where he wanted to see her sit every day.

"Don't get too excited nigga. I never said that I was staying," Marlee replied.

"Come on baby. It'll be fun working for me. We can ride together every morning and I can hit it in my office whenever I want to," RJ said, kissing her neck.

"Ugh. I would never fuck my boss," Marlee laughed.

"But, seriously baby. What do you think?" RJ asked.

"It's not bad RJ, but I just don't know. I love my job and I'll miss working with Sierra," Marlee replied.

"I can hire her too," he said seriously.

"It is not that real," Marlee laughed.

She looked and listened as RJ showed her how to renew, cancel, and start new contracts. He showed her how to take payments and how to order supplies for the office. Marlee couldn't believe how much his sister was getting paid to do hardly nothing. And she damn sure didn't need an assistant to do it. RJ was offering to get her an assistant too if she stayed, but it wasn't necessary.

"You can fix it up however you want to. This is all Joy's stuff," RJ said as he motioned to the wall art and stuff on the desk.

"I like that," Marlee complimented as she pointed to a plaque that said joy, hope, and faith.

"That's their names," RJ replied.

"Whose names?" Marlee questioned.

"My sisters. And ain't a damn thing joyful, hopeful, or faithful about them weird bitches." RJ frowned.

"I never knew their names. You never talk about them," Marlee noted.

"And I never will. Are you ready to eat?" RJ asked her.

"Yeah," Marlee replied as she grabbed her purse and followed him out.

She and RJ went to a Chinese restaurant not too far from the office and enjoyed their lunch. When they got back to the office, RJ grabbed an empty box from the storage room and started packing up his sister's belongings. He gave Marlee some Lysol wipes and she started wiping everything down.

"Hey. How's it going?" Banks asked when he stepped out of his office.

"Everything is good." Marlee smiled.

"Good enough for us to have a new employee?" Banks asked with raised brows.

"Hi daddy," Joy said when she sauntered into the opened area that used to be hers.

"Hey baby. I didn't know that you were coming over today." Banks smiled as he hugged her.

"Yeah, I was in the area and decided to stop by," Joy replied, as RJ scowled.

She turned her attention to Marlee and instantly remembered who she was. Marlee was pregnant the last time she saw her, and she didn't really get a good look at her. Joy wasn't one to give compliments, but Marlee was beautiful. Maybe it was the haircut, but she had a certain flare to her that made a person want to look twice.

"Come on back to my office," Banks suggested, trying to get her and RJ out of the same room.

He walked back to his office, assuming that Joy was following right behind him. Instead, she stayed behind to ask a few questions.

"Enlighten me. Who are you again?" Joy asked while pointing at Marlee.

"Who I am is of no concern to you. Now, be a good little girl and follow your daddy to his office like he told you to," Marlee replied while looking directly at her.

RJ and Raven had already warned her about Joy. She prided herself on being the mouth piece for her mother and sisters, but she had Marlee fucked up.

"You and daddy sure do know how to pick 'em," Joy hissed as she rushed down the hall to her father's office.

"I guess you can add her name to the beat down list too. I gave Aspen and Kassidy a pass since they've been behaving, but your sister can get it," Marlee warned.

"Fuck that bitch," RJ said as he grabbed Joy's stuff from the walls.

Her timing was perfect, and she could take all her shit with her when she left. And if she didn't, it was going straight to the trash. He hated that his father was dealing with them again, but they were his kids too. Banks had a heart of pure gold, which explained why he was doing anything to help Lauren. RJ knew that it was guilt that made his father do it. Banks felt bad for leaving her and then learning that she was sick. It wasn't his fault and he left her before anyone even knew that she had cancer. Lauren must have really thought that she was dying because she was an entirely different person. RJ and Marlee saw her and Patrice in the mall and she came up and spoke to him. She even bent down and kissed Tre's little hand in his stroller. RJ couldn't wait until she walked away to wipe his baby's hand and rid him of her germs.

"Her mama seems nice," Marlee said, pulling him away from his thoughts.

"The Lauren that you saw in the mall is not the same Lauren that I know. She was putting on a show or maybe the cancer got her scared," RJ noted, right as the phone rang.

He answered and listened to what the person on the other end had to say. He grabbed a pen and notepad from the desk and scribbled something on it before he hung up.

"What's wrong?" Marlee asked.

"That was one of our big contracts asking for some info. I need to run to my office right quick. Finish boxing that stuff up for me, baby," RJ said as he hurried to his office that was down the other end of the hall.

Marlee grabbed the desk phone and called to check on her baby first. He was with her mother and Alvin and she wanted to make sure that he was okay. Once she talked to her mother, Marlee resumed RJ's earlier task and continued to clean up the work area. She was almost done when she was startled by Joy's annoying voice.

"What the hell are you doing? Who told you to touch my stuff? At least Ivy knew her place when she came here. RJ needs to do a better job of training you!" Joy yelled.

"Bitches just won't let me be great," Marlee mumbled under her breath as she tried her best to ignore Joy.

Her man asked her to do something and that's exactly what she was doing. She opened the bottom drawer and pulled out a planner. Before she could put it into the box, Joy snatched it from her hand.

"Give me that! This is personal," Joy fumed.

Marlee tried to stay calm, but she failed. When Joy entered her personal space and tried to look in the drawer herself, Marlee was over it. She could tell that Joy was the type to always pop off and expect other people to just take it. Bad thing was, she had never met anyone like Marlee. When Joy purposely bumped her again, Marlee grabbed a handful of her hair and slung her to the floor.

"You needed to get a good ass whipping a long time ago. I can tell!" Marlee yelled as she threw a barrage of punches to Joy's face.

"Ahh! Get off me! Daddy!" Joy screamed, as Marlee slung her all around the office.

RJ had just hung up the phone when he heard all the commotion out in the hall. He rushed out of his office, surprised to see Marlee standing over his sister giving her exactly what she needed. RJ stood there with a satisfied smirk on his face as he watched it all unfold. Marlee was giving Joy the business and it was long overdue.

"RJ! Get her away from me!" Joy yelled as she tried to cover her face.

"Nah, my arm is fucked up. I can't do nothing for you," RJ chuckled.

"Daddy!" Joy screamed, right before Marlee silenced her with a punch to the mouth that split her lip.

"RJ! Why the hell are you just standing there boy?" Banks yelled when he walked out of his office and saw what was going on.

He'd just warned Joy about her mouth, but it seemed to have gotten her in trouble anyway. Marlee didn't bother anybody, so he knew that his daughter had to have provoked her. Marlee was a feisty one, and Joy had to find that out the hard way.

"Get your wife," Banks ordered his son.

RJ wasn't in a rush, so he took his time and pulled Marlee off Joy. When he looked down at his sister, he smiled at Marlee's handiwork. Joy's mouth was bleeding and she had scratches all over her face. Her eyeliner mixed with her tears made her look like a raccoon. Her designer shirt was ripped, and her black flowered bra was exposed. Her hair was all over her head and her earrings were somewhere on the floor.

"I want her arrested. Call the police daddy. I'm pressing charges," Joy cried as she buried her bloodied face in her father's chest.

"I wish the fuck you would. Lauren gon' be burying your stupid ass," RJ warned.

"Did you hear that daddy? He just threatened to kill me," Joy said, crying harder.

"Everybody just calm down. Nobody is calling the police or killing anybody. Go into the bathroom in my office and clean yourself up Joy," Banks said as he pulled her away from his chest.

He hated that his kids would probably never get along, but he was tired of trying. RJ seemed to take pleasure in his sister's pain and Banks hated that even more.

"And you want me to work here. I don't think so. I quit," Marlee said as she grabbed her purse.

"How can you quit a job that you never even started?" RJ asked her.

"Let's go RJ. Sorry Banks, but this ain't the job for me. I'll fuck around and get locked up," Marlee said as she walked away fussing.

Banks chuckled lowly because Marlee was a piece of work. He had never met a woman with so much spunk, but he loved her. His son was in for a surprise if he thought he could pull anything over on her because she wasn't having it.

"Man fuck!" RJ barked angrily as he followed his fiancée out of the building.

Banks was outright laughing after that, but he couldn't help it. He knew his son, and RJ wasn't giving up on Marlee coming to work there. RJ was about to do a lot of ass kissing and his father didn't blame him. When his phone rang a few seconds later, Banks sighed when he saw that it was Lauren calling. He was sure that Joy had told her what happened and now it was time for him to do some damage control.

Chapter 45

"Shit just went all the way left bruh," RJ said to Murk, who was in his passenger's seat.

"That's good for Joy. Bitch talk all that shit and can't even back it up," Murk replied.

He and RJ had just come from shooting pool and were now on their way to Desi's house. Marlee and the baby were over there with Desi and RJ had to pick them up. Legend had Murk's car for the weekend, so he had to ride with RJ too. Murk had spent the previous weekend laid up in Biloxi with one of his chicks and he owed Legend a favor for wearing his anklet.

"Her stupid ass hurried up and took all that shit out of there. I guess she won't be back around the office any time soon," RJ laughed.

"Marlee and Mat got them hands," Murk replied as he continued to text someone.

"What's up with you, bruh? You been acting weird all day. It ain't like you to be doing no texting like that. What's the deal?" RJ asked.

"That bitch Christie is pregnant again," Murk replied as he shook his head.

"Nigga, what? Baby number six and three of them are with Christie. You talk all that shit, but you love that girl. You don't ever stay the night with none of your other baby mamas, but you always stay the night with her. She's the only one who you don't want to have a boyfriend. All that hate shit you be talking is some straight bullshit," RJ said, calling him out.

"I already told you, bruh, the shit be good as fuck. I can't help it," Murk replied.

"You need to start using condoms. I mean, you take care of all your kids but damn. That's too much." RJ shook his head.

"I hate using condoms. Why can't they make a pill for men? I'll make sure I pop them bitches every day and never miss a dose," Murk swore.

"You say some stupid shit bruh," RJ laughed.

"Man, I'm going crazy with the five I already got. Desi banned them from the house after they tried to swim in her bathtub and had water everywhere."

"Damn," RJ said as he fell out laughing.

"I can't take no damn more," Murk sighed.

"Is she having it?" RJ asked.

"If she have an abortion, she gon' die," Murk noted seriously.

"Man, that's not true. Who told her that stupid shit?" RJ asked.

"I did because I'll kill the bitch if she even tries," Murk replied, making his cousin laugh again.

"Damn cuz. Baby number six it is," RJ said, right as Murk's phone rang.

"What nigga?" Murk asked as he answered the phone for his brother Legacy.

"That nigga Legend got popped, but he's alive and shit," Legacy replied, like it was normal.

"Where the fuck is my car?" Murk asked him.

"Man, fuck that ugly ass car. Lil bro laid up in the hospital and that's the only thing that you care about," Legacy fussed.

"I hope the police don't have my shit. I'm killing that lil bitch on site if they do. And be prepared to get slapped in your shit for talking reckless lil nigga," Murk warned before he hung up on him.

"What happened?" RJ asked.

"Legend stupid ass got shot," Murk replied.

"Again? I swear that lil nigga got nine lives," RJ said.

"That's because he's stupid as fuck. The nigga is reckless and don't even try to be discreet. I never in my life seen so many dope dealers who want everybody to know that they sell dope. Stupid ass niggas might as well trap in front of the police station," Murk fussed

"What hospital is he in?" RJ asked.

"Shit. I didn't even ask," Murk said as he dialed Legacy's number.

RJ called to tell Marlee and Desi what was going on. Once he found out what hospital his cousin was in, he relayed the message to them both. Marlee was dropping Tre off to her mother and then coming up there with Desi.

Once they got to the hospital, Ivy was the first person who RJ spotted. She was pacing the hallway with the phone up to her ear, talking to someone. When he got closer, he heard his father's deep baritone on the other end. Their grandmother and a few of their other family members were there, but RJ wanted to talk to his mother before he went and spoke to anyone else. She was still talking to his father, so he and Murk stood there and waited until she was done.

"I'm fine baby. He got shot three times, but all the bullets went straight through," Ivy said, answering one of the questions that RJ and Murk wanted to ask.

When she got off the phone, RJ gave her a hug, followed by Murk.

"Is my mama here auntie?" Murk asked.

"Yeah, she's in the room with Legend now," Ivy replied.

"Where did he get shot at?" RJ asked.

"Once in the chest and twice in the arm. That damn boy got my nerves so bad. I hate getting those kinds of phone calls. And where were the two of you? We've been here for hours," Ivy said.

"Man, Legacy just called me a few minutes ago," Murk replied.

"I swear, all that weed is frying that boys brain cells. I told him to call y'all when we first got here. I knew that I should have done it myself," Ivy fussed.

"Is Legend saying anything about what happened?" Murk asked.

"No. Did you really expect him to?" Ivy questioned with a smirk.

"How did he get here?" RJ asked.

"He drove himself," Ivy answered.

"Nigga probably got blood all over my damn car. Let me go in here and see what's up," Murk said.

"Y'all go speak to your grandma and everybody else. Stop being rude. And where's my baby at RJ?" Ivy asked.

"Marlee is bringing him by Tiffany before she comes up here," he replied.

"Good. He don't need to be around all these sick people germs," Ivy noted.

RJ and Murk went over and greeted their grandmother and other family members. Once they talked to them for a while, they walked into the room to see Legend. Ivy was sitting on the bed babying Legend like always, while Iris sat in the chair nearby. Murk looked over at Legacy, but he held his hands up in surrender.

"Chill bruh. My bad for what I said earlier," Legacy hurriedly apologized.

Murk was nuts and he wasn't in the mood to deal with him. He would swing on him in the hospital like it was nothing.

"The fuck happened nigga?" Murk asked his little brother.

"Lyfe!" Ivy scolded, just like she always did whenever he and RJ used foul language around her.

"You better respect my sister, nigga," Iris snapped angrily.

Their entire family knew how she felt about Ivy and it was not a game. She would go to war with her own mama for her baby sister and they all knew that. She didn't care about what her kids said and did in her presence, but Ivy wasn't with it. She was the only one who could call Murk by his real name and not face his wrath.

"I'm sorry auntie," Murk apologized.

A knock at the door a few seconds later interrupted their conversation. Murk opened the door and let Desi and Marlee in.

"Don't be trying to get killed before my wedding lil boy," Marlee joked when she walked into the room and kissed Legend.

"How are you feeling brother?" Desi asked as she too kissed his cheek.

"I don't know why they keep trying to kill me. Big pop in the sky ain't ready for a nigga just yet." Legend shrugged like he was confused by it all.

"They ain't trying to kill your stupid ass for nothing," Iris fussed, right as the doctor walked into the room.

"How are you feeling Legend?" the doctor asked as he looked at his numbers on the monitor.

"I'm good pop. I can't complain," Legend replied."Any pain anywhere?" the doctor questioned.

"Yeah pop. I'm hurting up in here. Last time I got shot, they gave me something stronger. I need the same thing I had before," Legend replied, sounding like he was already high.

"I can give you something stronger if what you have now isn't working. I'll send the nurse in shortly. Let me know if you need anything else. Other than that, we'll continue to monitor you for infection or any changes." The doctor smiled as he turned to walk away.

"Good looking pop. I appreciate that," Legend replied.

"Man, you need to chill out with calling everybody pop. Is anybody in here your daddy, nigga?" Murk questioned.

"His stupid ass don't know who his daddy is. Hell, I don't even know who the nigga is," Iris said, making Marlee and Desi laugh.

Murk and his mother and brothers didn't care what came out of their mouths. They were reckless with their words, but it was always funny as hell. They cursed like sailors around Iris, but she had a fit if they said anything in front of Ivy. Marlee thought it was cute the way she loved her sister. She even threatened to stab Lauren and her daughters if they came at Ivy wrong. There was no doubt in anyone's mind that she would have made good on her promise.

After staying there for more than an hour, Desi and Marlee left to go home. Marlee gave RJ the okay to stay a while longer, since Desi offered to go get Tre and bring her home. RJ knew that Murk wasn't leaving until he got some answers, and Legend wasn't talking as long as Ivy was there. He wasn't going to talk around anyone other than the people that he could speak freely in front of. When Ivy announced that she was leaving, Iris went to walk her out and Murk got right to the interrogation.

"The fuck happened Legend?" Murk asked.

"I don't even know pop. I was doing the same shit that I always do. I went to drop something off and talked to the dude who got it from me. Next thing I know, some nigga was pointing at the car and I'm shot the fuck up," Legend said as he coughed and winced in pain.

"That nigga probably set your stupid ass up. Who was it?" Murk asked.

"Nah pop. We been dealing for over a year with no static. I didn't even get out of the car," Legend noted.

"So, the nigga who was shooting didn't even see you?" Murk asked.

"Nah pop. I don't even know that fat black muthafucka, but it's on if I ever see his bitch ass again. I never forget a face," Legend said, as Murk and RJ looked at each other.

There was only one nigga that they knew who fit that description. Tyson had motive and he knew Murk's car. He was suspect number one in their eyes, and Murk was ready to retaliate. More than likely, Tyson probably thought that it was him and RJ in the car but got Legend instead. Once he got all the info that his brother had, Murk and RJ left soon after.

"You need to get rid of that flashy ass car. Everybody and their mama know who the shit belongs to," RJ said as they took the elevator down to the parking lot.

"I don't have a choice after what happened. Damn man. I knew I shouldn't have let that nigga use my shit," Murk fussed.

"What difference does it make who used it? If it wasn't Legend, it would have been you," RJ reasoned.

"That big planet of the apes looking nigga got balls to pull some shit like that. I hope his mama is ready to bury his punk ass," Murk fumed.

"Just let me get married before you do anything. I don't need you going to jail and Marlee having a fit. One more month bruh. That's all I need," RJ pleaded.

"You got that cuz. You know how I do it. I need to see how that nigga move before I do anything anyway. I'll make sure me and my brothers stay in one piece long enough for you and my girl to walk down the aisle. It's on right after that though," Murk swore.

The first thing he needed to do was get another car, but he wasn't in a hurry. He used Desi or one of his baby mama's cars sometimes, so he would have no problem getting around. As much as he loved his mirror tinted machinery, it was time to retire it. Too many bad things had happened over the years and it was no longer worth keeping it. Murk was going to be a man of his word and chill out long enough for Marlee and RJ to become husband and wife. Tyson had better get ready for war after that because he was on Murk's hit list.

As soon as he and Murk got to his car, RJ stopped when he heard someone speak to him. He was surprised when he turned around and saw Aspen standing there. He didn't think that she would ever speak to him again, but she'd obviously gotten over her hate for him. Murk wasn't interested in hearing their conversation, so he got into the car and waited for RJ to finish.

"What's up Aspen?" RJ spoke back.

"Nothing much. I just came to see my cousin. She just had a baby," Aspen replied.

"Cool. Well, have a good night," RJ said as he turned his back to her.

"Your big day is coming up, huh?" Aspen questioned, stopping him once again.

"Yeah, it is," RJ replied.

"Married. I can't believe that you're really getting married to someone else. I just thought that would be us one day," Aspen admitted.

"How, when you already had a man? A man that you've had the entire time that we were together. How can you get mad with me for leaving when you were living a double life?" RJ asked.

"I don't know what you heard, but that's not true," Aspen denied.

"No need to lie to me, my baby. I'm about to be a married man, so I don't care one way or the other." RJ shrugged as he left her standing there and got into his car.

He was happy to let Aspen know that she wasn't as perfect as she tried to appear. She was pissed about him leaving her for Marlee, but she wasn't the innocent victim that she tried to portray. She was his past and she belonged in his rearview mirror, just like she was now.

Chapter 46

Two weeks, according to the wedding tracker that was placed on RJ's page. That was how long it would be before he and Marlee were united in marriage. Kassidy had stayed her distance for a while, hoping that her best friend would come around. Months had passed with no word from him, and Kassidy's feelings were hurt. After telling RJ and his father everything that Aspen had told her, she was almost sure that their friendship would get back on track. Unfortunately, that never did happen. Although RJ told her that it was a wrap on their friendship, Kassidy thought she would give it one more try. Time changed things and maybe RJ felt differently now. After checking her appearance in the mirror, Kassidy got out of the car and walked up the stairs. After ringing the doorbell, she took a deep breath and waited for someone to open up.

"Hey Ivy." Kassidy smiled when she opened the door.

"Hey," Ivy said with a forced smile. "What are you doing here?"

Kassidy felt slighted by the other woman, but she didn't let it show. Ivy used to be happy to see her at one time. It looked like she was ready for her to get away from her house now."I hadn't seen or talked to you in a while, so I decided to stop over. Are you busy?" Kassidy asked.

"Just babysitting my grandson," Ivy replied.

"Oh. Where is he?" Kassidy asked excitedly.

"He's in his swing," Ivy said, not bothering to let her inside.

Things had changed, and Kassidy was seeing that for herself. Ivy would usually be happy to let her in, but she was standing in the door like she dared her to even try.

"Is something wrong Ivy?" Kassidy finally asked.

"Kassidy, listen, I know that I allowed you to come around in the past, but things are not the same anymore. You and my daughter-in-law don't get along and you and RJ aren't friends anymore. Your presence only causes confusion," Ivy admitted.

"Wow. RJ and I have been best friends for years. Me coming around was never an issue until he got with Marlee. If you ask me, she's the problem, not me. She's been bothered by me and RJ's friendship since day one," Kassidy replied.

"Stop lying to yourself Kassidy. I know how you feel about my son and I always have. I used to see you damn near cry whenever someone new entered the picture. You have a problem with every woman that RJ has ever had, and it was hard for you to hide it. But, things are different now. Marlee is not just some girl who he's gonna get tired of dealing with and leave behind. She's the mother of his child and soon to be wife. She's not going anywhere," Ivy noted.

"I never had a problem with Marlee. She was the one who hit me," Kassidy reminded her.

"And for good reason. I can't even lie Kassidy; I was crazy about you at one time, but you're the worst kind of person in my opinion. You're messy and you can't be trusted. I don't know why Aspen felt the need to confide in you, but I'm sure she's regretting that now. I'm happy that you and my son are no longer friends. He can do better," Ivy rambled.

When she learned that Kassidy was the one behind Banks finding out what Lauren was doing, she got upset. On one hand, she was happy that the truth was revealed. But, she saw Kassidy for who she really was, and her feelings changed after that.

"I was only trying to be a good friend and help," Kassidy replied, pulling Ivy's thoughts from the past and back to the present.

Ivy wanted to scream when she saw RJ's truck pulling up because she knew that he and Marlee had retuned to get Tre. They were going to Paris for their honeymoon and they went shopping to make sure they had everything they needed for their trip. Ivy was praying that

Marlee didn't try to kill Kassidy like she'd done to Joy. Her husband's daughter deserved it, but she was hoping that her daughter-in-law gave the other woman a pass. As long as Kassidy didn't say anything, she would probably live to see another day.

When they got out of the truck, both RJ and Marlee paused when they saw Kassidy standing there. Ivy was doing up some praying and she got nervous the closer Marlee got to them.

"Get rid of your trash RJ. You got two minutes before I come back out here and act a fool," Marlee said calmly as she bypassed Kassidy and went straight into the house.

Ivy exhaled and turned to follow her inside. RJ was filled with rage at Kassidy's nerve. He hadn't seen her since she showed up at his job to tell him and his father about Aspen and Lauren.

"You can't be that damn dumb. I haven't seen or talked to you in months. What made you think that it was okay to show up to my mama's house? Do you want my wife to kill you? I begged her not to come after you once she had my son," RJ ranted.

"All those years of friendship-,"

"Means absolutely nothing to me when it comes down to my wife," RJ said, finishing her sentence for her.

It was at that exact moment that the invisible white flag went up. A moment of surrender and Kassidy was giving up. All the years of loving him in secret, only to be treated like yesterday's trash. Kassidy remembered her mother telling her that she'd probably lost out on hundreds of good men while sitting around waiting for one. No, Kassidy never told RJ that she was in love with him, but her actions showed it. He'd never felt the same way and now she knew that he never would.

"It's cool RJ. It took me forever, but I get it now. You won't have to worry about me bothering you or your family again. Congrats on your upcoming wedding. I wish you all the best," Kassidy said as she tried her best to hold back the tears that wanted to flow.

She was done and there was no coming back. She wished him and Marlee well, but it was time for her to move on. Hopefully, the man of her dreams would find her soon. Until then, she had no problem being alone.

RJ watched as she pulled away and he didn't feel a thing. Kassidy had been his friend for years and he overlooked a lot of the things that she did. Her true colors really started to show when he got with Aspen and things only got worse. RJ had talked to her about it several times, but she was still on that dumb shit. When Marlee knocked her on her ass, she should have learned but, obviously, she hadn't. RJ was happy that she was out of his life. He didn't want anything to do with anybody who didn't mean him and his wife any good.

***

"You better be able to fit a pair of these shoes fat boy," Marlee said to Tre, as he smiled up at her from his swing.

"You know he gon' ball up his fat feet," RJ said as he watched her struggle to try the shoes on his son.

Marlee had gotten the shoes two months ago and she was hoping that one of them worked. They only had ten more days before the wedding and she needed everything to be perfect. The wedding planner was a Godsend and Marlee would recommend her to anyone. She made the entire process easy and as stress-free as possible.

"RJ, help me," Marlee begged as she continued to struggle with their son.

RJ got up from the bed and took Tre out of his swing. He told Marlee to hold him while he effortlessly slipped the shoe on their son's fat feet.

"Daddy got the magic touch," RJ said as he kissed his son's chubby cheek.

"Really Tre?" Marlee laughed as she looked at him.

She was happy that the shoe fit with a little room in the front. Tre's feet wouldn't grow that much in that short period of time. He had a little room in the shoe even if it did.

"Are they good?" RJ asked.

"Yeah, he's good to go," Marlee replied.

"Well, everything is almost perfect," RJ said as he looked at her.

"Please RJ. Let's not have this conversation again. It's just for one day. You act like I wear it all the time." Marlee frowned.

"I don't care Marlee. I love your hair. It was one of the things that attracted me to you," RJ noted.

"I thought you were attracted to all that ass that I was twerking on the dance floor," Marlee smirked.

"That too, but I'm serious baby. I love your mohawk. That's like your signature look. I don't want you to wear no fake hair. Why can't you just get a fresh color and cut?" RJ asked her.

"Why is that bothering you so much?" Marlee asked.

"Because Marlee. I love that you're different from the rest. I love that you don't wear your hair like everybody else. You put your clothes together like a professional, but it's always unique. You even impressed the wedding planner with some of your ideas. I don't want you to change who you are, even if it is just for one day," RJ said as he looked into her eyes.

"Aww baby. That was so sweet. If it means that much to you, then I'll wear the mohawk. I just gotta think of a hot ass color to get now," Marlee replied, right as her phone rang.

She scrunched up her face and turned the phone around to show RJ who it was. Ten days before she got married and she was just now hearing from her father. Marlee still hadn't told him about her plan to have her stepfather walk her down the aisle, but there was no time like the present.

"Hey daddy," Marlee said when she answered the phone for her father.

"Hey baby. How's everything going?" Matthew asked her.

"Everything is fine," Marlee replied.

"I'll be down there tomorrow and I'm staying until after the wedding. What do I need to do? I know I have to get fitted and all that stuff, but what about rehearsal? Don't we have to practice and all that?" Matthew asked.

"Yes, we do that the day before, but we need to talk daddy," Marlee said, as RJ took the baby from her.

Marlee got up and paced the floor as she prepared to break the difficult news to her father.

"Okay, baby girl. What's up?" Matthew asked her.

"I um, I've already asked Alvin to walk me down the aisle at my wedding," Marlee blurted out.

She closed her eyes and prepared for the hurricane known as Matthew to make landfall. She knew that it was coming, but his anger or lack thereof, was not changing her decision.

"Is this a fucking joke Marlee?" Matthew fumed.

"No daddy, it's not," Marlee replied.

"Alvin might be your mother's husband, but he is not your father," Matthew reminded her.

"I know he's not my biological father, but he's always been like a father to Mat and me," Marlee noted.

"I don't give a fuck what he's been like. I'm your father, not him. You must be crazy if you think I'm coming to your wedding to watch another man walk you down the aisle. Fuck that shit! I'm not even coming!" Matthew snapped angrily.

"What's new? You've never been to any of my other important events either. Why should this be any different? At least you have the decency to tell me that you're not coming, so I wouldn't be looking for you like I usually do," Marlee hissed.

"This is the wrong time for you to be dwelling on the past Marlee," Matthew said.

"No, this is the perfect time. I'm getting married in ten days and you just now decided to call me? You didn't even ask if I needed any financial help or nothing else. Knowing your track record, you probably wouldn't have even shown up if I did want you to escort me. I mean, why should you? It's not like you bothered to show up for my high school or college graduations. You didn't bother to show your face at my baby shower or the hospital when your first grandchild was born. But, you know who did show up daddy? Alvin, that's who. I never had to wonder if he was coming or not because I always saw him cheering me on from the front row. Being a father is more than just a title," Marlee argued as she quickened her pace.

"If that's your choice, I can't do nothing but respect it. Congrats and good luck with everything," Matthew said before hanging up.

"Pathetic deadbeat ass nigga," Marlee fumed as she threw her phone on the bed.

"I guess I need to add your pappy to my beat down list. That nigga better not come to our wedding on no bullshit," RJ spoke up.

"His sad ass ain't even coming and I don't give a fuck," Marlee fumed.

"Don't let that get you down baby. It's all good. In ten more days, you'll be calling me daddy anyway," RJ said, making her smile.

No matter how bad things seemed, he always found a way to make her feel better. There was no doubt in Marlee's mind that, in ten more days, she would be making one of the best decisions ever.

Chapter 47

With huge smiles on their faces, Marlee and RJ held hands and looked at each other before they leaped over the broom. The old tradition was important to both their grandmothers and they didn't have a problem making it a part of their special day. The guests in the huge church erupted in applause and cheers as soon as their feet touched the floor. The newlyweds glided down the aisle to the awaiting cars, followed by their small wedding party.

"It's official now baby. I got papers on that ass," RJ said as he pulled Marlee close and planted a sloppy kiss on her lips.

"Everything was so perfect. No rain and no drama," Marlee replied as she wiped her lipstick from his lips with a Kleenex that was in the back of the Rolls Royce that they were riding to the reception in.

"Yeah, now on to the after party," RJ said as he grabbed her hand and kissed it.

"Hold this mirror baby. I need to make sure my makeup is on point before we start taking all these damn pictures," Marlee said as she handed him the huge mirror that she had already had in the car.

"Who does their own makeup on their wedding day?" RJ laughed.

"This chick. I know I would have been too critical if somebody else would have done it, so it didn't make sense," Marlee replied.

Marlee grabbed her makeup bag and freshened up her look. RJ held the mirror for her and smiled as he watched her. Marlee had her mohawk colored platinum blonde and RJ had never seen a more beautiful bride. Her makeup was flawless, but she was even more beautiful without it. Being that she loved to go against the grain, Marlee opted out of the traditional white or off-white dresses. The specially made rose gold wedding dress hugged her curves perfectly, and RJ couldn't keep his eyes off her. He knew that she was about to go off, but he couldn't help himself. He put the mirror down and pulled her in for a kiss.

"Seriously RJ? Now you got lipstick on your lips and you messed mine up," Marlee fussed.

RJ didn't care though. He picked the mirror up and held it to her face while she got right again. When they pulled up to the reception hall, he understood why Marlee was so concerned with her appearance. The photographers were right in front waiting to take some more pictures. Mat was already outside waiting to get their bags from the car. Marlee wanted her and RJ to change after they were done taking pictures, so they could enjoy themselves. They didn't know who was all at their wedding because they really weren't looking.

"How long is this picture shit gonna last?" Murk complained, as they posed in a different area for more photos.

He was ready to get drunk and flirt, but they had been taking pictures for almost two hours. Finally, after taking a few shots by the waterfall, the photographer dismissed them and started taking random shots of their guests. Marlee and RJ went to change while everybody else hit the dance floor. Murk found him a prospect sooner than he thought and he wanted to know who she was.

"Who is that Desi? Is she related to y'all?" Murk asked as he pointed to the woman who was on the dance floor enticing him with her moves.

"That's my cousin, Nika. Her daddy and my mama are first cousins. I can't stand that messy bitch, so she's all yours," Desi replied.

Since Kallie had been into her man a lot lately, Yanni started hanging with their cousin, Nika. She was another known hoe in the family and she had met her match with Murk. Desi couldn't wait until he told her all about their time together, so she could rub it in Nika's face.

"That's cold. Nobody deserves that kind of treatment," Desmond said as he watched Murk finessing the other woman.

"Fuck that bitch. Did you call and check on Destini?" Desi asked him.

"Yeah. My mama said she was good. She said she can stay until tomorrow," Desmond replied as he kissed her neck.

"Aww. I'm gonna miss her," Desi pouted.

"That's because you spoiled her," Desmond replied.

"I couldn't help it. I fell in love with her cuteness," Desi said.

"And I fell in love with you," Desmond admitted as he looked deep into her eyes.

He never thought it would ever happen again after the unexpected passing of his wife, but it did. He fell head over heels in love with Desi and he didn't know what he would do without her. Without even trying, she came into his life when he was at his lowest and made life worth living again. She was a great woman to him and an even better mother to his daughter. His mother loved her and so did Destini's maternal grandmother. They were grateful that Desi took such good care of Destini and her love was genuine.

"Aww boo. I love you, too," Desi said as her eyes filled with unshed tears.

"Do you love me enough to share space with me?" Desmond asked, as they swayed to the music.

"We're already sharing space. We've been sleeping by each other's houses for months," Desi replied.

"I know Desi, but that doesn't make sense. We're paying rent at two separate apartments, but we're always together. We can buy a house and save money if we live under the same roof," Desmond reasoned.

"You want us to buy a house together," Desi repeated, just to be sure she heard him right.

"Yes, I do. I'm not going anywhere, and I hope you aren't either," Desmond said as he looked at her.

"I didn't plan on it." Desi smiled.

"Cool. Well, I guess we can start looking for us a house. And don't worry, we'll get something big enough for Murk too," Desmond replied.

"Me and Murk are not a package deal. He's my friend, not my responsibility," Desi pointed out.

"I don't know Desi. He might not take the news too well. He was your roommate before I came along, and I don't want to come in between that," Desmond noted.

"We were never roommates. He stayed over one night and just never left. Murk is about to be a father of six. Ain't no way in hell is he coming to stay with us with all that baggage. He can keep the apartment if he wants to. I'll talk to him about that later," Desi replied.

Desmond pulled her in for a kiss and she welcomed his soft lips. She had given up on love after Jerry, but Desmond made her want to try again. Destini was a gift from God and she loved her like she'd given birth to her. Desi thought it would be weird for everyone when Destini started calling her mama, but they embraced it just as she had. God saw fit for her to be a mother after all and she was so grateful. Desmond was life when she felt dead inside and she would always love him for that. She wanted her happily ever after and she wanted it with him.

"Don't be trying to steal me and my husband's shine bitch," Marlee joked when she and RJ walked up on them.

"Stop hating," Desi replied as she gave her cousin the finger.

From what Marlee could see, not too many people were sitting down. The reception was in full swing and she and RJ got on the dance floor and partied with their guests. Ivy had Tre in her arms as she and Iris danced, while Banks danced with his granddaughter, Paris. The hall looked like a huge club and the DJ was doing his thing. After hours of drinking, dancing, and eating, the beating of drums could be heard near the entrance. Everyone looked up towards the front door and cheered when the brass band and Indians entered the building. The party got even more lit after that, as everyone second lined around the huge dance floor. That had to be the work of Banks because Marlee and RJ didn't even think to do something so extravagant. It was the perfect way to end their perfect night and they couldn't have asked for anything better. The entertainment stayed there for about an hour before the lights were turned on. By then, Marlee's heels were nowhere to be found and she was sweating her makeup off.

"Baby, this damn reception was like a big ass concert," Raven said as she walked over fanning her face.

"Girl, yes, this shit was lit," Desi agreed.

The caterers were passing out cake and it was time for everyone to leave. It was after midnight and the reception started at six. It was supposed to end at ten, but Banks had pulled some strings. Marlee and RJ were walking around talking to a few people, when they heard cheers coming from the corner of the room. They rushed over to see what was going on, when they got over there and saw Banks down on one knee in front of Ivy.

"The fuck is this nigga doing? His ass is going straight to jail. He's already married," RJ said as he looked at his parents in shock and confusion.

Ivy was wiping tears from her eyes, as Banks slipped a ring on her finger.

"Are they engaged now?" Marlee asked RJ.

"I don't even know," RJ replied, right as his parents walked over to him.

"Baby, look. Don't you just love it?" Ivy gushed as she showed RJ and Marlee her ring.

"How can y'all be engaged and you're still married?" RJ asked while looking at his father.

"We're obviously not getting married until I'm divorced, but this was long overdue," Banks replied as he kissed Ivy's hand.

"Congrats guys. I'm happy for y'all," Marlee said as she hugged her in-laws.

"Yeah, I'm happy for y'all too," RJ said as he did the same.

"Thanks." Banks smiled happily.

"You better be lucky that you paid for everything. I would have been making you go half if you didn't. Proposing at my wedding reception," RJ laughed.

"I waited until the end," Banks said as he laughed with him.

They waited until the last of the guests had exited the building before they all did the same. Tre went home with Tiffany and Alvin, while Marlee and RJ went to the suite that they had rented for the night. Marlee prayed for a perfect day and she was thankful that her prayers were answered.

***

"Bitch, it was everything. I can't even lie. That bitch be acting stuck up sometimes, but she did that shit," Nika said as she and Yanni sat on her porch eating crawfish.

Yanni was green with envy as she listened to her cousin go on and on about Marlee's wedding. The wedding that she wasn't invited to. Her entire family was there while she sat at home with her crying baby. Yanni couldn't even lie; she missed doing things with her cousins and she hated to feel left out. She had regrets and she wasn't ashamed to admit that. There were times when she wanted to pick up the phone and give Marlee the apology that she was owed, but her pride wouldn't let her. She didn't even know if Marlee would accept, but she at least wanted to try. She was once a part of the inner circle, but now she was on the outside looking in. Jealousy was an ugly thing and Yanni knew that better than anyone. She always wanted something that someone else had, but it never worked out in her favor. That was why she made it a point to get Tyson. He was like Marlee's new toy and she wanted to play with it. Crazy thing was, the man who she really wanted was now her cousin's husband. She'd inadvertently pushed Marlee into the arms of the man who her heart truly desired.

"That's good. I'm happy for her," Yanni said, shocking her cousin with her response.

"Bitch what? Since when you started liking Marlee?" Nika questioned.

"Marlee never did anything to me. I was the one who fucked up with her," Yanni finally admitted.

"What the hell has gotten into you?" Nika asked with a frown.

"I'm just sick of all this dumb shit. I'm sick of my life and, most of all, I'm sick of Tyson. Marlee dodged a serious bullet and my stupid ass got hit with it. That's what I get for putting myself in the line of fire," Yanni replied.

"Damn cousin. It sounds like you've been to church and got saved. Let me find out my cousin is a Christian now," Nika joked, but Yanni was not in a playing mood.

She was displeased with her life and miserable. And suddenly, the ten dollars an hour that she made working for her cousin's husband was embarrassing to her now. Tyson didn't help with their daughter like he should have, and he had another baby on the way. Taj put her life on social media and she made it known that she was having another baby by her ex-husband. She and Tyson obviously had problems because she was always blasting him in every post. She was saying how much of a deadbeat father he was, but she was the dummy who was giving him another child.

"Was Kallie at the wedding?" Yanni asked.

She had been avoiding looking at the pictures on Instagram, but she gave in as she sat there with her cousin. Kallie had been moving differently since she lived with her man, but it was all good with Yanni.

"Everybody was there but you," Nika said, stating the obvious.

"This is so different, but it's pretty," Yanni said as she looked at some of the photos.

Marlee always did like to be different and her wedding reflected that. Instead of dresses, her girls were dressed in tuxedos like the men. They didn't wear the tuxedo pants, they wore skirts instead. It was cute as hell and Yanni had to compliment her cousin's creativity. Even her dress was beautiful, and she looked great in it. Yanni's eyes drifted to RJ and he looked genuinely happy. She was still trying to figure out how they met, but that was irrelevant at that point since they were married now.

"Girl, it was like a big ass club up in there. They had a brass band and everything. You know I met me somebody and had my own after party when I left. His ass is all types of crazy though." Nika frowned.

"Crazy how?" Yanni asked.

"Some of the shit that he wanted to do in the bedroom was ridiculous," Nika answered.

"But, I'm sure you did it anyway," Yanni said while rolling her eyes.

"You know I did, but fuck him. We stayed there until noon the next day and I thought it was all good. I tried to give him my number and he told me that he was good. Nigga said he got what he wanted, so there was no need for him to call me. I know niggas be thinking like that, but his stupid ass actually told me to my face. And I almost died when he called for a ride and Desi pulled up to get him." Nika frowned, making Yanni turn to look at her.

"Was he tall and skinny with dreads?" Yanni asked.

"Girl yes. You know him?" Nika asked.

"He's RJ's cousin and Desi's best friend. Whatever you did with him, Desi and everybody else knows now," Yanni said, making Nika's heart rate speed up.

Some of the things she did in that hotel room should have been illegal. She planned to take her secrets to her grave, but everybody probably knew by now. She and Desi never did get along and she was the last person that she wanted to know her business.

"It's whatever." Nika shrugged like she didn't care.

Yanni smirked, knowing that her cousin was in her feelings. When her phone rang and Craig's number appeared, Yanni excused herself and answered the call.

"I hope you got what I've been asking you for," Yanni said when she answered the phone.

"I got you and I hope you got me too. I got a room and I'm trying to see what that mouth do all night," Craig replied, making her roll her eyes.

"Whatever," Yanni replied.

"Whatever my ass. I'm doing you a favor. Ain't nothing free, my baby. You can't afford what he's charging, so I'm offering you a way out," Craig noted.

"Text me the information and I'll see you later," Yanni said before she hung up the phone.

She prayed that her mother would keep her baby for a while because she got in her feelings sometimes. Craig was doing her a huge favor and she needed him more than he knew. Once Nika left, Yanni took a shower and put her daughter to sleep. That was the only way her mother agreed to watch her. Yanni walked out of her house, right as Craig pulled up to get her. She had a debt to pay and she was looking forward to clearing her tab.

Chapter 48

Murk hated to get rid of his prized possession, but it was the best thing for him to do. He ended up selling his car to the same body shop that did his custom paint job and he got a nice chunk of change from it. If he was being honest with himself, he would have gotten rid of the car a long time ago. It was too small for him and all his kids and he had another one on the way. He ended up getting an all-black Escalade and he kind of liked having a bigger vehicle. He had his car parked at his mother's house now, since he was on a mission. He gave one of the local fiends something from his stash to let him borrow his car for a few hours. Murk hated to do dirt with anyone else, but he had an accomplice with him that night. He regretted the decision as soon as his unwanted visitor got into the car.

"The fuck is taking this nigga so long pop? I'm trying to go slide up in something tonight," Legend drawled from his place on the back seat. He had the car full of smoke and Murk was ready to put his stupid ass out.

"Shut the fuck up and put that shit out. How you trying to shoot if you're high?" Murk fussed.

"My aim is even better when I'm high pop. Stop stressing, I got this," Legend assured him.

They were in a blue Altima with tinted windows, but the car wasn't one that would make anyone look twice. New Orleans had a million of the same cars on the streets and there was nothing special about that one. Murk promised RJ that he would wait until after he got married to handle Tyson and the time had come. He and Marlee had been married for a month now and that was long enough. Murk spent days watching his every move and he knew his schedule like the back of his hand. To say that Tyson looked like he escaped from the zoo, the nigga had mad hoes. He laid up with a different chick every night and Murk knew where all of them lived. He was parked on Tyson's mama's block a few cars down from the house. Tyson was later than his normal time and Legend was getting impatient. When Murk showed him a picture of Tyson, Legend confirmed that he was the man who he'd seen standing outside when he went to make a sale, right before he got shot. He wanted to deal with Tyson himself and Murk reluctantly agreed to let him.

"Fuck!" Murk yelled as he pounded his fist on the steering wheel.

Tyson had come out of the house, but he was carrying his daughter when he did. Murk watched as he strapped the baby in her car seat and pulled off soon after. Murk started to follow him, but he made sure to stay a few cars behind.

"Don't trip pop. My aim is on point. I can hit his bitch ass while he's driving," Legend said as he cocked his gun.

"Put that shit up stupid ass nigga. He got a fucking baby in the car. You got nieces and nephews too, dumb ass," Murk chastised.

Murk continued to tail him until he pulled up to a house about ten minutes later. He didn't get out of the car, but the porch light to the house came on a few minutes later. Murk watched as Marlee's thot ass cousin walked out and up to Tyson's car. Being that he was a street nigga from birth, Murk saw that something was off about her. It was hot as hell outside, but she was wearing a hoodie. He and Legend watched as she opened the back door to get her baby out.

"The fuck! You see that shit bruh!" Murk yelled to his little brother.

"That bitch is foul pop," Legend replied as they watch Yanni slip something under the front seat of Tyson's car.

That explained why she had on the hoodie. She was hiding something underneath. She moved fast as hell and Tyson didn't even know what was going on. Once she got her baby out of the car, Yanni smiled brightly and waved as he pulled off.

"These hoes is scandalous," Murk said as he started following Tyson again.

"It's on now pop. Get close to that nigga so I can put his ass to sleep," Legend said as he pulled his hoodie over his head.

He didn't have to tell Murk twice. He pulled his hoodie over his head too before he sped up to catch up to Tyson. Legend was ready to light up the block and Murk was ready to let him. He was almost close enough to Tyson to put in some work, when a car came out of nowhere and ran right into the passenger's side of Tyson's car. Before Murk and Legend could register what was happening, a man dressed in all black jumped out of the car and started shooting. He didn't even try to cover his face because he obviously didn't plan to leave Tyson alive.

"Oh shit!" Murk yelled as he stomped on the brakes.

He put the car in reverse and started backing up and away from the bullets that were flying. He didn't know how many shots had rang out, but it seemed like they would never end. When they finally did die down, he and Legend were turning down a side street heading in the opposite direction.

"The fuck is that nigga Craig on?" Legend said, as Murk drove like he was being paid to do it.

"Who is Craig?" Murk questioned.

"I went to school with that nigga. He's a lame. This ain't even the life for him," Legend replied.

"When did your dumb ass ever go to school?" Murk asked.

"That nigga was there the few times that I did go. Damn pop. I wonder what he did dude to make him step out of character like that," Legend said.

"I don't know, but we obviously weren't the only ones who wanted that nigga dead," Murk noted.

"You think he's dead pop?" Legend asked.

"If he ain't, he's damn sure close to it," Murk said as he headed to his mother's house.

Once he dropped Legend off, he went and got the dude whose car he'd borrowed. He gave Murk a ride back to Desi's apartment, where his own truck was parked. He tried calling Desi, but she was by Marlee. That was perfect because Murk had to fill them in on what was going on. He knew that Marlee would know who to call to get the info, so he headed straight to his cousin's house as soon as he got into his truck.

***

"Man, that shit was wild," Murk said as he downed his glass of Hennessey and poured himself another one.

"All the dirt you be out there doing. I know that shit ain't got you shook up like that," RJ replied while looking at him sideways.

"This shit was different though, bruh. If I would have pulled up a little closer, I would have been getting shot up too. Dude jumped out of the car on some savage shit. The nigga had to be following him too. It wasn't a coincidence that the shit happened as soon as he dropped his daughter off," Murk noted.

"I don't even feel sorry for him. He did Craig dirty in front of everybody. That boy was embarrassed," Desi replied.

"It's been an hour and I still don't see nothing online," Marlee said as she scrolled through her phone.

"Call Kim," Desi suggested, speaking of Tyson's son's mother.

"Hell no. If it's not on the news, they gon' wonder how she knows about it," RJ reasoned.

"Yeah, that's true," Desi nodded.

"And y'all hoe ass cousin is foul. Bitch straight slipped dope under her baby daddy's car seat. The fuck is she on?" Murk wondered.

"She's probably in her feelings because his ex-wife is pregnant by him again. That nigga don't do shit for her baby anyway. She probably don't care if he gets locked up," Marlee replied.

"Damn man. I want to know what happened. I know somebody must have called the police. That was too many shots for them not to," Murk said.

They all sat around the kitchen and talked about the events of the night. Marlee kept checking the local news websites until she finally found something. The story was very vague, only saying that the police had responded to a shooting and there was only one victim. They didn't give names and didn't say if the person was dead or alive.

"This is Kim!" Marlee yelled when she saw her phone ringing.

"Speakerphone bitch," Desi instructed.

"Hey girl," Marlee said when she answered the phone.

"Girl, somebody shot my fat ass baby daddy up!" Kim yelled on the other end.

"When? Is he dead?" Marlee asked like she was surprised.

"No, but he'll wish he was. They found weed in his car and it was more than an average person smokes. That might not mean much to some but, for a convicted felon, that's some serious shit. Trinity said that somebody called the police to report that he had drugs in the car. Before they even got to him, somebody shot him up. I guess it's just not his day," Kim laughed.

That part of the story had Yanni's name written all over it. There was no limit to what she would do, and she just kept proving that.

"Do they know who did it?" Marlee asked.

"Nope. You know how they are in New Orleans. Everything is a drug deal gone bad," Kim replied.

"What else did Trinity say?" Marlee questioned.

"Not much. He got shot three times and went through surgery. They got all the bullets out, but he's going straight to central lockup once he's released. But, girl, I'll keep you posted if I hear anything else. I know Trinity will probably call me back before the night is out," Kim said before hanging up.

"That bitch Yanni is grimy." Desi frowned.

"I told y'all. That bitch came outside wearing a hoodie in ninety-degree weather. Me and Legend watched as she took something from under the hoodie and stuck it under the seat," Murk said, repeating what he'd told them earlier.

"I can see her being upset about him not taking care of her baby but damn. It wasn't that serious," Marlee spoke up.

"What did she expect from a nigga who fucked his girl's first cousin?" RJ questioned.

"Exactly. I don't have no sympathy for her dirty ass. Big boy is probably wondering where the dope came from too," Desi replied.

"He just got off papers not too long ago. He should be happy for that much," Marlee said.

"That don't mean nothing to them people. Shit, he gon' wait about two years just to get a court date. Orleans Parish Court is backed the fuck up," Murk noted.

"And y'all are sure that it was his sister's ex-boyfriend who shot him?" RJ asked.

"Legend recognized the nigga. I didn't know who the hell he was," Murk replied.

"I'm not surprised. Tyson used to handle him so bad. I guess the last straw was when he knocked him out in front of the whole block. You can't be embarrassing people like that. That bullying shit got a lot of people in their graves right now," Marlee pointed out.

"That's some real shit," RJ agreed, right as he heard his son start to whimper over the baby monitor.

"Let me fix him something to eat. He's been sleeping for a minute and I know he's hungry," Marlee said when RJ left to go get Tre.

He was eight months old now and eating some solid foods. Marlee had just fixed him some mashed potatoes, but she had to warm them up.

"What's up Vegas baby?" Murk said when RJ walked back in with his son.

He was tired of telling Murk about calling his son that, so he just let it fly. Tre laughed with anybody, so it was no surprise that he smiled at Murk with his two new teeth. He already had four at the top and his bottom two had just popped out.

"Hey handsome." Desi smiled as she kissed her little cousin's hand.

"Where's Desmond?" Marlee asked her.

"He took Destini to see her aunties. He said she's crying up a storm and won't let nobody touch her," Desi laughed.

"That's because she doesn't know them. They don't come around enough," Marlee said, speaking of Desmond's deceased wife's sisters.

They didn't like Desi and they were the only ones who seemed to have a problem with her. The one thing that Desi was afraid of had happened, but only with them. They accused Desmond of trying to replace their sister with Desi and making Destini call her mama. Their mother didn't feel that way and she loved Desi and how she cared for her granddaughter.

"Fuck them hoes. As long as they don't come around me with that dumb shit, I'm good. Desmond already cursed their stupid asses out," Desi replied.

"I hope they jump your bald head ass. Don't look for me to help you either," Murk hissed.

"Yeah right," Marlee laughed.

"That's real shit cuz. Bald head bitch trying to sneak and move out on me," Murk fussed.

"How am I sneaking when I told your illiterate ass what was up? And call me another bitch and I'm cutting your skinny ass," Desi threatened.

"The girl got a man, bruh. The fuck did you expect? You can't stay with her forever," RJ tried to reason.

"I already knew what it was when she first told me about the nigga. First, she moved him in with us and now she's trying to move out with him," Murk complained.

"Who the fuck is us? You stayed over one night and I couldn't get rid of your ass after that," Desi corrected.

"I thought you liked Desmond?" Marlee said.

"I do like him. That's my nigga. He's good people," Murk noted.

"What's the problem then?" Marlee asked.

"He's not the problem," Murk replied while looking at Desi.

"So, I'm the problem?" Desi asked while pointing to herself.

"Hot pussy ass. It's just like you to let some dick come in between us," Murk fussed.

"I'm not letting anything come between us, but I don't know what else you want me to do. I offered to let you keep the apartment in my name. With a record as long as yours, I know you can't go out and get one on your own. But, fuck it. I'll give up the apartment. You can move in with me and Desmond whenever we find us a house," Desi conceded.

"I'm not your charity case Desi. Don't be trying to feel sorry for me," Murk argued.

"Fuck you, Lyfe!" Desi shouted angrily.

"Now see, I was only fucking with your globe head ass. You taking shit too far now," Murk fumed.

"Man, leave that damn girl alone," RJ said as he and Marlee laughed at them going back and forth. It was all fun and games until Desi called him by his real name.

"I'm about to stop speaking to his ass again. I don't have time for this dumb shit," Desi ranted.

"Don't do me like that sis. I'm just fucking with you, girl. You know a nigga happy for your bald head ass. I'm not trying to move in with y'all though. I'm good with keeping the apartment," Murk said seriously.

"You and Desmond need to get at my sister. She can help y'all find a house," RJ said.

"Yeah, Marlee gave me her card. I'll set something up with her soon," Desi replied.

"My pops is selling his old house. Maybe y'all can work something out with him," RJ noted.

"That bitch is nice too. I might change my mind about moving in if y'all get that one," Murk joked.

"That's a lot of house for just a few people," Marlee acknowledged.

"Yeah but, if the price is right, we might just go for it." Desi shrugged.

"Our house is bigger than that one and it's only three of us. I'm trying to put some more babies in you, so we'll need the space," RJ said as he winked at Marlee

"This bitch is always blushing like that ain't her husband," Desi laughed.

She and Murk stayed over for a while and had dinner with RJ and Marlee. When Desmond called and said that he was on his way home, Desi left a few minutes after. Murk stayed behind for a little while until he got a call that put a huge smile on his face. They didn't have to ask where he was going because they already knew.

Chapter 49

"Ahh!" Marlee screamed as she and Sierra tackled Desi down to the floor.

"Y'all do too damn much," Mat said as she sat on the sofa holding her nephew.

Marlee had come over to visit and she was happy that Tre was with her. He usually stayed home with his father, so that was a pleasant surprise. Since Tyson was locked up, RJ was cool with Marlee being on the block again. He was facing up to ten years in prison unless his lawyer could work a miracle. Yanni was a sad ass bitch, but that was good for Tyson too. They did Marlee dirty, but karma was real.

"Y'all are so extra," Desi laughed, as Marlee helped her up from the floor.

"Cousin, I'm so happy for you. You deserve every good thing that happens to you," Marlee said as she wiped the tears from her eyes.

"Aww, you're about to make me cry too," Desi replied.

After speaking with RJ's father, she and Desmond were given the deal of a lifetime. He agreed to do owner financing on his home and they were only paying twelve hundred dollars a month. The house was huge with a small apartment added to the rear. Five bedrooms and three baths was more than enough room for Desi and her small family. The house was in near perfect condition, but some of the rooms needed to be painted. They had met Banks and his lawyer the day before and finalized the paperwork. Desi thought that things couldn't get any better until they walked out of the building. It was then that Desmond dropped down to one knee and asked her to be his wife.

"Desmond is so sweet. You couldn't have found yourself a better husband." Sierra smiled.

"I swear, I never pictured myself being as happy as I am now." Desi blushed.

"When is the wedding? You know you can count on me for whatever you need," Marlee said.

"That goes for me and Mat too, cousin," Sierra replied.

"Thanks y'all, but we're not doing anything big. We want to move into our new house as husband and wife, but we're bypassing the big wedding. We're using the money that we have saved up to get our house together," Desi replied.

"That's smart Desi." Mat nodded in approval.

"Yeah, we plan to be in the house within the next two months, so we'll probably go to the courthouse before then." Desi shrugged.

"Well, maybe we can throw y'all a dinner party afterwards. We can rent a hall or do it at our house by the water. Ask Desmond if he's okay with that and I'll take care of everything else," Marlee offered.

"That's sounds like a plan." Desi smiled.

"Now, on to the real issue here. What the hell are you gonna do with Murk? Does he know about the proposal yet?" Sierra asked.

"He knew before I did. He claims that Desmond asked his permission before he proposed. I don't know who the hell he thinks he is," Desi laughed.

"Is he still keeping the apartment?" Marlee asked her.

"I don't want him to," Desi replied.

"Why not? Girl, you better not be trying to play with that crazy ass boy. You know he thinks you're his real blood sister," Marlee noted.

"I know and he's my brother from another mother. I've been knowing him for almost two years, but it feels like a lifetime. I don't know how I'll feel if I don't see him every day. Am I crazy for wanting him to move in with me and my new husband?" Desi asked her favorite cousin and best friend.

"I don't think you're crazy, but you need to see how Desmond feels about it before you make any decisions," Marlee replied.

"He's good with it. He already said that the added apartment is for Murk before I even mentioned it," Desi noted.

"All that's fine and good, but how does Murk feel about moving in with y'all?" Mat asked.

"Stubborn bastard said no. He said his hoes can't walk around naked, so he doesn't want to come. I need to cancel the lease and force him out," Desi laughed.

"Damn man. Everything is changing. It's good changes, but I'm still in my feelings," Sierra pouted.

"Don't even start all that shit again," Mat said while rolling her eyes up to the ceiling.

"I can't help it. I'm gonna miss my bestie," Sierra fake cried while hugging Marlee.

"Stop being so dramatic Sierra. You're my best friend and sister-in-law. I'll still see you just as much as I see you now," Marlee pointed out.

"I know, but I'm so used to seeing you at work every day. I can't believe that you won't be there when I go back Monday." Sierra frowned.

"I know friend, but my hubby needed me," Marlee replied.

After hiring and firing two replacements after his sister quit, RJ was going crazy. He was trying to do his job as well as the job that Joy used to do, and it was overwhelming. After working until almost midnight one night, he begged Marlee to come work with him. He was stressing, and she didn't like that. She didn't even have to think about it for too long. She put in a two weeks' notice on her job and did what she had to do. She'd officially started by RJ two days before, and she actually liked it.

"I know and I'm happy for you. Everybody can't have a quickie with the boss on their lunch breaks," Sierra laughed.

"Shut up girl. I'm very professional when I'm there. I even wear a uniform," Marlee laughed.

"Baby, I know Yanni just wants to die. Have you seen her yet?" Desi asked.

"Yeah, but we didn't say anything to each other. I went to the break room to get something to drink and she was sitting there eating. She probably was shocked to see me with a uniform shirt on. I don't have nothing against Yanni, girl. She did me a favor and I'm happy. She tried it though," Marlee replied.

"She tried and failed. You don't just work for Banks Parking; you're Mrs. RJ Banks," Desi noted.

"They better act like they know!" Marlee yelled as she gave her a high five.

When Desmond called a few minutes later, Marlee was happy that he was okay with them having a small dinner once they were married. Marlee knew that RJ would be okay with it because he never told her no. She was so happy for her cousin and she wanted to make sure that she had everything that she needed. Desi had been through a lot and she deserved her happy ending.

***

Marlee looked at the phone and blew out a breath of frustration. She was still trying to play catch up with all the filing and paperwork, but she was off to a good start. Since Joy had left, none of the contracts had been filed and some had expired and were still in the active folder. She just needed to get everything up to date and it would be smooth sailing from there. The only thing she needed was for her husband to stop calling her every five minutes for nothing.

"Yes RJ," Marlee sighed when she answered the phone for him.

"Come give me a kiss," RJ said, making her remove the phone from her ear and stare at it.

"Really RJ? I'm busy as hell and you're calling me with that bullshit," Marlee fussed.

"I'm the boss here and at home and you better remember that. Don't forget who signs your paychecks," RJ joked.

"And don't forget who you're gonna be begging for some pussy when we're off the clock," Marlee countered.

"Why you gotta go there? I'm sorry baby. You know I'm just fucking with you," RJ said.

"I'm busy RJ. I'll see you in a little while for lunch," Marlee said before she hung up on him.

She would have plenty of free time to play around with him once she got caught up. Until then, she saw him at lunch or if they so happened to be in the break room at the same time. As soon as Marlee was done entertaining her husband, she got right back to it. She was able to clear out the file with the expired contracts and replace it with the active ones. She had a long list of calls that she had to return for people who wanted to use their services. Marlee had her head buried in paperwork until someone cleared their throat behind her. When she looked up and saw Joy, her attitude did a slight shift.

"Hi. Is my father in his office?" Joy asked politely, shocking Marlee with her newfound attitude.

Maybe that beatdown that she delivered to her a few months before was what she needed. Joy hadn't been back around since then, but she seemed to be a changed woman now.

"Yeah, he's here. You can go back there if you want to," Marlee replied.

Joy nodded and proceeded down the hall to her father's office. Marlee didn't know what was up with her, but she would have to ask RJ later. She knew that her mother had undergone surgery for her breast cancer and she was now doing chemo and radiation. Banks was true to his word and kept her on his insurance. He even offered to hire a nurse to assist her, but Lauren declined. Her mother had come down from Denver to help and she had been staying with them.

"My mama just dropped us off something to eat baby," RJ said as he walked up to Marlee's desk.

"From where?" Marlee asked.

"Her and my grandma went out to eat at some new place. She said the food was good, so I told her to bring us something back," RJ replied.

"I wish I would have known that she was out there. I would have gone outside to see my baby," Marlee said.

"His fat ass was sleeping. She said he ate and went straight to sleep," RJ laughed.

"Aww, he's getting so big." Marlee smiled.

"I know. I can't wait for his first party," RJ replied.

He was serious when he said that he wanted his son to have a circus party. The same lady who coordinated their wedding was doing Tre's first party too. She was good at what she did, and RJ didn't care that she was pricey. She was worth every penny that he paid her.

"I'll be in the break room in a minute. I have one more thing to do," Marlee said as she prepared to make one more phone call.

"Okay," he replied.

RJ grabbed their food from his office and went to the break room. Marlee joined him a short time later and they talked as they ate their food.

"Did you know that your sister Joy was here?" Marlee asked him.

"Nah. What did she want?" he questioned.

"She was looking for your daddy. I guess she's still in his office because she never came out," Marlee answered.

"Lauren ain't doing too good. They found another lump and it's bigger than the other one was. They want to send her to one of those special clinics and they need money to pay for it. My pops told me this morning," RJ informed her.

"I'm sorry to hear that. Is Banks gonna give it to her?" Marlee asked, even though she already knew the answer.

"Yeah, but he said he wants to write the check and pay the people himself," RJ replied.

"That's understandable," Marlee nodded.

"I know we haven't had the best relationship, but I hope she can beat it. I wouldn't wish cancer on my worst enemy," RJ replied.

He and Marlee finished up their meals and sat there and talked for a while. Yanni walked into the break room, right as RJ got up to throw their trash away. She didn't say anything to either of them as she got her food out of the fridge.

"I guess it's time for me to get back to work," Marlee said as she stood to her feet.

"Girl, you're married to the boss. You don't have to rush back from lunch. Take all the time you need," RJ replied as he kissed her lips.

"No special treatment RJ. I thought we talked about that already," Marlee said.

"I can't help it baby. You're my wife," RJ replied as he kissed her again.

"Don't you have a conference call?" she reminded him.

"Oh shit! I forgot all about that. See, that's why I was begging you to come work here. You deserve a raise already," RJ joked as he pecked her on the lips two more times before rushing back to his office.

Marlee laughed as she shook her head. She went to throw her water bottle away while Yanni was throwing her trash away. They almost bumped into each other, but Marlee moved before it happened.

"Sorry," Yanni mumbled.

"You're good," Marlee replied as she turned to walk away.

"I'm sorry for everything," Yanni blurted out, making Marlee stop and turn to look at her.

She had tears in her eyes when Marlee looked up at her and that was a first. Yanni was never the apologetic type, so Marlee was surprised. She always had a fuck everybody kind of attitude, but she really looked torn up.

"I forgave you a long time ago Iyana," Marlee replied truthfully.

"I miss you and Desi so much and I'm sorry," Yanni cried.

"I can't lie Yanni, I miss the way it used to be too. Tyson and nobody else was worth losing our bond. If you would have been straight up and told me that you used to fuck with him, I would have cut it off right then and there before feelings got involved. Any man that my family or friends have been with is off limits to me. But, it's all good. In the midst of my storm, God sent me a rainbow," Marlee replied.

"I just want things to go back to the way they used to be," Yanni sniffled while wiping her eyes.

"Honestly Yanni, I doubt if that will ever happen. I forgive you, but I don't trust you. We're first cousins, so I do want us to be cordial with one another. I can't give you much more than that," Marlee said truthfully before walking away.

Yanni nodded because she understood exactly what her cousin was saying. She had done a lot of fucked up things in her life and she was paying for them. Messing with Tyson started a downward spiral and she was having a hard time bouncing back. Thanks to the weed that Craig came through and got for her, Tyson was now a distant memory. At least for a while anyway. Yanni didn't bank on him getting shot when he left her house. That was just an added bonus. It was rumored that Craig had pulled the trigger and she believed it. His sudden move to Mississippi with his grandmother proved just how guilty he was. He had been begging Yanni to come see him, but she couldn't afford to miss any days from work. She was barely making it off of what she made now. Once she paid her baby's daycare and got diapers and whatever else she needed, she was back to square one. She had to beg her brother for money to get a bus pass and that was just pathetic.

Tyson did the bare minimum and that still wasn't much. Him being locked up was no different than when he was home. Yanni thought that having Tyson's baby was a good move financially, but things only seemed to get worse. She was barely making it before and her daughter was another bill that she did not need.

But Marlee, on the other hand, had hit the jackpot. She was living like a queen and RJ was definitely a king. He hated Yanni and he didn't try to hide it. She was surprised that she still had her job, but she was grateful. She was even more surprised when she found out that Marlee was working there. That was crazy in her opinion, since she was married to one of the bosses. Yanni was sure that her pay exceeded the little chump change that she was being paid every week. Maybe if they were still cool, Marlee could have helped her move up the ladder and get an inside position too. Sadly, that would never happen. RJ probably wouldn't allow it even if she wanted to. Yanni accepted her fate and everything that happened was her own fault. She should have known better than to burn her bridges, especially if she didn't know when or if she had to cross them again.

Chapter 50

Aspen sipped her wine as she looked through over two hundred pictures of Marlee and RJ's wedding. They had a link to the photographer's page put up and she scrolled through every one of them. She'd even looked through the ones that they took on their honeymoon in Paris. Admittedly, RJ's wedding was beautiful, but the moment was bittersweet. After spending five years of her life with him, Aspen thought it would be her whose hand he took in marriage. Now that they were married, all they talked about lately was their son's first birthday party. In only one years' time, her life had been completely altered. She usually wasn't one to dwell on things too long, but she was having a hard time getting over that. They were having a family game night at her aunt Patrice's house and everyone seemed to be having fun, but her.

"Girl, Patrice be serious as hell about these game nights," one of Aspen's cousins sat next to her and said.

Aspen was happy for the temporary distraction because she needed to focus on something else other than her ex.

"Girl, yes. She's a sore loser, so she always tries her best to win. I think she be cheating sometimes," Aspen laughed, right as Patrice stuck her head into the room.

"Come on Aspen. I'm about to show everybody why I'm the Monopoly champ!" her auntie yelled out to her.

Aspen decided to bury her feelings and enjoy spending time with her family. Thankfully, Aaron's annoying ass wasn't there, and neither was Blythe. Aaron had to stay at work late, and Blythe was supposed to be there a while ago. She was over an hour late, but Aspen knew that she was coming. Some of her cousins were there, so she could ignore her if she had to. Rosalyn spoke to her, but their relationship hadn't been the same since her wedding day. Even Nikki had been acting distant lately and Aspen didn't know why.

"Pick your game pieces and let's get started!" Patrice yelled to all who were playing.

As promised, she walked away the winner of the game and Aspen moved over to the card table soon after. They were only playing Uno, since nobody in the family gambled. Right when the first game was about to end, Blythe and her family walked in. Aspen groaned inwardly because she was not in the mood for her sister's slick ass mouth. Her husband and kids spoke to everyone right before going to the kitchen for food.

"Sorry we're late, but we had another stop to make first," Blythe announced, as if anyone cared.

Aspen was happy to see that her big sister appeared to be in a good mood. That meant that Blythe would lay off her and she welcomed the break. She knew that her sister meant well, but it was draining to hear the same stuff all the time. She was tired of hearing about how much Aaron loved her and how wrong she was doing him. They didn't know him like Aspen did and she was tired of telling them that; Aaron had issues that he refused to get help for. There was only so much that Aspen could do.

Since she had the abortion, she tried her best to distance herself from him. She had been studying for the law school admissions test, so she used that as her excuse. Aaron knew how important that was to her, so he gave her some space. There were times that he just wanted to be around her though. Sometimes, he would show up at her house unannounced and just sit there while she ignored him. He didn't mind, as long he got to see her. Since she had taken the test almost a month ago, she didn't have an excuse to give when he wanted to spend time with her.

"Where is Aaron?" Blythe's husband, Ricardo, asked when he sat next to Aspen.

"He had to work a little later than usual. He might pass through when he gets off," Aspen said, hoping that she was wrong.

Aaron was like another member of the family and they all knew and loved him. It wasn't unusual for anyone to ask about him, even when she was with RJ. He'd been around since he was a teenager and that was to be expected.

"When are the test results coming back?" Ricardo asked.

"I don't even know, but I'm going crazy waiting. It was only supposed to take a week, but I haven't heard anything yet. I hope no news means good news." Aspen smiled.

"You got that sis. You're smart, so I know you passed with flying colors. We'll have two lawyers in the family soon." Ricardo smiled.

"I sure do hope so," Aspen replied, right as the doorbell rang.

She got up, but she went to the back to refill her glass instead of answering the door. Blythe, Anisa, Patrice, and Nikki were in the kitchen, along with a few other family members. The four women were huddled in the corner whispering, but they stopped as soon as they saw Aspen.

"I'm just coming to get more wine. Y'all can finish talking about me when I leave," Aspen said, calling them out.

"We need to talk," Patrice looked at her and said.

"I'm listening," Aspen flippantly replied.

"Not here," Patrice said as she pulled her along and shoved her into one of the spare bedrooms.

When she saw her sisters and cousin following, Aspen got angry. "I thought you said that we needed to talk. They don't need to be in here," Aspen snapped.

"You are so selfish and inconsiderate," Blythe said, starting up with her mess.

"I'm leaving auntie. I did not come here for all this. I'll just call you later," Aspen said as she walked away.

She opened the door, but her aunt's next words stopped her movements. With her hand on the knob and the door slightly ajar, Aspen turned around to face her with tears in her eyes.

"How could you do that to Aaron? How could you take away the one thing that he wanted the most?" Patrice said as tears fell from her eyes.

"What are you talking about?" Aspen asked, although she already knew.

"I thought you had a miscarriage. How could you abort an innocent child?" Patrice sniffled, as Aspen looked at Nikki with fire in her eyes.

"I can't believe you, Aspen. I was feeling sorry for you thinking that you lost your baby. I can't believe you killed it," Anisa said angrily.

"That was nobody's business and I don't appreciate you opening your mouth Nikki," Aspen fumed.

"Besides telling me that she was your Uber driver, Nikki didn't do anything. I knew you were lying from the moment you opened your mouth. I'm certified and trained to spot people like you every day. You didn't look like you'd ever even stepped foot in a hospital. Imagine my surprise when I paid a visit to the place where Nikki picked you up from and found out that they were an abortion clinic. You were kind of smart about it too. Aaron's trip out of town was the perfect time for you to put your plan in motion. My heart goes out to him because he deserves better," Blythe spoke up.

"I don't expect y'all to understand," Aspen said as she lowered her head.

"I just don't get you, Aspen. You were going crazy trying to have a baby with RJ. Why was he good enough to have kids with, but not Aaron?" Anisa asked.

"Y'all don't understand. Aaron has problems that he needs to get help for. I'm afraid to go to sleep most nights when he's around. I couldn't bring an innocent child into that madness," Aspen replied.

"Why are you still with him then? You've had several chances to go, but you never did. Even when he tried to move on, you interfered in that too. Like I always say, you're selfish and inconsiderate. The same traits that mama had," Blythe spat.

"Aaron is a good man, Aspen. I know that some of the things he saw when he was in the military changed him a little, but he still doesn't deserve to be treated like that," Patrice pointed out.

"It's more than that auntie. He doesn't take his medicine and that only makes things worse. He has these crazy outbursts where he hits himself and it's just scary. Sometimes I'll wake up during the night and he'll be standing over me, staring like a madman," Aspen said.

"None of what you're saying just started happening though, Aspen. You could have left and never looked back.

You chose to stay, so it couldn't have been as bad as you're making it out to be," Anisa replied.

"I'll tell you what the problem is," Blythe said, sounding like she was in the courtroom. She paced back and forth in the room as if she were delivering her closing arguments to a jury.

"Yes Blythe, please do tell us what you think the problem is," Aspen said sarcastically.

"You don't want Aaron and you haven't wanted him for a while. He was a temporary fix for when RJ didn't act like you wanted him to. You kept him around because he was convenient. He was just something for you to do until the man that you really wanted came around. Now that RJ has moved on and got married, Aaron isn't needed anymore," Blythe rationalized.

"Aaron is not a placeholder Aspen and I'm tired of telling you that," Patrice spoke up.

"It's not just that. I don't have any room in my life for a baby right now. I'm trying to go to law school." Aspen frowned.

"And you knew that when you laid down and had unprotected sex," Blythe pointed out.

"Do you want Aaron or not? That's a simple question that needs to be answered," Anisa said.

"He really does love you, Aspen," Nikki spoke up for the first time.

"If you don't want him, he deserves to know. He deserves to move on and be happy with somebody else," Patrice noted.

"And you need to back off whenever he does. He deserves to have a family. You might not want it with him, but don't rob him of the opportunity to have it with someone who does," Blythe said.

Aspen felt a migraine coming on. She was being hit from every angle and it was a bit overwhelming. No, she didn't want Aaron and Blythe hit the nail on the head. He was a familiar place when things didn't work out like they should. Aspen remembered a time when she was madly in love with Aaron and didn't want to be away from him for too long. They did everything together and they were inseparable. That was before he went to the military and came back a changed man. She wanted the old Aaron back, but he was long gone. In his place was a man who sometimes stayed up all night holding a gun because he thought that someone was after him. She didn't have the heart to tell him that they were through, especially after she'd lied and told him what he'd wanted to hear for so long.

"You need to make some decisions Aspen. You need to think about someone else other than yourself for a change. Now I'm asking you, right here, right now. Do you want to be with Aaron or not?" Patrice asked, putting her on the spot.

Aspen looked at her sisters and cousin before she said anything. She knew that her answer was going to upset them, but she had to be honest with herself and everyone else.

"No, I don't want to be with him anymore," Aspen replied truthfully.

"It's gonna break his heart, but you have to keep it real with him, Aspen," Blythe said.

"I know. I'll have a talk with him," Aspen promised.

"Listen, I know I'm hard on you most of the time, but it's only because I love you. I don't want you to end up like our mother, but I see the pattern Aspen. You were too young to know what was going on, but I remember everything. My daddy took so much until he just couldn't take it anymore. He died of a broken heart long before he put that bullet in his head. Never play with someone else's feelings just because you're unsure about your own," Blythe said as tears cascaded down her cheeks.

She pulled her baby sister in for a hug and Anisa did the same. Aaron was family and they didn't want to see him get hurt. It was better for her to end it now and let him move on with his life. Stringing him along wasn't helping and it wasn't fair.

"Okay, now that we've had our waiting to exhale moment, it's time for us to get back to the games. I'm ready to whip some more ass in Monopoly," Patrice said as she clapped her hands dramatically.

"And don't forget about our monthly dinner date tomorrow night. It's my turn to treat," Anisa replied.

And just like that, the mood went from gloomy to cheerful. They all dried their eyes and walked out of the room and rejoined the other guests. Aspen was shocked when she walked into the living room and saw Aaron sitting there talking to her brother-in-law. He looked up at her and winked, and she smiled at him. He seemed to be in a better mood than he was the day before, when he had one of his screaming episodes. He and Ricardo were engaged in an animated conversation about sports and Aaron's smile was as big as the room. Aspen hated that she was going to be the one to remove it. There was no way around it though. She and Aaron just needed to go their separate ways. Instead of moping around and feeling down about it, Aspen made the best of her night. She played games and enjoyed her family until it was time for her to go home. She would deal with her situation later and pray for a decent outcome.

Chapter 51

"This is just so nerve wracking. It's been weeks and I still haven't heard anything," Aspen said as she twirled her pasta around her fork.

She was having dinner with her aunt and sisters at one of their favorite Italian restaurants. They got together once a month for dinner and each one took turns paying the bill. Aspen had been a ball of nerves as she awaited the results of her law school admissions test. Blythe had asked a few of her colleagues about the holdup and they told her that they were a little behind with the process. They assured her that she would hear something soon and she hoped that they were right.

"Stop stressing Aspen. You'll get in. You're smarter than I am, and I passed with flying colors," Blythe noted.

"I've already prayed about it and I believe it is done. My sister would be so proud of y'all right now. Two lawyers and a marketing executive. I'm proud of y'all too. It wasn't always easy, but y'all did it." Patrice smiled proudly.

"With your help." Aspen smiled as she grabbed her aunt's hand and kissed it.

"Yeah, if it weren't for you, I don't know how we would have made it. You didn't have any kids of your own and you didn't have to take us in. I'll always be grateful that you did," Blythe said sincerely.

"You and uncle James were everything that we could have asked for and more," Anisa said, speaking of her auntie's deceased husband.

"Aww, y'all are gonna make an old lady cry. I only did what I know your mother would have wanted me to do.

I only wish that she was here to see it," Patrice said as she wiped her eyes.

There wasn't a day that went by that she didn't think about her sister. She missed her so much and it was even harder around the holidays. Her three girls looked so much like her and that was the only thing that kept Patrice going most days. It was like she still had her sister there with her and that was something to be thankful for.

"We should go on a cruise. Just the four of us," Anisa suggested.

"Yes. That's sounds good to me," Aspen replied.

"I'm ready." Blythe smiled.

Aspen was happy that she and her family were in a good place, especially Blythe. After having their talk the night before, she understood everything that her sister was saying. She needed to put someone else first for once in her life and do the right thing. She had planned on having a talk with Aaron once game night was over, but he left. Aspen thought he was going to show up at her house, but he never did. She was ready to get the hard part over with and she was hoping that it happened soon. With her dream of attending law school hopefully becoming a reality soon, Aspen didn't even want to think about dating anyone. She wanted to focus on her career and pray that love came when the time was right.

"Everybody text me when y'all make it home," Patrice demanded before she honked her horn and drove away.

Aspen blew at her sisters before pulling out of the parking lot right behind her. As soon as she drove away, one of the girls who she'd taken the test with called her.

"Hey Toni," Aspen answered cheerily.

"Did you get in?" Toni asked.

"I don't know. I haven't received anything yet," Aspen replied.

"I just got my letter out of the mail. I guess it's just not my time right now," Toni sighed.

"Damn Toni. I'm sorry to hear that. Shit, you got me nervous now," Aspen replied.

"You'll do fine Aspen. You were one of the smartest ones in our study group. I just have to study harder and stop getting distracted so easily," Toni noted.

"I'm not home yet, but I'm almost there. I'm so nervous," Aspen said.

"You passed, I know you did. Just call and give me the good news when you open your letter," Toni said before they disconnected.

Aspen was driving above the speed limit at first, but she slowed down once she got off the phone. She was so impatient a little while ago. Now, she felt like she needed more time. When she finally pulled up in her driveway, she sat in the car for a little while. Messages from Blythe and Anisa came through their group chat minutes apart, alerting their aunt that they made it home. Aspen sent out a text telling them that she had made it home safely and also about her conversation with Toni. Her phone was going crazy with messages from her aunt and sisters, telling her to check her mailbox. Aspen finally worked up the nerve to get out of the car and walk over to her mailbox. As soon as she opened it, the letter that held her future inside was face up staring back at her. Her hand shook violently as she reached inside and pulled it out. Aspen fumbled with her keys and nervously let herself into the house. She kept her eyes on the letter the entire time, never noticing that her alarm didn't go off. She rushed into her room and turned on the light. The letter and everything that she was holding in her hands fell to the floor when she saw Aaron sitting at the foot of her bed.

"Aaron! What the hell are you doing here? How did you get into my house?" Aspen yelled angrily.

"Where have you been?" Aaron asked as he stared blankly at the wall.

"Did you hear what I just said Aaron? How did you get in here?" Aspen repeated.

"I tried so hard to be the man that you wanted me to be Aspen. I tried to make you feel loved, even when I didn't feel the same coming from you," Aaron said as his leg bounced uncontrollably.

Aspen knew right then and there that he was having another one of his mental melt downs. There was no way that she could have a conversation about breaking up with him now. He was a loose cannon, ready to fire. She wasn't in the mood to coddle him, but she really didn't have a choice. Aaron had to be handled with kid gloves when he got like that and Aspen knew just what to do.

"Just relax Aaron. Have you been taking your medicine?" Aspen asked as she rubbed the back of his head.

"Don't touch me! Keep your fucking hands off of me!" Aaron yelled as he jumped up and got in her face.

That part was new to Aspen because he was never the violent type, not towards her anyway. She jumped back a little as her heart beat erratically in her chest.

"Aaron, baby, please, just calm down," Aspen tried to reason.

"Baby? I'm not your fucking baby. You killed the only baby that I had. The one thing that I could call my own and you took that away from me!" Aaron yelled angrily, making Aspen's eyes wide with shock and fear.

"What are you talking about Aaron. I didn't kill our baby. I had a miscarriage," Aspen said, angering him even more.

"Lying ass bitch!" Aaron snapped as he backhanded her across the face.

Aspen screamed out in pain as she hit the hardwood floor. Never in her life had she ever been hit by a man. She would have never expected that Aaron, of all people, would be the first.

"I swear I'm telling you the truth," Aspen said as she held her stinging cheek.

"I heard you," Aaron replied.

"What?" Aspen asked as she looked up at him from her place on the floor.

"I heard everything when I came to Patrice's house last night. I saw when they pulled you into the room and I was about to knock until the door was slightly pulled open. I heard you admit to killing my baby and not wanting to be with me anymore," Aaron said sadly.

Aspen put her head down as the reality of the situation finally hit her. It must have been Aaron who was at the door when she went to refill her wine glass. She also remembered opening the door, attempting to leave when Blythe started up with her mess. She had no idea that Aaron was standing in the hall at the time, listening to everything that they were saying. No excuse that Aspen could give would have been good enough, so she didn't even try.

"I'm sorry," Aspen apologized as she lowered her head in shame.

"Sorry? Is that all you have to say for ruining my life? The only real family that I had, and you decided to take it away from me like you had that right. Everything that my boys ever said about you was right, but I didn't want to believe it. You're a selfish, inconsiderate bitch. Even still, I loved you more than I loved myself. I put your wants and needs before my own and I always have. And it's fucked up because I don't have shit to show for it but a broken heart and a dead baby," Aaron said as tears spilled from his eyes.

"Aaron please, just calm down and let's talk about this," Aspen begged.

He didn't seem to hear a word she said and that much was clear. He started pacing the floor and yelling out obscenities, as Aspen thought of a way to escape. She saw her phone on the floor not too far from where she was, and she rushed to grab it. When she stood to her feet and tried to make a run for the door, Aaron grabbed her hair and pulled her back.

"Tell me why I should let you live?" Aaron asked as he gripped her hair tighter and made her look him in the eye.

Aspen's eyes got wide when she saw him pull a gun from the small of his back. He didn't put the gun to her head but having it near her was just as frightening.

"Please Aaron, talk to me. We can get through this baby. We can work things out just like we always do," Aspen pleaded as she tried to finesse her way out of the situation.

If no one else could talk Aaron off the ledge, she knew that she could. She had done it too many times to count and she was always successful.

"No, not this time Aspen. You made it clear that you don't want me and, honestly, I can live with that. I've moved on before and I would have had no problem doing it again. What I can't live with is you waiting until I go out of town to kill my unborn child. You knew how much having a family of my own meant to me, but you didn't care. All you cared about was law school and a nigga who didn't even want you anymore. You wanted to have his baby, but I wasn't good enough for you to keep mine," Aaron rambled as he laughed sarcastically.

"That's not true. I would have loved to have your baby, but it just wasn't the right time. I'm sorry baby," Aspen replied in fear.

"Stop calling me baby!" Aaron snapped as he pulled her hair even tighter.

"Okay Aaron, I'm sorry, but we can fix this. Just tell me what I have to do to make everything better," Aspen replied in fear.

"After killing my baby, tell me why I shouldn't kill you? You didn't give my seed a chance at life, so why should you get to live. What makes you so special? Why shouldn't I do you the same way that you did my baby?" Aaron asked her.

"Because you love me," Aspen replied as she looked him in his eyes.

"Yeah and loving you just killed us both," Aaron cried as he pointed the gun at her head.

"No!" Aspen screamed before the bullet pierced her skull and silenced her cries.

Aaron was still holding her by her hair and he refused to let her body hit the floor. With the gun still in his hand, he picked Aspen's lifeless body up and carried her over to the bed. Blood was leaking from her head onto his arm and the floor, but he didn't care. Even in death, he treated her with the respect that he felt she deserved.

"You look beautiful," Aaron said, as he fixed her up in bed as if she were sleeping and not dead.

Her eyes were opened slightly, so Aaron used his hand to close them. He put her hands on her stomach and made sure that her hair was okay. Aspen was always beautiful to him and he wanted her to be found that way. Aaron went to unlock the door, so that whoever came in first would have no trouble getting in. He'd already disarmed the alarm, so that wouldn't be a problem. He was about to get in the bed and lie next to Aspen when he heard her phone start to ring. He picked it up from the floor and answered Patrice's call.

"Aspen?" Patrice asked when someone picked up the phone.

"No, it's Aaron," he replied.

"Oh, hey baby. Where is that girl? I'm sitting here waiting for her to call me and she never did. I'm on pins and needles trying to see if she passed that test or not," Patrice rambled.

"I'm happy that you called Patrice. I know I've told you before, but I just want to tell you again. I really thank you for taking me in when you did. You were always good to me and your love was genuine. That meant a lot to a kid who had nothing or nobody," Aaron replied.

"Aww, it was my pleasure sweetheart. You were always a good boy and never gave me any trouble," Patrice noted.

"Look in your backyard under the stairs and get the back pack that I left there. Everything in it is yours to keep. I closed both my banks accounts and sold my truck today. I cancelled my life insurance because they won't bury me anyway. They'll send you a check for whatever money is coming back from that too. You're my emergency contact and my beneficiary," Aaron rambled, even though Patrice tried to stop him several times.

"What are you talking about Aaron? What's going on?" Patrice asked him.

"I've done all that I can do and I'm tired," Aaron replied.

"It's okay baby, I understand. Where is Aspen?" Patrice asked as she frantically sent Blythe a text message.

Something wasn't right, and she needed her and her husband to go check on Aspen and Aaron. She knew that her niece was planning to end things with him and she had a feeling that he didn't take the news too well.

"Aspen is in bed," Aaron mumbled his reply.

"Can I speak to her?" Patrice asked.

"No, you can't," Aaron said while shaking his head as if she could see him.

"Why not Aaron? Is Aspen okay? I need to hear her voice Aaron. Just let me hear that she's okay," Patrice begged.

He started crying and yelling about how much he loved her, and Patrice was on edge. Blythe sent her a message saying that she and Ricardo were on their way over and she prayed that they got there in time.

"She's not okay," Aaron whimpered.

"Is she hurt Aaron? Please, get her some help if she's hurt. Everything will be okay baby, I promise," Patrice assured him.

"Everything will never be okay. Why did she have to kill our baby? We could have been a family. I've never had a real family before, besides yours. Was that too much to ask for?" Aaron questioned.

"No baby, it wasn't too much. You'll get that family that you want one day Aaron. Just don't give up," Patrice said as she nervously paced her floor.

"No, it's too late for all that now," Aaron said as he laid in the bed next to Aspen.

"It's never too late Aaron. As long as you have breath in your body, it's never too late."

"Just don't separate us, please. That's all that I ask of you. Give us a double service and bury us together," Aaron replied before he hung up the phone.

"Aaron, no!" Patrice yelled, but the call had already been disconnected.

"It's just you, me, and our baby now. I love you so much Aspen. You know that, don't you? I could never live with myself if I didn't have you. That's why I can't stay. I have to be with you. We couldn't be a family in life, but we'll be a family in death," Aaron said as he kissed her cheek.

He laid down next to her and intertwined his left hand in hers. He used his right hand and put the gun up to his head and closed his eyes. He pulled the trigger, ending his life and the pain that he had been feeling for years.

Chapter 52

RJ squeezed Marlee's hand as they walked into the church together. It all felt surreal as he gazed up front and saw the two caskets separated by a huge photo collage of the two deceased. They were happy and smiling then, but something had obviously changed over time. RJ always said that Aspen's man was unstable, but he didn't know just how right he was. He was shocked when he learned about Aspen's death the week before. It was even more shocking when he learned that Aaron was responsible. Lauren called and told his father and Banks broke the news to him. RJ waited a few days, but he eventually reached out to her sister, Blythe. She was heartbroken, of course, but she told him the entire story of what had gone down. It pained her to know that one of her predictions had come true. She always told Aspen that she would end up just like their mother and, unfortunately, she did.

"Hey Ms. Patrice. I'm sorry for your loss," RJ said as he walked up and hugged Aspen's aunt.

Patrice looked like she'd aged since the last time he saw her and that was only a few days ago. With Marlee's blessing, he passed by her house to see if there was anything that she needed him to do. She declined, but she thanked him for the offer. She had Aspen in life insurance, but the military covered Aaron's expenses.

"Thank you, baby, and thanks for coming. And you must be the wife." Patrice smiled at Marlee.

"Yes, ma'am." Marlee smiled while embracing the older woman.

"This is my wife Marlee," RJ said.

"It's nice to meet you, honey. Thanks for coming." Patrice smiled through her pain.

She felt like another piece of her heart had been ripped out of her chest, but she tried her best to be strong. She knew that Aaron had issues, but she didn't know that he was capable of doing something so horrible. As hurt as she was for Aspen, she was equally hurt for him. Aaron had been through so much in his life that he obviously felt like he couldn't take anymore. He never felt wanted from birth and Aspen didn't make him feel any better. Her family warned her about playing with his feelings, but she didn't listen. Being hardheaded had caused her demise and lots of heartache for her loved ones.

Patrice knew that many people wouldn't understand her decision to funeralize them together, but Aaron had no one else. Although that was his last wish, Patrice would have done it anyway. He was her family too and she didn't feel the need to explain that to anyone. Some of her own family members were not pleased with her decision, but she didn't care. They were calling Aaron a coward, but she disagreed. PTSD was real and not enough people knew enough about it. They were quick to call him crazy, but it was so much more than that. No one knew what Aaron was going through, but he needed help. He didn't think anything was wrong with him, but most people with problems didn't.

"Here's a little something from me and my pops. I hope it helps," RJ said as he handed her two cards.

"Thank you so much and tell your father the same." Patrice smiled.

RJ and Marlee walked away and went up to the front to view. He felt a huge lump in his throat as they got closer to the open caskets. Marlee squeezed his hand in hers as they looked down at Aspen's lifeless body. She was beautiful and appeared to be sleeping. The soft pink dress that she wore complemented the pink and white coffin that she was laid out in. Aaron looked equally as handsome in a navy suit and striped tie. Marlee wanted to cry as she looked at the two of them and the pictures that surrounded them. They dated back to their teen years, up until a few weeks before their deaths. They seemed to have had lots of happy times together, but not so much in the end.

"Come on baby. Let's sit down," Marlee said as she pulled on his hand.

RJ's face didn't hold any emotion, but she knew that he was hurt. Aspen was someone that he'd spent five years of his life with, so she understood his pain.

"Let's step outside for a minute. I'm not good with this kind of stuff," RJ replied.

He hated funerals and Marlee was aware of that. She didn't want to go, but her husband needed her. RJ looked like he wanted to throw up, so she hurriedly walked outside with him to get some fresh air.

"Are you good now?" Marlee asked as they stood outside of the church.

They were still in the visitation part of the service, so people were going in and out of the sanctuary. Some came out wailing, while others refused to even go in.

"Yeah, I'm good. I just hate the smell of funerals. I don't care if the service is in a church or a funeral home, the smell is always the same. And they all play that same sad tune. I don't think I'm staying for the entire service. I can't deal," RJ replied.

"Whatever you want to do is fine with me," Marlee assured him.

They found a bench to sit on as they watched people going into the church. Marlee was shocked when Lauren and his sisters walked up and spoke to him. They all seemed uncomfortable with each other, but at least they were cordial. Lauren looked so small and fragile and she hadn't been sick for very long. Her hair was struggling to grow back, but Marlee thought she looked cute with her shorter do. The chemo and radiation had pulled all her beautiful hair out only weeks after starting the treatments.

"That must be her uncle Keith," RJ said when he saw a prison van pull up with two guards riding up front.

The back door of the van opened a little while after it stopped, and two armed deputies got out. They looked around trying to make sure the area was secured before they helped Keith get out. He was cuffed at the wrists and ankles, so he kind of shuffled along. The two deputies who were in the front of the van got behind him as he was escorted into the church.

"That's who Lauren was stealing your father's money for. He's looks like a crackhead," Marlee spoke up.

"That nigga is a crackhead. Either she was desperate for attention or he spit some serious ass game to her," RJ replied.

"It was probably both. And what the hell do they need four men to escort him in for? Is he a serial killer or something?" Marlee asked.

"That nigga ain't nothing but a petty thief," RJ replied, right as they carried someone out of the church screaming and crying.

He and Marlee stood up to see who it was when they saw Keith being held up by the deputies. He was having an emotional breakdown and Marlee wanted to cry with him. He looked genuinely hurt and her heart went out to him. Aspen's aunt and sisters were trying to comfort him, but the deputies didn't let them get too close.

"Damn man," RJ said while shaking his head sadly.

When Blythe saw him and Marlee standing there, she walked over and said hello.

"I'm sorry for your loss," Marlee said as she and RJ both gave her a comforting hug.

"Thank you." Blythe smiled sadly.

"Are they not letting him stay?" RJ asked when he saw the deputies loading Keith back onto the van.

"No, he was only allowed to view. I told my auntie that I didn't think it was a good idea, but he begged her to let him come. All that money she paid just for him to look at two dead bodies for two minutes," Blythe said in disgust.

"They charge for that shit?" RJ asked.

"Everything is about money these days." Blythe shrugged.

"I know Ms. Patrice is trying to be strong, but how is she really holding up?" RJ asked.

"She's not. I'm trying to convince her to sell her house and move in with me. She's not going to be okay. Aspen was her baby. I hate that she's beating herself up over this," Blythe replied.

"Why? None of this is her fault," RJ noted.

"I said the same thing, but she doesn't agree. Aaron stole Aspen's house key from her key ring the night before he killed her. That was how he got into her house. He watched her disarming the alarm a few times and that's how he was able to already be in there when she got home. He left a note in his backpack saying all of that," Blythe said.

Aaron had left a detailed note explaining how he'd heard them talking at Patrice's house that night and how hurt he was about what Aspen did. The moment he left the house, he already knew what he was going to do. He resigned from his job and emptied out all of his bank accounts. He took Aspen's name off of everything and replaced it with Patrice's. He knew that insurance wouldn't pay a claim if he committed suicide, so he had that canceled as well. He sold his truck back to the dealership that he got it from and gave all the money that he had to Patrice.

"Damn. How did she find the backpack?" RJ questioned.

"She talked to him right before he killed himself and he told her where to look. My husband and I were the ones who found them," Blythe said as she wiped her teary eyes.

As long as she lived, she would never forget the scene that she had walked in on. If it weren't for all the blood, Aaron and Aspen appeared to be in bed sleeping. They were holding hands and the gun was on the bed right next to him. Blythe had warned her baby sister but, as usual, she didn't listen. Sadly, she had met the same fate as their mother, just as her sister had predicted. Blythe loved to be right in the courtroom, but that was one time she would have loved to be wrong.

"Damn man. I met dude a few times and I knew he wasn't right. He used to ask me all kinds of crazy questions, but I told him that I wasn't a threat. The last time I saw him, he told me that they were expecting a baby," RJ pointed out.

"She aborted it. Aaron suffered from PTSD. He was already kind of unstable, but that was his breaking point. He really wanted a family and he was so happy when they found out that she was pregnant. Aspen waited until he went out of town and got rid of it. Then she lied and said that she had a miscarriage. I tried to warn her, but she didn't listen," Blythe said as she broke down and cried.

RJ didn't know what to do, but Marlee pulled her in for a hug. Blythe was always the strength of her family, but it felt good to cry on someone else's shoulder for a change. Marlee rubbed her back to comfort her and she appreciated that. She didn't really know the other woman, but she'd helped her more than she would know.

"I'm sorry," Blythe said as she pulled away from Marlee and got herself together.

"No apology needed," Marlee said as she handed her a brand-new handkerchief from her purse.

"Thank you. I guess I better get back in here. The service is about to start." Blythe smiled as she walked away.

RJ wanted to walk away and go back to his car, but he decided against it. Instead, he grabbed Marlee's hand and made his way into the church to say his final farewell.

***

"That's fucked up what happened to Aspen, but you better be happy that you left her alone when you did. That nigga would have killed you too. I saw the way he was looking at you and shit," Murk said to RJ.

"It was just so sad. They had to call the ambulance for her auntie when they closed the casket," Marlee said as she tried to shake away the memory.

An entire week had passed since they attended Aspen's funeral and it still saddened her to talk about it.

"That shit was fucked up. She got accepted into law school and didn't even live long enough to know it," RJ replied.

"Yep, her auntie spoke at the funeral and told everybody. Aspen got the letter out of the mailbox and never even got a chance to open it," Marlee noted.

"That nigga was bat shit crazy. I was ready to lay his ass out in front of that gas station. But, killing that man's baby was low," Murk said.

"Yeah, but it didn't warrant death. That's just so heartbreaking," Desi replied.

She and Desmond had gone to Marlee and RJ's house for a little while, and Murk had joined them soon after. It was a lazy day of doing nothing, so they just sat around and talked. Desmond and Destini were in one of the spare bedrooms sleeping, while everyone else sat in the living room drinking.

"I heard that nigga Tyson took a plea deal for five years. He better pray that I find the Lord by the time his fat ass gets out. That other nigga couldn't shoot, but my aim is perfect," Murk replied.

"Kallie said that Yanni be catching the bus to Mississippi to go see Craig. I guess he moved away after he shot Tyson," Desi spoke up.

"Kallie is still talking everybody's business I see. She got a man and still ain't satisfied. That's just why I speak and keep it pushing. Bitch talks entirely too much for me." Marlee frowned.

"Yanni is dumb as fuck. It's bad enough that she's traveling to Mississippi behind some dick, but I wish a nigga would have me catching the bus," Desi said.

"She's another one who I speak to and keep it moving. I don't have nothing against them, but I'm mindful of the company that I keep now. Besides you, Sierra, Mat, and Raven, I don't really talk to too many females," Marlee noted.

"The fuck that mean Marlee. What, you talking to niggas now? Is that what you're saying?" RJ questioned angrily.

"Let me find out I married a retard. How the hell did you come to that conclusion based off what I said?" Marlee asked.

"I'm just saying. You talking about you don't talk to too many females. It makes it seem like you talking to niggas instead," RJ replied.

"Fuck all that. What's going on with this wedding Desi? Y'all keep switching the dates and shit. That nigga must have changed his mind. I told you nobody wanted to marry your bald head ass. That's my dude and all, but I'll have to kill him if he flake on you," Murk warned.

"Is murder your way of solving everything? Killing and babies. That's all your skinny ass is good for. We're getting married right before we move into our house. You better make up your mind about that apartment too. Once I turn in the keys, it's over for you," Desi replied.

"Nah, I'm good on the apartment thing. Me and Christie are trying to make something shake. We're getting us a spot together," Murk said, making RJ choke on his beer.

"Murk! Are you trying to kill my husband? Don't be giving him that kind of news while he's drinking," Marlee fussed as she patted RJ's back.

He was coughing like crazy until he finally caught his breath. His eyes were watering, and he used the tail of his shirt to wipe them.

"Shit, my bad cuz. I didn't think you were gonna react like that." Murk shrugged.

"The fuck you mean nigga? You ain't never live with a woman before in your life," RJ noted.

"Before Marlee, neither did you," Murk remined him.

"Damn, that's true, huh? But still, bruh, you've never been in a relationship before. I knew your ass loved Christie. Talking all that shit, but I told you!" RJ yelled.

"Yeah, I love the bitch. The fact that she's on baby number three says a lot. I don't usually double back like that," Murk admitted.

"Yes! I love you, Christie girl, wherever you are. Somebody finally tamed this wild animal!" Desi yelled excitedly.

"Don't get too excited. If this shit don't work out, I'll be knocking at your door with all my worldly possessions," Murk swore.

"It'll work as long as you keep your baby maker in your pants," Desi replied.

"I'm done with kids after this. I'm getting fixed," Murk said.

"You need to. Making all them bad ass kids. Me and Marlee saw your oldest son at the barber shop," Desi replied.

"He told me he wanted his mohawk colored like mine, but his mama told him no," Marlee smirked.

"Speaking of mohawks, what's up with Kassidy bruh? Bitch just dropped off the face of the earth like it was nothing. See, if she would have let me hit it, she could have still been coming around to stalk you," Murk said.

"We saw her the day after Aspen's funeral. I guess that was her boo that she was all hugged up with," Marlee replied.

"It's about time she got her one," Murk remarked.

"Did she speak to you RJ?" Desi smirked.

"I was waiting for her desperate ass to say something. I'm not pregnant no more. I would have laid that hoe out right in front of the animals," Marlee spat.

"What animals? Where did y'all see her at?" Desi asked.

"We took Tre and Raven's daughter to the zoo and she was there. She barely looked our way. I'm happy that she got her sew-in back and left the mohawk to the professionals," Marlee laughed.

"Kassidy know what it is. Bitch don't even comment under my posts no more. It took a while, but she finally got the hint," RJ said.

When Marlee's phone rang, she smiled when she saw that it was the party planner. Tre's party was coming up and she had sent Marlee an email of some of her ideas. She and RJ were pleased, and they were ready for her to send the invoice. She had even found a petting zoo that came out to the customers, and RJ was sold. While she was talking, Desmond walked into the room carrying Destini. She was whining until she saw Desi. She wiggled out of her father's arms and went straight to her. Marlee thought it was cute when Desmond sat next to Desi and put his head in her lap. They looked so cute together and Marlee loved to see her cousin happy.

"What's up with this wedding brother-in-law? I can't seem to get an answer out of Desi. I hope you ain't backing out," Murk spoke up.

"Never that. I'm ready right now, but she's trying to wait until we move into our house. We got the marriage license a week ago and it's good for thirty days," Desmond noted.

"Really Desi? So, you're the hold up?" Marlee asked when she got off the phone.

"I thought you wanted to wait until right before we moved," Desi said while looking at Desmond.

"Wait for what Desi? We're already living under the same roof since I gave up my apartment. We don't even know when we're moving. I know it won't be long, but I don't want to wait," Desmond noted.

"That's what the fuck I'm talking about. Drag her bald head ass down the aisle on some savage shit," Murk instigated.

"Shut up bastard," Desi snapped.

"Are we doing this or what? I can put a dinner together for next weekend. That's nothing to do," Marlee spoke up.

"What am I gonna wear?" Desi asked.

"That's easy Desi. We can hit the mall before I get Tre from by my mama," Marlee offered.

"I might not find anything that I like though," Desi replied.

"We can order online if we have to, but I think you can find a nice dress right in Saks," Marlee noted.

"Stop stalling Desi. What, are you scared?" RJ asked.

"Not at all. I'm ready. We can go to the courthouse Friday and do the dinner Saturday," Desi replied, making Desmond smile.

"Yes! I'm so happy for you, cousin. My girl is getting married!" Marlee cheered.

"It's about damn time," Murk mumbled.

"Come on Desi. We need to get going. You need something cute and sexy to wear," Marlee said.

"Go handle your business baby. I'll get Tre from by Tiffany," RJ replied.

"Let me go change her and put her shoes back on," Desi said as she stood with Destini in her arms.

"I just changed her, but you can leave her here. She's only gonna get in the way," Desmond said as he tried to take Destini from her.

Destini started screaming, prompting her father to let her go.

"You know she's not gonna let me leave without her. I'm taking her with me," Desi said as she kissed Destini's cheek.

Marlee smiled as she watched her cousin walk away with her baby on her hip. It might not have been biological, but Desi was Destini's mother in every sense of the word. Marlee was happy for her favorite cousin. Actually, she was just happy period. She had a great husband and a healthy baby boy. She had her dream house and a great job that paid her way too much for the little work that she did. It seemed that everyone around her was happy.

Well, almost everyone. She hadn't heard from her father since he learned that Alvin was walking her down the aisle. Marlee refused to reach out to him first. That was his job and she hadn't done anything wrong. She and Yanni spoke to each other, but it would never be back to the way it was before. She was cordial with Kallie too, but she knew how far to take things with her. Other than that, her family was closer than ever, and she had a great extended family through RJ. Her circle was small, but she wasn't complaining. If she had to, Marlee would gladly do it all over again.

EPILOGUE

Marlee smiled as she took pictures of Desi, Desmond, and their three-day old baby boy. Desi was happier than she'd ever been before and that was evident by the huge smile that was plastered on her face. After months of going back and forth with the surrogate agency, they finally found a perfect match. Desmond's sperm was used for the process and it only took one month before the procedure was successful. Their son, Desmond Jr., was released from the hospital earlier that morning and they had a small gathering at Desi's house to welcome him home. Desmond and Desi already had a baby shower, so their son had everything that he needed. Both parents agreed that two was enough, since they had their perfect pair.

"Can I hold him mommy? I want to hold the baby," Destini said as she sat on the sofa with her arms spread wide.

Desi had legally adopted her a few months after she and Desmond got married, but Destini had been hers long before then. Destini was almost four years old now and so smart for her age. She was still spoiled behind Desi and her son probably would be too.

"Okay baby. Sit back like a big girl and I'll let you hold him," Desi replied.

"You're a big sister now Destini." Marlee smiled as she took a picture of the siblings.

"Me too. I'm a big brother too!" Tre yelled out.

He was almost three and he loved for everyone to know that he was a big brother. Marlee and RJ had welcomed their daughter, Ryann, into the world four months ago and he was so helpful with his baby sister.

"Yes baby, you're a big brother too," Marlee said, making him smile.

Tre looked so much like RJ that it was scary. Marlee was happy that her daughter had some of her features, but she favored her father a lot too. Mat was crazy about her niece and nephew and she was always buying them something. Her and Sierra had just moved into their newly purchased home, so they didn't stay at Desi's gathering too long. They were still in the process of unpacking and Marlee helped as much as she could. Tiffany and Alvin went over there every day helping them decorate and put everything in place.

"No the fuck he didn't," Desi fussed when she saw Murk walking through her front door.

"That's a bad word mommy," Destini scolded as she looked at Desi.

"It is a bad word and don't you ever say it," Desi warned her.

"What's wrong baby?" Desmond asked as he helped Destini hold her baby brother, since his wife was no longer paying attention.

"This dumb ass is what's wrong," Desi replied as she and Marlee walked over to where Murk was standing.

RJ was standing there holding his baby girl and Murk stopped to talk to him.

"Where's my new nephew?" Murk asked when Desi walked over to him.

"Bring your ass over here nigga," Desi snarled as she grabbed him up by his shirt and pulled him away.

"The fuck is wrong with you Desi?" Murk frowned as he pulled away from her.

"Your dumb ass seems to be the one with the problem. Please tell me that you did not just walk into my house with one of your random hoes. I invited Christie to come over. What if she shows up and sees you here with another bitch?" Desi asked.

"Christie ain't coming over here. I told her ass to stay home and she better listen," Murk replied.

"I don't give a fuck what you told her. She's my friend and I'm not doing her dirty like that. I'm just as wrong as you are if I condone what you're doing. Now, either you get rid of that gutter rat or I will," Desi fussed as she poked him in the chest.

"I swear you been acting brand new since you grew some hair. Bitch was calm as fuck as long as she was bald head," Murk snapped.

Desi had grown her hair out a bit and was now wearing it curly at the top with faded sides. It looked great on her, but Murk swore that she'd changed since it had grown out a bit. He was still a thorn in Desi's side, but she loved her best friend like a brother.

"Don't make me embarrass your ass in here. Get rid of that bitch. Now!" Desi ordered.

"Alright man. Nigga can't do shit around here," Murk fussed as he walked away to where his female friend was standing.

Desi blew out a breath of frustration as she walked back over to where everybody else was. It seemed as if everyone had changed over the years, but Murk was the exception. Moving in with Christie was a huge mistake because he still didn't do right by her. He stayed at Desi's house at least once a week because Christie was always putting him out. Murk was up to seven kids, with four of them being with Christie. He was quick to say how much he loved her, but he was still a dog. Desi and Desmond tried to talk some sense into him all the time, but Murk was stuck in his pathetic ways.

"Murk is gonna give you and Desmond a heart attack," Marlee laughed when Desi walked back over to them.

"Who the hell was that and where is Christie?" Desmond asked as he watched Murk walking the other woman out of the house.

"I don't know who that was. I don't think Christie is coming," Desi replied.

"That's because he probably made her stay home," Desmond noted.

"He did," Desi replied.

It was funny as hell to her how her husband knew Murk just as well as she did. Desmond had to help Murk and his brothers out a few times when they got arrested, and Iris was no better. She stayed in some bullshit that Ivy had to help her out of too.

"Christie needs to give him a taste of his own medicine," Marlee spoke up.

"Are you trying to get Christie killed? That nigga will lose his shit if he even thought that she was messing around on him," RJ replied.

"But, how is that fair RJ? He's with a different bitch every week while she's at home taking care of four babies. Now, I won't say that he doesn't do his part as a father, but Murk is a horrible boyfriend," Marlee admitted.

"I agree baby, but Murk has been the same way since we were kids. I'm surprised that he even settled down and moved in with Christie at all. The nigga is crazy and always has been." RJ shrugged, right as his phone rang.

His mother was calling on Facetime, but he knew that she wasn't calling for him. Ivy and his father were in New York shopping and celebrating their first anniversary. She called at least three times a day to talk to Tre and see Ryann's face.

"Tre! Your grandma and grandpa are on the phone!" Marlee called out to him as soon as Ivy and Banks' faces appeared on the screen.

Marlee laughed as her son ran over and grabbed the phone from his father's hand. Every day since they left, Tre asked when they would be returning. Banks had him spoiled rotten and he always wanted to be around his grandfather. Tre was still the only grandson and Ryann was the youngest granddaughter. Banks' other daughters still didn't have any kids and they still lived together. Lauren ended up moving to Denver almost a year ago once she got a clean bill of health from her doctor. She was only supposed to be going for a visit to help her mother after surgery, but she ended up staying longer. A chance encounter at the pharmacy to get her mother's prescription turned out to be better than expected when she was asked out on a date by the pharmacist.

Lauren had given up on men after Banks and Keith, but she was happy once again. She vowed to do things differently with her new man and things had been going better than ever. She found a job as a receptionist and she was in a good place. Her daughters still lived in New Orleans, but they visited each other often. Lauren also kept up with her good friend Patrice. Thankfully, Blythe was able to convince her to sell her house after Aspen's death and she now lived with her. Anisa had gotten married and had a baby, so Patrice kept herself busy with her growing family. She mourned Aspen for a long time and it was still hard on her around birthdays and holidays. She took it one day at a time and, as time passed, things started to get better.

"I'm about to get going niece. I have to bring Ty'Yanni by her other grandmother, so she can go to her cousin's party. Congrats on the new baby. He's adorable," Yvette said when she walked over to them.

Tyson was still in jail, but his mother kept up with her grandkids. Taj had a boy that Tyson had never had the pleasure of meeting. His sister had a baby too, but her baby's father was killed before her daughter was even born. Yanni was still as pathetic as ever, but she had been trying to do better lately. She had made visiting Craig in Mississippi a regular occurrence until she popped up pregnant again. Yvette was already taking care of her and one baby and she wasn't trying to do it again. When Yanni quit her job, Yvette put her out and kept Ty'Yanni at home with her. Yanni ended up moving to Mississippi with Craig until her second daughter was born. Craig's family was pissed when the baby came out looking nothing like him.

Once they had a blood test done, they sent Yanni packing back to New Orleans when it came back that the baby was not his. Yanni never said who her daughter was for, but she took steps to get herself together after that. She took classes to become a phlebotomist and she had been working at a local hospital for a few months. She got herself a low-income apartment and was taking care of her kids on her own. Yvette helped a lot, but Yanni was doing okay for herself.

"Thanks auntie. I appreciate everything," Desi said as she and Marlee hugged her.

They kissed Ty'Yanni too and watched as they left. The rest of the day went on as planned and, thankfully, Murk was behaving. He ended up going to pick Christie up and Desi was happy that she was there. Her mother had her kids for a while and she was happy for a break. Most of the food was already gone, so Dionne and Tiffany started cleaning up the kitchen. Desmond had walked his family outside and Desi started putting her house back together. Kallie was holding her baby boy and Marlee was helping her clean. Kallie had gotten married a few months ago and had just learned that she was ten weeks pregnant. She and Desi were still cool, but Marlee still fed her with a long-handled spoon. She didn't trust Kallie and nothing that Desi said was changing her mind.

"You need me to do anything else before I go baby?" Dionne asked as she looked at Desi.

"No, mama, thanks for everything. I'm happy you gave Destini her bath and put her to bed already. I wasn't in the mood to do it myself," Desi replied.

"That lil girl is a mess. She be making a damn fool out of me," Dionne chuckled.

"Welcome to the club," Desi laughed.

Once she saw her mother and the rest of her guests off, Desi relaxed with her husband, cousin, and friends. Tre had gone home with Tiffany and Ryann was lying on her father's chest sleeping. Murk was trying his best to get rid of Christie, but she wasn't having it. Eventually, he gave up and they left and went home together. When Marlee saw her cousin yawning, she and RJ made their exit as well.

"Desi is so happy." Marlee smiled as she and RJ headed home.

"Yeah, she is. If a person doesn't know them personally, you would think she really gave birth to those kids. She's a good mother," RJ replied.

"She really is," Marlee agreed.

Desi was proof that you didn't have to be a biological mother in order to have maternal instincts. She was great with Destini and there was no doubt that she would be just as great with her son.

"And so are you." RJ smiled as he kissed his wife's hand.

"Aww, thanks baby." Marlee blushed.

She didn't believe in perfection, but she was content. She had her husband and kids and that was all she needed to make her happy. Marlee remembered when she couldn't even eat or sleep when Tyson and Yanni did her wrong. She would have never imagined that a weekend getaway to Vegas would lead to her having her happily ever after. RJ was a dream come true and if felt good to know that she was his one and only.

Made in the USA
San Bernardino,
CA

58586872R00268